LODESTAR

Also by Michael Flynn

In the Country of the Blind
The Nanotech Chronicles
Fallen Angels (with Larry Niven and Jerry Pournelle)
*Firestar**
*The Forest of Time and Other Stories**
*Rogue Star**

* denotes a Tor book

LODESTAR

Michael Flynn

A Tom Doherty Associates Book/New York

LODESTAR

Copyright © 2000 by Michael Flynn

Edited by David G. Hartwell

A Tor Book
Published by Tom Doherty Associates, LLC
175 Fifth Avenue
New York, NY 10010

www.tor.com

Tor® is a registered trademark of
Tom Doherty Associates, LLC.

ISBN 0-312-86137-0

First Edition: March 2000

Printed in the United States of America

0 9 8 7 6 5 4 3 2 1

Margie

The Pearl

LODESTAR

Characters

The van Huytens

Mariesa van Huyten, chairman-emeritus of Van Huyten Industries.
Harriet Gorley-van Huyten, Mariesa's mother.

Armando Herrera, butler at Silverpond.

Christiaan van Huyten V, chairman of Van Huyten Industries and
    Mariesa's older cousin.
Marianne Godwin-van Huyten, Christiaan's wife.
Adam Jaeger van Huyten, Chris's son, ex-president of Argonaut
    Labs.
Kathryn van Huyten, Adam's wife.
Wally Jenks, Adam's lawyer.

Brittany van Huyten-Armitage, Chris's sister.
Norbert Wainwright van Huyten, Mariesa's second cousin.

The Pooles

S. James ("Jimmy") Poole, computer security consultant, one of
    Belinda's Kids.
Tanuja ("Tani") Pandya, novelist, one of Belinda's Kids.
Steven James Poole, Jr., "Little Stevie," a rugrat.
Stassy, the cook.
Rada, the nurse.

Baleen

Billie Whistle, a cheesehead, chief gopher for Baleen.
David Desherite, chief financial backer of Baleen.

Red Hawkins, an otter, chief rigger and operative for Balleen.
Guang Shaoping, a manufacturing engineer.
Karl Wincock, a pharmer.

Skywatch

Daryll Blessing, distinguished elder scientist, honorary chairman.
John Inkling, American Astronomical Union.
George Krishnarahman, Arizona State University.
Cheng-I Yeh, physicist and one of Belinda's Kids.
Bernie Lefkowitz, physicist and one of Belinda's Kids.

The People's Crusades

Roberta ("Styx") Carson, a poet and progressive and once one of
    Belinda's Kids.
Phil Albright, head of The People's Crusades.

Isaac Kohl, resident nerd.
Ellis Harwood, a muscular progressive.

Van Huyten Industries

Dolores Pitchlynn, president of Pegasus Aerospace, LEO Board.
A. V. Deshpande, president of Argonaut Labs.
Charlie Schwar, CEO of Cerberus Security.

Glenn Academy

Forrest Calhoun, Superintendent.
Liz DuBois, ensign-instructor, orbital mechanics.
Debra Matusek, ensign-instructor, physical training.
Jacinta Rosario, first-year cadet, a silver apple.
Ursula Kitmann, first-year cadet, a dove within the sun.
Soren Thorvaldsson, first-year cadet.

Alonzo Sulbertson, third-year cadet.
Ludwig Schimmelpfennig, first-year cadet (Lou Penny).
Yungduk Morrisey, first-year cadet.
Noëlle Nieves, cadet colonel.
Total Meredith, third-year cadet, a huntress.

Lodestar Station

Leland ("Hobie") Hobart, superconductor chemist for Argonaut, one
    of Belinda's Kids
Charlene Joyce Hobart, Hobie's wife.
Nikolai Cunningham, superintendent of Lodestar Polar Base.
Krystal Delacroix, a newsgroupie.

LEO Station

Shahrakh "Rock" Shary, LEO site manager.
Robert Blackhall, plant engineer.
Ron Williams, metallurgist.
Olya Tsvetnikova, Energia electrician.

Aboard the *Dixie Belle*

Mighty Mouse,
Doctor Doom,   }   on the wild side.
The Eel,

The Five Fingers (Jimmy's List)

Norris Bosworth ("SuperNerd").
"Captain Cat."
Chen Wahsi (in Guangzhou, Guangdong Republic).
"Earp."

Pete Rodriguez ("Pedro the Jouster").
"Gloria,"
"Red,"   } friends of Bosworth.
"Walter,"

Other Players

Belinda Karr, senior principal, Karr Academies.
Edward Bullock, president of Klondike-American and other interests.
Ed Wilson, an entrepeneur, president of Wilson Enterprises.
Blaise Rutell, president of the U.S.
Solomon Dark, presidential advisor.

Acknowledgments

First, thanks to a number of friends and colleagues at The SAM Group, a quality management consulting firm, for the loan of their names and personalities, including: Dr. Mariesa Julien, Ed Sykes (as fine a program manager in real life as he was a fictional butler), Shahrakh "Rock" Shary, Bob Blackhall, Ron Williams, and others. Each of them is the salt of the earth, regardless of the role his or her namesake may have been called upon to play here. Visit them at http://www.thesamgroup.com.

Craig Purdy, of NASA's Goddard Space Flight Center/Wallops Island, provided a host of information and background papers on asteroid composition, material extraction, and microgravity manufacturing. Goddard and Goddard/Wallops does a lot of unglamorous and sometimes unsung work in earth and space sciences; but while the rest of us think about the future and sometimes write about it, the folks at Goddard actually go out and take a peek. You can take a peek, too, at http://www.nasa.gsfc.gov.

Greg Bennet, formerly at NASA's Neutral Bouyancy Tank in Houston, supplied me with the particulars of NBT training. Greg is also president of Lunar Resources Company, a private venture planning a mining colony on the moon. The Artemis Project is a registered trademark of the Lunar Resources Company, and "Artemis Mines" is mentioned in the text with their approval. Visit them at http://www.asi.org.

Dr. Stephen O'Neil, vice president of research at Micromotion, Inc., and one-time denizen of The Irish Pub, was kind enough to explain some of the near-future potentials in microelectromechanical devices (MEMS). Sometimes the future is closer than we think. Part of it can be found at http://www.micromo.com.

O! a kiss
Long as my exile, sweet as my revenge!
—Wm. Shakespeare
Coriolanus V. iii.

In time of peril, like the needle to the lodestone, obedience, irrespective of rank, generally flies to him who is best suited to command.

—Herman Melville
White Jacket

Sometimes, in the quiet hiss of the night, Jimmy Poole would wonder where it had all begun. There were causes and effects, options and choices. One thing led to another, but no one thing led to it all. It was a seamless whole, receding ever backward. From Jimmy's own bravado to Roberta's begging to Adam's obsession and OMC's secretiveness. Hunt the roots of it far enough and you'd have to blame the Big Bang for everything.

There was the time that Chase Coughlin snuck up on him in the locker room at school and saw him naked; and another, far more mystical evening, when Tani Pandya saw him naked. The naked truth, if he were inclined at the present to bad jokes.

The room was dark, save for the pearly light that washed through the window at the far end. Jimmy pushed himself out of his bed, careful not to disturb the sleeping form beside him, and floated dreamlike to the window. *This is all a dream*, a part of his mind insisted. *In the morning you'll wake up, and everything will be like it was.*

Though there was scant promise in that, either; because "the way it was" was not exactly pleasant.

At one point, he decided that the whole daisy chain of cause and effect had started with a football thrown deliberately at his head in 1995. It had hurt, and bloodied his nose; and afterward his dad had gushed apologies for three days running, half appalled at the damage he had done, half terrified that Jimmy might call NJ-DYFS.

Did you ever hold me in your arms, Dad? It was hard to remember; harder to believe. A big man, wide but never fat, hardened by years spent before forges and stamping presses, arms that had lifted glowering red lumps of metal destined to become engine blocks. Arms whose embrace could easily hurt and whose casual swat could raise welts. *I remember footballs thrown at my face—motivation to catch them. I remember, Get your nose out of those trash books! I remember, Hey, let's go bat some flies!*

I wanted to catch those balls. I really did. I wanted more than anything to make you happy, Jim Poole, All-State running back! Jim Poole, shop steward! Big footsteps, but not mind.

Maybe if Mom had been more assertive; but it's hard even to picture her, and every year it's grown harder. Quiet, kind, always ready to soothe a hurt; but faint and scarcely noticeable beside her husband. *She named me "Steven James," but I was always "Jimmy" growing up; so even that one, small victory was denied her.* She had not so much died as she had faded away.

In the meantime, a rah-rah childhood that grew more desperate with each passing year, as first prodding, then shame, finally threat failed to divert their son's bookish course. Shared looks that I thought then were disgust, but which time has revealed as genuine concern. Stolid, honest, hardworking, unable to comprehend what sort of child they had birthed; wanting only the best, but never imagining that as anything but the same small laurels that had marked Dad's own success.

Am I a big man now, Dad? Or just a wimp who happens to be rich and famous? You cash the checks I send you, and you write cards and letters at all the appropriate times, but do my triumphs mean anything to you? Or is the playing field so esoteric, so alien to your own world, that the respect I've earned is incomprehensible?

Outside, a river of stars poured across the endless night, giving no answer. Fitting, indeed, that night be endless and that he should spend his restlessness gazing into it.

There had been a moment of thoughtless braggadocio, when visions of glory and subtle revenge had turned his mind; but that was too late along the course. You couldn't light the priming there, but earlier. There had been the day when Chase was drafted, or earlier still when Styx had visited with her cabal to pick his pocket and Hobie had prodded his vanity. Each time, he had made choices—and they had been the right choices, he still believed, even though they had led him step by step to this night.

There had been others, too. People pursuing their own dreams, or fleeing from their own fears, who had set the thing in motion. If Adam van Huyten had not shaken the pillars, Styx might not have come calling, hat in hand, to entangle him. If Leland Hobart, single-mindedly chasing his Holy Grail, had not made the whole hack thinkable . . . If DeepSpace had not reached out, or Orbital Management ducked behind its shell . . . If something unhuman had not rigged the dice ten thousand years ago . . . Seen from that perspective, the whole thing had a sort of inevitability, like the third act of a Greek play, and choice and will were not even on the table.

But that perspective was *too* far off, as godlike as the stars that filled the night. By explaining everything, Fate explained nothing. Closer in, there were passions and pretensions, choices and consequences: a perspective more akin to the eternally crescent moon that hovered in a corner of the sky than to the distant stars. Close and familiar enough to be a comfort.

But what is it that causes the avalanche? The collisions of continents that raised the mountain? The warm, moist air that draped its flanks with snow? Or was it the sound, the clap, the shudder that shook the first clump free?

The more he thought about it, the more convinced he became that that first clump of snow was the call from Billie the cheesehead back in sixteen; and he wondered, as he so often did these days, how the world might have gone if he had only said no.

2 0 1 6 – 2 0 1 7

1.

The Sack of Troy

They were called the Five Fingers, but never in public. Partly, this was because no one was quite sure who they were; and partly it was because, if they really were who they were rumored to be, it would be unwise to say so. It was not even certain that there were only five—or even five. Certainly, S. James Poole of Poole sEcurity Consultants was on everyone's short list; but the suggestion that there might be four others his equal at fingering the Net was a notion he would not even laugh at.

Billie Whistle studied the man whose image sprawled across her pixwall like a Marxist hero. A fat man, but one who had recently discovered thin and wasn't entirely sure he wanted to go there. His skin was loose, almost like a dog's, giving him the appearance of a partly deflated balloon. His dirty-brown hair was combed forward over his forehead—a counterattack against the naked scalp creeping backward. A man, Billie decided, who had always neglected his body as a nuisance, but who in his early thirties had spotted the first hints of hardware crash on the distant horizon. *Welcome to my world*, she thought.

If what she saw bore any relationship to reality. Poole was seldom seen in the flesh. He could project whatever persona he wanted to show the world. "Fat computer greek" might be nothing more than clever camouflage, a comfortable screen morph masking something far different.

However, "buff and debonair" was a low-prob configuration. Geek was the default mode.

The geek tugged on his lower lip. "I don't understand," he said—accusatory, as if his misunderstanding must be another's fault. "Was the teep unsatisfactory? Security wasn't breached, I guarantee that."

"No, it wasn't that." Billie ran her left hand—the one that worked—through short, stubby hair shaved close to the scalp. The input sockets felt like tiny bumps under her fingers. Encephalic Interface for Electronic Input/Output. The phrenology of the twenty-first century. "I teeped using one of their mobiles—what the construction workers used to call Uncle Waldo—and Blackhall showed me some prime ziggy volume in the Hub's number four tank, but something didn't smell right."

Puzzlement on pale jowls. "Smell? Are they simming smells now?" Shock

21

that there might be enhancements he hadn't heard of. "What kind of sensory jacks you got, cheesehead?"

"It's just a figure of speech, Poole." And *cheesehead* borderlined rude when flatskulls said it. Holes in your head for the I/O jacks. Swiss cheese. Jack cheese. Someday she would learn the identity of the person who had coined that particular slang, and he would suffer, terribly. "I meant something didn't seem right," she said, "but I can't put my finger on what it was that bothered me. Something rotten in the state of Denmark."

Poole frowned at some inner thought. "Or in the state of LEO," he said.

"Baleen needs ziggy stere," she said. "But on-orbit volume is bidding at a premium, so choice is limited and . . ." Billie fell silent. She didn't want to sound like a beggar.

"You could try putting a fly on their wall," Poole suggested. "But that would be illegal." With just enough sly behind the smile that she could take it as a joke, a warning, or a suggestion, however she pleased. There were stories about Jimmy Poole. Rumors about how he had gotten his seed money. Nothing ever proven; and, if Jimmy really were one of the Five Fingers, nothing ever would be.

"Baleen is legit," she temporized. What Billie Whistle herself was—or had been—was none of his business. The fly on the wall comment had cut way too close to the bone. Yet, how could Poole know anything? She and David had worked off-line, and the off-line world was invisible to the digerati.

"So forget telepresence," he said. "Take the trip in real, honest-to-goodness, suck-the-air-from-your-lungs outer space. Lift a bonebag and nose around LEO Station in person."

"Lift tickets are pretty steep. Twenty-eight troy. That's four hundred and fifty federal dollars per kilo."

"Baleen can't be *that* undercapitalized. Not if you plan to lift manufacturing gear to ziggy." The pasty-white face on her wall was replaced for a moment by a montage of wealth-images: stacks of bills; Wall Street Big Board; cartoon of spats, tails, and top hat tycoon.

"Most of our liquidity is locked up in hardware at this point," she told him. "Renting a manufacturing loft was supposed to be a no-brainer."

Poole reappeared, this time as a collage. Poole enthroned before his drives and monitors. Poole looking shrewd. Poole looking thoughtful. Poole lecturing a hall full of suits. Poole cruising in a limo—dressed "stupy," as they used to say—with a dark-skinned Indo woman at his side. Poole with a roll of cash. Poole with a stack of plastic. "Maybe I'll surf over to your R & C. If it looks good, I'll post a P2I. That'll give you the cash you—"

"We don't have a public 'Review and Comment' web site," she told him.

His eyebrows climbed. "Still looking for a bonded referee? Because I know someone—"

"It's not that. We're keeping the whole enterprise private."

Poole looked thoughtful. "But a public posting by a bonded referee . . . That's as good as driving stakes on a claim. The referee can log in any Promise-to-Invest and sort suggestions and pass out awards or equity shares for the really good ones. Right now, you're vulnerable if anyone copycats—independently *or* by fingering things out."

"We know that, and we're prepared to take the chance. We don't keep anything proprietary on net-accessible drives. We've got a two-year head start on any potential competitor; but some of the Bigs, if they knew what we planned, could crash development out of pocket change and beat us to market. Besides, our principal would rather keep his name off the web. If we post, the referee publishes the names of all investors." There. Set the hook.

Poole pursed his lips. "Your investors are anonymous? All word-of-mouth? Either you have one blockbuster of a product in mind, or your principal has mighty deep pockets."

"Deep enough."

"Yet you hesitated over a simple LEO lift."

Billie looked away from her doid for a moment and wet her lips. "There's a limit to how much he can tap."

Poole sent another montage across the pixwall. The Scarlet Pimpernel. Zorro. *Who was that masked man*, asked a grainy, black-and-white cowboy; frowning over a silver bullet. "Sounds like the masked man could use a faithful companion."

Billie carefully adjusted her features into bland puzzlement. "What do you mean?"

Film showing medieval warriors triggering a trebuchet. A great stone ball hurtled across the pixwall, morphing into a second film clip of money raining upon a Las Vegas street. Frantic people danced and snatched at the fluttering bills. "If you need liquidity, I might send some capital your way."

"You would." She made it a statement, not a question. Patience, patience. Don't jerk the line.

"Sure. I've got tons of welfare money."

A pause. Deliberate, she was sure. A verbal vacuum meant to suck the question out of her. Reluctantly, she said, "Welfare money?"

"Right. It sits around all day not doing anything."

Billie pressed her lips together. As a joke, it bordered on tasteless. And from the wrong side of the border. What did he know about it anyway? He'd never been there. "We're not looking for extra partners," she said, more snappishly than she had intended.

"Sure," said the consultant. "That's why you have to think twice about a lift ticket." His face reappeared, in the upper right of the pixwall. "Let's say, I'm willing to take a flyer. But I'll expect a quo for my quid."

"Well . . ." Billie laced her voice with hesitation. "We've calculated a tentative ROI, based on a five year penetration of the estimated market before any viable competition emerges . . ."

"Virgin field?" A clip from a porno flick. A panting young girl and a superimposed marquee flashing FIVE YEAR PENETRATION.

"Untouched," she said.

Poole's face appeared on the virgin's body. This time, Billie thought she saw frank curiosity there. "And you expect me to invest, sight unseen?" The bawd morphed into an innocent, masking her face coquettishly with a fan. Right.

"I didn't expect you to invest at all," she pointed out. "We were discussing the security on my LEO teep. *You* brought it up. I'm not even sure our principal would agree to you buying in."

"You haven't heard what my quo is."

Billie tried not to shrug. For one thing, it always looked awkward and lopsided when she did. "What do you want?" she asked.

"I want you to go up to LEO in person. You said things didn't smell right. Okay, go up and sniff. Come back and tell me."

"In person? Me? I can't . . ." She stopped. *Can't* . . . She never spoke of herself that way. And yet, this was one task that lay beyond her.

Poole did not ask why. He just gave that impatient cough and said, "Send someone else, then. Whatever. Someone with eyes and ears and enough brains to know what they see and hear."

Now it was Billie's turn to be puzzled. "Why should it matter so much to you?"

Poole went blank on her. "Call me a patriotic Dane."

The way he said that, Billie knew she'd not learn his reasons anytime soon. "I'll have to clear this with our principal. Like I said, he may not want another partner."

The Poole-image spread its hands. It wasn't his problem. "You want investment money?" A figure appeared in the lower right corner of the Gyricon wall screen. At first, she thought Poole was being deliberately insulting; then she realized the number was in troy ounces, not federal dollars. She carefully kept anything from showing in her face. "No bones," said Poole, "no troy."

Billie drummed the fingers of her left hand on the arm of her mobile. She thought the cursor over to the pull-down and scrolled the Dun & Bradstreet database, popularly known as Deeby-deeby. She considered the virtual keypad, and the electro-encephalitic interface translated thought into input. She spelled out Poole's name in the searchword box by glancing at each letter. Then she pondered the GO button. A popper window appeared on the pixwall, and she moved it over to the left with a toss of her head.

Impressive, she thought. Like an iceberg, Poole's wealth was reputedly ninety percent unseen; but even the portion so teasingly on display was substantial. Poole ranked near the bottom of the "500" list, but this was widely regarded as a policy decision on his part.

Poole smiled. "Rich enough for you?" A film clip showed an old man staggering: I felt a disturbance in the Force.

Billie flushed. Poole was a spider. Anything that disturbed the web, he knew about it. Certainly any site linked to him would be on bounceback. *Time to cut this short.* She turned her attention to the telecomm monitor and thought the cursor to the disconnect button. "We'll be in touch," she said, and pondered the disconnect.

Annoyingly, Poole's face remained on her pixwall a moment longer. Long enough to wink at her. *Bastard,* she thought. He had to prove that he'd had control of the commlink all along.

She disconnected from the system and ran the disinfectant. Not that she thought Poole had penetrated her. His personal stone tablets did not have too many line items, but not screwing his own client was one of them. And no third party could have cut in while Poole held her dance card. He was that good. Still, it never hurt to be careful.

Inserting the stump of her arm into the socket of her power chair, she cruised into her kitchen, where the others waited.

"Well?" said Red Hawkins, the operative, "did he go for it?" David Desherite, Baleen's principal, said nothing, but stood against the sink with his arms crossed and an inquiring look on his face.

"We've got him," she said, "but there's a catch." She didn't look directly at David.

"Wot's the catch?" asked Red.

Billie positioned her wheelchair in front of the coffeemaker. "Go back in the living room. I'll make some coffee and we'll talk."

"Need help?" asked David.

"I'm the hostess," she told him, avoiding the question.

She blinked her eyes three times and her implants converted the synapse sequence to the electronic command: *Activate #1 VCSEL laser.* That was the one installed on her cap's forehead—dead center, like a third eye. She tilted her head so the microlaser's tiny red spot struck the coffee machine's receptor. The menu screen lit and Billie pointed at it with the stump of her right arm. She imagined wiggling her fingers and the microlasers on the arm cup established a handshake with the coffeemaker's A/S.

Handshake, she thought bitterly.

She twitched an imaginary middle finger to scroll the selections. VCSELs lased from the surface of a chip, not its edge, so they could pack a godawful number of them on the end of her arm and train their software to respond to impulses that no longer had wrist, hand, or fingers to work on. The screen displayed COFFEE—BLACK. She twitched YES, then 3CUPS. She had filled the bean magazine that morning and the hot water was permanently fixtured. *Next best thing to an IV drip.* (But that reminded her of real IV drips; and the smells of antiseptic and disinfectant wafted momentarily through her memory.)

With her "real" hand, she pulled three mugs from the cabinet under the coffee machine. In all the apartment's four rooms, there were no cabinets that could not be reached by a one-armed woman sitting in a wheelchair—thanks to Tyler Crayle and his foundation money.

It had cost a great deal to design this apartment and make it, if not user-friendly, at least not overtly hostile. Most days, she preferred to forget what taking that money had entailed. The move to Milwaukee, the loss of her flowing brown locks to the EI sockets, and the job that her benefactor had asked her to do for the Nameless Ones.

Not all costs were counted in troy ounces; some were carved from your soul.

She set the first cup under the spigot with her left hand, and when the screen said READY, she toggled again with her phantom limb. She filled the cups one by one and placed them carefully on the chair's built-in tray. Everything ready, she reinserted her right arm into the chair and imagined pushing on a joy stick. The chair rolled toward the doorway.

That job had been nearly three years ago, and Tyler Crayle had never called on her again. She had not walked the wild side since—not until David had approached her.

As for the move to Milwaukee, who cared what strangers called the mass of buildings she glimpsed through her windows? It might as easily have been Portland or Chattanooga or Ypsilanti. The world outside her walls barely existed. The world within her walls was as wide as all cyberspace. There was an old saying: In the virtch, no one knows you're a dog. Or a cheesehead. Or even a paraplegic, double-amputee cheesehead, who once might have been a knockout babe, a sharp techie, and a dynamite dancer.

David Desherite waited on the other side of the door, ready to take the tray from her. She rolled past before he could reach out. "I could have done that for you," he said as he trailed her.

"Yes, I know." He meant well; but on this one topic he was clueless.

Red had squatted by her audio tower, making himself at home. He had pulled μCDs out of their magazine slots, checking the titles. Irritated, she nodded to the player, connected, and selected a playlist—as easily as running an imaginary finger down a virtual roster. Red jumped when the unit began to play a symphony by Rodriguez. He turned and grinned at her.

"Built-in remote, eh? Wish I could play that trick, sheila."

"No," she told him flatly. "You really don't."

The Australian opened his mouth, then thought better of it. The other two served themselves from her tray and settled onto the stools that were the only human furniture in a room that more nearly resembled an art gallery. All things considered, she didn't need chairs and sofas. Or beds. And she didn't need Red tagging along when David indulged his foible for personal face-time. Not that Red had no right—Baleen's organization was flat and, aside from some deference to David as principal partner, there was no hierarchy; but Billie hadn't envisioned Red's grinning, bald head when she had imagined this meeting. Heat flushed her cheeks. And what did she really think would happen if she and David had been alone? David wasn't the only clueless one here.

"We tapped the Poole for a sack of troy," said Billie and told them how much. Red whistled. David was cautious.

"That's not pocket change. How far can we trust him?"

"About as far as you can throw him."

"How far is that?"

"Well . . ." She tried to be fair. "He *has* been losing weight lately."

Red's laugh was a donkey's bray.

"You said there was a catch," David prompted her.

"Yeah. He wants us to send a bonebag to LEO and 'check things out.' " She exchanged a significant glance with David and made a covert nod toward Red. David went all bland.

"Check things out . . . Why?"

"I told him something seemed funny to me. He made bagging a condition on the investment."

David nodded. "And what struck *you* as odd about LEO?"

"Shary was evasive. He wouldn't meet my eyes."

Red snickered. "You were Uncle Waldo. A telepresence mobile doesn't have eyes to meet. Just optics."

"I didn't mean it literally. And there was something else. I can't pin it down. But I keep thinking I *saw* something when Blackhall, the engineer, was showing me around."

"But you don't know what?" David said.

Billie shook her head. "A gut feeling."

Red laughed. "That might be what you had for breakfast today."

A flash of irritation crossed David's face, and he glanced at Red a moment. "So, Poole is paying us to satisfy your own uneasiness? What's in it for him?"

Billie shook her head. "He imitated a clam." But she thought, *Maybe the same things you're looking for.*

"Then I guess I should go up," said Red Hawkins. "I'm the bleeding operative. I'll be installing the equipment and rigging things. Besides, I helped build the damn station. I know my way around, and half the otters in ziggy know me."

David sipped his coffee. "That's a good reason why you shouldn't go. You have a motive for going up, but *not* for asking the kinds of questions you'll need to ask."

And besides, Billie thought, Red didn't have the kind of subtlety the job might call for. She thought Red was down with Baleen. He was the sort of man who, when he hired on, hired on all the way. Yet, like Baleen's product, he was more surface area than volume. What you saw was what you got, because there wasn't much else there.

"It's risky," she said.

"Oh,"—David waved a negligent hand—"what can Orbital Management Corporation do?"

"They could learn enough about Baleen to pirate our whole venture," she said. "I've got too much invested to feel easy about that." Yet what would Poole do if they took his cash, then failed to follow through? The whisper was that Poole no longer walked the wild side; but that didn't mean he'd forgotten how.

Red Hawkins toyed with his beard. It was a large, tightly curled affair, counterpoint to his barren skull. "She's got a point, mate. Everything I got's sunk in this game, too. Same with Shao and Karl."

"I'd make it good for you," said David. "You know that."

Red cocked his head and looked at him. "Then there wouldn't be much point to it, would there?"

David dropped his eyes. "I mean if it blows because I fooed. If Baleen goes down because the market wasn't right, that's different."

Red snorted. "Don't come the raw prawn with me, mate." David colored, but Red continued. "Aw, don't take it wrong, rich boy. I didn't come down in the rain. Besides, wot'd I do with that construction bonus besides blow it on feed, frosties, and features? This way I can get rich enough I can buy the bleeding brewery." He threw back his head and brayed. Billie and David traded looks past him.

"You *want* to go," Billie said.

David shook his head. "I *have* to go."

"We have too much riding on this to risk it over some personal weenie of yours."

David made an exasperated sound. "*Someone* has to go. You think something strange is going on, and Poole must think so, too, or he wouldn't have paid us to go look. Can we risk installing Baleen without resolving those doubts? So someone goes. It's got to be Baleen, and it's got to be someone with ziggy. That leaves out Shao and Karl. Red, you're too well-known. That leaves me."

"A couple months on Wilson's SpaceLab," said Red.

"And on Goddard and FreeFall Resort. I know ziggy, otter." David gave Red a level stare and the two held the pose a moment. Then Red tugged at his beard and nodded.

"Yeah," he said. "Maybe you do."

Billie regarded David: the confident pose, the glittering eyes, the easy smile; but behind it all, a hard and implacable anger. And she wondered not for the first time since she had thrown her life and fortune into Baleen whether Baleen was something in which David believed or whether it was just something he had fashioned to use in another cause, to which she was not privy.

After the others had gone, Billie saw the μCDs that Red had thoughtlessly yanked from their position in the player's magazine. She hated it when she had to deal with physical objects. It was a reminder of how helpless she really was. She could pretend all she wanted and lie about empowerment and throw euphemism on euphemism; but the truth was she only had one arm and one leg and they might as well have taken the other leg because she couldn't move it or feel it and the only time she was ever really free was living other people's dreams in an electronic wonderland.

There were empty slots in the magazine. Her ballet and other dance music had once been kept there. But three days after she had finished rehab, she had used her one good hand to yank those disks out one by one and snap them in two with the wheels of the chair that bound her.

She turned her mobile and faced the now-blank pixwall. So Poole was going to gift them with gold. Was that good news or not? It all depended on what sort of man Poole really was. What sort of person lay behind that carefully cultivated public persona? And why had a cruel fate made him so suddenly a fulcrum in Billie Whistle's own personal life?

2.

A Poole and His Money

S. James Poole, Poole sEcurity Consultants, broke the connection with Baleen, laughed, and spun his oversize chair around a full circle. He clapped his hands together. "Gotcha!" he told the darkened pee-phone screen. Tani Pandya, engrossed with the progress of their small child as he squirmed his way across the living room rug, did not even turn to look into his Sanctum.

"What have you got this time?" she asked.

It was a comfortable chair. Ergonomically designed so he could sit in it for long hours without butt-death, armrests shaped to avoid "carping." It felt good to sit there, like a king enthroned before his drives and monitors, juke boxes and virtch hats, here in the center of the happening world.

"Some little start-up," he told his wife. "I waved some gold in front of their faces and they promised to send someone up to LEO Station to suss things out for me." Well, the cheesehead he had talked to hadn't quite said yes, but the yes was there and they had both known it. Any internal head-bumping at Baleen would only be to convince themselves that they hadn't been bought.

"What *is* happening on LEO?" Tani said, rising to her knees and looking at him.

Jimmy gave her the Look. "If I knew that, I wouldn't be sending a cat's paw."

"I was speaking rhetorically—No, Stevie, that's too far." She scuttled across the room after the child. Stevie saw her coming and his mouth gaped in a hideous grin as he crawled faster. Laughing at the game? Jimmy wondered. Or screaming in terror at the gigantic creature chasing him? What went on in the mind of a newbie?

It was fascinating to watch Stevie develop. Very much a self-adapting algorithm. Exploring the environment, taking in data, incorporating that into his programming. Fear of heights. Fear of dark. Fear of loud, unexpected noises. More recently, fear of separation. How much of what makes us human, he wondered, is based on fear?

Stevie himself had been a loud, unexpected noise in Jimmy's life, and Jimmy knew not a little fear of his own because of it. Though the kid was largely self-booting, it was still up to Tani and him to oversee the programming of the operating system; and, while a certain amount of overwriting and revision was possible early in the development phase, the code had to be debugged well before release to the operational environment. You only had one opportunity to get it right. There was no erasing; no rebooting permitted.

He had tried to explain his anxiety to Tani once, and she had looked at him with that same mixture of horror and fascination with which she greeted everything he did and said. Later, she'd made memos in her writer's notebook. He knew she was mining him for her novel, and sometimes wondered whether, absent that book contract, the fascination would be missing from her gaze.

Jimmy eased himself from his chair, feeling unsteady for a moment, like an otter from LEO returning Earthside. Or at least what he imagined an orbital worker might feel. He bent down and swooped Stevie up before the rugrat could crawl into the Sanctum. Stevie stared at him wide-eyed. *Horror and fascination*, Jimmy thought. Frightened by the giant creature holding him; yet, eager to learn what it meant. Perhaps that was the only rational way to approach the world.

"*Something* is going on up there," he told Tani. "No one throws up a laager unless they're trying to hide something behind it. And not just any old something. They have a top of the line firewall dressed up to look industry standard. That would be like buying a custom-tailored suit and having a seamstress make it look off-the-rack."

Tani pushed herself to her feet. She was not a tall woman. Jimmy was short himself and he topped his wife by half a head. She had a soft, plumpish body and dusky skin, as if the Pillsbury doughboy had been born a girl in Bombay. Beauty is in the eye of the beholder was an old cliché; yet how did it become a cliché except by being true? Jimmy knew the mechanism. The face you saw when your genitals exploded became, like Pavlov's bell, associated with the pleasure; and soon enough, just as the dogs salivated when Pavlov rang his bell, Jimmy Poole had felt himself stir (not to mention salivate) when he saw Tani's face. Programmed by back-propagation from the solution set, just like a neural net.

But he was naggingly aware that there had to be more to love than that. Otherwise, he would have been deeply infatuated with his right hand.

"The only reason you care," Tani said, "is because you can't worm your way through and see for yourself." Quickly and efficiently, she checked Stevie's diaper, though she made no move to take him from Jimmy's arms. "It's your wounded pride."

Jimmy tried not to show his wounded pride. Tani could see right through him. She had that talent. She could always see the person behind the persona. That was why her first novel, *Taj Mahal*, had been such a popular and critical success. "I *could* worm through if I wanted to," he said, knowing even as he said it how phony and defensive it would sound. He tried to convince himself that it was true. He really could, if he tried; but that was theory and the only way to *prove* it one way or the other was to reactivate Crackman. "I've given up cracking. You know that." He held little Stevie out at arms' length. "Isn't that right, small person?"

The kid was too young yet for word recognition. In fact, he was remarkably silent on the whole speech issue. "Isn't that right?"

Stevie grinned and belched and a glob of something that had once been milk emerged and dribbled down his chin.

Coincidence and not commentary; yet, was it any wonder that the ancients had seen the will of the gods in chance concatenations?

Tani took the child from him and began cleaning him up. Well, she'd had plenty of practice on her husband, Jimmy admitted. He'd been pretty much of a slob in his earlier rev level. His kitchen had been on the Superfund list.

"Do you think the woman you spoke with will be able to uncover anything?"

"The cheesehead? Nah. You should have seen her face when I said she should go to Leo herself. Don't know if she was scared or angry. But Baleen will send somebody. They're just as curious as I am, even if it's just some fuzzy intuition on their part. They haven't tried to worm through the firewall, like—" He stopped.

"Like you have." She had turned from ministering to Stevie to look him in the eye. Once again, Jimmy had the icelike feeling that she was looking *into* him, not at him.

"I swear I'm not mousing them."

"Will you swear you *haven't*? Never mind. I don't want to hear the answer. But I don't want to see the feds at my door, taking you away, impounding everything we have to live on, and leaving me alone with a child. They'd do that, you know. They don't care. Half their budgets come from asset seizures."

In his teens and twenties, Jimmy Poole had known himself not merely immortal, but invulnerable as well. Now he had turned thirty and neither prospect seemed quite so certain anymore. He knew he could worm through Leo's laager, but he was no longer sure he could do it without leaving tracks. There were others out there now nearly as good as he was. Younger and hungrier than he was. Whoever had built the laager had possessed no small skill. No intruder could breach that handiwork without instigating an overwhelming curiosity on the author's part to find out who had done it.

"I already told you," he said with some irritation. "That's why I talked Baleen into sending a bonebag up there. I've got no more desire to be dragged away than you have to wave good-bye when they do."

And besides, he thought, as he watched little Stevie sit upright on the play mat where Tani placed him and heard him make a noise that only the wildest imagination could ever interpret as *Da!*, there were deprivations far more severe than any government could imagine.

* * *

When he stopped by Tani's office later, he saw that she had gone out. Her screen was dark, her notebooks locked away in her cabinet. Stevie was napping in the nursery under the watchful eye of Rada, his nanny. In the kitchen, Jimmy asked Stassy where Tani had gone and the Russian woman, her arms deep in a tray of dough, nodded with a flour-stained chin toward the backyard.

Tani was sitting on the knoll where the ground fell off toward the bay. Gulls circled overhead looking for a handout. In the distance, the San Mateo Bridge draped gracefully over the water. Tani had changed clothes. She wore baggy, "mainstreet" trousers and a bulky cable knit sweater. Jimmy watched while she tore little tufts of grass from the ground and threw them to the March winds.

She heard him coming and glanced briefly in his direction. A gray squirrel darted across the lawn, a zigzag path composed of random directions and times intermixed with sudden freezes. Jimmy scanned the sky, but there were no hawks circling, so it must have been his own approach that triggered the evasive action programming.

It's how the small survive. Enough of them anyway to keep gray squirreling a viable profession. It was something to keep in mind when survival was on the table.

Of course, hawks survived, too . . .

He plumped himself beside Tani on the grass. She drew her legs up under her chin and wrapped her arms around them. "Enjoying the view?" Jimmy asked. She shook her head in silence.

Jimmy let the silence grow. You had to give people their space: verbal and mental as well as physical. You couldn't push things. It had taken him many years and cost him a lot of pain to learn that.

He wore shorts, and the grass and clover in the lawn tickled his legs. He ran a hand through the tangled green mass. Tall or squat, leafy or flowered. A thousand different strategies for sucking sunlight and making sugar. And the bugs and the squirrels had as many strategies for stealing it. And the birds and the foxes were running their own agendas. Each plant and animal was different, like the automata in a self-organizing neural net.

"It goes in fits and starts," Tani said.

Jimmy nodded, knowing she meant her book.

"I write a chapter. Then, the next day, I want to delete it and start over. Jimmy, what if it never gels?"

"You can do it," he said. "Look at *Taj Mahal.*"

"That—wasn't the same thing. *Taj Mahal* flowed right out of me. This one doesn't."

Jimmy draped an arm around her shoulders, unsure how to offer comfort. Her first book. How it felt to be one of the "new immigrants." How her father's dreams had wrapped like chains around her ankles. The convenience store. The robbery. Azim Thomas grabbing Zipper's gun arm; Meat Tucker pulling

Tani back into the stock room. (He *owed* Meat for that one. Otherwise Tani would have been as dead as her father. He owed Azim, too.) Of course, *Taj Mahal* had flowed like blood and sweat and tears. She had lived it. Jimmy hadn't known such writing possible—static words, linear arrangement, no hyperlinks; yet they had *lived*—and afterward he had found his usual genre reading pallid and flat.

Jimmy wondered if half the problem was that her success had come too quickly and too easily. "Maybe," he suggested cautiously, "the virtch isn't the right world for you to write about."

She pushed him away. "Give up? Start over? I've put seven years of my life into this book! I've—" She stopped and looked away from him. "I've done a lot of research," she finished.

"*Taj Mahal* came alive because you lived it. You haven't lived in the virtch; you've only studied it, and you can't *write* with passion if you haven't *felt* the passion."

Tani sighed and leaned her back against him, allowing his arms to encircle her. "Maybe you're right. Passion. And drama. Something that will make the book stand out and grab people around the balls, so they sit up and notice."

"If you're going to grab people by the balls," Jimmy whispered into her sun-warmed tresses, "you can start with me. I promise to sit up and notice."

Tani laughed and leaned her head back so that she was almost lying in his arms. The sunlight danced in her eyes. Her teeth shone. She felt warm and soft against him. With one hand she stroked his cheek. With the other hand, she stroked . . .

"I've already done that," she said.

It was only much later, long after they had entertained the hawks and gray squirrels of the south bay, that Jimmy wondered if there wasn't another way to take her meaning.

3.

The Last Place on Earth, or Somewhere Damn Close to It

It should have been colder than it felt, but the parka kept Leland Hobart toasty warm. The wind howled and blew snow as gritty as sandpaper, that stung against exposed flesh before melting and settling into the fabric. There was probably a name for it, for this particular kind of ice. The Eskimos had a gazillion names for ice and snow. Wasn't that what everyone said? So did the Norse, come to that; and for much the same reason. *Welcome to it*, he thought as he plowed his way through the curling drifts toward the black hulk of the research station. *I'd rather have a hundred names for sunshine.*

It was a nor'easter, they said; except that Lodestar Base was so far north the winds blew from the southeast, instead. In fact, there wasn't much north of Bathurst Island except more north. And, in another sense, there wasn't even any north up that way, either.

The wooden and aluminum trestle swayed in the wind and Hobie studied its motion with narrow eyes. The contractor had sworn the trestle would withstand the worst the season would offer, but the rising storm was unseasonable. If the trestle went down, another year's work went down with it. Well, it had been a gamble to start work so early; but an early start meant more experimental uptime before the winter closed in again.

Only two seasons up here: winter and the Fourth of July.

He wondered if there was an older joke circulating among the Lodestar cadre.

The wind slacked off and dropped a fifth in pitch, sounding like someone blowing across the lip of a beer bottle. Probably the guy wires that held the trestle in place were humming. He reached out a thickly gloved hand and placed it on the nearest cable. It was hard to tell through the padding, but he thought he felt it vibrating.

A sharp tug at his waist drew his attention to the main hut, where Nikolai waited for him. Hobie waved and gave two return tugs on the lifeline. Quickly, he finished his inspection of the circular trestle and the electrical lines. Satisfied that everything was still holding together, he guided himself back toward the hut, hand over hand. Nikolai grabbed him when he was close enough and bundled him indoors.

"You shouldn't stay out so long, Dr. Hobart," the base superintendent told him when they had sealed themselves in and the banshee wind had been stifled. "That wind sucks the warmth right out of you. You can freeze to death before you know it, eh?"

Leland Hobart had pulled his gloves and goggles off and was rubbing his hands vigorously. "Next time, I'll bring my own mother with me."

Nikolai Cunningham shook his head. "Scientists."

"Puts me in my place," said Hobie, grinning. They entered the dressing room and shucked their parkas.

"I should've stayed in Manitoba," Cunningham said. "Winters were just as bad, but the project team actually paid attention when I talked. It's colder out there than you—"

"Don't worry, mama. Short and squat like me, we don't lose body heat as fast as you string beans."

Cunningham hung his parka on the wall hook next to a row of similar parkas. Each had a distinctive color or pattern on its back and a name stenciled between the shoulders. "Sure, but black as your skin already is, who'd know when the gangrene set in?"

That was skating a little close to thin ice, but Hobie knew Nick hadn't meant anything but some good-natured japing—playing the nines. Hobie scowled into the mirror and ran his stubby fingers through the short-cropped nap on his head. "Didn't think it showed." A face as black as vengeance. Nothing *but* the tar brush there. It was the sort of color that made some people cross the street when they saw him. The color of low expectations.

He looked like a football player, Hobie thought. A football player recently cut from the team. At thirty-two, he'd be an old man in the NFL. Hell, an offensive guard? He'd probably have retired on injuries years ago. Washed up, with nothing to do except buy into a car dealership in some medium-important city, so other guys could cash in on what little name recognition he might have built up. It had been a near thing, he remembered, avoiding that seduction. Now, instead of being an ex-jock, he was someone whose name was sometimes mentioned in the same sentence as "Nobel prize." No black man had ever won a Nobel prize in the sciences, a thought that appalled him in two different ways. And one of them was that spotlights scared him shitless.

"God designed me for sun and the tropics," he told Nick. "But high-temperature superconductors aren't ready for field-testing in Aruba quite yet."

Cunningham laughed and told him that most of the crew would be gathered in the mess hall to watch the latest morphy, "just bounced off the up-and-down." Humphrey Bogart and Harrison Ford snuggling with Mae West while they searched for the stolen Black Rock of Mecca. Hobie begged off, saying he was tired, and headed for his room in the next hut. Actually, he didn't care much for morphies. Hair *still* didn't look right on the computerized imagos. Give him a movie any day, with real actors in front of real cameras.

Hobie's quarters were lined with furs. Fake furs, but realistic enough to send some people into foaming fits. Beyond the thick insulation he could hear the moaning of the winds. With the space heater glowing in its niche and the muted windsong, the robes gave his room a snug closed-in feeling, as if he were with Peary or Amundsen on one of those turn of the century polar expeditions. *People used to die coming up to this 'hood.* Most of the islands and capes here in the archipelago had been named for people searching for the doomed Franklin expedition. The last place on earth, they used to call it. It was either that, Dr. Hobart thought, or someplace damn close to it. He pulled the book he had been reading from the shelf and propped himself on the bed. It was one of the great classics, *How Few Remain*, and he was almost finished with it. He particularly enjoyed the characterization of Frederick Douglass, and wondered sometimes at the parallels to his own attempts to live normally in a white world.

He glanced again at his reading shelf. Should have brought more books with him. He might have to break down and download something from Your-Library.com, though he disliked screening a book—*screading*, the kids said nowadays. He liked to slouch while he read, hard to do even with a flatscreen.

The robes billowed and Hobie heard the sound of the door closing. He put a thumb in his book and looked up just as Krystal Delacroix poked her head through the robes. "Do you have a few minutes, Dr. Hobart?"

Hobie sighed and put the book away. "Come in."

Krystal was twenty-three, thin, and pale with hair the color of straw. She wore "sensible" clothes, cut in the baggy, low-hanging style preferred on Main Street. The dark cuffs at her wrists and ankles contrasted with the light print of the blouse and pants. The floral scarf around her neck was tucked into her blouse. Paper notes and styluses peeked from the shirt pockets.

"You're not going to doid me?" asked Hobie with a worried look around his room. It looked remarkably like a room in which a man had lived alone for several weeks. "I'd want to clean up first."

Krystal pulled the scarf out and made to fasten it around her head. "Should I?" The digital optical input device was a small, silvery disc sewn into the fabric. A "third eye" for news groupies.

"I'd rather not." And Charli would die of embarrassment if he showed up on the netscape surrounded by such a mess.

The woman grinned. "Don't worry." She tossed the scarf on the back of the room's single chair. "But if you want to keep up public interest in your experiment, you have to get more pixels out on the newsgroups." She flopped on the other end of the bed-*cum*-couch and crossed her legs yogi-style. "Text-only is bo-o-o-ring."

"You can't do science with news releases," Hobie said.

"And you can't do news with science," Krystal shot back. "Talking head stuff. Induces audience MEGO."

"MEGO?"

"My Eyes Glaze Over. At least this gig has exotic locale. Snow. Ice. Remoteness. Nearest town's an island away; and that's stretching the definition of town. There's even a hint of risk." She mimicked holding an old hand-mike to her lips and said, "This is Krystal Delacroix, reporting from the ice-bound wastes of the Arctic. Geez, I wish my parents hadn't named me Krystal. It sounds so air. Not very mainstreet."

"Could have been worse," Hobie told her. "Could have been Tiffany."

She laughed. "Or Moon Unit."

"Well, that'd be okay if you were reporting from Artemis Mines."

"Hey, 'no flubber on that one, Charlie.' It's just that you can't lift in the org if the big hats don't take you serious. And sometimes the only thing they know about you is your name."

"Give 'em something else to remember. Something new or different; not the same old same old."

Krystal shook her head. "Too risky. 'Brick by brick you build a castle.' "

"Stones," he pointed out.

She looked puzzled and Hobie shrugged. Krystal had it all wrong. You grabbed what you could and blew your own horn; because in the end no one watched butts half as well as you watched your own. Sometimes he found the younger generation hard to read. So earnest and dutiful and play-together; not like the ragtag bunch he had grown up around. Back then "risky" had been a come-on, not a caution.

Krystal looked around the room. "Cozy," she said. "Do you have anything for internal combustion?" Hobie gave her a blank look and she made a bottle with her fist. "You know. Something to warm the insides?"

He pretended to misunderstand her. "I have some hot chocolate packets and a selection of teas."

Krystal opened her mouth, appeared to change her mind, and said, "Hot chocolate would be nice."

Hobie slid off the bed, drew two packets from the drawer and emptied one into his own mug, the other into his "guest mug." People sometimes acted funny when they realized he didn't drink alcohol. They always assumed there was some reason for it, some secret in his closet, and they became very quiet and understanding. It never seemed to occur to them that he just didn't like the taste of booze.

Hobie laughed to himself as he put the mugs under the faucet. You ought to have a reason to drink; you didn't need a reason not to.

The water dispenser was a Peltier system: a ceramic sandwich of semiconductors. Put a current through it, and one ceramic plate became hot while the other grew cold. The water that poured into the mugs was just short of boiling.

Old technology, he thought as he stirred the chocolate. Decades old. Used as heat sinks in electronic equipment. But the complementary process, the

Seebeck effect, generated electricity from nothing more than a temperature difference; and so had become a very useful power source on the orbital stations, where, between sunlight and shadow, they had the mother of all temperature differences. He had planned to use a Seebeck motor to power up his superconductor loop when it was time for ziggy.

"I thought the interview would go smoother," Krystal said, "if I knew more about your experiment."

He handed the guest mug to Krystal. "We've been over this already."

"Some of us need to hear things more than once to understand."

Hobie nodded and resumed his own seat on the careful end of the bed. Krystal had done several interviews and backgrounds since arriving at Lodestar Arctic Base. From the questions she had asked, Hobie figured she had done her homework and, for a newsgroupie, had a fair grasp of the technical issues. So she wasn't exactly Ms. Bubblehead of 2016. And that meant she was in his room running a hidden agenda.

Hobie smiled and relaxed a little. It was good to be back on familiar ground. Never trust anyone with only one agenda showing. "Where should I start?"

"Well, I know you're testing high-temperature superconductors." She tossed her head and laughed. "Except that calling what's outside right now 'high temperature' sounds a little whack."

Hobie blinked, realized she was serious, then realized she was right. Krystal's subscribers probably had a different perspective than he did. High temperature? *Context is all.*

"Right," he said. "Well. You probably don't want to hear about Luttinger liquids or non-Fermi fluids . . ."

Krystal laughed, a deliberate sound—though Hobie could not say why he thought so. "You scientists keep finding materials that become superconducting at higher and higher temperatures. Like outside . . ." She waved a hand at the furs. "But my screaders will want to know: What's on the horizon and how will it change their lives?"

It was an odd feeling, but as they talked Hobie thought there was a disconnect between her voice and her posture. Her questions seemed wooden, perfunctory; yet she nearly vibrated with intensity. He had seen enough scientists, newsers, and athletes hot on the trail of some prize to recognize the symptoms. Yet, what was the prize? Was she fishing for some scandal? He knew of nothing scandalous in Project Lodestar; but he had also learned a long time ago that newsers did not need a controversy to report one. Sometimes all they needed was a different perspective, a little imagination, and a dose of jaded cynicism. Hobie chose his next words with care and hoped he didn't sound like he was hiding something.

"Okay," he said, "lots of applications if superconduction ever goes commercial—large magnets, energy storage, motors, zero-loss transmission lines, maglev trains. All kinds of stuff."

Krystal put her mug aside and fanned her face with her hand. "Hot chocolate sure does warm you up." She fanned her face, which had grown distinctly flushed. "So what's the problem? Ductility. Wasn't that what you told me?"

Hobie nodded. "To get all those bennies I just mentioned, you have to draw wire. Okay, you can 'silk screen' thin-film circuits for computer boards. But, *most* applications. Unfortunately, the high temp ceramics tend to be brittle and inflexible. Then, a couple years ago, extending Anderson's work to anomalous spin liquids, I found a relation between the parameters of superconducting compounds and the chemical properties of the constituent materials—"

"That was your 'periodic table.' "

"Yes."

"The one that's going to win you the Nobel prize."

Hobie was not one to tempt fate. "Maybe. There's talk of it. The committee usually waits to see how significant a discovery really is before they—"

She placed a hand on his arm. "Don't worry," she said. "I'm sure you'll make it."

How had she gotten so close to him, he wondered? He couldn't remember her sliding down the bed. "Y-you see, each supercompound is, uh, quenched if the temperature gets too high. But it's also quenched if . . . If the magnetic field penetrates it." He tried to squirm to his left, but found he was already at the foot of the bed. "Normally, a superconductor *expels* magnetic fields. The Meissner effect. But above the critical point, the fields, uh, penetrate . . . And that means there's a critical current density, too, since a current through the wire generates its own magfield."

She was sitting alongside him now, touching him with her knee, her arm, her . . . There seemed to be a great deal of knee.

"So I c-c-correlated known c . . . compounds. A nominal scale against those three qualities, and . . ."

Krystal Delacroix ran her forefinger down Hobie's arm. He suddenly realized that she *was* on the trail of a prize. And *he* was the prize.

Hobie stood abruptly and Krystal slipped and fell on her elbow. He saw that she had unfastened the top two buttons of her blouse, and he tried to look and look away at the same time. "What do you want?" he demanded.

Krystal sat up straight. "I would think that was damn obvious."

Well, *duuh.* Hobie felt his cheeks burn. "I'm, uh, married?" And why should that come out sounding like a question?

"Yeah, right." Krystal resumed her yogi squat. Her flesh was pale, sickly. The only hint of color was the dark, rosy tips. Hobie turned away, concentrated on refilling his mug, losing himself in the details of preparation. Why did everyone think that black men lusted for a glimpse of white bosoms? "What does that mean?" he demanded.

"I mean there's 'married' and then there's *married.* Which one are you? What's her name? I've never heard you mention it. Where's her picture? I don't see anything pinned to your walls here. How many letters or E-mails have you gotten? Or sent?"

"That's none of your business, is it?" He turned again and faced her and saw that she had rebuttoned her blouse. The flush he had noticed earlier now occupied her entire face.

"Look," she said, "I'm sorry if I misread your signals, but . . ."

"I haven't been sending any signals."

". . . but do you know how *boring* it is up here? Nothing to do but watch that stupid compass needle dip and bob . . ."

"We *are* at the north magnetic pole . . ."

"Wizzy! But what do you do after the first hour? Watch another morphy? Pop on a virtch hat and play inside your own head?" The newsgroupie threw her arms up and then fell on her back on the bed. "I was just looking to kill some time. I thought you might be bored, too."

"Bored?" Hobie lowered himself into the chair. The room was close, the chair was not so far from the bed. "How can I be bored? If we can stabilize the field and maintain the R-vector orientation so it creates a repulsive force . . ." He could see that she wasn't listening and leaned forward in the chair. "Don't you see? We'd verify whether a self-driven ground launch is possible!"

Krystal shook her head. "That won't exactly grab Walt and Wanda Web-browser by the short curlies, will it?"

Hobie slouched back. "I tried to arrange a car chase and an arson, but Nick wouldn't go along with it."

Krystal gave him a narrow look. "Don't come across so high and mighty, Mr. Scientist. If the news doesn't entertain, it doesn't get watched. Maybe it was different back when people actually had to *read* newspapers or listen to whatever factoids got read to them on the tube. They couldn't surf-'n'-choose which bytes to 'act with; but that was then and this is now. People sign up for interest groups and their spyders search for keywords. They can't load you down if they don't know you're loaded. You want to get known? You need jingles—a theme song—and F/X, maybe even a prosper—"

Sure, and have someone direct a roller video . . . "What the hell's a prosper?" he snapped.

"Professional spokesperson. And maybe I should add another gotta."

"What's that?"

"You gotta keep your newsgroupie happy."

"Ah." Hobie cradled his mug in his hands and pondered his next move. What he was doing was important, but how could he get the newser to see that there was more at Lodestar Base than an exotic background shot and a black man doing things white folks *still* didn't expect black men to do?

When Hobie thought about his superloop—which was, he admitted, most of his waking hours—he thought about magsails lifting satellites from LEO to GEO without the need for fuel; about magships which, no longer dependent on free-fall ballistics, could sail at will with the solar wind. Even—when he dared to think about solving the problem of magnetic quenching at very high current densities—lift off straight from the Earth's magnetic pole to orbit, to the Moon, and even to Mars. That, more than anything else, was his Holy Grail.

But when Krystal thought about the superloop—if and when she did—Hobie suspected it was mostly in terms of web site hits. Did she even comprehend what it would mean if a ship did not have to lift its own fuel and oxidizer?

But she was right about keeping her happy. She was perfectly capable of spinning the news any which way. The Earth's spinning, molten core created a magnetic field. What did spinning news create? *Something that attracted readers.* So, it might as well be the right spin. He studied Krystal over the lip of his cup. When he thought about it, he had insulted her pretty badly. What was it the kids used to say when he was in high school? *Whatever works.*

"Would it help," he asked, "if I told you I was extremely flattered by your offer?"

It was a cold, clear day when they kicked the loop for the first time, one of those days when the sun was so impossibly bright that a man wondered how there could ever be all that ice around. Until stepping outside brought the reason home like a knife.

"Winds are calm," announced Weather. "Two klicks. Zero Beaufort.

Nick looked to Hobie and waited for his nod.

The loop would fly. Hobie knew it would. All the calculations, all the simulations, said so; but there were always those unexpected engineering malfs. Things never quite worked the way the equations predicted because there were always more variables in the real world than in the equations. He took a deep breath and let it out slowly. "Kick the amps," he told the base manager. Cunningham spoke briefly into his throat mike, listened, then gave Hobie the thumbs-up.

Really, there ought to have been hums and sparks. Dynamos and Jacob's ladders and van der Graaf generators. Copper wires and vacuum tubes . . . Thirties tech may have been dumb, but at least you knew when something big was going down. Maybe he ought to have had someone program electrical noises into the I/O system, the way they built computer keyboards to click like typewriters.

"We have lift," announced the tech monitoring the strain gauges. "Five kilos . . . Ten kilos . . . It's rising from its bed . . ." She brushed back her honeyed hair and shot Hobie a glance. Thumb met forefinger: A-OK.

Hobie turned to the window facing the test bed. He couldn't see anything yet. "Increase the amps," he said, "and start unreeling the tether."

A heartbeat or two went by; then he saw it. The loop of hobartium IV lifted from its cradle like a kite, playing off the lines of the Earth's magnetic field.

It rose smoothly and silently, tugging against its tethers, pulling on the load cells that recorded the its upward force. Soon, it was a bright circle in the sky. A strange, insubstantial kite.

"Easy," Hobie said. "You gotta keep the tension equalized around the circumference . . ." No one was listening to him. They had gotten all this in the briefings. All his nervous chatter could do was distract them. Hobie fell silent. The way you worked with professionals was: you told them what you needed, then you stepped aside.

From the corner of his eye, he noticed Krystal Delacroix capturing everything on her digital movie camera. The technicians hunched intently over their instruments . . . Nick presiding over the show like a maestro over a symphony . . . Hobie, the great composer, standing by and waiting for the flat note. He turned back to the window and tried to look visionary as he watched his creation sail the magnetic field lines. But he probably only looked worried.

"Why is the tension so important?"

He turned and Krystal was there. The silver doid on her headband was almost in his face. Talk about close-ups. "Because the orientation is an unstable equilibrium," he told her. "The loop wants to flip over. Too much wobble and it pancakes." Hobie flipped his hand from palm-up to palm-down.

"So, why not, like, fly it that way?" Her eyes said *duuuh?* which irritated Hobie.

"Because in the loop's self-stabilized position, the R-force is attractive, not repulsive. Instead of flying, the loop would be pulled to the ground."

"That would be serious, wouldn't it?"

Hobie knew the questions were meant to create sound bytes for the web site, but they still sounded herbie. Of course, he had spent years working things out. Walt and Wanda Webbrowser just wanted answers. If they wanted that much. "Yeah," he said as seriously as he could. "I won't be marketing personal levitation belts for a long time to come. Tip over and . . . whap! Faster than falling."

"Eight hundred newtons," announced the tech.

"I'm getting eccentricity," said another.

Hobie turned away from Krystal. "Quench it, now!"

The man at the power board ramped the amps and the loop went limp and dropped back to its cradle.

"Did something go wrong?" Krystal asked.

"Nah," Hobie answered absently. "This is science. Getting the answer's more important than whether the answer is yes or no. I'm trying to learn what sort of R-force I can get and how far short of theory it falls. If the loop pancakes and tangles, we lose uptime for maintenance." And there weren't enough hours in the day. Okay, there were thirteen hours, this time of year; but they flew like minutes.

"How important is the R-force, Hobie?"

She had briefed him earlier on the kinds of questions she would ask, but he was supposed to make the answers seem casual. The idea was that the site's Artificial Stupid would parse a surfer's question and cut to the .wav in which he answered the question most nearly like it. The more naive surfers would imagine they were engaged in a conversation with the Great Man himself. Hobie flashed Krystal a broad, friendly smile, even as Nick handed him the printout with the data from the run.

"Well, Krystal . . ." The A/S would insert the surfer's actual name. "I did some back of the envelope figures on the trip up here. Blue sky, but I'll write them up for a sidebar. Figure a five ton sail. That's the loop and its support structure. Throw on one ton of systems, like the attitude controls to keep the loop oriented, and a three ton payload. A satellite, maybe. Give it four thousand kilo-amps, you get something like three hundred and eighty kilo-newtons, straight up. Uh, that's three and a quarter gees, net acceleration; for a final velocity of eleven or twelve klicks."

"Which means . . . ?"

"Medium energy trans-Mars insertion trajectory. Your satellite's at the Red Planet in a hundred-fifty days."

Nick, at the command console, whistled. "That sounds pretty optimistic."

"It is. If I put four thousand kilo-amps into a loop of hobartium IV, the magfield overcomes the Meissner effect and quenches the loop. But the EVOP shows we're going in the right direction. Maybe hobartium V. Or X."

Krystal rolled her eyes, which Hobie figured meant they'd have to spend the evening together explaining "jargon." Though what jargon he had just used escaped him.

They ran several more test runs over the next few weeks, as March crept toward April and the temperature inched upward. The results varied, as Hobie had expected. The real world was statistical, and all data were both fuzzy and temporary. Measured force ran between five hundred and a thousand newtons. But that was only about half the time. Three of the runs pancaked, and four others would have if they hadn't quenched the system in time.

The last test run he watched from outside the compound. The arctic spring was in full bloom by then and ambient temperatures were approaching the quench point, even with the insulation and reflective sheathing. The kicker tripped and squirted current into the loop and the flaccid ring slowly stiffened out into a hoop and rose from its platform.

A good run. He saw that immediately, even with no instruments. He stood with his parka hood thrown back so the wind could tousle his hair, looking skyward with his fists on his hips.

Canted precisely against the Earth's magnetic field, unruffled by any wind, balanced exactly on the cusp, the loop ascended into the sky. The tethers ran out and straightened, holding it bound so the R-force could be measured.

Then, it was loose!

Slipping away like an invisible Frisbee through the cold, bright sky. Superconductors had no resistance, so the current was still running through the loop, even though it was disconnected. It floated gracefully toward the south until something happened. A random breeze nudging it off the unstable equilibrium; the drag of the tethers; the sunlight warming it to quenching temperatures? Who could say? It flipped, collapsed, and fell in a tangle into Penny Strait.

Krystal, who had jerked her head around to follow the escaping loop with her head-scarf camera, turned back to Hobie.

"Tough luck, Hobie," she said with genuine sympathy. "You'll have to go on orbit now and fab another. But Nick told me we were almost at the seasonal limit for test conditions. Too bad the tether broke."

Hobie didn't say anything. *Maybe* they could have gotten another run or two, but the forecast showed wind moving in for the next two weeks; so chances were this would have been the last run, anyway.

The tether hadn't broken, though. Hobie had pulled the decoupler with his own hand.

He shaded his eyes and looked toward the sparkling chop of the Strait. Heroic pose for the web surfers. *Someday*, he promised himself. Someday we make it all the way.

4.

The Winner of Our Discontent

March is an ambiguous month; no longer winter, but not yet willing to declare for spring. It often brought snow—snow lay on the grounds now—but it was a half-hearted snow, a spiteful, final flurry that covered hummocks and bushes and turned the meadow into a rippling, white ocean. During the day it softened and ran under the patient sun, and during the night it froze once more, so that footprints and bird tracks and other blemishes were neatly airbrushed into a recurrently pristine surface. Some of the children had tested it, walking atop the icy crust with slow, careful, sliding steps. Two had broken through and were now happily flailing about in the ankle-deep fluff. The youngest, Pauline's Virginia, had nearly reached the entrance to the hedge-maze. Dimly, their shouts and cries passed through the frost-rimmed window glass.

I might have been a grandmother by now.

Mariesa Gorley van Huyten released the curtain, and it fell back into place, blocking the view of the estate grounds. *Had I ever become a mother.*

The library at Silverpond was paneled in dark woods, and when the curtain fell, the sense of gloom deepened. She ran a hand along one of the wingback chairs that flanked the window. The library had a faint odor; ink, slowly acidizing paper, leather bindings and upholstery, cigars anciently smoked. Floor to ceiling bookshelves lined every wall but one—and on that wall cabinets held rare and fragile folios. Conrad van Huyten, her great-grandfather, had been a bibliophile. Willem, his son, had been less a lover of books and more a lover of their contents. *Knowledge is power,* he had told young Mariesa more than once. And so beautifully crafted books had given way to merely crafty ones.

The old man had not often been wrong; but he had been wrong about that. Sometimes all that knowledge showed you was how powerless you were. Mariesa entered the alcove in the corner of the room, where Gramper's old floor globe sat—the one she had marked up all those years ago with black circles showing known or suspected impact craters. Gramper had lectured her quite sternly over the vandalism and, despite his vaunted insight and acumen, he had never seen the screeching warning she had drawn. *Helpless,* she thought, tracing the broad circle of the Chesapeake Bay strike. Eocene, that one; the seventh-largest known, it had scattered its debris across the east coast. Baltimore, Washington, Norfolk, scores of smaller cities would all be wiped away were its twin to come now. The tsunami would scour clean Maryland's eastern shore; in the west, break against the foothills of the Blue Ridge; bore north up the Susquehanna Valley like a Roto-Rooter, and drop a rain of iron and glass from Cape Cod to Cape Fear. Mariesa shivered, even though the March chill was safely outdoors.

She had been naive herself. Not all impacts had left marks. Tunguska had not; neither had the Micronesia Bolide of 1992. And even of those that had, the eons had covered many. They were underground, or underwater. Every now and then universities, or oil companies, or space researchers stumbled across them. Seismic profiles had uncovered the Chesapeake strike only in '96. And satellite images had shown that Aorounga Crater in Chad was a multiple hit. And how many craters did the vast, anonymous ocean hide? Her fingers touched the circular Aral Sea, traced the double circle of the Gulf of Mexico. Here: a semicircular arc, like a bite taken out of Quebec's west coast . . . Were the Belcher Islands the central peak of a vast, sunken astrobleme? And there: the Madelaines in the Gulf of St. Lawrence—did the Northumberland Strait mark the lip of another long-vanished crater?

Mariesa gave the globe a sudden spin—eastward, as always—and the fearful pockmarks blurred. *What can we do about it?* she had once asked her small circle of confidants, others who had understood the catastrophic potential of an asteroid strike.

Nothing.
What could we do about it?
Swat them aside.
Go somewhere else.

Her eyes fell to the reading table beside the globe, where twin oversize books were displayed. *Or both,* she thought. The older book's cover featured a Plank-model SSTO lifting off. *A Passion to Break the Sky* (1996–2006). The early years, she thought wryly, scanning the subtitle. Now *there* had been presumption! The years had still been early when that was written. She picked up the newer companion volume and flipped through its pages of glossy photographs and graphics. Scenes of Shuttle-C's lifting specially modified external tanks into orbit. Scenes of construction workers rigging the tanks into position, creating the Hub and Pinwheel of LEO Station. Scenes, too, of Goddard City; of FreeFall Hotel & SkyResort; of Celestial Dragon, with its "wagons in a circle" design; of half-finished Europa and Tsiolkovskigrad. A score of stand-alone modules sporting various corporate and national logos. *Boom towns,* she thought.

The cover was a panoramic view of LEO Station during its spin-up in 2013:

bright flares from the rocket motors on the tips of the Pinwheel and the slightest blur of motion just beginning. The title, in bold, white lettering: *Castles in the Air (2007–2015)*.

What would they call the next volume? she wondered. Beside her, the globe slowly eased to a stop and its buckshot face lured her unwilling eyes. *Too Little: Too Late.*

But, no. If *that* came to pass no one would be publishing coffee table books for a very long time after.

"There you are!"

Mariesa looked up at the voice and saw her cousin Chris leaning against the doorway. He was a tall man, with startling gray-green eyes and hair cropped short and combed forward in the faddish Roman emperor look. "You've found me," she said.

"The others are waiting." He stepped aside and swept a bow.

Mariesa sighed and followed him into the hallway. "Let's get this over with."

"Now, Riesey," Chris chided her as they walked, "it's not so bad. I had to endure it two years ago. Now it's your turn. And besides, consider the alternative."

She chuckled at his macabre joke. As they turned into the ballroom and the laughter and chatter from the veranda at the farther end reached her, she asked, "Has everyone arrived?"

"Everyone who is coming."

A freight of meaning in those leaden words. "Did Adam come?"

Chris shook his head and his features closed up. "No."

"I'm sorry to hear that."

"He knows he isn't welcome."

Mariesa stopped and laid a hand on his arm. "Chris, he's your own son."

"That only makes it worse, what he did."

She looked at the grim set of his mouth and the diamond hardness of his eyes and knew there was no point in pleading Adam's case. Nor was she sure she wanted to. The betrayal had struck her hard. And yet, it was sad to see the walls go up between a father and son.

Chris walked on ahead but Mariesa paused before following. The ballroom, floored in hardwood and bordered by polished green marble in decorative patterns, ran from the great bay window in the front of the house to the enclosed veranda in the back. On the flanking walls, portraits alternated with tall, thin mirrors. The Hall of Dead Van Huytens, she had called it when she was a child, a name that had reduced her grandfather to helpless rolls of laughter.

Gramper was one of the men on the wall now. Willem Riesse van Huyten was the last space but one. Beside him, Conrad wore a high, starched collar and long, waxed moustaches. Christiaan III was the one in the frock coat, opposite the entry to the dining room. Albert Henry, in his powdered wig, hung across the room from him. *That's a lot of dead van Huytens up there,* she thought.

And they weren't all there. Old Henryk, the founder, graced the boardroom at Van Huyten Industries. And there were others relegated by scandal or lack of consequence to storerooms and attics.

And they weren't all dead. The last portrait, to Gramper's left, was her own. She had been posed in her light blue Simyonna gown, gazing solemnly upward against a backdrop of stars. Chris had commissioned it after taking the reins of VHI from her—perhaps as an apology. As a youngster, Mariesa would pose before one of the mirrors, pretending that her reflection was another portrait. Yet, when the moment finally came, it had felt too much like the breath of mortality. As if it were the hanging, she thought wryly, and not the burial that mattered.

A discreet cough begged her attention. Armando Herrera, her butler, stood by with a package in his hands. Armando was slim and dark-haired, with eyes like obsidian. He wore an evening coat and red waistband of Mexican cut, and managed to look both professional and subtly dangerous at the same time. "This was left by the front door, miss," he said, proferring the package.

It was wrapped in plain, brown paper and tied with twine. *Aunt Mariesa* was written across the face in a hand that she instantly recognized. "Did you see who brought it?"

"No, miss. Shall I put it with the others?"

Over her shoulder, Mariesa could see Chris chatting with his sister on the veranda. "No. Take it up to the Roost. I'll look at it later. No point in opening sores just now."

Considering that the van Huytens had been around for three hundred years, they were not very thick on the ground. Two dozen or so, eked out by spouses and a few close family friends, had gathered on the veranda at Silverpond. Supposedly there were more remote cousins with whom all contact had been lost; but, all in all, the van Huytens had exercised the same dour, Dutch restraint in their procreation as they had in their other personal habits.

Dominating the buffet table was a large ice sculpture of a phoenix rising. Crystalline wings were spread; frozen flames clutched in vain. Beautifully done. It would melt eventually; it was melting already. It should have been captured in marble. What possessed a person, Mariesa wondered, to invest so much artistry into so transient a medium? Or was the transience itself part of the art, and buffet table ice sculpture a sort of performance piece?

Surrounding the sculpture were fruit plates, salad bowls, and cheese boards. Chafing dishes exuding delicious odors. A roasted beef tended by a cheerful, rotund carving chef. Mariesa smiled at Gerard, the *chef de cuisine*. "It looks delicious, as always." The caterer nodded his thanks.

Harriet sat in her wheelchair by the windows with eyes closed and her head tilted back, the sunlight giving her skin an unaccustomed glow. A red blanket enclosed her waist and legs. She wore a pale scarf around her shoulders, held in place by a brooch in the form of a rose. Harriet's Sterling, her prize-winning silver hybrid, had become her trademark. On the lapel of her navy jacket, a more restrained gold pin depicted an Orbiter—a souvenir of a long-ago lark. Had she worn it today as a subtle reminder that she had once, if briefly, visited orbit, while Mariesa never had? It was hard to tell with Harriet. Scoring points off her daughter had become an old habit and no longer required conscious thought.

Mariesa leaned over and kissed her mother on the cheek. The flesh seemed cold, despite the sunlight. Harriet's eyes fluttered open and she smiled softly with the right side of her face. Mariesa patted her hand and said, "May I get you something, Mummy?"

"No, dear," Harriet said in a slurred voice as she returned the caress. "Nothing for now."

Mariesa circulated among uncles, aunts, nephews, nieces, and cousins at various degrees and removes. She chatted briefly with each, sometimes pro forma, sometimes with genuine affection. Of them all, she had always liked Great-aunt Wilhemina the best; but Wilhelmina was gone now and, with her, the last of Gramper's generation.

Brittany van Huyten-Amitage, her face and bust an accolade to the surgeon's art, offered an insincere cheek and murmured something about her turn being next. Mariesa smiled noncommittally. Brittany's husband, Hugh, famously wore the most elaborate set of antlers this side of Yellowstone Park. Either he didn't mind or he didn't know of Brittany's horizontal hobbies or— Mariesa watched his eyes track Tracy Bellingham's cleavage across the room— he took it as tacit permission to do the same.

Brittany had been carefully polite; Pauline was barely so. A few clipped, formal phrases to observe the social conventions, and Pauline turned away. Later, Mariesa saw her patiently tugging Virginia out of her snow-encrusted playsuit and wondered how so spiteful a woman could have borne so darling a child.

Norbert had secluded himself in a corner, where he nibbled at a buffet plate sparsely filled with fruits and dry vegetables. When he saw Mariesa, he made room for her and said portentiously, "Beware the Ides of March," in what he no doubt imagined to be arch wit. Mariesa sat beside him with her own plate.

"Adam didn't come," she said.

Norbert's patrician smile dimmed. "Yes, I noticed. Knew his father would be here, I s'pose." His Boston Brahmin upbringing showed in the flatness of his vowels and his tendency to lose an occasional R. Sometimes Mariesa wanted to shake him by his lapels and shout, *You're Dutch, you twit! You're not a Yankee!* But everyone was entitled to cultivate his own eccenticities.

"He sent a present. Adam did. Left it on the front porch earlier this evening."

Norbert shook his head. He was a dry man, apparently without passion. Brittany had once said that Norbert carried the famous van Huyten reserve to such an extreme that the rest of them seemed given to utter abandon in comparison. "Too bad," he said. "Who'll take the reins when ouah generation passes? Bryce is too young. Have to hire outside the family. Ha'd to trust an outsider." His thoughts turned inward and his lips grew long. "Ha'd to trust family, too, I s'pose."

"I'm sure there's an explanation for what Adam did."

Norbert nodded slowly. "Maybe. I wish Chris would unbend, but he won't listen to me. And Adam is just as pigheaded. After all, it's not everyone who can say he was fired by his own fahther."

Mariesa sighed. She wished she knew more, but she no longer ran VHI and, while Chris kept her informed on most matters, on this one issue he had maintained an utter silence.

Mariesa was engaged in after-dinner conversation with Tracy Bellingham, her one-time college roommate, and Wayne Coper, her sometime companion, when Brittany tapped her on the arm and said, "Here it comes," with a satisfied voice and a nod toward the pantry.

Oohs and aahs and Armando wheeled in a serving cart bearing a flaming cake. How much of Brittany's *ooh* was directed at the pastry chef's artistry and how much at the buff young man pushing it, Mariesa did not dare to guess. All she could think of as she stared at the birthday cake was, *Dear Lord the fire marshall ought to be here!*

Everybody broke into "Happy Birthday" and clapped and shouted. Make a wish. Make a wish.

I wish there weren't so many candles . . . Mariesa studied their flaming ranks. Atlanta must have looked like this when Sherman went through. *Don't count them,* she thought. *They're only true if you count them.*

"Go ahead, dear," said Harriet. "Make a wish." The baby-cousins jumped up and down with excitement. There was little enough of the adult world they understood, but birthdays were one.

Mariesa thought about the pockmarked globe in her library; about a rain of fire and death igniting the forests and the cities until the *world* might look like this very cake. *Let it not be.* She sucked in a breath and blew as hard as she could, sweeping back and forth across the flames. Fifty-nine winked out into thin streamers of smoke. The last candle danced, flickered and bowed, only to brighten and burn with a steady, yellow flame when her breath finally failed.

Mariesa sagged back, sucking in her breath, and stared at the bale flame.

"Tough luck," said Chris sympathetically. "Looks like you don't get your wish."

* * *

Cool, wet spring was losing ground to hot, dry summer when Mariesa and the Sky Watch Committee visited the White House. In the past, conservative presidents had invited her because she was a successful CEO; liberals, because she was a woman CEO. Jim Champion had invited her because he had genuinely liked her company; Donaldson, because he wanted her cooperation in his grandiose plans. One president, more mercenary than most, had hoped to shake some loose change into campaign coffers. But never before had she come to the president's house hat in hand.

Nor had she ever been kept waiting in the hallway outside the Oval Office; and to judge by his carefully controlled expression, neither had Daryll Blessing, Ph.D. Blessing strode the hallway, pausing by each of the portraits—TR, FDR, JFK: an alphabet soup of presidents—as though he had come only to view the art and was *not* killing time. Only his brusque strides and the rapping of his signature blackthorn cane revealed his impatience. The rest of the Sky Watch Executive Committee occupied the benches and chairs that lined the hall, each immersed in thought. Inkling, from the American Astronomical Union, skimmed a magazine he had brought with him. (Had he known they would be kept waiting, or did he always keep an astronomy journal handy?) Krishnarahman, from ASU, dozed, or appeared to. Mariesa, for her part, simply waited.

Finishing his art tour at last, Blessing lowered himself onto the bench beside Mariesa. He huffed, as if out of breath, and touched a hand to pure white hair brushed back in the Naughty Ought "birdwing" style—a style too late by half a decade, and by a generation plus. The honorary chairman of Sky Watch left the mundane operational details to Inkling and the others, but the president's veto had roused him from his quasi-retirement. "I'm not used to waiting," he said.

Mariesa counseled patience, but the old astrophysicist was not listening. Several decades of speeches, news conferences, and sound-biting had conditioned him to speech habits that were more pronouncement than dialogue. The hazard of becoming a Grand Old Man was that you began to think of yourself that way. Mariesa was no admirer of President Rutell; but he *was* the President of the United States and he just *might* have other pressing issues facing him besides this meeting. The perennial crisis with the Social Security trust fund was coming to a head—again—with the first wave of boomer retirements, and each of the major parties was pondering the best way to duck the issue.

Shortly, they were ushered into the Oval Office, where the president stood to greet them. He pumped Dr. Blessing's hand and led him with great solicitude to a large, comfortable chair facing the big desk. If anyone noticed that this good deed excused him from shaking Mariesa's hand, no one remarked on it, and Mariesa was not so foolish as to stand about with her hand outstretched.

No Victorian matron ever mastered the calculated snub half so well as Rutell and his circle. She found a seat at the edge of the little group and resolved to maintain silence for the duration. If she spoke up, it would become a debate; and SkyWatch was here to persuade, not to argue.

Seated once more, Rutell hunched forward over his desk with his hands clasped and his teeth on display. The desk was flanked by the American and Presidential flags. There was enough paperwork scattered atop it to show that Rutell was a busy man, but it was stacked and organized to show that he had everything well in hand. "Well, now," he said cheerfully, "to what do I owe the honor of this visit?"

Blaise Rutell looked older than his forty-eight years. There were wrinkles and gray streaks here and there that had not been evident the day he stepped into Donaldson's unexpired term. Well, they said the office aged one; though aside from the impeachment crisis and the Balkan truce talks early on, few squalls had ruffled the sails of his presidency. He had managed the mild recession in November of '11 without aggravating it too much—a lot to ask of a man who considered himself an activist—and had surfed to election in his own right on the recovery that followed. Now, with no end in sight to the expansion, he looked to ride the wave into a second elected term that would, barring the unforeseen, make him the second-longest serving president in U.S. history.

Daryll Blessing spoke for the committee, as they had agreed he would. "We've come to discuss your veto of the SkyWatch funding in the new appropriation bill," the old man said. "We fear you've been misinformed, and would like you to reconsider." Rutell smiled, looked interested, and said nothing. Encouraged, Blessing went on. "Mr. President, do you know what a Near Earth Asteroid is?"

Rutell shrugged and spread his hands. "Of course, I do. Calhoun's Rock. Several others. Their orbits bring them close to Earth."

Donaldson had smiled a lot, too, Mariesa remembered as she studied the wall of teeth Rutell presented. Donaldson's smiles had been phony, but this was the genuine article. Rutell's family was monied and connected. He had gone to properly ivied schools, networked with the right people, harvested the fruits of influence planted by his father and his grandmother, and along the way absorbed the notion that graduates of his school were Wiser and More Compassionate, and were thus better suited to make decisions for others. It was the smile of a man who never doubted his own rightness.

"More than close, Mr. President," Blessing said.

"Ah. You're talking about the Impact Scenario."

"Yes, the Impact Scenario."

As always, when the subject arose, Mariesa felt herself tense. The trembling wasn't as bad as it used to be. Once there had been nightmares and cold sweats, and her fears had driven her to horrid extremes. Little by little, she had leavened the terror with reason; but she still felt a sense of urgency, of precious days wasted. *You shall know neither the day, nor the hour.*

But you knew that there would be a day, and there would be an hour.

"Our NEO studies," said Krishnarahman, "reveal a probability distribution of both size and approach that is disturbing." His voice was an odd mixture of Hindustani melody and cowboy twang, as befitted an Arizona-born son of immigrants. "We can project the likelihood of an impact of a given size body over the next—"

"Tell me, professor," said Rutell, interrupting the lecture, "in all of recorded history, how many people have been killed by a meteor?"

"Well," said Krishnarahman, looking flustered, "that would be difficult to—"

"Because there haven't been any." Rutell smiled and leaned back in his chair. "Compared to floods, fires, and earthquakes, falling rocks don't seem to be a major risk." He smiled—a reasonable man asking others to be reasonable with him.

"Because it *hasn't* happened doesn't mean it *won't* happen," suggested Inkling.

Rutell shook his head. "Ifs and buts, gentlemen. Give me some *solid* reasons why I should spend the taxpayers' money on your hobby."

That Rutell gave a fig for the taxpayers' money was unlikely enough that Mariesa had to swallow a laugh. More likely, he wanted that money for a vital, contributor-favoring program.

"Sodom and Gomorrah," Blessing huffed.

Rutell frowned. "What do you mean?"

The old man worked his lips before he spoke. "The description in the Bible," he said portentiously, "corresponds well to a bolide exploding just overhead."

"The Bible. Oh." Rutell shook his head, and Mariesa wondered if he would dismiss the suggestion as a violation of church and state. "There's no crater there, is there?"

Blessing shrugged. "Unless the Dead Sea covers it. However, Tunguska left no crater, either. I only suggested a scenario." He waved his cane. "Merely a scenario. My point was that very little history ever gets recorded in sufficient detail. The actual death toll from meteors might be . . ."

"Astronomical?" suggested Rutell.

Blessing flushed. He had doled out enough condescension to recognize it from the other end. "This is not a joking matter, sir. Consider the dinosaurs!"

Rutell made a face. "I consider them every time I face Congress." Even Mariesa had to admit that was a good line and joined in the chuckles that followed. "But seriously, gentlemen . . . and lady. I understand that there is no consensus on the fate of the dinosaurs. I was briefed thoroughly on NEOs and dinosaurs when I was vice president and Calhoun's Rock was all the news. Paleontologists, in particular, don't accept the impact theory."

"Professional jealousy," said Blessing, "because it was a physicist who proposed it."

"Hmm. A physicist who never studied the fossil record or considered alternate explanations, and who spent a lifetime assassinating the characters of his opponents. I understand some geologists doubt that the famed Chixulub formation is even a crater at all. 'The Pemex number five cores are uninterrupted across the K/T boundary,' if I remember the briefing papers correctly."

Mariesa narrowed her eyes as she listened. This was knowledge too particular and too ready to pretend he recalled it from briefings six years ago. The president had been carefully prepped for this meeting.

"True, the asteroid hypothesis has been losing favor," Inkling admitted, "ever since we learned how much iridium volcanoes emit. The Deccan Traps . . . not to mention the Siberian Traps—which correlate nicely with the Permian extinction . . . Well, the important thing is not whether a giant impactor upset the dinosaurs' ecosystem sixty-five million years ago. The point is what even a modest impactor might do to us, tomorrow."

Rutell nodded. "Nicely put, doctor. Still, if the past is any guide, it's not a very *likely* scenario. And focusing on dramatic, *external* causes of extinctions distracts us from the damage humanity itself is doing to the environment."

"With all due respect, Mr. President," Blessing said, "a giant meteor would create severe ecological damage all its own."

Rutell cocked his head. "I thought you were one of us, Dr. Blessing."

Dr. Blessing straightened in his chair. Thunderclouds gathered on his brow. "I don't see where the one concern excludes the other."

"Perhaps not for you, Dr. Blessing; but the public is more easily fooled. Especially if our opponents seize on the issue to downplay the real problems."

He does not plan to reverse the veto, Mariesa realized. He agreed to hear us as a courtesy, but he never planned to listen. Mariesa broke her vow of silence. It didn't matter now if she drew his attention.

"There is another factor that must be taken into account," she said. Rutell cocked his head and looked at her, as if surprised to hear her speak. Mariesa noticed the others looking at her, too. She took a breath and plunged ahead. "Some near earth objects have changed orbits over the past two decades. They may have been consciously diverted . . ."

"Diverted . . ." the president said.

". . . into orbits that bring them closer to Earth."

"Consciously . . ." The president exchanged glances with Blessing. "If you mean the Visitor Hypothesis, that's even more speculative than the Impact Hypothesis. Those features that Dr. Mendes discovered on Calhoun's Rock could be natural, couldn't they?"

Blessing pursed his lips and spared Mariesa an irritated glance before addressing the president. "The Tunnel and the Inscriptions are almost certainly artificial," he said. "As you know, I was senior author of the paper that examined the evidence."

And the holder of the press conference. Mariesa thought, *and the writer of the Sunday supplement pieces* . . . Junior researchers tested that particular limb before Blessing crawled out with them. But he had crawled out—and long before anyone else of note.

Which Rutell knew very well. He spread his wall of teeth again. It was a defensive wall, Mariesa suddenly realized, one which held any assaulting doubts at bay. "Yes, Dr. Blessing, you've written about the possibility of alien contact for a great many years. Since long before the FarTrip expedition. It's something of a cause célèbre with you. Almost a religion."

Almost wishful thinking. The thought was left unspoken, but they all heard it. The old man's pale jowls flushed, and Mariesa could see the left hand, resting on the crook of the cane, tremble. Inkling must have seen it, too, because he spoke quickly into the silence. "The scientific consensus is that the Visitor Hypothesis warrants serious investigation."

" 'Serious investigation.' That means 'increased funding,' doesn't it?" Rutell spoke with a breezy, we're-all-insiders chuckle. No one joined him and he turned immediately earnest. "And we *are* investigating," he went on. "The first robot probes will rendezvous with your asteroids later this year. Why not wait to see what they find? That way you can have some real data to plan from."

Oh, he was a reasonable man, Mariesa thought. So are they all; all reasonable men. "I only hope we don't wait too long," she said.

Rutell smiled in her direction. "And your concern about asteroids is also on record."

Meaning her phobia. Mariesa had gotten accustomed enough to the mention that she no longer blushed. She had borne guarded looks and whispered comments for two years after her private fears had been made public. Now less was said aloud, but the thought lurked behind the eyes of the people she encountered. She gave Rutell a smile as pleasant as his own. "The truth may lie," she said, "somewhere between my obsession and your complacency." Gauging his reaction, she decided that accusing Rutell of complacency was like accusing a fish of being wet. The self-assurance of the Northeastern Establishment was proof against most *facts*, let alone against a troubling theory and a few unanswered questions. "In the meantime," she said, knowing it was pointless to argue, "what harm can it do to maintain the funding for SkyWatch? At the very least, it will build up a solid database for planetary science, and, at most, it may provide us with advance warning—if the worst does come to pass."

"If the worst *does* come to pass, what good would an advance warning be? We can't do anything about it." Rutell's clean, patrician features closed up momentarily. "I think . . . for myself . . . I'd rather not know it was coming."

Mariesa did not mention gigawatt lasers in orbit. Donaldson's secret project was still a sore subject, and some of the soreness was in her own heart. "Nevertheless, continued funding—"

Rutell leaned back in the presidential swivel chair and linked presidential hands behind his head. "I thought it was improper," he said with just a touch of levity, "for the government to fund private ventures. Let the marketplace decide whether asteroid searches are worth doing."

"That the government ought not to do *many* things," Mariesa told him evenly, "does not imply that the government ought not to do *anything*."

Rutell regarded her with arching eyebrows. "Perhaps I've misjudged you."

Mariesa held his gaze. "Perhaps."

Rutell nodded once, twice; then he gathered himself. "There'll be a technical corrections bill in the fall," he said in a voice hearty with finality. "Clean up all the loose ends these bills always seem to have. Why don't you bring the issue up then?"

It was the kiss-off, of course. With four parties sharing power in the House, it was difficult to build a consensus in favor of anything; and all too easy to build one against. The situation in the Senate was little better. *Pushing the rider through the first time was a first class bitch,* Mariesa thought. *We'd never make it on a second try.*

The committee stood under the shaded canopy outside the White House while they waited for the electric cart that would ferry them through the security zone to where their car was impounded. The sunlight was so bright that, under the canopy, it almost seemed dark, and shadows accented their features. The wind was a blowtorch, raising a sheen of perspiration on their brows and necks and wilting the new-sprung flowers. The heavy scent suggested funeral parlors. Inkling spoke first.

"Well," he said bitterly, "that was a waste of time."

Blessing looked up sharply from his study of the ground. "It might have gone better if only the professionals had come."

He meant her, Mariesa thought. Representative of the *Amateur* Astronomical Association on the SkyWatch governing board. Though what a science degree had to do with lobbying presidents escaped her. Blessing's own disappointment was speaking. He had imagined that his partisanship on the president's behalf entitled him to more than merely a polite hearing. "The president and I," Mariesa snapped, "may have been the only professionals in the room."

She saw the hurt glance Krishnarahman gave her, and instantly regretted the remark. It was *her* disappointment speaking, too; and she had not gone into the room expecting much at all.

Blessing leaned forward on his cane, almost as if he would topple without it. He jabbed a free finger toward her. "You shouldn't have come, Mariesa. I don't care how savvy you are when it comes to politicking—I admit, science doesn't go in for that sort of thing—but you're not exactly in Blaise Rutell's political corner. I'm sure it roused the man's suspicions. I know you and I both want the same thing when it comes to SkyWatch—strange bedfellows, heh?—but it was probably not a good tactic. There's a time to stay in the background."

Krishnarahman said, "Dr. Blessing, I don't think that—"

Blessing sighed. "And you didn't help the cause, either, George, with your minilectures on likelihood distributions. Politicians don't think in quantitative terms." Inkling, listening in, looked away before Blessing could bring up his mention of the Deccan Traps. The traffic beyond the security zone swooshed like a distant river. Far off, horns honked in lieu of geese.

Mariesa kept careful rein on her temper. *You pompous, old jackass . . .* Did Blessing really believe that any answer but No had ever been in the offing? Was his self-image as a mover and shaker so ingrained that his only possible explanation for failure lay in his three companions?

We didn't fail, she told herself. One cannot fail when the outcome is fore-doomed.

Inkling clapped his hands together and rubbed them, a Pontius Pilate gesture. "What next?"

Krishnarahman shrugged. "ASU will continue participation, using our own money. I'll see to that. I'm sure the Planetary Society and others will contribute to a fund. Remember how the Society saved the SETI program by organizing a private effort? And of course many of our members will continue to watch and report at their own expense. It's just that designing the shared databases, collating the reports, analyzing the—"

"Yes," said Mariesa with sudden inspiration. "Maybe the president was right."

Mariesa barely recognized her old office these days. Chris had remodeled everything since taking the reins of VHI. The dark woods had given way to a lighter and brighter decor. The office was done up now with cacti in big pots, with intricate Mexican fabrics hanging on the wall, with a sort of faux adobe drywall. Her large, traditional desk had been replaced by some arrangement of surfaces and seats that only careful study would recognize as a desk at all. *That* must be a credenza. And *that* was surely a workstation. Her Scrooge McDuck clock was gone, and her "sci-fi" art. Instead, Mexican and Navajo art—and a single engineering drawing of a frog, labeled "Frog Prints." The only artifact she recognized was the calendar pylon in the corner. Too useful to replace, it seemed like an alien monolith set in the old *Frontera*.

Outside the broad picture windows, the slopes of First Watchung Mountain were thick with newborn summer. The mayapples and foamflowers had faded, but the bright pinxter and violets were in bloom. At the edge of the tree line, where the forest faded to meadowlands, a young doe grazed on staghorn sumac. A solitary goose, having wandered around from the pond in front of the building, watched the deer suspiciously between nibbles of grass. At least, Mariesa thought as she viewed the panorama over the lip of her teacup, at least this has not changed.

Chris settled into the chair opposite with his own cup in hand, and Mariesa transferred her study from the face of the mountain to the face of the CEO. He looked drawn and worried, she thought. Discontented in a way she had never seen him. Perhaps he was learning the difference between being president of Argonaut Labs and being CEO of Van Huyten Industries. All the juggling and politicking and compromising and consensus-building; one eye on the stock market, another on the Van Huyten Trust, and the third on the Goal that the inner circle had aimed for what seemed a lifetime ago.

"So," he asked, "how did the meeting with Rutell go?" His voice was hearty, but his eyes seemed distracted. Like the president of the United States, the CEO of Van Huyten Industries had a great deal on his plate, and a meeting with his flaky cousin had not been scheduled with the rest of the spinach. Mariesa knew firsthand how little casual time Chris must have.

"Oh." Mariesa sipped her tea and set it down on the low, wooden table that separated them. "Not well. He had his mind made up. Daryll couldn't dissuade him."

Chris looked sympathetic. "Too bad. But it's what I try to tell Dolores. Don't grow dependent on government money."

"Thank you," said Mariesa, somewhat tartly.

Chris lifted an eyebrow. "Hmm? Oh, I should tell you about that, right? But Dolores says the gravy is flowing and *someone's* going to slurp it up and the only thing we gain by not dipping our beak is that our competitors get a leg-up courtesy of the U.S. taxpayer. I can't deny she's done well playing that game—she kept Pegasus Aerospace on Leo's board when O&P lost their seat. Hard to argue with success. But a change of heart in the next Congress and suddenly money dries up, programs are canceled, and people are laid off. Or worse, you have to divert resources to lobbying and stroking and currying favors. All because you start thinking that profits are something you negotiate with the government." His lips pursed, as if he had tasted something sour. "Do you know how many man-hours we spent parsing the new Orbital Safety Precautionary Act? When we were done with all the eligibility rules and the exclusions and the exemptions and the cut-offs and the other 'technicalia,' it added up to one big special favor for one big company: Bullock's Orbital Management Corporation. And how many man-hours did *Bullock's* people waste crafting all those rules—before slipping them under the table to the staffers writing the bill? Not to mention dreaming up a drop-dead title for the act so they could smear their opponents as 'anti-safety.' " His fist struck the arm of his chair.

Mariesa started to rise. "I seem to have come at a bad time."

Chris waved her down again. "No, no. Don't mind me. You came here to vent your frustrations and I upstaged you. Sorry." He rubbed his face with both hands, then gazed into the distance, and it seemed to take a moment for him to recall her purpose. "SkyWatch," he said after a silence. "That's different game." He smiled without humor or rancor. "Doesn't generate its own income; so, yeah, you do have to go begging funds. You *will* continue. I mean, you won't give up watching; and the Planetary Society and the rest . . . ?"

"Certainly, but . . ."

Chris swallowed his tea and set his cup beside her own. "But," he suggested.

"But we were counting on that funding to prepare a common database and purchase new 'salamander' supercomputers. You know that the orbital dynamics of so many minor bodies are chaotic and—"

"Yes, yes. Well, I already vented about dependency on the government. You don't want to hear a replay. What you want is . . . Do you want me to guess, or are you going to tell me?"

Mariesa sighed. "Could VHI underwrite the cost?"

Chris nodded. "I thought so. You can't do this out of your own allowance?"

"Chris, you know how the Trust is set up. I get the use of a great many conveniences, from butlers to mansions; but it is all paid directly by the Trust. When I was CEO, the corporation paid me a salary most years. But now . . ."

"Now you're a poor little rich girl. You can think about the arrangement every April fifteenth. You don't pay an income tax if you don't have an income; your butler does. Meanwhile, this is how our cousins have always gotten on."

"Yes, but—"

"Yes, but they don't have grand plans to save the world."

Mariesa waited before replying. "Chris, you were one of the planners," she said quietly.

"I thought I was." He looked out the window and his voice took on a suddenly wistful tone. "Remember those days? Setting up the deals with Daedalus and Energia and Pratt & Whitney and the rest? The underground of frustrated NASA and Air Force people? The Fifty Year Plan? Fifty years!" He wagged his head. "Talk about hubris! Remember the special pins for the Steering Committee, and the nighttime meetings during the management retreats? It's a wonder we didn't have a secret handshake." His smile faded slowly. "Of course, that was before I learned there was an inner circle. Hell, maybe there *was* a secret handshake."

She hesitated, uncertain of his mood, trying to read the mind behind the steel eyes. "Chris, I admit I made mistakes—"

"Hunh." Chris folded his hands prayerlike. It was his habit when he was being thoughtful. "Those mistakes of yours have the board spooked. Yes, even six years later. They blame you for the loss of Daedalus Aerospace and the resignations of Steve and Belinda and the others. The brain drain hurt us, Riesey; and the board hasn't forgotten. They'll look very hard at any funds lobbed in your direction."

"The money wouldn't be for me . . ."

Chris waved off her objection. "Don't split hairs. Anything that reminds them of asteroids will remind them of what you and Donaldson cooked up. I'd rather they didn't think about it."

Sometimes she would rather not think about it herself. A good friend had died because of her obsession. "Does this mean you're abandoning the Goal?" she asked quietly.

Chris leaned back in his chair, an ergonomic affair of light woods and padding. Mariesa wondered if he was conscious of the distancing he implied. "Riesey, I may be more dedicated to the Goal than you—because I won't endanger it with half-baked shortcuts. We had a plan—a good plan, God bless Keith McReynolds. Solar power satellites on-line by 2033. If you had told me they were to double as an asteroid defensive shield—"

"You would have thought I was loony."

Chris grunted. "All right," he conceded with a nod. "I'm a hard sell. Regardless, it was an *organic* plan. It had to grow at its own pace. You tried to force it. You can't hatch chicks faster by turning a blowtorch on the eggs. Even if that battle laser Donaldson gave you hadn't been destroyed in the *soyuski* raid, what would we have gained? Some useful tests-of-concept on high power lasers in extreme temperature-vacuum-radiation environments; some software validation for target acquisition and asteroid tracking. Had there been no strings attached, it would have been modestly useful. *But it would not have advanced the Goal by a single month.* It wasn't powersat time yet."

"It seemed . . ."

". . . like a good idea at the time. Yes." He brooded for a moment, his eyes and brows a stormcloud. "Being lied to, that's what hurt the worst."

"Chris, I've been saying I'm sorry for five years."

"Practice makes perfect." There was no grin to take the hardness from his words. He shook his head and emerged from his chair. He walked to the window and stood there with his hands clasped behind his back. "I'm a real son of a bitch. That's what everyone says, isn't it? Fired my own son. And now I won't even let you apologize."

"Chris . . ."

He faced her. "Do me a favor, Riesey. Turn around. See that pixel-picture?"

Aside from the "Frog Prints," the pixure of Leo Station during spin-up was the solitary piece of decor in the room that did not evoke kachinas, cactus, or adobe. It hung on the wall opposite the desk, where her Scrooge McDuck clock had once been. Chris walked over to it and touched the frame with his fingertips.

"Plans within plans within plans. You were too subtle, Mariesa. You should have told us."

"Do you think Jimmy Undershot or some of the other presidents would have agreed—"

Chris held up a hand. "We've been through that. Maybe they would have

been spooked. Maybe not. Now"—he snapped a finger against the pixure—
"we've lost our 'base camp,' thanks to Adam. Oh, *someone* will build SPSs.
The infrastructure is growing in that direction, and I trust Detweiler's projections. But I doubt that anyone else is thinking in terms of powersats that double
as asteroid-killer battle lasers." He grimaced. "I would've been perfectly happy
to buy into any SPS consortium that had a chance of making money; but,
damn it, you've convinced me we need the asteroid shield, too. So—unless
you plan on winning over Bullock and Rutell and the others—regaining LEO
Station is number one priority right now. As long as Bullock calls the shots
on the Consortium, we're stymied. *Damn Adam!*" He gave a sudden, violent
shove to the pixure and it swung precariously to and fro. Chris turned away
from the wall and jammed his hands in his pockets. He walked to his desk and
kicked at a strut. Then he sat down and rubbed his ankle. "That hurt."

Mariesa had not moved from her seat. She didn't know if he meant the kick
or the betrayal. "He's your son . . ."

"I don't have a son."

"Face him, don't run away."

He gave her a suspicious look. "Have you been talking to Marianne?" He
didn't wait for an answer, perhaps he didn't want an answer. Chris swung a
keyboard on a below-desk gooseneck up to work level and typed a few lines.
A printer whirred and Chris studied the printout carefully before signing it.
Then he carried it to Mariesa.

"Here," he said, "is my authorization. Chairman's discretionary budget. Enter
your private key to transfer the funds into SkyWatch's account."

Mariesa scanned the document. "It's . . ."

"Not enough?"

"Generous. And we'll find additional donors, I'm sure."

Chris returned to the swinging picture and steadied it. "I had it hung there
deliberately," he said, "so I would have to look at it every damn day I sat
behind that desk. So I would never forget what had to be done." He looked
over his shoulder at her. "And you know what really frosts me?"

Mariesa shook her head.

"LEO Consortium reported rents and other income way over what we had
projected for fiscal '15. I don't mind Bullock snatching the station out of our
hands half as much as I mind him doing a better job with it."

For most of the year, the evening sun did nothing more than darken the
reflecting pond with the shadow of the mansion; but once each summer, at
the solstice, setting past the notch at the western end of Skunktown Mountain,
its rays turned the water to glistening lava. Gramper had always treated the
day as a sort of family holiday, and Mariesa could remember racing about on
the lawn with Chris and Brittany while Gramper and Mathilde, Piet and Harriet, and the other grown-ups sat in lawn chairs and waved cigars and drinks

at each other while they debated who knew what. The custom had become less frequent with Grandma Mathilde's death and with Aunt Beatrice's growing coolness toward the rest of the family, and had ceased entirely when the old man passed on, and what had once been a single family became three separate households. *Exunum plurum*, Mariesa thought as she wheeled Harriet onto the patio that overlooked the pond. The family gathered now only for funerals and such and for meetings of the Trust.

Harriet sighed and gathered her blanket around her shoulders. Mariesa reached down and adjusted the folds. Harriet smiled at her with half her mouth but did not try to say anything. Mariesa set the brakes on the wheelchair, then found a patio chair and set it beside her mother.

In silence, they watched the pond redden.

Like water into wine, Mariesa thought. Runamuck Creek was clear where it wound through the meadows north and east of the house, but Silverpond itself grew slowly more crimson. The first of the evening breezes swept off hillsides, raked the wild grasses and reeds aound the pond, and swept across the meadows, bringing with it the pungency of milkweed and fresh-mown hay. Queen Anne's lace rippled like a restless crowd.

Harriet sighed. "Not many more like this," she said, slurring her words like a drunkard.

Mariesa digested the words, and rejected them. Strange, how that thought bothered her. She and Harriet had hardly been close; had seldom shared mother-daughter moments. For years, they had been virtual strangers and, on some things, outright opponents. Manipulations, mind games, and matchmaking. Yet, on those occasions when they had touched, no touch had ever gone so deep. Each day since the stroke, Mariesa had cried a little bit, preparing herself so that when the day finally came, it would not be so keenly felt.

"Have you thought about my suggestion, Mother? About FreeFall Resort? They say zero gravity reduces the stress on the heart."

Harriet jerked her head in a parody of no. "Such phoowishness. I coon't weave." (And how that slurring must frustrate her! Harriet had always prized careful diction.)

Mariesa reached across and laid her hand on her mother's arm. Leave Silverpond, or leave Mariesa? It might not even be true what they said about increased lifespan. Radiation exposure was certainly greater in orbit. And how did zero gravity affect blockages, growths? It might be easier on the heart, but harder on the cells. No one had studied it. Too few long-term residents as yet.

"At least, you could have a MEMS implant. It would monitor your blood chemistry and signal Dr. Maloof if anything happened. It could even search the hospital deebies and reserve facilities."

"I don't need . . ." And Mariesa leaned closer to hear what her mother didn't need, plucking meaning from the sounds, listening to the voice it once had been. "I don't need some gizmo wandering loose inside my body to tell me I'm sick. And Armando is quite capable of calling the emergency squad, should the need arise."

"It's all the rage these days," Mariesa said, patting her mother gently on the arm. "Why, I've gotten one myself."

Harriet shot her a suspicious glance and considered her for a moment. Her lips parted as if to ask a question, but all she said was, "You always were one for the modern things." Closing her eyes, she sighed. "I miss the activity we used to have. When you had all those meetings. And the parties for the children. Even a husband, for a while . . ."

Harriet had complained incessantly about the bother, and Barry Fast had been not the least of her complaints; but if she chose to remember an alternate history, so what? There was little left for her now but memories and they might as well be as pleasant as imagination could make them.

"Yes, Barry had his charms," Harriet went on. "A climber, but . . ." She shrugged. "And Belinda. She never comes here anymore. You've not quarreled, have you? Even Chris—though I suppose he is busy these days. He's inherited all your worries, hasn't he?"

"He is the winner of our discontent," Mariesa said dryly.

"What? Oh, Riesey, I never un'erstand ha'f the things you say." Harriet fell silent, as if the speaking had worn her out. She whispered something under her breath.

"What was that, Mother? What did you say?"

"Children's voices. Can you hear them? It seems like only last week they were here. That nice young girl, Jenny. And the boy who liked computers. What was his name?"

"Jimmy Poole," Mariesa told her. Wealthy, so they said; but Mariesa wondered if he would ever make a mark on the wider world.

"Yes, that was him. He was such a sad little boy. I hope he's happier now. And that angry black boy—Azim, wasn't it? He won a medal . . ."

"The Congressional Medal of Honor."

"Yes. I remember their faces so clearly, but not always their names. What do you suppose that means?"

"I don't know, Mother."

"Could you ask Sykes to bring me a lemonade?"

"Sykes retired, Mother. Don't you remember? We gave him a big party."

Harriet clucked. "Now how could I forget that, but remember the children so clearly? Who was that girl who looked like pipe cleaners all twisted together? She had a boy's name, I think. Billie? Yes, Billie Whistle, that was it."

"That was a few years later. She wasn't one of the first group." Should she tell Harriet that young Billie had been virtually paralyzed in an automobile accident and whatever future she might have had, had been brutally crushed into a wheelchair? No, let her remember them as they had been. Full of possibilities.

Mariesa listened while Harriet rambled. Sometimes Mariesa supplied a name to go with the memory. Leland Hobart. Chase Coughlin. Cheng-I Yeh. Tanuja Pandya. Leilah Frazetti. She didn't know why her mother had fixated on them.

She remembered how carefully Belinda had identified her "special promise" children each year. *Those pushing the edge,* Barry had put it once. The intellectual edge, the artistic edge, the creative edge, the empathetic edge. The smartest, the brightest, the most daring, the most desperate. But those earliest ones, they were children no longer and hadn't been for years. They were in their thirties, now, well-settled in their careers. Most of them.

"And the girl in black." Harriet had come at last to the one name Mariesa knew she would come to. "The one who wrote the poetry. Roberta. She had some silly nickname for herself. She was always your favorite."

"They were all favorites, Mother."

"No, this one was special. She was the daughter you never had."

The pang Mariesa felt was composed equally of pain and pleasure. She laid a hand across the emptiness where her womb had been. Should she remind Harriet of the miscarriage and the grandson she never saw? But that would be cruel. A reminder of what all her schemes and maneuvers had wrought in the end. "Why do you say that, Mother?"

"Because she alone had the power to hurt you. That is how one recognizes daughters."

Prudence

It had been a lousy day from the get-go and there weren't enough hours left for it to get any better. The Boeing 830 banked and dipped into the turgid cloud layer shrouding the L.A. basin. Jacinta Rosario worked imaginary pedals with her feet and treated the tray table as a surrogate yoke. The night sky outside the windows was swallowed by haze and Jacinta looked past the curve of the wing, hoping to see the matching constellations of the Greater Los Angeles Area spread out below.

No such luck. It looked like haze all the way down. She tried to imagine what the pilot would do next; tried to feel the motion of the plane the way the pilot did. *Absorb care into the task*, the Seventh Precept read. If she *became* the airliner, she could forget that she was out on her own and how difficult a path lay before her. *Initial descent*, she decided. It didn't feel like another loop around. They had broken the holding pattern—at last!—and were making their approach.

"We're starting our final descent into LAX," the chief steward announced over the speakers and Jacinta smiled over her small triumph. "Time to pack things up, folks. The weather down there is overcast and raining, so it'll probably be a little bumpy going in. We're sorry about the delay, but . . ."

But it's not our fault. Jacinta stopped listening. She'd heard three thousand miles of excuses masquerading as apologies, and that was enough for her, thank you very much. Who *cared* whose fault it was? It was just bad luck. Snow in Newark had forced her to wait: for the equipment, then for the flight crew, then for a departure window. It was somehow fitting that a late Pacific storm would delay her arrival. What it all added up to was: she had missed her connection to Bakersfield. It would be easier—certainly more comfortable— if there were someone to blame; but the only candidate in sight was God; and He, by the evidence so far, was not paying attention. Well, the Twelfth Precept was: *Fix the problem, not the blame.*

The postures of the other passengers expressed weariness, boredom, or irritation. For most, Los Angeles was a destination, not a connection, so it didn't matter if they were a couple hours late. She sighed, gathered her papers, and stuffed them into the flight bag under her seat. The man in the aisle seat beside her glanced her way.

"Something pretty important, I guess, the way you've been studying them."

Over and over, the whole long flight out. They read the same each time; but her heart soared too each time she read the words. Was her spirit that obvious? Jacinta set her face into more composed lines while she sized him up. Mid to late sixties, she guessed. Carrying more pounds than he ought to. He'd spent the whole flight from Newark reading westerns, so he was no great thinker. On the other hand, he didn't sound like someone coming on to a seventeen-year-old woman traveling alone. It was the forty-somethings you had to look out for.

"Yes, sir. Pretty important." The man raised his eyebrows at the "sir," but he didn't make a fuss about it one way or the other, so she added, "I'm starting at Glenn Academy for the spring term."

The man nodded. "Good for you. Bucking for space pilot? I hear the competition's real fierce."

"Yes, sir." She smiled for him. "But so am I."

Fierce but frightened. She had never been so far from her sisters before. What happened when you missed a connection? Did the airline make arrangements? Was there another flight they could put her on? Who should she ask? She walked off the jetway into the waiting area, trying to look confident. It was the Lost Lamb that attracted the predators.

Maybe she looked too confident. No one came to offer help. *You're eighteen years old. Well, almost.* What was it the grown-ups liked to say? *Just do it.* Of course, grown-ups didn't have *precepts*, just slogans, but sometimes they managed to capture a truth. Twin TV screens listed arrivals and departures, and she drifted over to them. So many departures were listed as DELAYED that for a moment she dared hope her Bakersfield flight was still on the ground. But, no . . . Gone. Departed. Adios, señor airplane.

"There's a later flight," a male voice said over her shoulder.

She turned to scowl at a dark-haired boy her own age wearing a sheepskin-lined leather jacket. Fake sheepskin, she hoped for his sake. "How would you know where I'm going?" she said in the Voice of Polite Distance.

"He doesn't even know where *he's* going," said the young woman with long, blonde hair and strikingly violet eyes who stood beside him. She wore a gimme cap in Aurora purple with gold thread spelling out *RS-135 Neta Snook*.

"Chaos theory," said the boy agreeably. "In an ultimate sense, none of us know where we're going. Too many variables over too many years. But in the short term, precise predictions are possible. Bakersfield. Glenn Academy." He smiled broadly. "Right?"

The blonde woman said, "Stickers of SSTOs and Black Horses all over your flight bag were Sherlock's subtle clue. Hi, I'm Ursula Kitmann and cutey-pie here is Soren Thorvaldsson. We're cadets, too. Just met on the flight out here. We were on our way to the commuter gates when Soren noticed you."

"Hey," said Soren. "Worth noticing."

Jacinta accepted the outstretched hands in the Posture of Possible Friendship. She explained about the storm in Newark. "Tell me about it," Soren complained. "I came from Minneapolis, where it's clear as a bell. But the *plane* I was supposed to come in on was held up in Atlanta because its *crew* was waiting in Chicago for another plane that was stuck in Boston."

Ursula shrugged and said, "Same story, different cities. The air traffic system's stacked like dominoes. One local foo and the whole thing dominoes."

"So," said Soren, "we're all in the same boat—I mean, in the same plane. If"—a nod toward the flight board—"we can wangle seats on the Midnight Special."

"Which is way over in the commuter concourse," Ursula added. "We've got plenty of time, but the sooner we get there, the sooner we can confirm seats. It'd be a hell of a thing to get this close and miss First Muster. They can give your place away if you're a no-show. Did you know that?"

Of course, she knew that. Hadn't she read and reread the admission papers for the last few hours? She didn't think an air traffic foo would count against her; but she had come too far to be turned back. Since the other two clearly knew their way around airports, Jacinta followed them down the concourse. Yet, it would be so easy to throw her anxiety on their shoulders; to accept their lead. *You are not a duckling. You do not imprint. Stand beside; never behind.* The recitative comforted her and she quickened her pace to walk next to Soren. "Have you been here before?" she asked. "This airport, I mean."

Soren's locks danced when he shook his head. Ursula only shrugged. "Every time Mom and Dad traded me off," she said. "Until they decided which of them didn't want me more than the other." She closed her mouth abruptly and frowned, as if she had said more than she had intended. *Knowledge grows from experience,* Jacinta thought, *not from superiority; but experience always has a price.*

At the gate for the Bakersfield flight, they found four frazzed businessmen, a cheesehead, a woman shepherding a pair of unruly todds, and three more cadets. There were plenty of seats available, as it turned out. Cancellations, failed connections, and no-shows had opened up enough spaces to accommodate them. The checker-in told them the flight was on hold until eleven-thirty, but that could be lifted at any time if a crew could be gotten. There was a thunderstorm in the mountains, but it looked to be breaking up.

Ursula groaned. "An hour and a half?"

"Law of averages," Soren told her with his infectious smile. "We were late for our scheduled flight, so we're early for this one. On the average, we're on time. Hey, 'Cinta! If they need a crew . . . Do you have a jump jet license?" He grinned and Jacinta could not keep an answering smile from briefly surfacing.

The businessmen exchanged arcana about stock markets and system audits; and the cheesehead had his induction cap on and was pondering his laptop.

The other three cadets introduced themselves. The willowy girl with the elfin face was Marta Molnar. She had flown all the way from Budapest, and spoke with an oddly pleasant accent. Square-jawed Jason Holzstreicher had a solid but unfinished look, as if he had been whittled casually from a log of white ash. Alonzo Sulbertson, who was medium height, slim and black, was a lordly third-year student. The gold and ruby pin in his collar proclaimed him a veteran of at least one orbital training flight. That alone marked him a demigod.

Experience, not superiority, Jacinta reminded herself. Prudence, temperance, knowledge, and fortitude would one day win her a brooch like that one.

It was natural that they klatsched. Six young men and women sharing a common dream? How could they not? Mutual attraction, like gravity, drew them into a circle. They perched on the chairs or squatted cross-legged on the floor. Every now and then the laughing three-year-old dodging her weary mother would break through the ring.

Molnar spoke with the worldly cynicism of the European—a jaded attitude that Jacinta recognized as False Confidence. Kitmann was brashly cheerful, occasionally sarcastic. When someone commented on the delays, cancellations and rebookings, she smiled and said, "I like to do things the hard way." Jacinta noticed the small, discreet pin on her collar—the Dove Within the Sun— and adjusted her own Maiden's Shawl to display the Silver Apple; but if the other sister noticed, she gave no sign, and custom required that one not be forward about such things.

Holzstreicher exuded a confidence in voice and body language that bordered on arrogance. The Macho Man. Like Soren, he had a pilot's license already. He spoke loudly and interrupted inappropriately and deferred only when the quiet Sulbertson spoke. Jacinta noticed that Soren, otherwise sassy and ready with oddball jokes, also deferred to the upperclassman. *Alpha male*, she thought, studying the black man. *At least a local maximum.* Sulbertson—sensing her gaze?—glanced at her and Jacinta withdrew her attention.

They were, Jacinta realized, perilously close to bonding; and she wasn't sure she wanted to do that with a random group of people she had barely met. *Choose your friends*, she recited to herself, *as you choose your foes, for both you will keep for life.* She shifted her posture slightly, creating distance, and passed more often when the verbal buck came her way. Sulbertson may have sensed something, because she caught him casting curious looks her way from time to time.

As the Observer, she found her attention drawn more and more to Soren. The Minnesotan, like the others, was her age within a year or two; yet he seemed younger. Maybe it was his eyes or his baby-faced good looks. Maybe it was his openness. Maybe it was his terrible jokes. ("I need to borrow your brain," he said to Sulbertson when the discussion had paused on orbital dynamics, "but I promise to give it back.") But gradually she became convinced that he was closer to his center than any of the others, except perhaps Sulbertson, whose extra years gave him some additional anchorage. Usually, the Joker masked insecurity. Molnar's continental urbanity certainly did. The Hungarian girl, half a world away from anything familiar, shouted loneliness with her very posture, even while she smiled and chatted. But when Soren made a bad joke, it was not simply to draw attention. He made bad jokes because he knew they were bad and found humor in that badness. The second derivative of humor in the calculus of laughs. There was something in his mind that saw and pounced on juxtapositions, and made quirky connections. He was altogether the most attractive of her chance companions.

Realizing that, Jacinta stood abruptly. "I'm hungry," she announced. "Anyone want a hot dog or something?"

Head shakes and nods. Holzstreicher said, "Get me a Coke." Sulbertson pulled a ten from his pocket and said, "My treat. Dog and a coke. Ketchup on the dog."

"I'll have a hot dog, too," Soren said, turning his deep, dark eyes on her. "Nothing on my dog, please. I like my nitriles straight up."

"Watch my flight bag, wouldja?" She hadn't asked anyone in particular, but she noticed as she walked away that it was Soren who pulled it closer to him and was annoyed to find that that pleased her.

The snack bar was a short walk down the concourse, set in a narrow niche in the wall. The SPP grating had been pulled half-shut, as if to announce imminent closure, but the owner had shown pity for the stranded travelers. Jacinta was not the only one who squeezed inside with a late-night snack in mind. There were two lines, each several customers deep, and Jacinta took her place in one. A portly, balding, sixtyish man and a younger woman wearing a headband around raven-black hair serviced the customers. The television showed the Weather Channel—everyone's topic of interest, it seemed.

The lines inched forward. The buzz of conversation, the cheerful chatter of the Weather Channel, the occasional cluster of gate announcements blended into an inarticulate background. The time-lapse on the 3V monitor showed the downpour as it tracked across the L.A. basin, broke up, and retreated sullenly toward the northeast. The virtual POV rotated and moved through the storm cell up into the hills, turned, and came back through from another direction. Then coverage shifted to the Pacific Northwest and the conversation in line shifted to bitching and moaning about missed connections and late departures. Jacinta tuned them out.

She reached the head of the line and the bald man asked her what she wanted, but the black woman said, "Let me take this one, Carl," and traded places with him. The woman—Jacinta judged her to be nearly thirty—brushed some sweat off her forehead with the back of her wrist.

"A service, sister?" she asked.

Startled, Jacinta looked closer and saw the silver apple pinned to the woman's blouse. She didn't know why she was so surprised. Though most of their retreats were in the northeast, silver apples could be found across the country. As the First Precept read: *The apple is never far from the tree.*

"Are you stuck here overnight, sister?" the woman asked in the Voice of Intimacy in Public.

"I don't think so. My flight's on hold; but we'll be going out in a little while. To Bakersfield," she added. "I'm Jacinta Rosario from the North Orange Retreat. I'm starting at Glenn Academy this spring."

"Make us proud," her sister said. "Fledgling?" Jacinta nodded. "This weather could change any minute," the older sister told her. "If you do need help tonight, you know our edress. I'm Darlene. We have a retreat nearby, in Torrance. One call and we'll come get you."

Jacinta would rather die than ask help on her fledging. The sisterhood taught that the hand was always open and always ready, but there was an unspoken stigma on those who reached for it too quickly. Dependency, even on one's sisters, was a last resort. She answered formally in the Voice of Independence. "I will remember your kind offer." Darlene nodded, as if in approval, then turned away to fill her order.

Jacinta made her way back to the gate more confident than she had been since the bus had stuck in the snow on the way to Newark Airport. She and Darlene had exchanged only a few words; yet she felt closer to the sister than to any of the young cadets she had shared the last hour with. Not that she disliked Kitmann and the others. They seemed decent enough; though the black man had a certain dangerous sleepiness to him. The Drowsing Panther. And Soren was definitely shoog. What did grown-ups say? Buff? No, not buff. "Dreamy," maybe. He had that unfocused, boyish look. Grown-ups probably tousled his hair all the time. *Remember this Type, sisters. The Little Boy. It will call on your mother-instinct.*

But did mothers feel this way, Jacinta wondered, about their sons?

It was a shock to find the waiting area empty and the plane gone.

She stood dumbly with the cardboard tray in her hands and surveyed the lounge. Gone. All of them. Her flight bag, too. Even the podium was closed down. The marquee announced DEPARTED in red, running capitals under the flight number and destination. DEPARTED . . . DEPARTED . . .

The drinks on her tray toppled and fell, creating a fan of Coke and ice across the tiles.

Alone and friendless, three thousand miles from home. Everything she had was in her flight bag; everything that had not been shipped ahead. How would she get to the Academy now? She would be late for First Muster and lose her place. She could feel the tears work their way like sap up her trunk; and she clenched fists over her bosom, opened the palms like spears, and called upon her Inner Strength.

There would be a flight out in the morning; but she would need someplace to spend the night. Not a hotel. Her cash card had gone with her flight bag. *Stupid!* The retreat? Surely the sisterhood would not hold her to blame if she sought refuge this one night?

No; though they might cluck to themselves outside her presence. Perhaps she wasn't ready to fledge, they would say. Never aloud, but the thought would be there. Her hand touched the jacket pocket where she carried her copy of *The Precepts of Mother Smythe*. *Dependency is the only sin*, she recited silently. *"It's not my fault," the one, true failure.* Slowly, calm returned. What can I do now? That was the key question. The only question.

The hand on her shoulder broke her concentration and caused her to suck in her breath. "Looks like we got a problem."

She turned, assuming the Posture of Readiness. A predator spotting a young girl alone; Sister Darlene coming to see her off; Soren having stayed behind when she didn't make it back in time . . . Expecting anything, she did not expect what she saw.

Alonzo Sulbertson, the third-year student, had his own flight bag over his shoulder. Dark eyes lodged in a dark face; black hair cropped nearly bald. His broad, turned-up lips blending into his coloring, so that he seemed almost a man without features. Until he smiled and the white of his teeth showed.

"Looks like we both missed the plane," he said.

"Wh . . ." She would not blubber in front of a man. It triggered the Guardian in them. Another moment passed before she could trust her voice. "What happened?"

"They lifted the hold all of a sudden; but it was a short window—too many flights backed up—so they couldn't wait. Doesn't take long, getting those little commuter hover jets boarded and out. Didn't you hear the announcement?"

The acoustics had been poor in the snack bar; the speakers had not been clear; the Weather Channel announcer had drowned it out; she had not been listening closely. The world was full of excuses. "No," was all she said.

"That kid, Thorvaldsson, ran down the concourse but he didn't see you in line."

"There were two lines," she said, "I was in the back." *He didn't look hard enough. He should have checked . . .* But, no; she wouldn't play the Blame Game.

Sulbertson shook his head. "Tough luck. Got any plans?"

Instantly, she drew into herself. "Sure."

"Yeah." Sulbertson looked uncomfortable and glanced away for a moment. "Look," he said, "when I missed the plane I went to the pee-phones and rezzed a car. It's a fair drive over the mountains, but it's doable. If we start now, we'll be at the Academy not much later than the others. They'll still have to get a cab from the airport down the Fifty-Eight toward Mojave. This time of night, that won't be easy."

"We?"

He shrugged. "Long drive. Goes faster with someone to talk to."

"My flight bag's gone."

"Yeah. Thorvaldsson took it with him, like he was guarding it with his life. What're you getting at?"

She crouched and began gathering up the spilled food. *The consequences of your own actions are your own responsibility.* "My cash card was in my flight bag."

He gave her a puzzled look. "And . . . ?"

Jacinta sucked in her lip. "I can't help pay for the car."

Sulbertson squatted, too, and began helping her. He picked a hot dog off the floor and studied it for a moment before passing it to her. "Didn't ask you to."

"Then I'll help with the driving."

"In the dark and the rain and you don't know the roads over the San Gabriels . . . ?" He waved a hand. "Don't worry about it."

She stood with the tray of trash and dumped it in a nearby can. "I don't want to owe you."

He cocked his head and his smile faded. "A little fussy who you accept favors from?"

Her chin tilted up. "Yes."

"Like a black man?"

"It's not that. I just don't like to owe people."

"Get used to it," he suggested. He turned to go.

"Wait."

"What?"

"How come *you* missed the plane?"

He shrugged and dropped his glance. "Well. You know. I was . . ." He jerked a thumb toward the rest rooms. Jacinta shook her head.

"That's damn good eyes, Sulbertson, if you saw Soren take my flight bag aboard. You had to be right here in the waiting area when they boarded."

"All right, I was. So what?"

"So you stayed behind on purpose. Why?"

"Why?" This time his smile seemed amused. "'Cause I gave you the money for the dogs and I wanted to get my change back."

It was an unlikely answer, and Jacinta wondered what she was getting into as she followed him down the concourse. Had he seized an opportunity to be alone with her for the long drive? He moved with easy, languid strides. How easily he had taken charge! Some men had a sense of lordship, as if all they surveyed was in their gift. Even when they didn't exercise that right, the *posture* of ownership was there, informing their actions.

The rain had started up again by the time they were northbound on the 405. The windshield wipers on the Ford Wraith slapped like a metronome—a lulling sound unsuited to a long night drive. Jacinta wondered why, with all the technological changes cars had gone through—onboard navcomps, heads-up displays, modular engines, aerogel bodies that gave strength *and* lightness— they hadn't found a better way to keep the windshield clear of rain and snow.

They had driven mostly in silence, if you didn't count the navcomp's voice whispering cues and warnings in seductive, androgynous tones. Jacinta sat closed in on herself, pondering the fact that she was alone, without resources, with a man she had barely met. From time to time, she glanced at him and saw how easily he sat. Both hands on the wheel, watching the road ahead, but with a casual manner. Totally in charge. Finally, he caught her looking.

"If I wanted silence for the ride," he said, "I could have asked Harpo Marx to tag along."

"Who?"

"Never mind." Sulbertson focused on his driving again and another few minutes went by. Then he said, "Is it me?"

"You what?"

"Making you so uncomfortable. You sit like you were carved from wood. 'Bout as talkative as a log, too."

Rain crawled like worms down the side window, creating strange, jewellike sparkles each time they passed a street lamp. "No," she said, lying only in part. "Just . . . the circumstances. Everything has gone wrong on this trip."

"Everything?"

"Do you want the list?" Start with all the things she had forgotten to pack. No. Start with all the people who hadn't come to see her off. Her sisters had come, yes; but *only* her sisters. Mom hadn't approved of the silver apples, called them a cult, but did her disapproval have to run so deep that she would not even come to the airport to see her daughter leave?

"Prepare to merge with northbound traffic from I-Five," the navcomp murmured. Sulbertson grinned. "Thanks, darling." He looked around—at the road ahead and behind—then his eyes came her way again. "So you're not always so standoffish. Is that what you're saying?"

"I don't know what you mean."

"I mean the little walls you build between yourself and everyone else. Earlier, with the rest of the cadets, I could almost see you laying the bricks."

Jacinta crossed her arms. "You could see that, could you?"

"There. You're doing it again. With your body language and your tone of voice. It's like you're putting yourself somewhere else. I couldn't put my finger on it earlier, but that's it. You're frightened and alone and—"

"I am *not!*"

Sulbertson jumped a little. She had used the Voice of Independence. This time when he peered at her, his eyes were narrow and thoughtful. "And you're doing it on purpose, aren't you?"

She had parted her lips to tell him it was no business of his when the navcomp interrupted.

"Bulletin," the voice sang cheerfully. "Emergency route change. Prepare to exit on the Fourteen in one mile. Recomputing travel times . . ." A right turn arrow with the legend "One Mile" appeared in the heads-up display on the lower windshield and began to blink.

Sulbertson frowned and punched the traffic bulletin button on the console. ". . . combined with slick roads and fog, causing the chain-reaction accident on the Grapevine," announced the synthetic voice. "Traffic is stopped in both directions." Then, after a pause: "California Highway Patrol reports that—" Sulbertson cut the announcement off. "Damn," he said. "Hey, navigator— that's you, Rosario—check the overview map. I think the new route takes us in the back way."

Jacinta leaned forward and frowned over the unfamiliar icons—incomprehensible unless you already knew their meanings. She touched a magnifying glass and the map on the navcomp screen zoomed in. Experimentation proved it to be a three-step toggle: close-up, normal, and wide angle.

"Check for traffic behind, signal, then shift to the right-hand lane," the computer advised. "Prepare to exit in half a mile."

Sulbertson laughed. "They always put those little warnings in there. 'Check for traffic . . .' 'Make a *legal* U-turn . . .' I really hope nobody out there driving is dim-bulb enough to need them. But . . . 'Here there be lawyers,' like it says on the old maps. How about that route, navigator?"

"Um. It looks like it bends east for a while, then goes north toward Edwards and intersects with, uh, Fifty-Eight."

"Yeah, that's what I thought." Sulbertson drifted across the highway and off the exit onto the new road. "Not an interstate, but not a bad road, either."

It was wrong to tempt the Fates with words. The Fourteen would have been a very good road indeed, Jacinta thought, had it not been for the several tons of mud that had broken loose and flowed across it. Hills rose on either side of the road. Now one rose directly in front, too. Red taillights were jumbled all together where the cars had stopped or pulled aside. It was single digits in the morning, but a fair number of cars had halted in front of the mud. Sulbertson stopped the Wraith and they stared at the obstacle. Lightning flashed above them. Rain drummed on the roof of the car and blew in sheets across the road. The wipers rocked hypnotically and the navcomp displayed now-useless messages on the heads-up. Jacinta felt a small flower of despair blossom within her. She would never make it to the academy now.

"Must have just happened," Sulbertson said.

"How do you know?" Her voice came out dull and flat. Not one of the canonical Voices, at all.

"No bulletin download yet on the traffic—" Even before he could finish, the onboard announced that the highway had been closed and promised to recalculate another route. Sulbertson pointed a finger at it. "*Now* you tell us. Better shut it down," he added. "There *isn't* any other route. Poor thing'll go crazy trying to compute the incomputable. It'll try to take us all the way around to Barstow; and there's no guarantee that the San Bernardinos are any better." He looked at the mudslide again. "Jeez, I hope nobody was under that when it went."

Jacinta pressed the red toggle and the map screen blinked and faded. The car's cab darkened. She hadn't realized how much the navcomp screen had lighted the interior. "Now what?"

Sulbertson scowled and drummed on the steering wheel with his two forefingers. "This mess won't be cleared up for a couple days," he decided. "Interstate Five will probably be open in an hour or two. What say we turn back to the Golden State and wait. Catch a little shut-eye, maybe."

"Do you mean in a motel?" she asked in the Voice of Caution.

Sulbertson made an exasperated sound in his throat. "No, you can sleep in the damn car, if that's what you want." He swiped the magcard through the reader and looked into the Facemaker so the car's onboard knew he was the legal renter. The engine restarted, and he backed up and cut across the median to the southbound lanes. The ground was soft and the wheels dug in, sliding a little in the mud before he managed to coax the car back onto the pavement. "What's with you, anyway?" he asked when they had started back down the highway. "It's not like I'm trying to get into your pants, you know."

"That's not for you to decide."

"Looks like I can't win for losing. But do you mind telling me who stacked your particular deck?"

"Is there something wrong with chastity?"

"What? Hell, no. I approve of it, mostly."

"Well," said Jacinta, folding her arms and looking straight ahead, "I approve of it wholly."

Sulbertson took his hands off the wheel long enough to make a shrug. "How did we get started on this? Look, if you don't do the deed, that's no skin off my nose. I never asked, and you're not my type, anyway."

The hiss of the tires on the rain-slick pavement was the only break in the silence. Jacinta closed her eyes and recited the Fourteen Precepts to herself, one after the other. She reviewed the Sixteen Archetypes and pushed the image of Alonzo Sulbertson firmly back into his proper box. Finally, Jacinta broke the silence. "It's not the same," she said.

"Huh? What's not the same as what?"

"Chastity isn't celibacy."

"Well. That's good news for someone, I'm sure."

"Good news for *me*." She twisted sideways in her seat to face him and turned her scarf to show the pin. "I'm a silver apple. Do you understand what that means?"

He frowned and spared her a glance. "That's one of those new sisterhoods, isn't it?"

"It means we have each other. It means we don't have to go on being the cannon fodder for your sexual revolution—"

"Hey, it wasn't *my* revolution."

"—or being the playgrounds for 'recreational' sex. Do you know what it is to be sweet-talked, used, and then dumped into single-parent households, like my mother? Do you know how *smug* boys can be when they know they can walk away and a jaded society will only shrug? Well, the silver apples expect better. They taught me confidence and self-reliance and let me know I wasn't alone in my choices."

Sulbertson heaved a sigh. "All I said was"—raising fingers to tally his points—"one, it's late; two, both direct routes are blocked; three, the Golden State will clear long before the Antelope Valley; four, we'll have to wait a couple hours, regardless; and five, we might as well get some shut-eye while we do. If you have a better plan, I'd be glad to hear it."

Jacinta deflated and sank in her seat, hugging herself. Three thousand miles and most of a day of travel piled on her like sandbags. She wished she could close her eyes and wake up at the academy. That was the seduction. It was so much *easier* to depend on others. If you took no responsibility, you would accept no blame. And while a blameless life was something to aspire to, there was a wide gulf between *deserving* none and *accepting* none. "I'm sorry I blorked at you," she said. "I'm usually not so fused, but it's . . ."

"Yeah, we're all tired. Long day."

"If I'd been listening to the announcements, we'd've made the plane and be snug in the dorms by now."

"It can happen to anyone."

"Why *did* you stay behind?"

"Here's the cloverleaf coming up," he said. "Jeez, it looks so delicate. I heard it collapsed one time in a quake and some cop went right over the edge on his cycle. Keep an eye out for a place to stop." He peered up through the windshield. "I think the rain may be letting—" A strobe flash of lightning proved him a liar, and Jacinta laughed at the look on his face. "Okay," he said after the thunder had died, "so I'm no weatherman." Then, as if the shared laughter had been a signal, he said, "You asked why I stayed? Because we don't leave our own behind. I was senior cadet present; so it was my responsibility."

"An officer, as well as a gentleman." The Voice of Light Humor.

The look he gave her was unreadable, not one she recognized from her training. "I like to think so."

Shortly, they reached the butt-end of the traffic blocked by the accident. The Highway Patrol had set up flares and cops in yellow slickers were waving people to the shoulder or guiding them through an Authorized Vehicles Only U-turn through the median. "That must drive their onboards crazy," Sulbertson said with a chuckle. He rolled his window down a crack and called to one of the officers. Another hour or two, the trooper told him when he asked how long the wait would be.

"Pretty bad?" Sulbertson asked.

The cop stepped up close to the rental car as an ambulance rolled up the lane they had cleared for emergency vehicles. "Yeah. Pretty bad."

"I'm trained in EMT work," Sulbertson offered. "Second class license."

"Nah, squad's on the job. We got all the help we need, dude; but thanks for the offer."

The rain was spraying into the car through the window crack. Another flash of lightning turned everything black and white for an instant. It threw shadows. The crack followed so closely that Jacinta was sure it had struck somewhere close by. It was as if God was hunting for her.

"What caused it?" Sulbertson asked the patrolman. "The download said slick roads and fog."

"Half right. A commuter plane went down in the pass. Fog kept cars from seeing it until they plowed right into it. Look, I've got three miles of wrecked cars to—"

"A commuter flight?" Jacinta leaned across Sulbertson with a sudden, unreal sense of urgency. "What flight was that? What flight?"

The cop looked startled by her intensity. "I forget the flight number," he said. "It was flying L.A. to Bakersfield, but turned back when the storm reformed. Way I heard, wind shear caught it and pushed it down into the highway."

Sulbertson rolled the window down farther and the wind blew the rain into the car. "We rented this car because we missed that flight. Some friends were on board. Were there any survivors?"

"Not that I heard. You had friends on board? Man, that's phat nasty. You were damn lucky to miss the flight."

"Yeah," said Sulbertson, slumping in his seat with a stunned look on his face. "Damned lucky." The rain, spraying on his face, looked like tears.

Friends? Jacinta thought. No, she had barely met them. Holzstreicher, she felt sure she would never have liked. Not merely a man, but a *male*, with all the macho B/S that implied. And Molnar was too standoffish, a Euro-snob. And Kitmann . . . The Doves Within the Sun were a religious sisterhood. The two of them would have clashed sooner or later. Even Soren, she felt sure— his jokes would have tested her patience in the end.

So she was fortunate not to have formed a bond with any of them. They were strangers, for whom she might feel pity; nothing more. But then, unreasonably, she laid her head into her hands and wept. Not because she had known them and had taken them into her heart; but because she hadn't, and she hadn't.

5.

Face Time

The face on the screen looked very sincere, but Jimmy Poole wondered if that meant much more than the name that had come with it. Was it even a real person, or just an electric dream? The nose was long, the cheekbones high. The skin was lightly tanned; the eyes, a peculiar gray. The hair looked real, too, and morphies tended to have fakey hair—slick and solid, as if lamination had suddenly become the hot tonsorial fashion. High prob scenario: he was looking at a real face with a phony name. Jimmy didn't like that. It smelled.

Smelled like a government job. Jimmy began to worry. Why would Baleen's principal be a false persona? Entrapment? Step warily! "And just what is it you want Poole sEcurity to do, Mr., ah, Desherite?" As he spoke, his left hand danced across the macro pad, montage-ing help-wanted ads and other images of work for hire on the receiver screen.

Desherite frowned at the twist Jimmy had given his name. "You sound like you don't believe me."

"You haven't told me anything but your name," Jimmy pointed out.

"That's right." It was a flat statement, almost as if Desherite didn't care that his mask had been ripped aside, almost as if he had called with no other purpose. Jimmy didn't mind ripping masks aside, but it bothered him when there was no face behind them.

His web ferret flashed another message. The node trace on "Desherite's" call had hit a cat's cradle and lost the skein. So his caller couldn't be pinned down, geographically *or* topologically. He might be half a world away; or next door. A false ID calling from nowhere.

There had been a time when, as Crackman, Jimmy had sought such customers out. But if age had not brought wisdom, it had at least brought caution, which, as Tani had once told him, was a working start. With his left hand, Jimmy digitized the face on the screen and sent the ferret into the master dataface at *The New York Times*. If "Desherite" was a professional spook, his pixure would never have appeared in public, but it was worth a shot.

Jimmy decided on a straightforward approach. When no other strategy suggested itself, honesty was always an option. "David Desherite," he announced, "is a shell persona. Knock on the door and there's no one home." Three quick

macros, and his Artificial Stupid dipped into the screen art deeby and threw
an old black-and-white horror movie clip on his bounceback screen: a castle
door creaking slowly open into an empty room. Jimmy enjoyed shuffling visuals. There was nothing more boring on-screen than a talking head. And the
barrage of images and sound bytes sometimes disoriented his callers, to Poole's
advantage.

It didn't seem to bother the Face, though. The guy must be in his forties—
always assuming the mug was the Jenuine Bean—but he took it as well as a
thirtysomething. There was an intensity to his gaze that drew Jimmy in, the
feeling that this was a happening dude.

The Face blew his breath out and frowned. "It's worked well enough until
now," he said.

"*I* haven't seen it until now."

His caller propped his head on his right hand, an index finger curling up
his cheek. "What's the flaw?" he asked. He seemed less upset than intrigued.

Jimmy shrugged. "No depth." To an inquiring look, he added, "Desherite's
got an employment history, college record, high school transcript, birth certificate . . . On the surface, it looks good; but there's nothing underneath." The
A/S illustrated that with a striptease by the Invisible Woman.

"Example?" Oh, he was a kool kustomer, this Desherite. But what was his
game?

"Take your residences. My ferret automatically researches anyone who calls
me, so it moused the public real estate deebies. The people you claim for
parents lived at your address of record, but according to the Realtor's ad, that
house had only enough bedrooms for three kids, not four."

"I bunked with my brother." The Face spoke with amusement, as if he did
not expect the explanation to stand up.

"You mean one of your sisters. Well, maybe you had a more interesting
home life than most guys. But that's only second-layer stuff. Dig deeper. 'Desherite's' *never* gotten a parking ticket? *Never* ducked jury duty? *Never* hit on a
web site? *Never* downloaded a video. *Never* subscribed to a printzine *or* a web-
zine? If 'Desherite' *is* a real person, he doesn't have a life."

His caller was nodding. "What about census records or the IRS?"

Was this the trap? Did they think he'd be herbie enough to mouse in
there? Not without very careful planning. Entry was illegal to any but authorized law enforcement agents and singles-bar bouncers hired for White
House security. "Couldn't say. But the smart money bets no Desherite in there,
either."

The Face thought awhile. Poole used the pause to check his sensors. The
laager around the phone call was beginning to attract interest. Three mice and
a worm were nibbling at the edge. Jimmy's security A/S gave them a virus and
sent them back to infect their sources. Time to shift the scene. He squirted a
code to Desherite's machine, converting both systems to a new encryption

scheme. Desherite must have had a phat system, because Jimmy saw the man's eyebrows go up and then tighten in a frown. Most of his callers never noticed when he code danced.

Money, or power. Or both. *Do I want to play this man's game?*

"All right," said Desherite. "Maybe I should have come to you first. Can you craft me an unbreakable persona? One that's down to the bone?"

" 'Can you' is the wrong question." His trademark line, it graced all his ads. Jimmy swung his chair back and forth and kicked his legs. "You're asking me to finger locked deebies."

"The people I'll need to fool won't be stopped by 'No Trespassing' signs, *and* they know keyholders. I don't *think* I'll look important enough to trigger an in-depth analysis of my persona; but I'll be putting myself somewhere where, if I think wrong, I'll be in Shit City without my hip boots."

Jimmy smiled even as he shook his head. " 'Homey don't play that no more.' "

For a wonder, he didn't have to explain the allusion. *He's one of us,* Jimmy reminded himself. At the older end of the generation, but still one of us.

"If it helps you make up your mind," Desherite suggested, "what I want to do is in a worthy cause. It may be a little illegal, but it's not immoral."

Jimmy shrugged. Illegal could put him in jail. Immoral could get him elected to high office. The important thing was not whether it was right, but whether it would work.

The flashnote on his auxilliary screen caught his eye. His ferret had come back from *The New York Times* dataface with three pixures, none of them Desherite. Two were newsgroup "candid" shots; one was a formally-posed publicity still. Congruence was only seventy-two percent, but most of the difference was the beard and moustache and the change in hair and eye color, and those could be altered. Jimmy read the name, then worked hard to keep anything from showing in his face.

"Down to the bone," Jimmy suggested, "is only half the problem." He paused for the other to ask what the other half was, but Desherite merely waited for him to explain, which bugged him. "You've got to suture self," he said.

Rapid eyeblinks, followed by a frown. "Suit myself?"

Jimmy snickered at finally eliciting a reaction. "No. You've got to *suture.* You've got to cut off all connection between yourself and your regular persona, so if anyone tracks your backtrail, it leads them *only* to the persona you want them to see."

"My 'regular persona.' That's what you call a person's true identity?"

"No, 'true identity' is what people call their favorite persona."

"I'll . . . remember that." Desherite cocked his head. "Does this mean you'll take the job?"

Caution closed Jimmy's lips. "This means," he said slowly, "I'll think about it."

Desherite shrugged. "You want us to put bones on Leo to suss around? Fine. It's my bones that have to go. I'll want a meeting."

"What are we doing now?"

"Face to face."

Jimmy rocked forward in his chair. "Interface to interface isn't good enough? These are the Terrible Teens. Get used to it."

"Call me eccentric. If we go on this project, I'll be trusting you with . . . Well, something invaluable. I want to look you straight in the eye when we deal."

Almost, Jimmy told him to blow off; but he glanced again at the name the ferret had fingered and reconsidered. Given what this man had already done, Jimmy felt a deep curiousity to learn what he was about to do. Might be time to shift some portfolios to catch the money that would shake loose. Whether he took the job or not, knowledge was always useful. "How soon can you come to San Jose?" Jimmy wasn't about to drag his own personal bones any farther than he had to.

"Make it San Francisco."

They settled on Le Maison Raoul for Saturday. "Dress mainstreet," Jimmy advised his caller. "This is California."

Afterwards, he spun his chair a full three-sixty and leaped like a gymnast finishing the parallel bars. A tough problem, suturing *that* persona! No wonder whatever loser had crafted the falsie had bungled. Probably he'd been afraid to try too hard.

Government deebies. Very secure. Even to glance their way would be unwise. Risky business even for legal games. Yet there must be a way. Skate along the edge, or just a little over. Not too far. He had promised Tani. But, *kool beans, what a problem!*

He left the Sanctum and prowled the living room while he thought. He could use a guardian angel for the suture—one that could fly any inquiry over to the right file. It was inserting the Desherite persona into deep cover that niggled at him. If the Bad Guys had access to keyholders, they could easily check tax returns and other stuff he didn't dare finger. Had "Desherite" filed during the last couple years? Had to. Wilson and other employers-of-record would have withheld tax. The Feds might be slow, but someday they would wonder why that particular Citizen ID Number had never filed any earlier returns. Bomb the archives? Best place to hide a body was at a massacre. But they'd look long and hard for the charlie with the nuts to pull *that* hack, and Jimmy knew it was not ego to think that he would be on the short list of Those Who Could.

In the kitchen, he rummaged in the cereal cabinet until he found a box of Sugar Pops. He poured a bowl and began eating them with his fingers. Stassy, the cook, watched with something bordering on disgust. Jimmy grinned at the woman and held the bowl out. "Core a show," he said in what he imagined was Russian. "Cochise?" Stassy's look said that Tani would soon hear of this. "Diet nazi," he muttered under his breath. But a diet meant nothing if you didn't break it now and then.

Jimmy left the kitchen and went to the rear of the large family room. The curtains on the bay window were pulled back, letting in the sun and the sight of the rolling lawn in the back of the lot. Fine green grass sloping down toward a copse of trees—city greenbelt land, but Jimmy had exclusive access. Tani sat on a blanket, hunched over her laptop, while little Stevie crawled through the grass under Rada's watchful eye. Jimmy watched them in silence. He bounced up and down on the balls of his feet, as if he were built on springs.

Risk all this? That was crazy. "Desherite" didn't know what he was asking. Play it safe, Jimmy thought. Play for time. Check things out. Did he want bones on Leo bad enough to finger a false persona?

Desherite's eyes had burned with a righteous anger, the alluring draw of a go-to-hell attitude. Ten times better to be that man's ally than his opponent. But a hundred times better to stay on the sidelines.

So it was crazy, yes; but it was phat stoopid, too. He stepped closer to the window and watched his family play. Tani doesn't understand, he thought. She didn't understand how *alive* it felt on the wild side, where "safe" was just another word for "dead."

The cable car clanged its bell as it made the turn onto Columbus Avenue. Three rows toward the front of the car, David Desherite turned to look at something along the street and Jimmy Poole, SuperSpy, ducked his head behind a hardcopy newssheet. He squirmed with suppressed excitement and tried to keep from bouncing in his seat. No point in catching the attention of the man he was shadowing. He had wanted to observe his new client before getting down and dirty—to learn something about the man—and being noticed would spoil that.

Fingering Desherite's flight number had been the work of a moment. Jimmy marked his quarry coming out of the jetway and followed him to the BART line that ran up the median of the 101 freeway. Then, from the smooth, quiet maglev train to the clanging, bouncing Powell-Mason cable car. The twenty-first century and the nineteenth, side by side. Go figure.

Peeking around the corner of his prop, Jimmy compared the man to the pixures his search engines had found. He had to admit that Desherite's disguise was good. Not so over-the-top as to draw attention to itself, but enough subtle touches that only someone who knew the man well would see the real face behind the hairstyle and the colored contact lenses. The faint scar on the right cheek was a stroke of brilliance. Misdirection was always the best disguise. More people would remember that scar than the face it accented. Fooling a Facemaker, though; that would be something else. That would mean tampering with deebies.

Desherite shifted again and Jimmy ducked behind the wall of newsprint. He chuckled to himself. Desherite obviously intended to ride the cable car to the end of the line and then take the Sausalito ferry. Jimmy thought he could avoid Desherite on the boat. It wasn't as big as the Staten Island ferries of his childhood, but it wasn't a canoe, either. The tricky part would be the couple of blocks walking between the turntable and wharf 45. He bent the corner of his paper to sneak another glance.

And Desherite was looking directly at him!

Jimmy knew when to fold a hand. He lowered his paper and tried to look astonished to see Desherite riding the very same cable car as he was. Desherite, for his part, threw his head back and laughed—which drew uneasy stares from those around him and taught Jimmy something important about his would-be client. This man was way too easily amused.

Nevertheless, Desherite played the game until they were aboard the ferry and sliding across San Francisco Bay on a cushion of air. Jimmy stood near the bow enjoying the fine mist raised by the fan deck below. It was not a popular spot. Most people did not care for the damp, but Jimmy rather enjoyed it, and it helped him keep cool in the bright afternoon sun. Shortly, Desherite leaned an elbow on the rail beside him and cocked his head. "So. You're Jimmy Poole."

Jimmy had endured enough mocking voices in high school to recognize even the gentler variety. Taunting voices; condescending voices; patronizing voices. From people like Chase Coughlin, barely bright enough to pour from a shoe with the instructions written on the heel. No one laughed at S. James Poole! Not any more. Not twice.

"So," he said as casually as possible, "you're Adam van Huyten."

He gave "Desherite" credit: the man barely changed expression and answered without missing a beat. "I see I'm hiring the right person."

That was better, but not good enough. "You haven't hired me, 'Desherite.' You're buying my services."

Van Huyten shrugged, conceding the point. "All right. I'm buying. Are you selling?"

Jimmy looked away, suddenly wary. The euphoria he had felt earlier in the week had evaporated. Dancing with wolves was one thing; but the wolves had to buy in, too. "You're talking risky business."

"I thought 'risky' was your forté."

"Think what you like. Those rumors were never proven. I'm married now. I have a kid. It changes you." Until this very moment, Jimmy hadn't realized how deeply it had. Silently, he watched Alcatraz Island fall behind the hydrofoil. Prison. Behind him, he heard the faint cries of children. Or were they gulls? He had always thought of "Crackman, the Gonzo Hacker" as a persona he could still suit up if the spirit moved him. That he could still be dangerous if he wanted to be.

"Look," said van Huyten, "the bonebagging was your idea. I might have written off Billie's suspicions if *you* hadn't asked for a look-see, too. So you must have your own reservations about siting on-orbit."

Jimmy shook his head. "It's not that. 'My only site is where I sit.' But there's one stoopid security laager around Leo, and you don't make hidey-holes unless you're hiding something."

Adam van Huyten cocked his head. "I thought you gave up hacking."

"Cracking," Jimmy corrected him. "Hacking is legit. I was just browsing; but you can't help it, if you run into something like that, to poke at it a little bit out of curiosity."

"Uh-huh. You want a bonebag up because you won't crack it on the virtch. I understand. I have two children myself, though they're both in college now. But that brings us back to the original question. You want bones upstairs and, for various reasons, it's my bones that have to go. 'Desherite' has worked so far because Ed Wilson pulled strings on SkyLab, but I can't depend on inside help if I step into Bullock territory. And Bullock, like I said, has connections who can deep-check deebies legally. Or at least, quasi-legally. So, will you do the backfill for Desherite or not?"

Jimmy sighed. "Maybe I don't want to find out about Leo that bad."

Van Huyten turned away. "Then we're wasting time."

"Wait."

Van Huyten stopped and Jimmy felt himself impaled by the man's eyes. Fierce, narrow, focused like a laser beam. He felt like a butterfly on a board. *I don't want to be involved with this man.* Whatever van Huyten was up to, it was phat nasty. He could feel the *drive* pouring off him like heat.

"I'm waiting."

Jimmy swallowed and stared into the distance. It was a mistake to meet like this. There was no way to walk out. Dive overboard and the lifter fans were likely to suck you in. Why had he come in the first place? Did it really matter if he was still who he used to be? What did he have to prove? Sure, Crackman's life was more electric, more "there," than S. James Poole, Bourgeois Slug; but this whole thing could be a setup. He glanced at Adam van Huyten, the man who sold out Van Huyten Industries and handed Leo Station to Bullock's OMC. If Crackman did crack again, could he trust this man? Someone who had betrayed his own father would not think twice about throwing a subcontractor to the hungry wolves. If the job fooed, the Powers That Be would trade van Huyten for the legendary Crackman in a New York minute. Netmasters like Jimmy threatened their control over the carotids of information, while someone like Adam van Huyten, whatever else he might have done, was still One of the Boys.

"There are some things you can do legal," he said. At least legal to the extent that maintaining a phony identity was legal in itself.

A cough and a shrug. "Such as . . . ?"

"When I followed you from the airport, I expected you to take a limo. But you took the BART maglev up the 101 instead."

The eyes grew impatient and the voice hard. "I support mass transit. So what?"

"*Who* likes trains: David Desherite or Adam van Huyten?"

Van Huyten's eyes narrowed. "A lot of people ride commuter rail."

"Sure. That's just one datum. It divides the pond in two: train-phreaks and everyone else. But it also means David Desherite is a fish swimming in a slightly smaller pond. Are there any foods you don't like?"

"I'm not crazy about asparagus." This came out slowly. Curiosity dominated his voice now. The eyes blazed less fiercely. The unholy magnetism was quenched.

"Then 'Desherite' should order asparagus—and not make a face when he swallows. Train riders who hate asparagus . . . The pond gets smaller. Look, dude, people aren't just faces. They're habits, preferences, turns of phrase, mannerisms. You can fool a lot of people with the persona you have now. You can fool millions of people. You can fool all the people who never knew Adam van Huyten and a good chunk of those who did. But the rest . . . They'll scratch their heads and wonder why you remind them so much of good ol' Adam. And if they start to wonder, they might look closer. You don't want that. But you don't want to go overboard, either," he added quickly. "It's just as bad if people notice that you're the exact opposite of Adam van Huyten."

Van Huyten nodded slowly. "I see . . . What else?" And now Jimmy heard a new note: respect. Jimmy fought hard to remain still, to keep his dignity. In the old days, he would bounce like a ping-pong ball and his voice would climb an octave or two.

"I made a few notes while I followed you. Little stuff, like that thing with the train. But you'll have to do your own inventory. That cheesehead assistant of yours is in on this, isn't she? Maybe she can help." (Whoops. Van Huyten stiffened a little at that and Jimmy wondered if he had just insulted his client's significant other. You never knew. Unplug the wiring and that would be one phat face. Jimmy wondered if her body measured up.)

Van Huyten's eyes had become falcon's claws, clutching Jimmy and pulling him away as easily as a captured field mouse. "Whistle doesn't know anything," he said. "And you won't tell her anything. As far as she and the rest of Baleen are concerned, I'm David Desherite. Do you understand?"

The voice had not risen. No threats had been made. But Jimmy swallowed and had to stop himself from backing away. "Understood," he said.

Van Huyten nodded. "Okay. Then what?"

It took Jimmy a moment to recover his poise. That was another thing that van Huyten ought to pay for. Jimmy did not enjoy feeling threatened. "That . . . depends on how long you want to run Desherite. If it's for the rest of your life—"

The other man snorted and looked up at the approaching shoreline. "Not."

"Good, because for *that* you need somebody like the CIA to set it up. Here's how I see it. No one on Leo is going to look up paper records or do a door-to-door for old friends and neighbors. Even if they do, that'll take longer than you'll be upstairs. So as long as you game the virtch you should be okay."

The forward nacelle on the fan deck caught a swell, splashing them. Van Huyten grimaced and took a step back, shaking his sodden jacket sleeve. Jimmy hardly noticed. "Another thing is your face."

Van Huyten's free hand went to his cheek, lingered there briefly. "My face . . ."

"Your disguise is good, but it won't fool a Facemaker. Recognition algorithms rely on fundamental physical dimensions. Everybody's mug, phizz, or kisser is a unique point in thirty-eight dimensional face-space. Nothing short of plastic surgery can change that; and even plastic surgery diddles only a couple of eigenfaces—nose shape, or the chin, or the cheekbones. But, to alter the distance between the eyes or the height of the forehead . . . ? Forget about it. The best you can hope for is a slightly muddy recognition set."

"I'm not herbert," van Huyten said sharply. "Desherite's inserted in the master datafaces at Cerberus Security, at Hertz, at . . ."

"Sure, *but Adam's face is in there, too.* That's how I made you. You see the problem? One thing they check real close is ID on lift passengers. Can't have some loony-tune tote a popper on board an SSTO. So there's a chance their Facemaker will come back with Adam van Huyten's name in its net along with Desherite's."

"So . . ."

"So, you have to set things up so *only* Desherite pops up in a search; because any search that nets *two* IDs will get them looking at you real, real close."

"You keep saying 'you,'" van Huyten said. "I'm waiting for 'we.'"

"You don't get it, do you? If worming through Leo's firewall is too risky for me, why should I sign on for this?"

"Then why did you set up this meeting? Why did you come?"

"Curiosity. When I found out who you were, I wanted to know what you were up to."

"I told you. A worthy cause."

"What, the Boy Scouts? United Way?"

Van Huyten made a fist and struck the rail. He turned away from Jimmy and studied, first the superstructure of the ferry boat, then the gulls flying overhead. *Looking for auguries,* Jimmy thought. When van Huyten turned back, his eyes were again on fire. *He'd make a hell of a preacher. Or a stump politician.*

"If you want to see the cards, you put your money on the table."

Jimmy swallowed. Slowly, he nodded. "Crafting a net persona is perfectly legal. Some brand mascots have their own 'personal histories.' Joe Latex, the camel they use in the condom ads, he's got a virtual birth certificate and everything. And I *know* . . . uh, I *think* the bios for the Centerfile Playgirls are fake. So phantom records may be okay, as long as you don't diddle with the real deebies. Set up a lurker in the vestibule so that, if anyone wants to see your tax return from five years ago, it'll lead 'em around the corner to an alley and show 'em a fake return. That way you haven't tampered with actual IRS files. Not that they wouldn't be pissed, legal or not . . . Uh, if you plan to use this persona for, uh, extralegal purposes, I can't know about it. Anything on the wild side, you got to contact a cracker named Crackman."

Van Huyten shook his head. "No. Absolutely not. It was bad enough coming to you. I can't risk Baleen on the honor of some outlaw hacker I haven't even met, not even for—"

Jimmy sighed and tried to spell it out. "*You* don't contact Crackman. *David Desherite* contacts Crackman. *Adam van Huyten* contacts Jimmy Poole." There. Did he have to make it plainer than that?

A moment passed before amusement curled van Huyten's lip. Then he shook his head and laughed. "It fits," he said. "In a world where image is reality, we have to keep our images straight. How long?"

"Three months."

Desherite frowned. "No sooner?"

"Depends. You want to slip past a Facemaker, or what?"

Desherite considered that. "All right. I can keep the lid on my partners that long." He held his hand out. Jimmy looked at the hand.

"My money's on the table," he told van Huyten.

"And now you want to see the cards . . ."

Was he sure he wanted to see them? Maybe the less he knew, the better. But it was too late to weenie. "I don't need to see your cards. I just want to know what game we're playing."

"Fair enough. It's the best game there is." And van Huyten's eyes glittered as they bored into Jimmy Poole's soul. "Revenge," he said.

Jimmy clasped the other's hand with sudden enthusiasm. "Dude!" he said.

6.

You Sure Can't See Them Northern Lights Deep in the Heart of Texas

The subdivision where Hobie lived consisted of mass-produced housing remarkable only for its affordability and its accessibility. The homes, bunched around branching cul-de-sacs, had once been considered a step in the right direction; but years of damp and heat and the occasional hurricane had rubbed them like gum erasers, so that now they seemed faded. Four models had been used—in levro and dextro versions—to create a bit of architectural diversity; but the grim alternation up and down the streets only accentuated their essential sameness. Hobie had lived there for five years now and still did not know the subdivision's name, or even if it had one. It was no longer the sort of place people aspired to. But Argonaut Labs, out along NASA Highway One, was an easy fifteen minute drive, and it was usually against the flow of traffic; and that made it convenient when he had to run over for a few minutes.

He found Charlene in the family room, leafing through a magazine with the sort of aggressive impatience that meant the magazine was only a prop. Pages turned with angry tugs, and too often to pretend they were being read. Hobie froze halfway down the stairs to the split level. Marriage had taught him only a little bit about women. Subtleties of expression and body language were beyond him. But subtle, this body was not.

"Where do you think you're going?"

Hobie groped for a response. Charli never asked a question without a specific answer in mind. He never guessed right and had developed the habit of waiting for the answer to suggest itself.

"Because if you're going up to change for dinner, it's too late. I called the Ganeshes and made our apologies. I told them you had a sudden emergency at the lab." She looked at him with eyes of fire. Her mouth was pressed into a tight, wide line and her face set in hard planes. Only now did Hobie notice that she was dressed in a long, deep-violet sheath slit up the side to mid-thigh. A string of pearls encircled her throat; a perfect cameo adorned her breast. Pearl-white gloves matching the choker and the cameo lay beside her on the sofa. Her hair had been done up, too, he saw. Piled high, with a braid encoiling it like a snake—the latest hair fashion from Detroit. Her perfume, one of the popular Odours of Earthe, was a pleasant forest glade, grown now a bit dank and moldy from the heat.

Hobie thought, *I am in very deep shit.*

"What have you got to say for yourself?"

He opened his mouth, but no sounds came out. He was no lightning thinker, like Otul Ganesh or Adam van Huyten. When he chewed on an idea, he was like a cow chewing its cud: slowly, and over and over, until it was properly digested. But he lived in a world that valued quick response, and his long silences had often been mistaken for dullness.

"L-Ladawan was having a p-problem with an experiment and asked m-me to help out." As always when he tried to force the words out faster than they came, they fell tripping over one another, stumbling from his lips. A football jock, slow to speak, a stutterer. Black as the proverbial ace of spades. A combination that had branded him in everyone's eyes, including his own. His answer sounded weak, even to him.

"On a Saturday?" Charlene did not understand researchers. She was strictly a punch in, punch out person, and the last thing to occupy her weekends were thoughts of work. "Why did he call *you?*"

"B-because I'm the p-program manager," he reminded her. He did not correct her on Ladawan's gender. Why clutter anger with suspicion?

"Oh, and don't I know *that*," she said, "with your beeper going off all the time. 'Hobie!' " she mimicked in a high-pitched, whiny voice, " 'Our shoelaces came untied! What should we do, Hobie?' "

"You're not being fair to them," Hobie pointed out, and he finally took the last few steps into the room.

"I'm not interested in being fair to *them*!" Charli shouted, flinging the magazine across the room. "All I asked for was one night out with our friends. Is that too much? You're gone for months at a time, up in orbit or up at the north pole, and I have to sit here on my thumb, and then what happens? You get beeped and run off and 'I'll be back in half an hour' turns into four."

Her light coffee skin had flushed a darker shade. Her eyes glittered like the sun off Galveston Bay. *You're beautiful when you're angry*, he thought. Her neckline plunged deep between her breasts and Hobie ached to plunge his hand there, too. To soften those angry lips with his tongue.

"C-Call Otul," he said. "Tell him I got delayed at the lab. Otul should understand that better than anyone. Tell him I'll be c-cleaned and ready in, um, half an hour. Ask him to change the rez. Another restaurant, if he has to. I'll jump in the shower. Why don't you lay out my clothes for me? Save time." And she'd told him often enough that he couldn't match clothing to save his life.

Charlene stared at him a moment. Her eyes were mere smouldering coals now. "What if Otul and Peg are gone already?"

"Then we'll go somewhere ourselves."

"We will. Just like that. Why?"

"Why?" Had he heard right? Did she want to go out or not? "Because you look so stupy," he blurted. "Because I want to strut into some restaurant and everyone looks at me and thinks, *He must be one bean dude to have such a fine-looking lady.* 'Cause every guy there'll have to look at his woman and think how he must've got the leftovers."

Charlene softened visibly; and Hobie relaxed. You can't go wrong telling a woman how beautiful she is. Not that Charli had a beauty jones; but she had spent the entire afternoon duding up, and no one likes to waste an investment like that.

Later that evening, when the excuses had been made and accepted; when the veal had been eaten and the sherry drunk; when the stories and the jokes had been bandied about, and the Hobarts and the Ganeshes had gone their separate ways, she allowed him inside her.

Maybe it was the heat. Maybe it was the sherry. Maybe it was some motion of quid pro quo for the rare night out; or noblesse oblige because she was feeling pleased with herself. Or maybe it was that long nights grew lonely for her, too; and she did love him after all, if not as intensely as during their fumble-fingered courtship, then perhaps as sincerely. Not a word was spoken, but her hands sought him out and brought him up, and she straddled him right there in the living room of their home with all the fine clothing scattered on the shag carpet around them.

Hobie accepted what the gods granted and prayed that it would go on. He lost himself within her, enveloped by her heat; rubbed by the coarse mat of her hair; pressed upon by her softness; dizzy with the odors of earth and body. Neither of them were given to talking at such moments.

Hobie did not know why Charli angry aroused him so. But it was a puzzle, and he was a man who gnawed at puzzles. Angry or not, she had the same centimeters—up and down and around and around. She carried the same kilos; had the same soft coloring, the same dark hair. So the parameters were identical, either way. Yet her anger could bring him to an edge he normally never felt.

And that meant the truth of it lay in the unmeasurables. Was it that he so seldom saw fire in her any more that, even when directed at him, he welcomed it? Or was there a touch of the masochist in his heart?

When the moment passed, she did not roll off right away, but rocked back on her heels. Sitting atop him, like a queen enthroned, radiant with spent passion. He ran his hands along the thighs that bound him.

"G-G-God, you're beautiful," he said, adding no qualifiers.

There was a lake behind the main building at Argonaut Laboratories. Properly, a marsh: brackish and given to rushes and cattails. Geese frequented it, and migrating herons. Small scuttling things darted in and out of the reeds, though gators sometimes found their way up from the bay and more scuttling things darted in than out. Once the joggers had been treated to the sight of an old bull gator snapping up a goose who hadn't got the log/alligator distinction quite right. Someone put up a sign: Gators–1; Geese–0, until the Professionally Offended had come by with charges of insensitivity. Adam had told them to take the matter up with the gator, who had, after all, performed the insensitive act. The P/Os had declined, but the sign came down anyway. The gator acquired the name Snappy John and the joggers took the bend at the south end of the marsh a little wider than before, until it became evident that the old gent was no longer in residence. The joke was that he had gotten a promotion to Human Resources.

" 'Labor' is the root of 'laboratory'," Hobie told Otul Ganesh after they had completed their daily laps around the pond. "But this is the only way any of us get to work up a sweat."

"You're speaking of your own research group, of course," Otul replied. He was doing his winding down exercises. Hobie watched him from his seat on the park bench. About a dozen others were spotted at some point around the circuit. Some, like Hobie, were resting.

"Oh, yeah," Hobie said. "All the heavy lifting your guys do. I forgot." He pointed to the other walkers, joggers, and runners. "Have you joined the pool yet? Closest guess to who drops dead first and when."

"In this heat?" Otul considered the problem. "Okay, I can see where you can define a metric to measure closest to 'when', but how do you decide closest to 'who'? That's a discrete multinomial."

"Affinity diagram," Hobie told him. "With a topology defining a proximity space."

Otul looked at him. "You're a topologist, now?"

"No, Doug worked it out. People wonder where the labor comes in for you physicists or us chemists. Ever see a *mathematician* actually work? Me, neither."

Otul wiped his face with his towel. "So, how does it work, Doug's proximity?"

"Easy. You and me, we're friends, right? We do stuff together. That puts you within the closure of the Hobart proximity. So if someone picks me in the pool and you're the one who does the frog, that's close."

"Or vice versa."

The rear door at Argonaut opened and a figure in a light gray suit stepped out and looked around. "Or vice versa," Hobie agreed. "Problem is, the metric isn't necessarily commutative. Maury falls within Jeff's closure set, but not the other way 'round because Maury sucks up to Jeff, but *not* vice versa. Get it?" The suit headed toward them.

"What I get," Otul said, "is that Doug has way too much time on his hands."

The approaching suit resolved into A. V. Deshpande, known to all behind his back as "Audio/Visual." Round without being plump, he was a short, tan man whose perpetual smile had grown more fixed since being named president of the labs. Hobie steeled himself for the encounter.

Not that he disliked Argonaut's new president, or even that he thought the man not up to the job. Some observers, and not all of them partisans, had always rated him higher than Adam van Huyten. But Adam had possessed a sort of magnetism that A. V. lacked, and morale had plummeted since he'd been kicked out. Desh caught some of the fallout. There was a nagging suspicion that his everlasting smile was one of unseemly satisfaction.

"Welcome back, Leland," Desh shook his hand in a perfunctory fashion. "How did you find Bathurst Island?"

Hobie deadpanned. "Oh, I just pointed my compass north and kept going until there wasn't any more north left." Otul snickered.

"I finished reviewing your recordings—very impressive, let me say—and your report. Did you forget we had a meeting for one o'clock to discuss the results?"

Hobie checked his watch: 1:05. Desh thought that effective management meant keeping careful track of how people spent their time. That was another difference between Desh and his predecessor.

"Relativity," suggested Otul. "We were running. Our velocity caused time to slow down for us, and we have returned to the building to find that a longer time has elapsed for you."

Hobie looked at his friend. "That's good," he said. "I like it."

Otul saluted. "Relativity, my dear Watson."

"I'm paying you people," the president said, shaking his head, "to come up with notions like that . . . Leland," he continued, "I had some questions about the proposal you submitted."

"Sure," he said. Desh signed his paycheck—or, more precisely, authorized the automated funds transfer—but he was also one of the sharpest minds in Argonauts. One of the reasons Hobie had been unhappy to see him promoted was that it took the man out of the lab. "Do you want to go back to your office?"

Desh lowered himself to the bench and loosened his tie somewhat. "No, this should not take long. How close are you to a realizable product?"

"We're ready for test-of-concept phase. Scale model parasols. Hobartium IV doesn't have the mojo for anything more massive."

"Parasols?" asked Otul. "This what you were talking about at dinner the other day?"

Hobie nodded. "Would've said more; but Charli . . . You know."

"Yes," said A. V. "The parasol proposal. You weren't very clear on the benefits. No, no . . ." He waved his hands. "The experimental protocols were clear enough, but what earthly use will they be? Kincaid needs to know for the submittal and I couldn't explain it very well."

"No *earthly* use, at all," Hobie said. "Way it works is this—Otul, stick around; you'll find this interesting. You make a superloop." Hobie made a circle using the thumbs and forefingers of both hands. "Then you lay a current on it. That gives you a magfield. You put it out in the solar wind. Charged particles, right?"

"I know what the solar wind is," Desh said dryly.

"The particles play off the loop's magfield, producing a drag—"

"Yes!" said Otul. "Turn the dipole configuration between the axial and the normal orientation—"

"—And you get a sort of variable anti-gravity machine," finished Hobie.

"What?" That was A. V. with a charitable degree of skepticism. "Not perpetual motion?"

Hobie grinned. "Well, current in a superconductor *is* a sort of perpetual motion."

"Like that bunny," Otul said. "It keeps going and going . . ."

"I'm glad you two are having such a good time."

"No flubber, Desh," Hobie said. "The wind drag on the magnetosphere boundary acts as a thrust against the Sun's gravity. When the superloop is operating, depending on the dipole angle, the spacecraft can behave like the Sun has any mass, including none at all."

Otul closed his eyes and concentrated. "Alpha would equal . . . ah, one minus the drag over mass-gravity."

Hobie looked at him. "You're good."

"It comes from clean living and a pure heart. So you adjust the drag to equal the Sun's gravity; the outward thrust from the wind equals the inward pull from gravity; and . . . whoosh!"

"No whoosh," said Hobie.

"Oh. Right. Vacuum. No sound. But . . . acceleration in a straight line. No ellipse."

"Better yet," said Hobie. "Spaceships can sit still."

Otul's eyes widened. "Oh!"

"*That's* the part I didn't understand," said A. V. "Why spacecraft that sit still?"

"Otul?" said Hobie. "You're the physicist."

The physicist pondered for a moment. "Well . . . Spacecraft have to keep moving along their orbits; otherwise they fall into the primary. Like . . ." Otul pointed to the joggers rounding the pond. "Say, you have to keep jogging or Snappy John'll pull you into the pond. That makes rendezvous tricky. Only two forces to play with—chemical oxidation and gravity. The first one is expensive, like most chemistry . . ."

Hobie snorted but made no comment.

". . . but gravity is free and universal. So ships and satellites coast—until they need to shift orbits or correct for orbital decay. But velocity is inseparable from altitude. At three hundred klicks Earth orbit, you need, oh, just under eight meters per second to maintain altitude. If you try to go faster, you just make your orbit more elliptical, which actually slows you down. So suppose— Who's that out there? Betsy? Suppose Betsy wants to rendezvous with Vick, over the other side of the pond. Orbital dynamics keeps them moving, slowing as they coast out to perigee, speeding up as they fall in to perigee. Now, Betsy can't carry enough fuel to accelerate for very long—"

"Dunno," said Hobie. "She looks like she's carrying plenty of fuel to me."

"So she has to time her short burst of speed just right, so that she coasts to a point on Vick's orbit just as he reaches the same point. Tricky."

Desh nodded. "I see. But if she can stand still . . ."

"Right. She moves into Vick's orbit any time she pleases, then just jogs in place until he comes around."

"And that's what the superloop can give us," Hobie finished. "We exploit a 'third force,' one that's also free and universal. We can accelerate as long as we want and—by 'tacking' against the solar wind—in nearly any direction we want. Costs of interorbital transfer drop by orders of magnitude."

A. V. tugged on his lower lip. "That sounds . . . profitable."

Hobie raised his eyes to the sky. One step at a time. He had never had to hammer these points home with Adam. "It works in the Earth's magnetic field, too. You can use sails to lift satellites from LEO to GEO. You give your satellite a magnetic kick at perigee to get higher altitude at apogee—it's like pumping on a swing. When you get the right altitude, you do a chemical burn at apogee for your insertion. It's slow—might take seventy, eighty days to complete the maneuver; but you don't need to spend fuel just to lift fuel."

Desh nodded. "All right. Very good. Work up a projection. Resources. Cost estimates. Gantt chart. Have Tracy calculate a tentative ROI. Have it roughed out before you lift to LEO."

"Lift?" Hobie said, suddenly confused. "You want me to bonebag?"

Desh nodded. "You'll want experimental verification. Build a few of these . . . 'parasols' and put them out."

"Come on, A. V., gimme a break. I just spent three months up on Bathurst. Charli's gonna forget what I look like. Why not teep?"

"Some things are easier in person." Desh's smile turned bland. "If this has the potential you think, I'd rather not use on-site technicians that report to OMC."

"Then why not run the experiments on Goddard City?"

"VHI doesn't control Goddard, either," Desh pointed out.

"No," said Hobie, "but the Goddard board isn't *hostile* to VHI."

Desh laid a hand to Hobie's shoulder. "Stick with chemistry, Dr. Hobart. It's cleaner than politics."

What Hobie really wanted to do was develop hobartium V. He was a chemist, not an aerospace engineer. Yet, if this was what it took to move Desh behind his project, he'd scatter parasols like dandelion seeds. In between times, he'd tweak his apparatus on the space station to run different compounds in the search for the elusive global maximum. Guilt washed over him, as if he were contemplating a visit to a lover. "I ought to stay dirtside," he said, but he did not hear much conviction in his own voice.

Desh seemed disappointed. "I know how you feel." But how would he? Did A. V. spend long tours away from his wife? Did he stretch bonds that were maybe not too strong to begin with? "I know how you feel," Desh said again. "You'll do the planning down here, of course. And build any auxiliary controls or gauging that don't require ziggy. But I need someone to go up to LEO, and you are my most plausible candidate."

Hobie studied him for a long moment. "I'll work up the project plan for you. Three months, I think I'll have a workable experiment for test-of-concept. As for the rest . . . I'll think about it."

"Three months . . . ?" Desh sounded disappointed.

"Depends," Hobie told him. "You want parasols that work?"

Desh clapped him on the arm. "All right. Don't spend too long thinking," he said. "Oh, one other thing. While you're up on LEO, can you check on the other VHI experiments? As a courtesy to your colleagues."

Hobie watched Desh walk back to the lab building.

"What was that all about?" Otul asked.

"Inquiring minds want to know," Hobie answered. It was the weirdest thing, but Hobie didn't think Desh believed much in the magsail parasol idea. He had only been looking for a reason to send someone's bones into orbit.

Houston in June, and the sun had cast its arrogant eye upon it. It was a sweltering, humid heat wave. Eggs did not so much fry on the sidewalks as poach. Tempers grew prickly and iced tea, tepid, and so much sweat condensed on drinking glasses that it was a toss-up whether the inside or the outside was wetter. Air conditioners had given up in despair. A few months ago, Hobie had been shivering behind layers of fake fur while the snow drifted high against the walls of Lodestar Base. Now he had to wring out his handkerchief. On the average, he reflected wryly, he was comfortable.

The glass sliding doors at one end of the family room were not only decorative access to the backyard, were also excellent heat traps. Charli sat on the sofa opposite. She was stripped to a halter top and short shorts, and beads of sweat stood out on her face and torso. In theory, it should have been alluring and seductive, but in the sweaty, dank reality it was not.

"I don't understand why you have to go," Charli said.

"I haven't decided if I will." He couldn't decide what annoyed Charlene more. That he might be going to Leo for another three-month turn or that he hadn't told her himself. She had heard it secondhand from Peggy Ganesh.

Charli gave him The Look. "Of course, you have," she said. "You just don't know it yet."

"I'd rather stay here with you."

"Yeah. Right."

It was too hot. Tempers were short. Petty irritations rubbed raw, like chafed thighs. "More lemonade?"

"It's gone."

"I'll make some more."

"Suit yourself."

Hobie pushed himself out of his slingback chair and climbed the stairs to the kitchen. There was a sort of balcony there that overlooked the rec room. Hobie pulled the ice tray from the magnetic refrigerator, dumped it all into a pitcher, and set the icemaker to make more. He left the door open while he made the drinks and enjoyed the guilty luxury of the cool air that spilled out. Over the railing, he could see Charlene unfasten her halter and dab at herself with a handkerchief. Great, now she was making *him* sweat. His eyes carressed her, ran down the glistening flat of her stomach. He squeezed the pulp of the lemon into the pitcher.

When he brought the lemonade down to the family room, Charlene had already refastened her halter. Hobie handed her a tall, sweaty glass, sweetened the way she liked it. She sipped from it and said, "Who is Krystal Delacroix?"

"Who?"

"Krystal. Delacroix. She's obviously a big fan of yours."

Hobie shook his head. "Don't know her."

"Really. She hired our firm yesterday to do some webstering. You know: survey a site, lay out a floor plan, weave the hyperlinks and trapdoors. You *do* know what I do for a living, don't you?"

Hobie lowered himself into his slingchair. "And she's a fan of mine? I didn't know chemists had fans."

"Her whole site's dedicated to you."

Hobie lowered his glass and stared at her. "Oh!"

"Oh?"

"She was up at Lodestar Base. I remember her now."

"Only now. She must not have been very memorable."

Hobie shrugged and wouldn't look directly at her. "Just a newser. She told me I needed to hype myself on the net. Build a constituency to support my work." He laughed. "She even said I should have a theme song."

"Well, you've got one."

"What?"

"A theme song. Retro-rap. 'Hobie, the Master of Cool'."

Now he put his lemonade glass on the side table next to his chair and leaned forward. "You're kidding."

"Could I kid about something as serious as a theme song?"

Hobie threw his head back and laughed. "I'll be damned."

"Was she good looking?"

"Krystal? She was white. Still is, I guess."

"So, that don't make her ugly. White women, they're trophies. A brother gets feeling big, first thing he wants is a little light meat."

Hobie's face set like stone. "You mind what you're saying, girl."

Her eyes narrowed to rifle sights. "Why's this woman setting you up a site? What'd you do for her that she does that for you? What happened when the two of you were snowed in together up there at that north pole?"

"Was more than just the two of us. Twenty men and women. Krystal wanted action, she didn't need Hobie to find it."

"She admires you for your brain, then?"

Hobie stood. "Some people do, you know. It's how she makes her living, running those sites. She . . . 'builds' a news story, jazzes it up a little, arranges hyperlinks to make it sort of an interactive game for surfers. She doesn't need any reason past making money to put up a site for me."

"Uh-huh." But the way she said it did not sound like an affirmation. Hobie reached out and took her by the arm, but she shrugged him off. "Don't touch me."

"Charli . . ."

"I said don't touch me!" She turned and stalked from the room. Hobie stood still for a moment, then turned, grabbed his lemonade and threw it. It was a plastic cup—it didn't shatter—but it splashed lemonade up the stairwell. He left the room without bothering to clean up.

He found Charli in the bedroom upstairs standing cross-armed, with her back facing the door. She did not move, even when Hobie came up close behind her. He wrapped his arms around her, and still she remained a statue. Hobie felt himself at a loss. There was no logic, no reason. She had cited no evidence of anything, except that Krystal Delacroix had chosen to promote Hobie on the newsnet. What sort of counterargument could you bring against that?

"You know it's you I love," he said, forming the words slowly so he would not stammer. He bent his head and kissed her where her neck joined her shoulder. He might have been kissing ebony; she was no more responsive than wood. "I don't know how I can prove that to you."

Yes, he did. Words were cheap. They might be lies. Truth lay in action, in the pure deed itself. He turned her so she faced him and laid her hands on her shoulders. "Just you, babe."

He kissed her and she did not resist. Hobie pressed the kiss and wrapped her again in his arms, pulling her tight, sweaty body against his. The heat and the sweat had reduced all odors to those of flesh and musk. Primal odors. There was a taste of lemon in her mouth. He moved his lips to her throat and he heard her sigh.

Later, Hobie lay on the bed with his eyes wide open, irritated with Charli, with Krystal Delacroix, most of all with himself. Somehow, incongruously, he recalled a remark he had heard years ago on one of his visits to old Mir. He had been explaining superconductors to that rigger, Flaco Mercado, and how lower temperatures increased conductivity. Someone, not Flaco but one of his friends, had remarked that women were just the opposite. The colder they became, the greater their resistance. Hobie lay there quietly, not thinking of very much at all.

Along the way, he did fall asleep, because when he opened his eyes again, night had fallen and with it the air temperature. Perversely, it had actually grown chilly. Hobie eased from the bed and pulled the sheet up over his wife's bare body; then he threw on a robe and retreated to his office.

The view from his office window was only more houses and a sparse line of cottonwoods along the nearby creek. But the sky was clear and brilliant. After an uncounted number of heartbeats, a brighter light appeared from behind his roof and tracked across the sky until it vanished over the horizon. LEO, he wondered? Tsiolkovsky? Goddard?

Up north, at Lodestar Base, the sky was often ablaze with color, as the solar wind roared across the Earth's magnetic field and spun in toward the pole. The northern lights. Hobie stared hard at the horizon, but the only lights there were the glow of Houston itself. He turned away.

It didn't matter. He was too far south to see the lights, even if Houston were to vanish from the face of the Earth.

There was a trophy on the wall above his desk. A two-foot length of pipe, bent almost into a hairpin. Charli nagged him now and then to take it down, but he never did. A skinny white kid with tattoos up and down both arms had ambushed Hobie after a football game, years ago. A skinhead. He had yelled something foul and swung; but Hobie had caught the pipe in his hand, twisted it from the creep's grip and, without thinking, bent the pipe in two.

It was an impressive feat. Certainly, the skin had been impressed.

Hobie held his two hands in front of him and turned them palm up.

He looked again at the pipe in its wooden picture frame.

He'd kept it ever since. He was never quite sure why. To remind himself, sure. But of what?

7.

At the last minute, Mariesa almost turned and left the bookshop. But then Roberta looked up from the paperback she was signing and noticed her standing in the doorway. The wave—neither friendly nor unfriendly—indicated a nearby chair, so Mariesa shifted her portfolio to the other arm and sat down to wait.

It was a small shop, the sort Roberta favored. The air was thick with the odor of oxidizing paper, and the books on the shelves ran to tooled leather bindings with gold leaf titles and raised bands on the spine. Roberta sat behind a dark wood table with a stack of her own books beside her. Not that she needed them: most of the autograph seekers seemed already to have copies. Mariesa wondered how the bookseller felt about that.

The fans waiting in line were mostly Roberta's age, but there was a sprinkling of twentysomethings looking impossibly serious and artistic, as that age so often did. Mariesa smiled faintly, remembering a younger Roberta. The rebels of one generation became icons to the next—and fossils to the one after that. One fellow who might have been in his forties was the geezer of the group. Mariesa herself felt like a time traveller, a refugee from a far land called the Sixties. No one else present would remember the hope and despair of those days— Moon landings vying with assassinations for the soul of a country until hopelessness and cynicism and irony won. She could feel sidelong glances brush across her. What's the old lady doing *here*? She couldn't possibly be *street*! Mariesa made eye contact with one young woman, who looked hastily away.

Roberta Carson was thin, solemn, and dark, with a long face that seldom changed its expression from a neutral wariness. Black hair fell in bangs across pale brows and recessed eyes. She dressed more brightly now than when Mariesa had first met her. The relentlessly black dresses and makeup were seen less often. But then, Roberta's *life* had more light in it now than it once did. If her face was one that had never learned to smile spontaneously, it was at least no longer one from which pain seeped as from an inner sore. An adored father who had run out; a mother who—well, she hadn't been neglectful, and Mariesa acknowledged that Beth Carson had done her limited best; but she hadn't

spared a great deal of time for her child. There had been long years of es-
trangement and in the end there had been words never said, wounds never
healed, and rifts never closed.

Mariesa looked up as Phil Albright took the chair beside her. He handed
Mariesa a glass of iced tea, keeping one for himself. "I saw you come in," he
explained. Roberta glanced their way and her face glowed like the sun come
from behind a cloud.

Biologically, Phil was old enough to be Roberta's father, though if Phil was
a replacement for the vanished Mark Carson, he was also much more than
that. But at fifty-eight, the "chief coordinator" of The People's Crusades did
not look at all well. His dark, wiry hair had turned a dusty gray. The solid bar
of his eyebrows that had always given him a dangerous, brooding look now
made him look older than he was.

"How have you been, Phil?" she asked. Polite conversation was expected.
After all, she had asked for this meeting.

The Crusader grimaced. "Oh, my prostate's been acting up. That's the problem with being a man. We fall apart faster than you. You, on the other hand,
are looking remarkably fit."

"That's because I don't worry myself to death over minute hazards lurking
in my meals."

Phil laughed, winning a few glances from the remaining poetry fans. One
of them recognized Albright. Mariesa saw him nudge his companion and point
to Phil, whispering. "Better safe than sorry," Phil said. "But you're right. A lot
of well-meaning activism was wasted on—okay—on trivia. I'm glad I took
your advice a few years back—"

" 'Don't sweat the small stuff,' " she quoted.

"—but I'd already been thinking that way myself. The Crusades have been
much more effective since we learned to focus and not hare off on every
unsubstantiated claim; so I guess your advice backfired on you."

Mariesa smiled. She had almost forgotten what it was like to spar with Phil
Albright. She wiped the condensation from the glass with the napkin that had
come with it. "Phil, I think you are mistaken on a great many issues; but you
are dead on target on a lot of others. I'd call it an even trade."

He lifted his glass to her. "I'll take that as a compliment."

"I support your EarthSafe solar plants—"

"Sure. Because you want to build solar power satellites and hope to piggyback on our groundside research. That's fine by me. Maybe you'll never get to
build those—what'd you call them in the EnergAge website interview a few
months ago?"

"Stars of light."

"Right. Maybe you'll never get to build them. The jury's still out on need
and eco-impact. In the meantime, I'll cash your check as happily as I would

any other donation." His comment was delivered with a smile that faltered momentarily, perhaps with the memory of other checks cashed with less happy consequence. "Almost any other," he added.

The jury was still out on SPS satellites, Mariesa believed, because Phil kept it out. No one could prove a negative and that was what his "Precautionary Principle" amounted to. Phil disliked Big Things and a gigawatt power station in geosynch orbit did not fall under Small Is Beautiful. That Phil also believed in an activist government was a bit of cognitive dissonance on his part, since the federal government was not exactly small, either. But then every human alive was a mass of contradictions. Only the dead were eternally consistent.

After Roberta had finished her autographing, the three of them took refuge at a coffee shop named Common Grounds that was just around the corner. Such places were no longer as faddish as they once were, but with alcohol consumption declining, they had become the preferred locale for gathering and gossip. The hostess showed them to a booth and left them alone to ponder the menu. Mariesa, studying the list of flavors, could remember when coffee was a single line item on a menu. There were enough varieties listed that it would take days to sample them all—though at least one could be certain of staying awake while doing so! A small box in the corner listed several teas, but the clear implication was that tea-drinkers were weenies.

They gave their order to the hostess and chatted about inconsequentials while they waited. Phil and Roberta had taken seats opposite her, as if their closeness strengthened each other. Which perhaps it did. It certainly helped Roberta to lay out three differently colored pills for Phil to take. The Crusader grimaced apologetically at Mariesa before swallowing each and chasing them with water. "Minimal medication," he said, setting the water glass down, "does not mean zero medication."

Mariesa did not need reassurances either way on that score. One did what was necessary. But she could see where Phil might feel the need for explanation. That was what made broaching any topic with him a delicate affair. Hot topics underlay the surface like intellectual minefields. She tried to guide the conversation in a suitable direction.

"A dear friend of mine has contracted neo-encephalitis," she said. There were some topics where men and women of good will could meet, regardless how they disagreed elsewhere. "You've met him, I think. John Redmond? He was my CLO."

"John E.? That's too damn bad." Phil shook his head. "I really thought when we identified the vector we were on our way to a cure . . . But we overused antibiotics so much in the past that this new bug is resistant."

And we don't drain swamps the way we used to, because they're wetlands now . . . Mariesa said nothing because she did not want to start a debate. The causal chain was complex—a virus of a parasite of an insect—otherwise half the country would be dozing off by now. And which of the many mixed factors one cited was defined as much by politics as by epidemiology. How the tsetse fly ever became established in the bayous and everglades of the Gulf Coast might never be known with any certainty.

"We waited too long," Roberta said. "Remember the jokes? Chronic Fatigue Syndrome is because Boomers won't take Geritol."

"No one imagined back then," Mariesa said, "the connections between CFS and African sleeping sickness, so no one—Ah, here's our coffee." She wondered briefly whether the renewed popularity of coffee bars was related to fear of the sleeping sickness.

The hostess brought a tray of pots and cups and set them down on the table. Mariesa lifted her cup. "Confusion to the enemy," she said. The others tapped their cups against hers.

"Dig up Attwood's bones," Roberta answered.

Mariesa sipped her brew in silence. Old Cyrus Attwood was dead six years now, but his spirit lived on in his nephew; and Klon-Am was, if anything, more formidable than it had been under that half-crazed old man. Ed Bullock had even managed somehow to seduce Adam. Chris could claim the takeover of Leo Station as *his* worry now; but to Mariesa, it was as if her only child had been abducted by trolls.

Phil Albright set his cup down and looked expectantly at Mariesa. In the background, an air by Mozart struggled against the random percussion of cups and spoons. Mariesa took a breath and began her pitch. "Rutell line-itemed the funding for SkyWatch," she said.

"I heard." Phil's tone was noncommittal.

Of course, he'd heard. With his connections, Phil had probably known before SkyWatch, perhaps even before Rutell himself. Rumor held that Rutell and Albright were especially thick. "We've started raising private money," Mariesa continued, "from a variety of sources. Donations. Corporate contributions. University bequests."

"And selling asteroids . . ." Albright favored her with his quirky grin. "Naming asteroids for money is tacky, but at least it doesn't hurt anyone. But your latest scheme . . . I don't know how you persuaded UN Deep Space to sell mining rights, but they belong to all the people of the Earth, not only to those rich enough to buy them."

Common ownership. The easy answers came to mind, but remained unspoken. Phil knew them as well as she did. On the one hand: the tragedy of the commons. On the other: wealth untapped, jobs uncreated, people condemned to everlasting poverty. Depletion versus neglect, with no middle ground. But she hadn't set this meeting up to spar over worldviews. Not in front of Roberta. Mariesa glanced at the younger woman.

Roberta sat watching quietly. Mariesa felt, as she often did on these encounters, that the black shadows of Roberta's eyes were the barrels of twin cannons. There had been a time, years ago, when a much younger Roberta had found Silverpond a treasured refuge; and another time, when she had treasured it as a target for frustrations that had no other outlet. Mariesa settled now for mutual respect, though she wondered how fragile that yet might be.

"More like a futures option," Mariesa explained. "The investor has ten years to proof the claim by landing a robot prospector and showing ballistic capabilities to recover the—"

Phil shook his head. "I can hear some of my Crusaders already. 'Strip mining the sky!' " He waved his hands in mock horror. "Me, I think it's a scam. Who on Earth has the capability of proofing a claim like that?"

Mariesa shrugged. There had been a lot of that wink-wink-nudge-nudge during the negotiations, too. The Conference of Chinese States wanted the fees and royalties allocated by population; the West, by resources invested; the Russians, by historical contributions to space travel. That any treaty at all had emerged was due in no small part to the belief that there would be no pie to split beyond the initial filing fees. Small change to the UN operating budget. That asteroid ore might ever be delivered to Earth orbit was a notion beyond their horizons. Indeed, in the long run, it didn't matter to Mariesa, either; though the capability to *reach* asteroids and *build* on them and *move* them might one day prove crucial. And so, providing an incentive to develop those capabilities had become part of the Plan. Mariesa lifted her cup. "We'll know in ten years, won't we?"

Phil's grin faltered. "Roberta will." The words slipped out easily, but Mariesa noticed the worried glance that Roberta spared him before she turned to Mariesa and asked, "So why this meeting? To line Phil up behind the asteroid mining treaty? Because we haven't studied all the ramifications—"

"No. You brought that up. I came on another subject entirely. I want a Crusade."

For once in her life, she had rendered Phil Albright speechless, but his mouth had opened before the realization that no words were coming. "A Crusade," he managed at last.

"To locate and track NEOs."

"NEOs," Phil suggested.

"Near Earth Objects. Potential impactors."

Phil said, "Ah," and lifted his coffee cup.

Roberta nodded. "I thought so. Mariesa, you don't care one bit if a single asteroid is ever mined. There's only one thing you really care about."

Mariesa said nothing. It was odd. She barely trembled now at the thought of Impact, where it had once transfixed her with unreasoning horror. They said that the worst part of fear was dread. Remove the waiting, remove the uncertainty, and the fear vanished with it. So as she had grown more certain, she had also grown less terrified. Unless she had only grown old and tired.

Not vanished entirely, she noted, as she raised her coffee to her lips. The black liquid rippled in concentric rings, and she set the cup down quickly, making a clatter on the saucer and spilling a tiny bit.

"A subject has to be pretty important for us to preach a Crusade," Phil commented.

"This subject might be the most important ever."

Phil's eyebrows lowered. "So you say. But then it's been a pet project of yours for a long time."

"I'm not alone."

"Nooo. I've spoken with Daryll Blessing. It's not entirely crackpot, I admit."

Mariesa tamped down the irritation. *Thank you, so very much.*

"Impact," said Phil, as if tasting the word. "You're right. It would be the ultimate ecotastrophe if it ever happened. But Mars and the Earth have been sweeping this neighborhood of the solar system for billions of years. Anything big that could hit us already has. Just small junk left."

" 'Small' is a relative term," Mariesa told him, "and, in this case, not necessarily beautiful. You needn't have the end of the world to have a catastrophe."

"No. . . ." The admission was reluctant. "Still, they say the odds are low . . ."

" 'They' say . . . But, Phil, those odds are based on random chance. What if it's not random? What if asteroids are being thrown at us?"

The famous eyebrows went from lowering to raised. "You mean Darryl's Visitors? I respect Darryl, so I'll grant you the hypothesis: that aliens visited the solar system ten millennia ago. But what has that to do with NEOs?"

"SkyWatch has identified twenty-three asteroids that have changed course to become Earth-grazers. We know of at least one that was almost certainly altered by aliens."

"Out along the eastern spur of the Jersey Turnpike," Roberta said, "we can identify twenty-three boulders that have fallen close to the roadway. We know of at least one boulder that has been spray-painted by fraternities." Mariesa gave the woman a sharp glance but Roberta did not flinch. "Hey," she spread her hands, "just pointing out there's no *logical* connection."

Phil pursed his lips and looked thoughtful. "Aliens," he said. "Jesus. I always thought about it when I was a kid. Did you know that, Mariesa? Me, a space junkie. Later, I used to dream that wise, benevolent galactic beings would come and show us the error of our ways. Save us from ourselves. Aliens would have put war and pollution and all the rest of that crap behind them. They could have taught us . . ."

"Phil!" That was Roberta, astonishment on her face. "You never told me that!"

Phil grinned sheepishly. "Because I outgrew it. No one's going to come and save us. We have to get off our butts and do it ourselves." He shook his head. "Now here they are. Or were. Maybe." He drained his coffee and set the cup down with an air of finality. "But aiming asteroids at Earth? Any beings advanced enough to cross interstellar space are bound to be benevolent. Interstellar war and conquest . . . The economics aren't there. What's so funny, Mariesa?"

"Oh, I was just imagining two Indians watching a Spanish galleon approach the shore; and one says to the other, 'Anyone with the power to cross intercontinental oceans must have progressed beyond warfare.' "

Phil grunted, as if punched. "And you think they're throwing rocks at us?"

"We think," Mariesa said carefully, emphasizing the "we" just a bit, "that the Visitors have shifted the orbits of some asteroids. We don't know why."

"But you believe it's a threat," Roberta insisted.

"The new orbits are all closer to Earth," Mariesa reminded them both.

"Daryll told me it's only to get our attention." Phil's voice fell equidistant between amusement, curiosity, and astonishment, but it also echoed concern. "But, tell me, how do you know they've all been pushed closer to Earth? *Those are the only ones you've looked for.* Maybe some rocks were shifted so they'd graze Mars or Venus. Maybe some were kicked the other way—into the outer darkness. You didn't look for orbital changes in other directions, did you?"

It was an astonishing question to come from the likes of Phil Albright. No one in SkyWatch had even suggested it. She had to grope for an answer. "But . . . why move them at all, if not to threaten us or to gain our attention?"

Phil shrugged. "I'm not an alien. Why do people climb Mount Everest? Because it's there. Maybe it's a celestial game of chicken. But those are human reasons. Alien reasons might be incomprehensible. Maybe it's an art form—'dancing rocks'—and has nothing to do with us at all."

"Dancing rocks," said Roberta with a quiet smile. "I like that."

Mariesa shrugged. "Darryl's a world-class planetary scientist. I'm an old lady who used to run a big holding company. He's an expert on orbits and stellar composition. I'm an expert on strategic planning and resource allocation. *Neither* of us is an expert on the motivation of aliens."

"If there were any aliens," Phil pointed out.

"If there were any. But even if the Visitors were benevolent . . . Phil, even the best-laid plans can go wrong given ten thousand years of perturbations. We don't know, but that's the whole point. We need to keep watching, and tracking, and projecting—so we *will* know. Phil, I need allies in this. Rutell gutted our budget. Our private foundation needs seed money. VHI will donate; so will the Planetary Society and others. I want to make it a Crusade, too."

Albright leaned back in his chair. He frowned and rubbed at his chin, his thick eyebrows knitted together over his brow. "SkyWatch is essentially harmless," he announced, after a thoughtful pause. "It will help advance science, and—at the margin—might even save our butts someday. That's the plus side. On the downside . . . There's no emotional hook to get the kids pumped for the old door-to-door. It will help advance science—and some of our members won't like that. And . . ." He looked squarely at Mariesa. ". . . You're involved up to your eyebrows. Some of our members don't like *that*, either."

Mariesa looked at Roberta, who shook her head. Roberta swept the long black hair from her face. "Not me," she said. "Not any more. Yes, Phil, I know what you need to do. Go ahead. I'll meet you in the hallway."

Albright rose and bowed his head a fraction to Mariesa. "I'll think about your proposal, Mariesa, but I don't hold much hope for it. If it was just me . . ." He sighed. "For the sake of a young boy's fantasies . . . But I'm not a dictator. Not a CEO, like you were." He shook her hand briefly and scurried out of the dining room. Mariesa thought he walked rather briskly.

When she turned back to Roberta, the younger woman was smiling sadly. "He's got to take those pills; but they make him pee orange."

"He's not well, is he."

Roberta began setting the empty cups and saucers on the side of the table, where the waitress could take them more easily. "No." She didn't raise her eyes when she spoke.

"May I ask . . . ?"

The last cup made a clatter when she set it down. "He's just damn-all wearing out." Roberta raised her head and the eyes were rimmed in tears. "He drives himself, and he drives himself. He doesn't know how to slow down, let alone quit." She swiped at her eyes with her sleeve. "Don't tell him I cry. He thinks we're both resigned to the inevitable. He thinks I've come to grips with it."

Mariesa reached across the table and laid a hand on her arm. "Have you?"

An abrupt shake of the head. "Not even a little bit."

"What about him?"

"He says he has. But sometimes I catch him lying awake at night. Sometimes he falls into a funk and I can't shake him. Jesus, I'm glad you made me go back to him. If I hadn't, he'd be facing this alone, and I don't think I could have stood that."

"I didn't *make* you do anything."

"He's younger than you are."

There was a challenge there. Mariesa could hear it in the spaces between the words. But what could she say? That the van Huytens were long-lived stock? That blind chance created a distribution of lifespans and some were bound to be on the short end and others on the high end? But Roberta was not looking for comfort or for explanations. "I'm sorry," Mariesa said. "I've always respected Phil, even when we've disagreed."

She laughed. "Don't tell me that. Even I haven't *always* respected him. He's pulled some pretty shabby stunts. But so have you. And so have I." Another swipe at the hair, and a look half apology, half defiance.

"You had to lash out. I was convenient."

"Yeah, yeah. My mother was dead, and you were her surrogate. I know. I worked *that* out a long time ago. You know—" She hesitated while the waitress cleared the table. Her eyes danced here and there, never looking directly at Mariesa; but never looking away. Mariesa took the check, but did not examine it. "You know, I was afraid to poke too deep," Roberta said when they were alone once more. "My poetry comes from somewhere. I don't *craft* it. It just comes welling up. I thought if I ever *understood* why I felt the way I did . . . What if it killed the poetry? What if I purged the anger and . . . there was nothing else there?" The gaze that punctuated the declaration was measured for defiance, but Mariesa saw fear there, too. Yes, what if it had? How many "well-adjusted" people preached new visions?

Mariesa folded the check and unfolded it, pretended to study it. Years ago, when Prometheus had planned a future for the girl who had called herself Styx—when she had imagined Roberta as a voice for the new era—Mariesa had pondered the same problem herself. A young girl feeling herself boxed in might find the right vision for a race boxed into one world, and therefore vulnerable to whatever the universe hurled at it. It would have been so easy to step in with largesse. But, Mariesa had refrained from meddling in young Styx's life. *She has to open the box herself*, she had told Keith McReynolds, who had been her chief financial officer then. *I can't open it for her.*

"But there was more there than anger, wasn't there? There always was."

"I suppose."

"You know, Glenn Academy has a cultural program. They bring in all sorts of artists . . ."

"Including poets. That was supposed to be my role, wasn't it? Back when you had everyone's life planned for them." The comment was tossed off lightly, but the old wound throbbed beneath the words. "Some of the poems I wrote back then . . . I don't think they'd welcome me at the Academy."

Mariesa waved a hand. "I can call in a favor or two, if you wish."

Roberta laughed. "You never stop trying, do you? All right. I've been collecting folk songs from orbit. That should do the trick."

"Thank you."

"This asteroid business is really important to you, isn't it?" Roberta asked. "Phil and I gave you at least a half dozen openings for snappy comebacks, but you just sat there and smiled. Ten years ago, you would have started a debate—or a lecture."

"Perhaps I don't feel things as intently as I once did." Was that the price, she wondered. Was terror muted only because all feeling was muted? *I have not been the same since the day Will Gregorson died defending LEO Station from the consequence of my foolishness.* And Roberta had stayed with her that terrible evening and listened to her rant and weep. She traded a glance with Roberta and found an answer of sorts. She did not want an argument with this woman; not when argument had once been all there was. "It could be the most important thing the world ever does."

Roberta shrugged. "Maybe."

"You don't believe there ever were any aliens, do you?"

Another shrug and a face that never gave much away. "Oh, it's an exciting notion, in an intellectual sort of way. Aliens puttering with rocks tens of thousands of years ago . . . But what *practical* difference does it make? Life or"— a moment's hesitation—"or death. Justice. Dignity. Would anything important really change? Look," she said, rising, "Gotta go. Phil's waiting for me." Roberta picked her purse up from the floor and hung the strap across her shoulder. "I'll work on him. Some of the Cadre—Isaac, Melanie, Suletha maybe—will want to keep SkyWatch going. The others . . . Well, they approve of Dr. Blessing. I might be able to bring them around."

Mariesa rose with her. Hands were extended; grips were awkward. "Thank you . . ."

"But why am I doing it, if I don't believe in your aliens?" Roberta's grin was self-mocking. It was a grin that hid things. "Because you sent me back to Phil after he—After I learned he wasn't perfect And I *hate* owing people."

Mariesa watched the young woman leave. That wasn't the wounded, boxed-in girl any more; nor the angry, spiteful one who had taunted Mariesa and nearly destroyed the Plan. She was an attractive woman—not in the conventional physical sense, but in the intensity in her demeanor. Roberta had found something in herself. She had a core now. Harder than it ought to have been, but a core. Spinning, like the Earth's core; creating a magnetic field that drew others in. She had the power, whether she knew it yet or not. Others could align on her. But which of all the lights in all the starry heavens was her pole?

8.

The Morph, the Merrier

Billie Whistle sat alone in her apartment and 'faced the world. It was her life. Teeping, virtching, 'facing—she was, by God! connected. She was plugged! She could be anywhere; do anything; she could fly across the net with the speed of thought, walk the virtual streets of imagined cities, chat in oak-panelled clubs with other morphs as false as her own. Oh, this was the life, if you granted that she had one.

Morphing, she could be blonde instead of dark, flashing long, silky hair and a sultry look. She could be whole instead of—let's be brutal—crippled. She could show off two long, gleaming legs with perfectly shaped calves. She could even—there was a VR site for this—dance *en pointe*.

But she never went to the dance rooms. Those were for wannabes, who craved the experience without the discipline. They were not for anyone who had ever felt their real bodies fly.

Her morph was preprogrammed. An A/S kept the imago smiling and pleasant, and a good thing, too, because there were days when she was not fit company—days when she hated all the stumbling, clumsy, two-legged oafs who did not even dream they possessed what she could never have again.

Baleen's boardroom lay somewhere out in the virtch, in a deeply encrypted region called the Briarpatch. Only Baleen (and Poole sEcurity) had the edress and key. With Poole warding the snoops, it was as secure as any room could be; and whether Poole himself snooped was now a moot point. The room was meticulously appointed: a library in an English country estate. Dark woods, comfortable-looking chairs, shelves full of books hyperlinked to various deebies—and none of it "monet." The visuals fractaled when you zoomed downscale, and never went pixel. Wearing goggs and 'phones, the room even had depth and acoustics, so that, for all practical purposes, Billie was *there*, "in the flash," in a place that never was.

All five of them were there, and maybe a sixth. Five misfits who had some-how fit together. The Baleen Board. Indeed, the whole of Baleen.

Red Hawkins used his own image for his screen morph. Why touch up what's already perfect, he had told her once; and Billie had never decided if he was engaged in conceit or self-mockery. Though, having finally met the man in person, Billie thought his virtual trousers were more handsomely filled than realism would require.

Red handled his imago awkwardly. The lips moved when he spoke, though not always in synch with the words; sometimes an arm performed a wooden gesture—what virtchuosos called an algore: the basic A/S algorithms that came with commercial morphs. Good enough for standard motions; but simming body language and expression were beyond Red's rudimentary skills.

But if Red Hawkins was a window mannequin, what was Guang Shaoping? One time, a bird on the virtchroom's windowsill; another, a book on the library shelf. Often, Baleen's chemical engineer 'faced as a Chinese ideogram—a disconcerting construct with which to hold a conversation. Today, for reasons only he could know, he was a bright, cottonball cumulus gracing the sky outside the window. While the background—mostly high, wispy mare's tails—moved left to right in the virtual wind, Shao's imago remained fixed, as if the cloud had been nailed to a point in the sky. Subtle shapes ran through it, suggesting faces and animals and objects. In childhood, Billie had delighted in discovering such figures in the billowing clouds; now she had to remind herself that the shapes were there because Shao put them there.

"The first line of business," said David Desherite, "is the simulation testing. Billie?"

David, like Red, 'faced as himself: tailored sports coat and sweater, open-neck shirt, cross-legged comfortable in a tall chair. The dress-up "casual" of the thoughtlessly rich. And yet—it was not something that Billie could put her finger on—but he seemed more "David" when he morphed. His head was a trifle wider; the hair, a more assertive cut; the scar, more vivid. It seemed, too, that David's imago had changed subtly over the past few months; as if he were evolving into another life form.

"I've finished the final round," Billie told her partners as she gloved a book on the library shelf. The hyperlink accessed Baleen's deeby, and the latest test report popped on a side screen.

"About bloody time," she heard Red mutter.

"I moved it as fast as I could," she said. "There were problems!" And she put enough vehemence into the words that she very nearly convinced herself. Yet, she was keenly aware of how she had stretched the schedule. Interface incompatibility. Undefined term. Corrupted file. Bit flip. So sorry. Her partners—all but David—had chafed at the delay, anxious to push on. That a virtchuoso like Jimmy Poole undoubtedly smirked backstage only salted the raw wound to her pride.

But she had endured shame and guilt, both. *Buy me time,* David had asked her, and without asking why she had thrown her own reputation onto the ticking schedule. And it had hurt. She had always given good measure in her work and it was not in her to do less than her best. David had to know that.

Billie initialized the sim and a blue-line cube appeared in the air before the group. "The full scale simulation tested the interlinked modules modeling Shao's equipment, Karl's microorganisms, and—"

"Cut to the chase," Red demanded. "Did it work?"

"Oh, it'll work, honey," purred Karl Wincock, the fifth partner, whose image lounged insouciantly in a tall-backed leather reading chair. "My little bugs just loooove that old mercury. They'd smack their lips, if they had any." Karl illustrated lip-smacking, running a tongue around the full, red blossom of her mouth.

Wincock was Baleen's pharmer, and no one was better at tailoring and growing microorganisms; but Billie was sure he was a man. So why did he use a sex-kitten screen morph with a short, tight skirt and let-it-all-hang-out blouse? Did it say something about the inner Karl? Was his gender bent? Or did he only want to tip people off balance? Sometimes Billie wondered how David had ever organized this strange crew. Only Hawkins was halfway normal; but only halfway.

"Those were lab tests," David pointed out to Karl. "Ziggy costs too much to lift a full manufacturing plant without preliminary models and feasibility studies."

"The sealed experiment on SpaceLab last February . . ."

"Provided data for Billie's sim, but you can't do a linear scale-up from a 'getaway pack.'"

"David is correct," the cloud announced. "The wise man tries the strength of the rungs before trusting his weight to the ladder."

A donkey's bray. "You get that out of a fortune cookie, mate?"

Billie lost patience with the bickering and started the sim. Fuck 'em. She may have dragged her feet along the way, but she was damn proud of the results she'd gotten.

A red coloration—the simulated microorganisms—stained one face of the cube. The red darkened and thickened; then a thousand crimson filaments spread through the aerogel's voids and channels and convolutions, twisting and folding until they permeated the entire volume. A heads-up datasplay tracked time, penetration, potency, and a dozen other metrics. In the end, the cube was solid red with a fine network of blue lines, and looked like nothing so much as excised muscle tissue.

Aerogels were mostly empty space, which gave them astonishing strength-to-weight ratios. It also made them useful as filter material. Dope its many cavities and channels with Karl's microbes and it would sieve a factory's waste stream for toxics the way a whale's baleen sieved the ocean for krill. And the residue, concentrated as it was, could be harvested and recycled.

Baleen had enormous potential, for public health and private profit; and, while Billie would shun neither the fame nor the fortune that she expected— she had invested nearly all her savings and capital in the venture—it was the thought of cleansing the world's waterways that brought what few smiles her life deployed. It was, in a way, her atonement for old sins. And new.

Billie contemplated the sim for a moment before, on impulse, rerunning it— this time with a conical geometry for the "plug." Really, it was a remarkable thing they had accomplished. Who would have predicted it that day when David had contacted her and asked her to troll the net for likely investments and she had come across Karl's proposal? Did the others feel the same sense of wonder as she did?

"Was there any thickening or self-poisoning?" asked David.

Billie started because she hadn't thought that anyone else had been paying attention; but now she became aware that the chatter had died away.

"No," she said. "The model predicts, absent a gravity field, an even film layer throughout, including the innermost capillaries. Expected variation: plus or minus point-four percent. No clogging or die-off choke points. And none of the aerogel capillaries pinch off—also thanks to ziggy."

The cloud beyond the window billowed, suggesting unicorns and angels in the ripples and streamers. A voice spoke from the shining luminescence. "Yet, the wise man knows that reality embraces many facets unsuspected by theory."

Red Hawkins's mannequin grunted. "That's Shakespeare, not yer bleedin' Confucius." It astonished Billie that Red not only knew the names, but recognized the paraphrased quote.

Virtual wind carved a fleeting smile into the featureless cloud. "Both Karl's theory and Billie's simulation may have overlooked significant factors," the aerogel engineer pointed out. "And so a pilot run is needed."

Shao was right. Ideas that worked in the lab sometimes failed on scale-up to commercial quantities. How many cubic meters of aerogel would Shao's equipment blow between P/Ms? How much mercury would Karl's bugs eat before surfeit? How many generations of microbes could Baleen breed from the mother culture before cloning another? Cost of ownership—purchase price *plus* the cost of maintaining and replacing—had to come in *below* the cost of traditional abatement and hazmat disposal. Who would buy effluent filters that needed changing every hour? Billie had calculated risks from process FMEAs and from deebies of elemental reliabilities and laid them on nested process maps from block diagram down to fault tree. But in the end, someone had to blow gel and breed bugs and count the chickens *after* hatching. It was time for Red and Shao to take the baton from Karl and her.

"The pilot run will have to wait a little while longer," David told them, "until I visit LEO and suss things out."

"Oh, for the love of . . ." Karl's bawd flipped the bird. "Rich boy, it's been months since Poole asked you to do that. You could have lifted your bones for him any time."

"There were . . . some things I had to take care of first."

Billie wondered what those things were. She had tarnished her reputation to "buy time" so he could take care of them and she resented, just a little, that he had not confided his reasons to her. She studied David's morph, but not in any hope of trolling a cue. There was never any expression on a morph but what its handler placed there.

". . . capital sitting idle," Shaoping was saying, "while Desherite plays tourist."

"Delay costs money," said Wincock. Billie saw that a shimmering PERT of the project time line now floated in the boardroom's air. Two-thirds of the nodes were darkened; one was blood red. *Bottleneck at <Loft Rental>*. "Maybe that doesn't twitch the rich," Karl went on, "but for the rest of us it means income not incoming. The four of us are risking more of our personal assets than rich boy is. Bacon and eggs, if you know what I mean."

"She means," Red commented, "the hen's involved, but the pig's committed."

Hawkins always said "she" when he talked about Karl. Billie didn't know if he was trying to yank any chains or not. In any event, Wincock never took offense and sometimes played to it. His imago hooked a leg over the arm of its chair, revealing a band of pale thigh at the top of its dark silk stocking. Billie admired the detail work on the morph even while it left her cold. Karl might be the beanest dude that ever spliced a gene, but he was not someone she ever wanted to know.

"There was no point lifting until the sims were complete," David reminded them. "I'll be going up next week, and once I've checked things out—"

Karl's imago shrugged. "I'm flat-ass tired of sitting on my butt. My bugs are ready. Billie's sims have checked out—finally. Shaoping's equipment is built, ground-tested, and HPSD-bonded. It's sitting in a *warehouse*, sucking rent. And we're paying Red here to play with himself, because he can't install the equipment yet. I say, let's lift."

David's imago leaned forward, as earnest as if it had been a real person. "Remember the issue, people! We can't afford to keep an operator aloft full time, not with the three or four month rotations the law requires; so we have to teep and use Leo's own bonebags for whatever needs human attention. And in this context, 'LEO' means Bullock's Orbital Management Corporation. I'd like to be sure they don't pick our pocket the way they plucked the station itself from VHI."

Red grunted. "They needed a traitor in VHI to hand them the keys."

David did not answer for a moment. "VHI," he said, "has problems, too."

"I don't see the foo, honey." Karl pouted large, red lips. "If LEO makes you twitchy, let's shift the scene to Goddard. Or Tsiolkovsky."

"We'd be restarting negotiations from scratch if we switched now."

"If we'd gone with Goddard in the first place, we'd be blowing smoke by now."

"Spilt milk," David said.

Billie wondered if Karl was adamant about switching sites. Karl had always thought himself the Indispensible Man—and, indeed, cheeseheads, operatives, and aerogel engineers were thicker on the ground than pharmers with Karl's mojo. He may have entertained go-it-alone fantasies. Except, without David's money, he could never have put together the team to make his toxic-eating bugs a commercial reality. He'd never even thought of the aerogel angle, let alone the benefits of ziggy.

But if they did vote to shift the scene, what would David do? David had a hard-on for LEO. Did jerking it mean more to him than Baleen? To hell with him, if it did. Yet, would Poole cover the nut if Desherite's money walked? The only reason Poole had bought in was his own curiosity over LEO. Did the others realize that?

She was holding a conversation with an icon, a sex-kitten, and a department store dummy. Body language was hard to judge. Karl might be floating a trial balloon, or he might be dead serious.

The silence deepened, each partner immersed in thought, each imago inert. Red spoke first. "When'd you say you were going up, mate?"

"Next week," said David. "A seat opened up on the *Valeri Chkalov* lifting from Jo-burg. I'll have to stay up a week before the return drop; but I expect we'll get closure and lift our plant by late November, which, given the delays in the final sims, puts us only two months behind schedule."

Red's imago made a stylized shrug. "That's fine with me. How about it, Karl-baby? It's like the swagman told the stationkeeper's daughter. We're too far in to pull out now."

The others conceded the point, one by one, and Billie let out a soft breath. David went on to the second line of business and the meeting ground its thorough way toward closure.

Afterward, Guang Shaoping lingered until only Billie and David were present. Amorphous shapes within the cloud hinted at tattered sails and broken masts. "The superior man," the cloud whispered before logging off, "sets not his mind for anything, nor against anything; but follows what is right."

When they were alone—or as alone as they would ever be while Jimmy Poole lurked—David turned to Billie and his teeth gleamed—a Kai enhancement. "One more hurdle overcome, Sancho."

"Yes," she said. "I'm glad I could help." There was no touching in cyberspace; only the image of touching. Eyes were not windows, but shields. Closeness was an illusion. David could as easily be in Kathmandu as sitting across the room from her. It was an illusion she could not bear and, after a few inconsequential words of farewell, she thought the word, "Ephthata!" and her goggs opened to real-time view . . .

* * *

And reality returned and smashed her back inside the confines of her wheel-chair.

The boardroom vanished, replaced by the bedroom she used as a workcenter. Racks of equipment in soft, sand-colored hues lined every wall but the pixwall itself: monitors and processors; modems, digitizers, scanners, zappers, tree-drives, Y-cores; cables hanging like monkey vines in a jungle, nearly hiding the wallpaper where endless repetitions of Karel Janácek's "Prague Castle" emerged dreamlike from morning mist. The flickering of diagnostics on the self-assessment monitors was sunlight dappled by waving canopy leaves; the soft sounds of drives spinning up or down was the wind. The occasional scritch-ings of write-to operations were insects.

Billie caught her lip between her teeth. Her thoughts kept turning on the fly-on-the-wall she had encrypted into Baleen's operating software. David had insisted, gently, persistently, until she had surrendered to him. But he had never explained and she had never asked, and sometimes she wondered why he hadn't, and why she hadn't. *David*, she thought, *I've put my trust in you. I've placed my soul in the cup of your hands. Don't open them.*

It had been a long time since there had been people she could trust. She could measure it in the heartbeats since that terrifying afternoon on the Turn-pike when, pinned and mangled and sprayed with her father's arterial blood, and with her sister's screams beside her ending in a horrible, liquid gurgle, she had watched the light slowly fade from her mother's puzzled eyes. *It was a miracle you lived*, the doctors all assured her. But if so, it was a puny, miserable sort of miracle, as if God had just barely the mojo to pull it off. Water changed into . . . grape Kool-Aid! *Thanks a lot, Mr. Deity, sir.* But what exactly was the fucking point? Maybe life was better than being dead. Not a whole lot better, mind you; but still a cut above worm food. She didn't really mind living through the experience crippled half as much as she minded the eternity she had spent watching her family die. *That* was the cruelty which she could not forgive.

The house gave no sounds. Not even the creak of a settling frame. Certainly no voices; no smell of cooking pot roast. No jangly roll music from little sister's room. No door slamming and Tom's home from L.A.! She hadn't seen Tom since the hospital, hadn't even sent him her new address. God, what could they talk about but Mom and Dad and Jill? No, it was better if big brother joined the rest of them in the outer darkness and she made a clean break with all of her past.

They'd been driving to the airport to pick Tom up. Laughing.

Somehow her apartment seemed less real than the boardroom in the virtch. It was certainly less crowded and less noisy. The virtch was a better place altogether to spend her time than here, alone with herself and her thoughts.

You should have said something to David before logging off . . .

For some time, Billie sat in front of the blank screen, wondering what star she had locked her navcomp on when she had signed on with Baleen. David Desherite, venture capitalist. Or the image of one.

But what should I have said?

Did she really think David would jolly her? That he found stumps and scars erotic? Yet, *something* drew her toward him. Not his hard, flat stomach or tight buns; but a flame that blazed behind his eyes. Some nights she feared him, imagining herself a moth, even while she longed for his presence beside her. She was a cheesehead and she had sockets in her brain; but she had one socket that hadn't been plugged in a very long time.

She rolled out of her workroom into the living room. (But you had to have a life to have a living room, didn't you?) Two stools sat against the wall for her rare visitors; otherwise, sculptures and objets d'art. A reproduction of Pyotr Valyshev's elaborately Ukrainian "Glass Egg" sat atop a steel pedestal. On the wall: Chong's "E pluribus," with the flag's fifty-one stars replaced by ethnic icons from thunderbird to shamrock to yin-and-yang. Every object in the room but one was a tribute to grace and beauty. The one exception being herself.

A few moments' thought uploaded *Mardi Gras* to her μCD player, and the dolorous baritone notes of Rytter Cleef singing the role of Beau Landry flooded the room with "On Death's Krewe." On the monitor, a gaily-costumed man bent over a body stretched out on the stage.

> *What are you behind this mask?*
> *Dare I see?*
> *Speak not! Lost love, lost life.*
> *Loss left cold upon the street . . .*

Too bad, Landry; but that's the price you agreed to for a night of unparalleled love.

. . . *Follows what is right* . . . Shaoping's parting comment had been meant for David and his fixation on Leo; but it was a poor sort of zinger that only zapped one person.

The comment might, for example, have been directed at the lurking S. James Poole. Jimmy was the most silent of silent partners. He claimed his only interest lay in groping Leo, but who knew? Privy to Baleen now, he could easily pirate the key information from their deeby, set up a front company in Ecuador or Kenya, and beat them to market. Poole was said to have lost his ethical cherry early and often, and things moved faster when you didn't have to do the R & D yourself. That might be why Wincock had tried to fasttrack the project just now. In case Poole was making an end run.

. . . *Follows what is right* . . . But, wittingly or not, Shao had zapped her, too; because Baleen's present predicament was rooted in her one moment of desperation and weakness. That was an irony that only Billie could appreciate. Her one-time employers wouldn't know of Baleen; and Baleen didn't know of the Nameless Ones.

She wasn't the only virtchuoso who had ever walked the wild side. Some had made a career of it. There were stories about Poole. Yet if Poole had done the dirty, he had done it for thrills, not because he was desperate. Not because he had bare cupboards and an apartment no longer friendly to his body's new configuration. Not because he had crushing medical bills and no way to pay them. Not because he had to wait in line so some government droid could sneer at every request. To the SBA, she was not "culturally deprived." General Assistance had scolded her against having an independent income.

Finally, she had realized that she had become a beggar, and vowed never again to give others such power over her. Dependency was a sucking trap. And if someone showed her a way out—dangled that much troy, and an accessible apartment, and computer equipment that was phat stoopid—and the only price was to winkle a few documents in restricted deebies, she would have been pure herbert to turn it down. So, she tickled money and stock in one direction and memos and records in another. Started a dummycorp, enticed an interest, moved assets *faster than a speeding bullet*. (Now which shell was that pea under?) In the end, a space station had changed hands and she had understood the awe Archimedes must have felt when he suddenly realized what leverage could do. No one had been hurt, except a rich guy who had never known what hurt felt like—and he was probably a better human being for it.

Still, there was a sort of cosmic justice in the way that the change of ownership on Leo had spun around like a boomerang and whacked her own fledgling company upside the head.

Jimmy Poole's reputation, deserved or not, was a comfort to Billie Whistle. He was a touchstone—an ethical standard kept in a pure nitrogen atmosphere in a vault at NIST. As long as Jimmy Poole existed, she could stare at Billie Whistle in her morning mirror without flinching over what she had once done.

Fortitude

The summer sun peeled heat off the desert in shimmering waves, causing the distant mountain peaks to waver and dance. Illusive pools of black water glistened on hardpan flats. Dust devils capered among cactus and yucca, but the wind that stirred them brought no relief to the sweating cadets.

Sometimes, lying exhausted on her bunk at the end of the day, Jacinta wondered if she had chosen the right life. It was not the physical regimen (though that was hard and uncompromising) nor was it the vagaries of the differential calculus (beside which obstacle courses and scaling towers faded to insignificance). No, it was the looks she saw in others' eyes or the words behind her back that she never quite caught. As if she did not belong there.

She ought to have been dead and, try as she might, she could think of no merit on her part that had won her survival. Chance ruled the universe and chance, on a whim, might have sent her plunging to a fiery death with Soren and the others, placing her *under* the desert rather than *on* it. That was a thought she shared with no one, not even with cadet captain Alonzo Sulbertson, who alone might have understood her bewilderment.

Yet at night, when an impossible canvas of stars spread above her, or when the training clippers lifted with their crews of upperclassmen, or when beautiful and exotic airframes soared overhead from the test fields at nearby Edwards, chance or no, she knew no other life was possible. Fortitude. She would see it through, ghosts or no; spread her wings as far as she could, and soar.

> *I left my momma far behind*
> *To march through dust; but I don't mind!*

They drilled. Across the hardpan flats, twisting and turning to barely intelligible commands, feet striking in crude approximation of simultaneity, kicking up a bitter, alkali cloud. It coated Jacinta's hair and face and forced its way into her nose and throat until she thought she could no longer breathe.

"This is absolute air," cadet Ludwig Schimmelpfennig complained one time while he stumped beside her under the blistering sun. "What's marching got to do with astrogation or flying clippers?"

Jacinta didn't answer him. The other cadets called him "Lou Penny," but privately, Jacinta had labeled him the Bitchmeister. There was no aspect of

Glenn Academy with which he could not find fault; and the academy would
be so much better run, if only the Powers That Be would accede to his wisdom.

Though when it came to close order drill in the high desert he had a point.
She hadn't expected so much mouse at the academy. But bits and pieces of
military training, like the fossilized relics of extinct species, kept popping up
in what was supposed to be a no-foolin' twenty-first century curriculum.

The cadet drill sergeant ordered a countermarch and the first-year cadets
went through the evolution with a bit more polish than they had shown at
the semester's start. The first rank turned smartly about and the files twisted
back on themselves. Yungduk Morrisey, Jacinta's corporal, smiled at her as he
passed to the rear. Jacinta acknowledged his attention without returning it. If
Morrisey had the yen to jolly with her, he'd have to do it in his dreams.

> *I don't know, but I've been told*
> *Outer space is mighty cold!*

They climbed and crawled. Through obstacles, across rope bridges, up walls.
There was not an object in known space that they did not have to go over,
go around, or go through. Jacinta learned what a cactus felt like. She learned
how cold the desert grew at night. She learned how to wriggle through conduits
that would give a snake serious pause. She learned how far down the ground
could be.

"Climb, Rosario!" Ensign-instructor Debra Matusek bellowed from the base
of the scaling tower. "No sightseeing!"

Jacinta wrapped her right arm and leg around the climbing rope and hung
for a moment to catch her breath. She would be sore tomorrow, no doubt
about it. Maybe a little less sore than five months ago; but sore enough. Far
below, Ms. Matusek was a small person, indeed. Jacinta held her left hand out
so her thumb covered the ensign.

"I could squash you like a bug," she chortled wickedly.

Now how could anyone climb a rope that fast? Matusek was beside her on
the wall, gripping the next line over. "I couldn't hear that, kay-det," she said.

The instructor was not even breathing hard. Jacinta muttered something
under her breath.

"What was that, kay-det? Are my ears going bad?"

"I said, 'this is mouse.' " Jacinta stuck her chin out, daring refutation. "I'm
climbing against gravity. There's no gravity in space."

Matusek's eyes widened. "You don't say? Why, I'll . . . Hey, Jorge!" she called
the other instructor. "Kay-det says there's no gravity in space!" Jorge Izquierdo
slapped his forehead with the flat of his hand. Matusek turned to Jacinta and
smiled sweetly. "Three gigs, kay-det. Permanent, until you can tell me why
what you just said was too stupid for words." Matusek rappelled to the ground.
"Up and over, Rosario! Rest period's over!"

Break my body, burn my brain!
I sneer at problems, laugh at pain!

They studied. When they weren't slamming their bodies, they were banging their brains. There weren't many lectures. Nineteenth century mass production methods? No, the modern era meant customized, one-off manufacture. A few lectures to put everyone on the same wavelength; occasional discussion groups; some one-on-ones with the instructor. But mostly structured modules over the campus intranet: sims and scenarios, problem sets, reference materials, chat rooms, frustrating conversations with Artificial Stupids. The whole thing was set up like a computer game. You could work at your own pace, identifying problems and solving them, advancing from level to level; but, like climbing that forsaken tower, you better get up and over.

At first, Jacinta worked from the terminal in her room. She was used to doing for herself, and the silver apples emphasized self-reliance. Yet, early on, she stuck dead on an engine burn calculation. She jiggled newtons and kilos until she dreamed in mass fractions, but she could not bring herself to launch the simulated rocket because she had no confidence in her answer. There was not enough information. "Real world," Lou Penny said confidently, "you *don't* always have all the skinny before you gotta act," and launched his virtual rocket on his best guesstimate.

It was a beautiful sight, narrowcast over the bunny class intranet. Jacinta watched it climb and climb and . . . run out of fuel and turn and crash in a fireball no less spectacular for being virtched. Later, in the common room, the Bitchmeister claimed the question was unfair; and Jacinta had sighed and said if she only knew what the forsaken *fuel* was she could look up its specific impulse in the deeby; and Kenn Rowley said no-brainer, it was Aerozine 50 with a Nitro Tet oxidizer—I_{sp} was 320 seconds—and the *real* problem was the unknown fuel mass; and Yungduk Morrisey went whaddaya mean "unknown" and rattled off the figures—and at that point they all stopped talking and stared at each other.

Ever since, Jacinta and the others had worked together in the common room. You never knew who might have the one crucial piece of information. And it could be that not all problems had to do with launching ships.

When I'm dead, don't bury me!
I'll float in space eternally!

They kept house. Though not very well. Cadet captain Sulbertson could explain in detail every shortcoming of her room, from uniform coveralls out of place in the closet to assignment logbooks not retrieved on a moment's notice. This, at least, Jacinta tolerated. You didn't want clutter in a cramped orbital ship.

"You can't find it, cadet?" Sulbertson leaned forward, invading her space. He wore white cotton gloves with a damning black smudge on the forefinger. Jacinta suspected the gloves were made that way.

"No, captain. I mean, Yes, captain! I mean, I can find it if you give me a minute." The logbook was on her desk. She'd been working Principles of Rocketry shortly before the surprise inspection. It was underneath those papers. She was sure. Dimly, Jacinta could hear the sounds of scrambling cadets down the hallway in the dorm. *It's not fair*, she told herself. *He always stops here first and that gives the others time to get ready.* Sulbertson took special joy in harrassing her.

She was feeling sorry for herself. *The sorriest thing in the world*, Mother Smythe had called that. *Self-pity is self-defeating.* Jacinta squared her shoulders. "Start counting, captain," she said in the Voice of Confidence.

Sulbertson cocked his head. His big, white eyes regarded her and he pursed his lips. "All right. Go! Gig, mark one . . . Gig, mark two . . ."

Jacinta broke for the desk, threw the papers aside, and—Bone! There was the logbook!—she whirled and thrust it into Sulbertson's hands. Sulbertson noted the problem most recently worked and handed it back to her. "Good enough, Rosario. Delete two gigs for taking the chance. Add one gig for the messy floor." He indicated the papers she had scattered in grabbing the log.

"Yes, captain," she said. "Thank you, captain."

When Sulbertson inspected the dorms, he never let on, by word or gesture, that he and Jacinta had ever shared an evening of tears. Punctilious and precise, he went by the book, checking and inspecting and—invariably—rubbing his white glove across the one surface she hadn't dusted. Even when, as sometimes happened, he spared her a backward glance on leaving, his eyes were never those that had wept for an hour on her shoulder over friends they had never had.

The whole thing was clearly designed to drive off as many bunnies as possible. Send them hopping back to mommy—those who had one—before spending troy on the real training on-orbit, *mano a mano* under an experienced captain-instructor. Snap inspections, arbitrary penalties, impossible assignments, petty harrassment. Foo a test, a courtesy, leave the least little thing out of place in your room, and you got gigged. Rack the gigs and you couldn't leave the campus to sample the sizzling night life of Tehachapi. The meek might indeed one day inherit the Earth, but Outer Space was evidently reserved for the anal-retentive.

September rolled around and the fall term newboos began to trickle in by ones and twos. Jacinta was assigned along with a few other underclassmen to escort the new arrivals to their dormitories. Ensign Dubois handed her a thinpad and stylus. She pronounced her name "duh boyz" and had no doubt heard all the usual jokes. "Names and billets. They sign here . . ." Pointing to a box on the electronic form. ". . . and here. You check them off there, and there. These . . ." A hardcopy flimsy. ". . . are your talking points."

Jacinta scanned the sheet. Welcome aboard. Here's your room. There's the head. That's the showers. Class orientation is scheduled for . . . Yadda-yadda-yadda. "No problemo, ma'am. Not exactly rocket science." She saluted.

You were supposed to salute—more military mouse. Salute anything with rank on its cuffs, including ensigns themselves only a few years released into the wild. Ensign Liz Dubois grinned at the rocket science comment. She taught orbital mechanics.

Danger, danger. Whom the gods notice . . . Jacinta began edging toward the door.

"Speaking of rocket science . . ." Dubois said, stopping Jacinta before she could make her escape. "Having any problems with the new module?"

"None I can't handle, ma'am." Using the Posture and Voice of Confidence.

"Hmm. Don't forget, I monitor your log. You haven't mastered the second problem set yet."

"I will." Did the confidence quaver just a bit there? She refused to let it quaver.

Dubois shook her head. "Needs more'n grit and determination, gal." She stabbed a finger at Jacinta. "A satellite's perigee," she said suddenly, "is three hundred klicks above mean sea level. Its apogee is thirteen hundred klicks. That's pretty damn eccentric, isn't it, cadet?"

One of Dubois's more charming habits was that of springing snap questions, any time, any place. You didn't have to be in class to be on the spot. In fact, you didn't even have to be *taking* her class. Jacinta had seen upperclassmen stopped and quizzed, and suspected that even visitors were put on the grill from time to time.

But . . . an apogee four times higher than perigee? That *was* some kind of eccentricity. Except that Dubois would never ask anything so straightforward.

"Um, it certainly *sounds* eccentric . . ." Jacinta carefully studied the other woman, looking for a clue that the comment was warm or cold; but Dubois had the most difficult body language she had ever encountered. "But . . ." Jacinta closed her eyes and pictured the orbit. An ellipse, one focus at Earth's center. Shy turn grazing the Earth; far turn way out there . . . Oh! ". . . But eccentricity is measured from the focus of the ellipse, not from mean sea level, and the focus is at the center of the Earth. When you add in the Earth's radius—"

Dubois nodded. "That's enough, Rosario. It's understanding that matters. You can teach a *machine* to do the arithmetic."

That was bone with Jacinta. She had forgotten the Earth's radius.

* * *

A half dozen other guides waited in the admin building. Yungduk, as usual, thought he was in charge, and tried to get them lined up like they were in review. Jacinta and the others ignored him.

"He wants us to line up like ducklings," Lou Penny whispered. "Get it? Young duck? Ducklings?"

Jacinta ignored him, too.

When the cadet colonel entered reception, Yungduk jumped up and saluted. So did some of the others. You didn't have to leap to attention, but you did have to show respect; so Jacinta sat straighter and gave the woman a polite salute. Lou kept his nose to his thinpad and pretended not to notice. The colonel looked them over, appraising them, before giving an as-you-were.

There was a test in all of this, Jacinta was sure; though what it was, she didn't know. The academy's unofficial motto was: You're never not in class. So everything you said and did went into your assessment. Lou and some others grumbled about Big Brother, but Jacinta was used to it from her years in the silver apple retreat.

Cadet Colonel Noëlle Nieves at twenty-two was about as far from Big Brother as you could get. Little Sister, maybe. Short and solid, but fine-featured, with a dusky complexion and a cloud of brown, curly hair that turned kinky in the back and told of family roots on three continents. Her eyes, set in a long, square face with a strong jaw, were by turns severe, laughing and mischievous. It was said, after lights out, that the colonel's bunny days were legend among the staff instructors; but whatever stunts she had pulled were a closely-guarded secret.

"Which one of you cadets," asked Colonel Nieves, "has Ursula Kitmann on your list?"

The others scrolled their thinpads while Jacinta sat numb in shock. *Ursula Kitmann?* A face rose before her: a young woman with long, blonde hair and violet eyes; but a face grown sketchy and indistinct. *Ursula Kitmann?* Echoes of hurt buried beneath brash cheer. Jacinta hadn't known anyone had survived the crash. She had never even checked.

"I do," said Kenn Rowley.

"When she gets here," said Colonel Nieves, "the superintendent wants to see her right away."

"Yes, ma'am."

"Wait." Jacinta had found a voice, though it wasn't one of the canonical Voices. "Wait." Rowley, Yungduk, the colonel, they were all looking at her. "I'd like to escort applicant Kitmann, ma'am."

"You would," the colonel said, letting a question curl into the words. "You are . . . ?"

"Cadet Rosario, ma'am."

Colonel Nieves regarded her silently while an inner clock ticked forever in Jacinta's breast. "I see," the colonel said after what must have been only a moment. "All right. Do it."

After Nieves left, Jacinta sat remembering the night of the crash, the night she had sealed off from conscious thought. She and Lonzo had survived the accident by missing the plane.

Ursula Kitmann liked to do things the hard way.

Now, here is a mystery. How can one gauge the changes in a person barely met, and known not at all? Start with the coarse physical features. The golden hair was shorter and bore a streak of platinum when the light struck it just so. The jaunty, confident walk had grown a limp. Stitches on cheek and jaw had faded to red scars. But what of the inner person? Had the glint in the eye faded, too? The brass confidence? Had the mind survived the crash even half so well as the body?

There were two signs Jacinta could read. First, Kitmann wore not a discrete pin, but a broad scarf around her neck on which a white dove traversed a golden sun. Second, she had flown the LAX to Bakersfield route. A vagrant breeze lifted Kitmann's hair as they crossed the quad to her assigned dormitory and Jacinta noticed that something plastic had replaced the woman's right ear.

So. Ursula. How was the plane crash?

How did you open a conversation? Jacinta wondered about Soren and the others—but could find no words to broach the subject. If Jacinta suffered nighttime bouts of self-blame and denial for having survived, what must Kitmann feel? It was better to leave the topic unspoken, the scabs untouched. Eventually, names unspoken gave answer to questions unasked.

"What did Superman have to say?" Jacinta asked, seeking a neutral ground on which they might meet again. The superintendent did not see every incoming cadet-applicant, and Kitmann had come out of the office even more solemn than she had been going in.

Kitmann tossed her head and, briefly, the prosthetic ear rebuked Jacinta. "That's an awfully flip way to talk about a man like Forrest Calhoun."

Frost in the desert, defying the heat and the sandpaper breeze. The ice in Kitmann's voice froze Jacinta's heart. Yet, what had she done to offend Kitmann? Squaring her shoulders, she pointed to the rose-colored buildings on the south side of the quad with the Spanish tile roofs. "Those are the classrooms and infocenter." She used the Voice of Polite Distance. "Northside are the dorms. Your billet is in Gagarin Hall—that's the first one on the right."

"Wait." Kitmann stopped and held a hand up. They had come to the monument that dominated the center of the quad. "*Ad Astra*" was its name. The base was a bubbled mass of plated aerogel that climbed upward, growing thinner and smokier, arcing toward the east—the open side of the quad. Streaks of red copper near the feathery apex suggested the exhaust plume of a space-craft in lift phase. At the very tip, cleverly foreshortened to suggest an even greater height, a bright figure yearned for orbit.

The accepted wisdom held the figure to be an SSTO, but no one knew for sure. It wasn't fully visible from the ground. Every year, at least one cadet would get caught trying to climb the plume to find out. Kitmann slowly approached and reached out to touch the smooth-black iron.

While Jacinta waited patiently for her charge to finish gawking, she noted the hobble in Kitmann's walk, marked the stiffness in her arm. *You'll never make it,* she thought—and was instantly ashamed. Yet, it was the truth, wasn't it? The regime was too demanding; the instructors cut no slack. Kitmann's broken and cobbled body wouldn't take the grueling pace. Those recalcitrant tears in Ursula's eyes must mean that Kitmann knew it, too. It was pointless to start what she could never finish.

But Jacinta's thought had been as much desire as fact. She *wanted* Kitmann gone. She didn't know why, only that the other woman's presence distressed her. Jacinta told herself that it was concern for Kitmann's health.

Ursula placed a hand on Jacinta's arm and said, cryptically, "Only three of us left."

Kitmann tried hard. Over the next few weeks, Jacinta gauged her progress. They were often together in the same training group—with no formal division into classes, everyone moved at her own pace—and while Kitmann did well enough at the theory and the problems and the sims, the physical mouse could prove insurmountable—in the case of the scaling tower, literally so.

"Something I should know about, kay-det?" Ensign Matusek asked one day while Jacinta awaited her turn at the "Wailing Wall." High above, Kitmann dangled under the scorching sun. An arm shifted to a higher grip, and Jacinta could see the muscles bunch as she strained to lift herself another length.

"She should give up," Jacinta volunteered in the Voice of Concern, "before she hurts herself."

Matusek shrugged. "Seems I watched you one time 'bout in the same situation."

"That was different."

"Could be right, kay-det. Kitmann stopped because she gave out, not because she gave up." She scowled at the Wall. "Morrisey! You and Rosario get up there and help Kitmann down."

She and Yungduk monkeyed the ropes on either side of the newboo, Jacinta on the left, Morrisey on the right. Part of Jacinta's mind expressed grim satisfaction at how quickly and smoothly she ascended. Scaling had become almost contemptuously easy for her. All it needed was practice, and Matusek nipping at your heels.

Kitmann, red-faced and huffing, hung on knotted arms that trembled under the strain of her weight. She wouldn't look at her rescuers, but fixed her gaze on the top of the Wall. "We're supposed to help you down," Morrisey said.

"No, thanks, corporal. I can make it." Kitmann pulled; her feet scraped for purchase on the the thick hemp cable. A harsh grunt escaped her. But she didn't move.

"You're favoring your left arm," Jacinta said. "Twine your legs around the rope. That'll take some of the strain off."

"No flubber, Kitmann," said Morrisey. "Ensign told us to bring you down. You don't want Matusek mad at us, do you? Besides, even if you do make it to the top, all there is, is you have to rappel down the other side."

"I can make it." The statement emerged through clenched teeth.

"Sure you can," said Morrisey, "but not today."

Maybe not ever, Jacinta thought.

Kitmann looked from one to the other. Then she began to lower herself. But again she tried to avoid putting all her weight on her left arm, so she slipped and slid down the rope a few feet.

Morrisey said, "Shit," and skinnied down the rope to catch up. Jacinta followed.

"I think I have a rope burn," Kitmann said calmly when they reached her.

"Look," said Morrisey. "We'll help take some of your weight. Rosario, hang onto her. I'll go up top and get a line. Kitmann, put your arms on her shoulder."

"I won't let go of the rope."

"One arm, then. You're used up. That's why the ensign sent us. It's not like you're the first cadet to need a carry-down. An otter has to learn to rely on her mates."

Kitmann nodded and, with marked hesitation, put her left arm around Jacinta's shoulders.

Jacinta almost lost her own grip on the rope. The arm wasn't real. It felt fuzzy where it touched the bare skin of her neck. And it was the wrong temperature. Jacinta shot Kitmann a horrified glance, saw silent defiance, and made no comment while they waited for Morrisey.

After they worked their way to the bottom and unclipped the safety lines, Kitmann dropped to the sand. Ensign Izquierdo brought the first aid kit and checked the rope burn on her right arm. *The natural arm*, thought Jacinta. She couldn't keep her eyes off the prosthetic. It moved and flexed like the real thing. It even had tiny hairs and goosebumps. She couldn't see where it attached. Near the shoulder, under the sleeves of the blouse; or was the seam itself artfully hidden among the other scars that zorroed Kitmann's body?

Matusek clapped her hands. "All right, gawkers. Next rank, up against the wall!"

That was Jacinta's rank. She squeezed Kitmann's arm—the "wrong" arm—

but the other woman turned her head at the pressure. "I'll find you later," Jacinta said. "We need to talk."

The violet eyes gave no answer. Jacinta did not take that as a no.

Evenings were their own and everyone relaxed in different ways. Some sacked out; others klatsched in the commons. Computer games were popular— especially flight sims—and so was surfing and trolling. Scratch teams on the athletic field played whatever sport was seasonal. A few cadets played instruments, and both a bounce band and a wind quintent were active. Jacinta found Kitmann on her knees in the chapel.

Okay, Jacinta thought as she watched from the back of the room, everyone was entitled to her own notion of a good time; but Jacinta had no use for self-abasement. As the Eighth Precept held, *You are taller on your feet than on your knees.* Groveling got you nothing but dirt in your face.

The "chapel" was a medium-sized room in the recreation building done up in soft colors and woods and a variety of leafy plants. It was a room where you could be alone with yourself, if that was what you wanted, or you could participate in scheduled communal services, real or teeped. Pixwalls and threedy tanks let the room's walls emulate church, meeting house, mosque, synagogue, or pagoda as the spirit moved. The deeby even had the auditorium at the Society for Ethical Humanism in Manhattan, complete with its niche statues and stained glass windows of great philosophers. It looked, Jacinta had thought when Kenn Rowley showed it to her, more like a church than some churches.

Kitmann had called up a Catholic setting; not surprising, since the doves within the sun were affiliated with an order of nuns. Jacinta didn't know who had come up with the idea of "signing up for a term" rather than making a lifetime commitment. Maybe the religious orders had been inspired by the secular sodalities that had sprung up in the cities; or perhaps the whole sisterhood thing had started in postulant-hungry convents and seeped from there into the secular world. No one seemed to know. One day there were women's shelters and support groups and hot lines; the next, there were the sisterhoods, precipitating like crystals from a supersaturated solution.

Kitmann had chosen an interactive program. She knelt on a prie-dieu beside a threedy holoscreen and spoke in a low voice to the robed deaconess that flickered in the tank.

Granted, a trained neural net could emulate conversation with astonishing fidelity, but it was only a simulation. Outside the boundaries of its knowledge base, a net floundered with random replies—which was why pilots seldom discussed philosophy with their onboard navcomps.

The hologram turned in her direction. "Hello," it said in a pleasant contralto. "Have you come to join us?"

Jacinta fought the eerie shiver that crawled up her spine. *It's reacting to the infrared sensors. Input reads a second IR source at 98.6°F. Deeby says that's human bod-temp. Triangulation gives location. RAM access to the greeting file pulls up a standard I/O statement. That program did not actually greet me.*

But it needed I/O to function—just like people. "No," Jacinta said, "I was looking for Ursula."

Kitmann rose from her knees. "We'll talk later, Priscilla."

"Are you sure?"

"We'll talk later, Priscilla."

"System shutdown confirmed." The dancing lasers blinked out and the "Christmas tree" inside the threedy tank slowed to a stop. The holoscreen placard read: SYSTEM STANDBY MODE.

Jacinta pointed to the screen. "You think they'll ever ordain one of those?"

"It's only a program," said Kitmann. "A construct based on the original Priscilla from *Acts.* Sometimes I talk with Chloe or Phoebe or other early deaconesses, or with the women-apostles, like Magdalen, or Salome, or the Marys."

"Just making a joke." *And you don't have to get snooty.* "I was looking for you."

Kitmann folded her arms. "You must have been looking hard to find me here."

"I—How's the rope burn?"

Kitmann displayed the angry, red welt on her arm, almost like a trophy. "I've been burned worse." Her defiant gaze faltered. "A *lot* worse."

Jacinta flinched. "Look, up on the tower, I couldn't help notice . . ."

"My new arm?" Kitmann held the *faux* limb up, turned it, flexed the fingers. "Hot spit, isn't it?" She was wearing a short sleeve blouse and Jacinta could see arm muscles move under the skin. Yet, they weren't muscles and it wasn't skin. "It's tougher than the real thing. The 'muscle tissue' is MEMS technology—micro-electro-mechanical systems. An Artificial Stupid neural net in the titanium 'bone' runs the electronics that extend and contract the MEMS. And an interface like cheeseheads use runs the Stupid—except it's implanted in my arm instead of a skullcap. I'm an official, government-sanctioned guinea pig."

"What if . . . it doesn't work?"

Kitmann leaned toward her. "Then how will I be worse off?" she asked in flat, measured tones. Then she laughed and straightened up. "I thought about getting a hook. You know, like that cartoon pirate? That way, I could gaff any boys that got too jolly. Or go fishing . . ." She held her arm out. "Go ahead, feel it."

Jacinta hesitated a moment; then ran her hand along the 'skin' of the bare forearm. It felt soft and fuzzy, like velvet. But it was cold, not human. Ambient temperature, like a lizard. Kitmann shivered at the touch.

"That . . . tickles. There are sensors in the 'skin,' you know. Pressure, temperature. They had to train me to feel those; just like I trained the neural net.

I would think about a hand or arm motion and the interface would pick up the neural signals and translate it to electronics. Then the Stupid would try this or that and the tutor program would encourage it until it got it right. But it was weirder the other way. They'd apply a heat source, or a pin, or an ice cube or something, and I would get . . . feelings." A momentary disquiet passed across her face. "I can't describe them. It would be like describing the smell of A-flat, or the sound of purple. But I would go, 'Oh, a pin. I must be feeling pain.' Or, 'An ice cube. That must be cold.' After a while, my brain would recognize the inputs automatically; but it's not . . . an *immediate* sensation. It's like the way a tone-deaf woman hears a Beethoven symphony. Hey, you want to see something? I can make all the MEMS stand up." Kitmann held her arm straight up at the elbow and concentrated. Then, like a dog's hair bristling, the forearm became . . . fuzzy. It looked like a bottle swab. Kitmann laughed. "You should see the look on your face."

Jacinta shook her head. "You should see the look on yours." She shivered. "It's creepy." The arm or the look? Jacinta didn't know.

Kitmann thought she meant the arm. "It looks a lot less creepy from my side. I guess you'd be happier if I was wearing a wood carving; or maybe part of a department store mannequin. Or better yet, I could just wave a stump around. Then you could feel sorry for the poor crip. Hey, this flubber isn't so bad. I can crush soda cans with my hand . . ."

"That's no big deal."

"Full?" Kitman grabbed Jacinta by the wrist and squeezed. Jacinta winced and tried to pull away. Kitmann's hand was a band of velvet iron. "Feel that? The bionic woman, that's me." Kitmann released the arm.

Jacinta rubbed her wrist. "That hurt."

The violet eyes were unreadable. "You don't know what hurt is."

A long silence followed, which Jacinta broke when she said, "Look, I'm sorry I missed the plane."

"That's not what hurt. What did you want to see me about?"

"You're afraid to put too much stress on that arm, aren't you?"

Kitmann rubbed her arm just below the elbow. "Longitudinal stress hurts at the joint. I'll get used to it."

"You could hurt yourself."

"And your point is . . . ?"

Jacinta took a deep breath. "You won't make it." Kitmann pulled back. In the dead silence that followed, the two locked gazes. Jacinta was the first to look down. "No matter how hard you try and no matter how much pain you put up with, you won't make it."

Kitmann shook her head. "I won't give up."

"You should. For your own sake," Jacinta said, using the Voice of Concern.

Kitmann was not attuned to the nuances of tonalities. She stood back a step and studied Jacinta. "You don't want me here. That's it. *You* don't want me here because I—"

"No—"

"But, hey! I'm used to not being wanted. My bio-mother and bio-father used to trade me off like a chunk of hot plutonium after they fissioned the family. Until the doves took me in, I never lived anywhere longer than nine months."

"Kitmann . . . !"

"The name's Ursula, but you have to pick it up and use it. Excuse me, I've got a life waiting." Kitmann shoved—with her left arm—and Jacinta staggered back into one of the benches that served as pews. "Don't chase after me," she said. The violet eyes were wet, her cheeks flushed. "Stay here." She looked away. "I thought there were three of us left; but I guess I was wrong."

The dove banged the door closed and Jacinta sat alone in the chapel. Somehow, Kitmann had to understand that she *didn't* have a life waiting; at least, not here.

Afterward, Jacinta tracked cadet captain Sulbertson to the simulator room and asked him if there was some way to help Kitmann see reason before inevitable failure killed her spirit. But Sulbertson only leaned back in the simulator's command chair and rubbed his chin.

"How many times you go down 'n see her in rehab?"

"Captain, I didn't know that anyone survived the crash."

"Uh-huh. Did you ask her about the others?"

"I—" Jacinta looked away. "I couldn't. I tried, but . . ."

And Sulbertson shrugged, as if, somehow, questions had been answered.

They found Kitmann the next morning, unconscious, at the base of the scaling tower. She had gone out in the night to try again, and at some point had lost her grip and fallen to the ground, suffering a concussion and a broken collar bone. The Aid Squad was on it, and the cadets in the morning training class encircled the unconscious body, whispering among themselves. It was Bucktail Smith who pointed out that she had fallen on the far side of the tower. It was one of those things that everyone had seen, but no one had noticed. Until Smith spoke up, the implication had not sunk in. Kitmann had made it over the top.

Which made it a shame that she was to be expelled.

"Cowboy" Calhoun was a legend in his own time. He knew it and he gloried in it. Others could take the aw-shucks-it-was-nothing route. It *wasn't* nothing. He had done some damn important somethings, and the mementos in his office were to remind visitors of that. Test pilot on high performance airframes. Early flight tests on SSTOs, when no one was sure they could lift enough fuel to come back down. Pilot on the Skopje Rescue. "The Farthest Man from Earth" during the long, lonely FarTrip expedition—where, with Ignacio Mendes and Iron Mike Krasnarov, he had discovered the first hints of the Visitors. He even had photographs from his stint at the first, *ad hoc* spaceflight academy, the one at Ames Field, where he had trained Chase Coughlin and others.

So, yeah, he was a legend in his own time, but his time had passed, and he knew that, too. Now he was Superintendent of Glenn Academy—ensuring that the next generation of ballistic pilots would not be a bunch of freaking cowboys like he had been. Age had whitened his hair in places. He still flew, but no longer on the knife edge. Orbital transfers and dockings; but not max-Q; not the rotation maneuver or the Swoop of Death; not the new frames or the new fuels or the new materials, where no one knew where the edges were until men and women the likes of Calhoun-that-was pushed the envelope out over those edges and pulled it back before it fooed, and where the smallest misstep might end in a blackened hole in the talc of the high desert.

Calhoun's desk was cluttered, but organized, the habits of a man who might need to find something fast in an emergency. The icons on his virtual desk were equally well arranged. He looked up from a paper he had been reading.

"C'mon in, gal. I don't bite." A trace of Texas lingered far in the back of his throat. Jacinta took a seat before his desk. A black and white photograph sat there: a bearded man in dungarees and battered, broad-brimmed hat grinning beside a large cotton bale. *First Bale, 1976,* the inscription read. A young boy, perhaps twelve, stood cross-armed beside him.

"You have his face," she said.

Calhoun studied the photograph. "Could be stamped in worse molds," he allowed. He swiveled his chair to face her. "Rosario, right? What did you want to see me about?"

"Ursula Kitmann."

"Ah." He leaned back in his chair. "And what about Kitmann?"

Jacinta took a deep breath. "I don't think you should expel her."

Calhoun blinked. "From what I've heard, I would've thought you'd be happy to see her go."

"I—think she made a mistake coming back. Or at least, coming so soon after . . . you know."

Calhoun cocked his head and his eyes became thoughtful. "Go on."

"You know she has an artificial arm?"

Calhoun nodded. "Among other things."

"Well, I sort of told her how she'd never be able to . . . That because of her injuries, she'd . . ."

Calhoun nodded. "I know."

"So it's my fault. If I hadn't made a point about her failing, maybe she wouldn't have gone out that night."

The superintendent sighed and pushed back from his desk. His gaze wandered to the class photographs on the wall. "Flight-testing airframes was the easier job. It doesn't hurt so much when one of those crashes and burns. Rosario, no one is responsible for what Kitmann did except Kitmann. She didn't have to prove anything. Not to you and not to me, and certainly not to the others that were on that flight with her. It's not her fault and it's not your fault that you both lived when others died. *She* made the decision, and not all your guilty feelings can take that responsibility from her. Show her that much respect."

"You could give her another chance. Sure, she made a mistake climbing the tower before she was ready; but she won't do it again."

"Damn straight, but it'll be something else. It wasn't the physical handicap that did her in, Rosario. Work in ziggy is hard. It requires stamina, patience, and upper body strength. Trust me, I know. Body strength . . . Well, that was marginal, but we were working on a therapy program to bring it up. We don't insist that everyone go at the same pace. Stamina? She's got plenty of that."

"She's determined to see this through, no matter what. The others, they're calling her 'No Quit-mann'."

"Then I wish they'd find someone else to admire. Look, I'm not dropping her because she failed to finish the tower climb and fell on the way down. I'm dropping her because she showed bad judgement. Climbing at night? Alone? That's not fortitude, that's stupid! And we don't need stupid cadets—who push things because they don't have the patience to take them at their own pace."

Jacinta could see that the superintendent was adamant. It was all for the best, she told herself. Better that Ursula be disappointed now, when she could at least blame a moment of foolishness, than to be disappointed later, after she had given it her best shot. "Just one thing, Mr. Calhoun," she said as she rose. "If doing something stupid is grounds for expulsion, there isn't one of us safe for the term."

The smile the superintendent gave her was a sad one. "Including me," he said.

Everybody said how the super's decision was bump and maybe they ought to pull a strike, or run a demo, or hold a vigil, or something; but it was Kitmann herself who stuck up for Calhoun and said that if she'd been headmistress, she'd have done the same. But it was bump anyway. And, yeah, people die and loves die, but the hardest of all was when dreams died. Ursula had been kicked hard in her life, even before her parents' divorce, but had learned to land on her feet and plot her own orbit; and she kept going because her course was fixed on a lodestar that drew her on. Spaceflight. Piloting hot machines. Ziggy. And, maybe, seeing new worlds. That was gone, now. Lost. And without that pole star, would her life spin off in some uncharted direction?

When Ursula's last day came, Jacinta checked a car out of the common pool and drove Ursula to Bakersfield, where they got maudlin drunk together in the airport lounge and Jacinta apologized at long last—because she had never once tried to find out if anyone had survived and had tried to wipe from her mind people the memory of whom was all that was left.

Neither of them were surprised when Lonzo Sulbertson showed up, and the three of them sat in the lounge trading stories of this and that. They talked about ziggy and the Visitors and Mariesa van Huyten selling asteroids and whether the *Ares* would ever get built; about Tsiolkovsky spinning up and Lonzo making his first moon flight. They talked about everything there was to talk about, except the last time the three of them had waited together for a jump jet in an airport.

Until the very end, when Ursula paused at the jetway and told them, "It's only the two of you left, now. Make us proud."

Then she boarded the jumper, and the rotors on the fan deck spun up and the plane lifted as gently as a leaf before the pilot kicked over the baffles and converted to horizontal flight.

Jancinta and Lonzo watched the plane out of sight. *I should be leaving, too,* Jacinta thought. *I don't belong here.* Then, sober, they sought their separate cars and drove back to the academy, each alone.

9.

A Loft Aloft

Shahrakh Shary was a middle-aged man with a swarthy complexion, a large, prominent nose, and a larger, even more prominent smile. His thick, brushed-back hair, insufficient to the head, surrendered crown and temples to the elements. The logo on his white jumpsuit—an abstraction of geometric figures—suggested the letters OMC without crassly spelling them out. *The corporation formerly known as Orbital Management*, Hobie thought as he floated from the lock of the *Artic Shaw* into LEO Station's Westport.

"Good to see you again, Doctor Hobart," Shary said. "How was your goddam trip?" The Hub was ziggy and Shary floated, with an otter's casual disdain for orientation, upside down with respect to Hobie. "Blackhall bunked you with a metallurgist down in Red-17B," he said, leading him aside from the flow of traffic. "That's Mars-level. You'll be more comfortable with a little spin gravity."

Hobie arched a brow. "Doubling up, are we?"

"We had to convert some residential floors to microgravity research," Shary explained. "It's a goddam Chinese puzzle up here, doc. We're always reconfiguring. Not enough room. They should've installed eight spoke-pairs instead of two when they built the place." Teeth showed briefly in a smile of frustration. "We, ah, had to move your equipment to make space for the goddam Smithsonian. But it's still ziggy," he added quickly. "We only moved it to Hub 4-D."

Hobie frowned. "So that's why my output's been low. . . . You're supposed to clear things with me before disconnecting my equipment. You know that, Rock."

"But everything's back to normal now." Shary looked so anxious that Hobie had to laugh to reassure him. VHI and Klon-Am—Shary's parent company— might be bitter rivals, but Hobie had always liked the orbital facility's site manager.

"I'm sure everything is fine. I'll run the checklist after I get settled in."

"Ah . . . One more thing . . ." Shary held out a clip-on ID card with Hobie's name, pixure, and affiliation on it. The ID had a chip imprinted on it.

"Big Brother is watching!" Hobie said without humor.

Shary grimaced. "You know goddam management. Dell'Bosco, my boss, he doesn't want VHI snooping around anything proprietary. The card will chirp like a bird if you approach a restricted zone, that's all."

Hobie eyed the card with distaste. "Used to be," he said, "otters stuck together." He clipped the badge to his coveralls. "Well, you're the ringmaster, Rock. When can we get together and discuss my project? I'll need to see you, your plant engineer, electrical, and mechanical. Who's bonebag this trimester?"

"Just me and Plant," Shary said. "You remember Blackhall. The rest of the staff is Uncle Waldo."

"We'd all be Waldo if we could," Hobie said.

"Goddam right," said Shary.

Westport was separated from the rest of the station by an internal lock at the first ring frame, in case of docking mishaps. East of that, stockrooms and warehouses occupied most of the rest of the tank, giving way in Hub-1D to microgravity manufacturing and research.

When he reached Hub-2, Hobie saw what Rock had meant by the Chinese puzzle remark. The interior was packed with self-contained experiments and robot manufacturing plants. With cost-to-orbit down to corporate pocket change, people were trying things in ziggy that would have been unthinkable a generation ago. Super-hard metals for balls and races, longer-lasting cutting tools, very large crystals, cobalt/rare-earth magnets. . . . Blackhall had used every cubic meter of space, fitting the sometimes oddly-shaped equipments like a farmer building a stone wall.

There were even installations *behind* the installations. Probably self-contained, Hobie guessed, with no physical material needing removal or replenishment. If the only output was data, all that was needed was a utility connection and a fibrop to the comm link.

He counted five waldos floating in the various bays: groundside plant managers or researchers visiting their facilities. The waldos were spheres about the size of a soccer ball, and each possessed a rack of manipulators and an array of optical and other sensors. *That's the way to do it.* Hobie thought. *Goggles by day: wife by night.*

None of the waldos reacted to his presence, so Hobie waited out of politeness. Signals had to pinball through the Iridium Network until they reached a line o' sight talker to the Earthside teeper; then the bounceback took just as long. Sometimes, when traffic was heavy, reaction could take entire seconds.

Still nothing. Could be all five teepers were trolling deebies; though you didn't need a *mobile* unit to access databases. After a few more moments without a response, Hobie headed for Hub-3 feeling a little miffed. Someone could have at least said hello. . . .

The Hub—five former shuttle LOH tanks—ran one hundred fifty-one meters east to west, all of it ziggy. The center tank rotated on a pair of giant Kingsbury magnetic bearings and, seen through the open manlock, tumbled like an amusement park barrel-o'-fun. But after Hobie passed through the spin decoupler and grabbed a ring on the other side, Hub-3 seemed to stop turning—and when he looked back at Hub-2, it was the rest of the station that was rolling instead. Hobie smiled at the illusion, which never failed to amuse him.

One of the waldos in Hub-2 chose that moment to rotate on its gyros and, with a hiss of airjets, hurtle directly toward Hobie. Hobie grabbed a stanchion and pulled himself out of the way with centimeters to spare. "Hey!" he said. "Watch where you're going, Uncle!"

The "soccer ball" braked to a belated halt a few feet past him. "Doctor Hobart!" said a voice. "I didn't see you."

Yeah, right. There'd been plenty of time for Waldo to notice Hobie floating in the doorway, time lag or no time lag; but why make an issue of it? "Have we met, Uncle?" he asked.

"Chan Fulin," the speaker grille informed him. "From Tien Jinshu Tzuzhi, in Guandong. We meet last year, at directionally solidified materials conference in Melbourne."

"Dr. Chan. Of course, I remember you." Actually, he only thought he did. There had been a lot of topics discussed at the Melbourne symposium. They exchanged a few pleasantries about colleagues before parting.

The center bay of Hub-3 was known as "Rome" because all roads led there: the east and west Hub and all four spokes of the pinwheel. The spokes were mounted in two pairs, one hundred eighty degrees apart. The two spokes in each pair were braced to each other and connected by tunnels at the tips and halfway down. In effect, each was a twenty-three story office tower. A rotation of 2.2 r.p.m. produced spin gravity running from micro in the attic to Mars near the basement.

The spoke entry ways were painted in bright pastels. In the early days, Hobie remembered, otters would get confused turning around in the Hub and go down the wrong spoke—sometimes even back down one they had just come up. Now the garish and contrasting patterns broke the symmetry and helped everyone orient. Signs by the hatchways gave directions to certain facilities. "Sector General," the emergency clinic, was on Blue-14 through 16, and "Ukraine," the greenhouse and garden, was (appropriately enough) on Green-8 through 10. Gold-8 to 10 housed the control center.

On a hunch, Hobie approached the Gold spoke entrance and his card warbled like a robin in spring. Hobie glowered at the forbidden portal. The exercise facilities were below the control center. How was he supposed to reach Pump-U-Up? He'd have to go down to Blue basement, cross through the inter-spoke pressure tube, then climb up.

If nothing else, he'd get his exercise that way . . .

*   *   *

Hobie had a damn good plan. Harvest his latest slug; draw wire, assemble the parasols and release them; then—back home to Charli. He'd spent two months on the details—bills of materials, activity sequencing, timelines—to ensure the optimum use of his time aloft. But no plan, as von Clausewitz famously said, survives contact with the enemy. Not that OMC was an enemy in any overt sense. As subcontractor to the LEO Consortium, they sold onboard services to all comers. But nothing in the book said they had to bust their hump when the customer was VHI; and so, few indeed were the humps busted.

Hobie hit his first speed bump after he harvested the slug of hobartium V that had grown in his absence. To verify its properties, he needed use of the met lab, but Blackhall, the sharp-faced plant engineer with the north-of-England accent and the perpetually bland expression, pleaded that the labs were already overburdened and no time could be spared. When Hobie pointed out that his contract had requisitioned those resources two months ago, Blackhall answered that the situation had changed.

You shouldn't accept a contract you don't have the mojo to fill. Hobie didn't voice the thought. He had seen enough activity since arrival to convince himself that Leo was pressing hard against capacity; but that could easily mask foot-dragging where VHI was concerned. At Argonaut, Hobie had heard all the stories about Klon-Am. He wasn't sure how true they were. Believe everything, and you had to hold Bullock responsible for the slave trade, the Spanish Inquisition, and the birth of disco.

Things went faster when he bent the rules. Hobie stopped trying to book facilities through Blackhall and simply went piggyback with other users. Few of them minded sharing time with him, especially in the small hours. They usually didn't need the same instrument at the same time; it gave them someone to chat with; and maybe they, too, resented OMC's heavy hand.

Williams, the Matthias-Selene metallurgist on graveyard shift, was a balding, gnomish man with a short, wide face, a ferocious white moustache, and a Brooklyn accent thicker than an egg cream. He gave Hobie free run of the facilities. Located near the top of Red spoke, the met lab boasted only one-seventh-g, so equipment was installed in two tiers, with retractable stirrups and bicycle seats for the second tier. Williams would, despite his age, leap from "ground floor" to "mezzanine" with the grace of a mountain goat.

Matthias-Selene was housed in one of the standalone tanks co-orbiting with Leo Station. The "suborbs," otters called them. They used solar mirros to melt ore and magnetic molds to shape the material without the distortions caused by gravity. By law, the Leo Consortium had to provide services, such as the metallurgical lab.

"How's your sample working out, *paisan'*?" Williams asked.

"Not too good," Hobie admitted, pointing to the blow-up on the electron microscope's pixcreen. "Microfractures." At this magnification, the cracks looked like the Grand Canyon, and might as well have been. This compound would never draw wire.

And it damn well should have! Hobie had drawn good wire from the previous slug; wire that had performed well in the Bathurst Island tests. According to his theory, this compound should have had even better ductility. He had timed this whole trip around that one expectation.

So maybe his theory was wrong and there was a discontinuity in the response surface. Hobie contemplated the possibility. The feeling in his gut was not entirely due to microgravity.

"Too bad," said Williams. "You still want the GC breakdown?"

Hobie glanced at the upload that had appeared on his screen. "Thanks."

"Hey, who loves ya, babe?" Williams bounced up to the Brinell tester and resumed his own work. Hobie turned to the GC spectrum and began marking off the peaks with his light pen. Yttrium . . . Gadolinium . . . But why bother? What did it matter now? Facts trump theory. That was how it went, wasn't it? Maybe he should have stuck with football. Get his face on bubble gum cards.

He stylused the numbers onto his personal cliputer screen. The A/S processed his scrawl and the pocket deeby came back with the phase diagrams. Hobie scowled at the result, rotated the display, projected it onto a different set of axes, and scowled some more. The alloy was on the wrong side of the predicted bifurcation plane.

He wiped and re-entered the data, using the keyboard this time. Small buttons beneath thick, clumsy fingers, but he proofread each datum before confirming. The screen blinked at him and redrew the phase diagrams.

No change.

It was hard to visualize a three-dimensional space over a six-dimensional manifold; but in simple, 2-D terms, his slug was living on the wrong side of the tracks.

When he compared the raw material proportions from the spectrum against the specifications, he saw that the actuals were all on the low side. He said a bad word under his breath. No wonder the stuff had been too brittle! It wasn't hobartium V at all, but a compound he hadn't even considered workable. He grinned in satisfaction. Just goes to show. When the facts seem to trump a well-confirmed theory, sometimes the thing to do was get more facts.

So the slug was a bogie. A defective. Damn bad luck with the proportions, but you couldn't expect precision when it came to metering slurries. Mechanical parts had too much play. He called up the equipment capability studies from the station deeby and scrolled down until he found *Pumps, metering, slurry applications* and . . .

. . . The measured proportions fell outside the natural process variation.

Hobie frowned. Not bad luck, then, but a malfunction. Maybe the slurries hadn't had the right viscosity. Or the flow rates had been improperly targeted. Or the lines had gotten plugged. Hobie jotted a few notes to himself in the corner of the printout. What sort of caretending had his equipment been getting? Based on his treatment since arrival, the answer had to be, not too freaking much.

Hobie slammed his stylus on the writing table and it bounced and floated in the air. Curious, Williams glanced down from his perch on the mezzanine. "You okay, *paisan'*?"

"Yeah," Hobie said. "Just great." Foot-dragging was one thing; but this bordered on sabotage. He rocked back in his saddle, leaned against the inspection station's back support, and contemplated the brightly painted bulkhead.

He'd have to grow another slug—this time with the correct proportions, and he'd damn well oversee the mixing himself! He snatched the stylus fom the air before it had fallen more than a few inches. But that meant extending his stay, and maybe pissing Charli off more than she already was. Her smile when he had left . . . LOX wouldn't have sublimated in its warmth. Yet, if he didn't grow another slug, his whole visit was a waste of time.

Hobie scanned the printout Williams had given him. Funny how all the errors were on the short side. Like flipping six coins and getting six tails. Possible, but only one chance in sixty-four. He scowled over the frequency distribution with growing anger. Could the OMC station personnel have short-filled the hoppers on him? Sometimes people were careless, especially with someone else's experiment. He crumpled the hardcopy in his fists, which earned him another glance from Williams.

Desh had asked him to check on other VHI experiments and production units while he was here. *Just a courtesy, as long as you're making the trip.* Now Hobie wondered if that might have been the whole reason for the trip. Did Desh think the OMC techs were neglecting VHI installations? Then why not say so up front? That was one of the things about A. V. Deshpande that irritated Hobie. The man doled out information like it was praesodynium, and held his objectives too close to his chest. Adam hadn't been like that.

Well, *maybe* Adam hadn't been like that.

Hobie sighed and gathered his things. If Desh wanted things checked out, Hobie would check things out. But there had to be a couple hundred experiments and manufacturing plants in LEO, ranging from steamer trunk size to most of a module bay, and a lot of them required some tending by OMC's mission specialists. Feed in the materials, remove the product, repair the equipment. Now and then, someone goofed and didn't follow procedures. The smart money was on stupidity, not maliciousness.

One of the great things about spin gravity, Hobie had long ago decided, was that you didn't have to suck baby bottles when you were thirsty. The lounge on Green-13 ran about one-third Earth-normal, so you could actually pour a cup of juice and drink it like a normal person. You just had to be a little careful pouring. The Coriolis effect gave the liquid stream a slight curve, so you had to hold the cup a little to the side.

Hobie was kicking in the lounge when Chase Coughlin showed up in the doorway. "Well, well, well," said Chase. "If it isn't the Master of Cool, himself."

Hobie covered his face with his hand. "Pilots got so much free time they surf obscure websites?"

"Hey," said Chase, taking a chair, "could be worse." Thin and gangly, the pilot wore his hair in a defiantly old-fashioned punk cut. A conservative at heart, Hobie decided, studying the other's hatchet face, the shaved sides, the ear studs . . . Chase had favored that style when he was still the class hood back at dear old Witherspoon High. Now, he wore red Pegasus coveralls with four bands on the sleeves.

Hobie shook his head. "How could it be worse?"

"It's retro rap, right? So you're cool. But what did *we* say back in the Naughty Oughts? 'Phat stoopid,' right? You could a been Phat Hobie, the Master of Stoopid."

"Doesn't have the right ring to it," Hobie agreed. "What do the kids say these days?"

"Street," said Chase. "As in 'mainstreet,' which I guess is supposed to be hip, or reliable, or something. Or they say 'bone,' when something's real good."

"Hobie, the King of the Street . . ." Hobie tried out the sound of it.

"Hobie, the Big Boner," suggested Chase.

"Give it up," Hobie said. "What brings you slumming?"

"Just back from the Moon with *LTV Alan Shepard* and a shitload of moon-rock gas."

"Helium-3," Hobie supplied helpfully.

"Whatever . . . Now I got a two day turnaround for maintenance while they load up some potassium flouride invoiced to Selene Industries."

"Why you taking KF to the moon?"

"Dam'f I know. I'm just the pilot. I suppose they got a use for it." He slumped in his seat, sighed, and ran a hand through his hair. "No fun landing on the Moon these days. Not like when Ned and me snuck over back in nine. They got a regular landing field now, and a Space Traffic Control tower and everything. Might as well be flying to Buffalo."

"Oh, *man!*" Hobie looked carefully at his friend. "No gray hair . . . But you must be gettin' *old*, you moaning about the good old days like that."

Chase laughed. "No flubber, charlie." He rose and went to the dispensers, returning with a can of near-beer. Somehow, even in one-third gee, he managed to slack. Chase frowned at the label as he resumed his seat. "Zero proof," he read.

"I guess," Hobie told him, "that means the taste is just a hypothesis."

Chase snorted. "Hey. Whaddaya think, Hobe? Anybody set up a still in this joint yet to goose the juice?" He popped the can. "They say Wheezer Hottle-meyer opened one of these in ziggy and he shot all the way to the west-end docks."

Hobie grunted. "I don't think there is any such person. I think you made him up."

Chase looked innocent. "Hey, if Wheezer didn't do these things, who would?" He took a drink, and scowled as he set it down. "I'm not cut out to be a truck driver, Hobe," he announced. "Flying damned lunar transfer vessels like some damned FedEx droid. Carting moon gas or KF or grabbing pods of PV cells the Luna catapult pops up to L1. Know what I'd like to fly?"

"No, what?"

Chase's voice grew wistful. "Something no one's ever flown before. Some-thing that doesn't have any damned manuals; something where you don't know where the edges are."

Hobie considered his friend for a moment, reading the frustration around his eyes, in the set of his jaw. Yeah, where could Chase go where Ned DuBois's footprint wasn't already there? "Tell you what, my man," he said with a mag-nanimous wave of his fruit punch. "If I ever invent a new kind of spaceship, you'll be the first to fly it."

Chase snorted, and Hobie hid a smile.

"Hey," said Chase. "You'll never guess who I ran into . . . Meat. Remember him? I lifted him and Flaco to Goddard City a couple weeks ago on the *Ruth Law*. That ol' headbanger *still* wears his freakin' pony." Chase shook his head. Hobie studied his friend's punk cut but said nothing.

"How's ol' Flaco these days?"

Chase shrugged. "Guy's a grind. But what can you say about someone whose big dream is to move to New Jersey? He and Serafina popped another kid," Chase went on. "A girl, this time. Cute, I gotta admit, but cute don't cut it when you've got it to do. Hey! I ever show you my little hell-raiser . . . ?"

Hobie glanced at the pixure Chase retrieved from his pocket and agreed that the kid did have a look in his eye that said he had just raised a little hell—or was about to. "You're right about one thing," he said, handing it back. "Poor kid looks too much like you to qualify for cute."

Chase tucked the pixure away. Next to his heart, Hobie noticed. But Chase gazed at it for a moment before he did; and who could ever have predicted such tender looks from the punk who used to beat up on Jimmy Poole? He looked at Hobie. "How 'bout you and Charli? You—?"

"No."

A flat answer that cut off all discussion. And was that pity in Chase's eye? The hell with him, if it was. It was none of his business anyway. Hobie's fist gripped his cup hard so that his knuckles paled against the dark skin. He had always dreamed that one day he would play the same role in his son's life that

Big Mike had played in his, but the few times he had raised the topic, Charli had avoided an answer; and her silence, repeated often enough, had become an answer: There would be no children. The blood of Big Mike Hobart would end with him.

"Meat told me," Chase said, "that he put in for Maintenance here on LEO, but the skinny was that O & P guys have zero chance of bidding in now that OMC wear the big hats. The Pegasus rep on the sceening committee imitated a clam, and the job went to a Bullock droid. Meat was pissed. Blamed me for it, too." The near-beer gurgled down Chase's throat. "Ah, that would taste good, if it had any taste."

"Why'd he blame you?" Hobie asked.

Chase waved the can. "Who knows? Because I work for 'the old gray mare,' I guess." His hand slapped the flying stallion logo on his red jumpsuit. "But am I Dolores Pitchlynn? No. I'm too damn young and too damn pretty. And I don't move in Madame President's exalted circles, thank you very much. Maybe Bullock has Pegasus cowed, so Old Lady Pitchlynn—What's so funny, Hobe?"

" 'Bullock has Pegasus cowed.' "

Chase scratched his head. "Okay, I guess we all got to laugh at something . . ."

"I feel Meat's pain," Hobie said. "I'm not getting much joy from the OMC folks here on Leo. 'Sure thing, Dr. Hobart. Right away.' And then I wait forever to get any action. I'm supposed to inspect the other VHI installations while I'm here. So I asked Blackhall for a list and you would have thought I asked him for the liver of his firstborn. How long does it take to print out a freaking list of facilities and locations?"

Chase scratched himself. "Life's a bitch. Be a lot better if everyone was the Jenuine Bean, like you'n me."

A white man dressed in an unfamiliar sea-green jumpsuit emerged from the stairwell behind Chase. Tall, with a long nose and a faint scar on his right cheek, his hair a little long for ziggy. He stiffened on noticing Hobie, then turned abruptly and left the lounge.

Hobie had seen enough reactions like that over the years. He was convinced that the percentage of such people had been dropping, but a smaller percentage of a larger population could still mean a lot of assholes. It was the other man's problem, not his. Still, he could not help asking Chase, "Who was that? Tall, white dude in sea green. You know him?"

"Sea green? Some outfit called Baleen. Guy's named David Desherite, I think. Choo-choo Honnycott brought him up yesterday on the Orville Wright."

Hobie knew no one by that name. Yet, he could not shake the odd conviction that he knew the man from somewhere, and that, under some other circumstance, he would have recognized him immediately.

*   *   *

In his dreams Hobie wandered through a stripped and deserted station. He swam from bay to bay, clambered up and down the spokes. He called out, but heard only distant echoes of his voice and the thudding clang of locks closing somewhere far off.

He ducked through a manlock and on the other side it was his home in Houston, equally bare and deserted. Empty closets and barren dresser tops and a sense of long abandonment. He hollered for Charli and was answered by the sound of a car's engine starting. He floated to the window and pulled the drapes aside, but there was nothing in the driveway and the cul-de-sac was empty. As he stood there, his own heart as hollow and abandoned as his surroundings, night fell and the scene outside darkened. Houselights and streetlamps slowly changed to stars and he was back aboard Leo, gazing through the starward porthole in Hub-5.

Never did care for that girl, Big Mike's voice said.

Hobie turned, but there was no one there in the empty bay. *Dad?* he called. And the echo came back, faint and distant, like the voice of an unseen child: *Dad?*

Hobie's work was refuge from such dreams. Monitoring the Jahn-Teller distortions in his growing slug, electron-doping the Cu^{++} cuprates, sampling and testing the slurries and feed rates, and *no one* touched the equipment but him. It was meticulous and painstaking and while he was absorbed in the task, no other thoughts could intrude.

Every now and then, Hobie would notice the Baleen man, and each time the man would turn away. Once in the cafeteria, Desherite put his back to Hobie. Another time, in the Gold-15 recreation room the man abandoned the stationary bike, threw his towel over his head, and scurried out of the room.

It began to get on Hobie's nerves.

The final speedbump was a killer, and Rock Shary broke the news personally. He even brought Hobie down Gold spoke to the manager's office on Gold-8, as if to say it was impersonal authority speaking and not the Rock himself. Rock didn't seem especially happy.

His office was more of a cubicle, and he couldn't even call it his own. Not only did he share it with a dozen or more teepers, who lurked in various deebies and equipments, but also with his plant engineer, Bob Blackhall. "You see how it is?" Rock asked in frustration. "Even I have to double up."

The office was a circular room eight meters across and three deep. If you left out the stairwell opening; that was one hundred thirty-five cubic meters of office space at just under 0.2 gee. Roomy enough, until you added desks, equipment, lighting, and Bob Blackhall. Two of OMC's senior mission specialists hung their hats there, too; though they were usually out babysitting tenant equipment. Still, Hobie couldn't feel *too* sorry for Rock. Hobie's first lift had been on a Mark II Plank out of Fernando de Noronha, on what had been for all practical purposes a test flight; and his "office" had been in the Kristal module on Old Mir, where "roomy" meant you breathed in when the others breathed out.

"I don't get it, Rock" Hobie said. "All I need is the station shuttle to plant my parasols. Once they're activated they'll climb to GEO on their own and I teep them so they hold station in the solar wind."

"It's the goddam legal questions," Shary told him.

"Which could have been mentioned way back when the contracts were signed."

"Maybe the contracts people didn't know what it meant. Nobody tells me. What happens if your parasols collide with other satellites while they're climbing? If we help you hang them out, the Consortium might be liable."

"That's bullshit, and you know it, Rock. A few perigee kicks at north magnetic and my toys will be out of everyone's way."

Shary bit his lip. "But until then . . ."

"I thought we were friends, Rock."

Shary dropped his eyes. "We are friends." He clapped Hobie on the bicep. "Goddam Blackhall has the toughest job up here," Shary said, gazing down the stairwell with an inscrutable look on his face. "You saw what a jigsaw puzzles we have. Production quotas for Klon-Am facilities. Babysitting tenants. Experimental packages for the goddam academics. *Plus* keeping the air fresh and the water clean. Blackhall's under a lot of pressure. There's not enough goddam room for what we have on board." Rock gave Hobie a searching look. "You understand? Not enough room. So Matthias-Selene and the others, they set up their own tanks outside. Motorola even broke their goddam lease to move out. We have some of the mission specialists double-bunking just to free up another couple floors and it's still not enough. We can't squeeze any more out of Hub-1 and Hub-5 without losing goddam warehouse space for vital supplies and—" Shary ran out of steam. "Goddamn." For the first time, Rock's verbal tick sounded like a genuine curse. The plant manager looked so dejected that Hobie wanted to wrap his arm around his shoulder and tell him everything would be all right.

Still, the new slug was harvested; the wire drawn. It needed only the assembly of loop to frame and the parasols would be ready for emplacement. Hobie had too put much personal sweat into the project and had risked too much at home to let any obstacle, even lawyers, stand in his way.

Climbing down to the lounge afterward, Hobie discovered Chase Coughlin bumping heads with some of the technicians. When they saw him, Williams, the Matthias-Selene metallurgist, began a rhythmic drumming on the table, and Chase, doing a credible moonwalk, chanted:

"Hobie Hobart, the Master of Cool!
Hobie Hobart! He nobody's fool!"

Olya Tsvetnikova, electrical maintenance, kept up a background: "So cool . . . So cool . . . Ooh, ooooh, so cool . . ."

Hobie grunted and plopped into another seat at the table. "Don't quit your day jobs."

An OMC man running a game on one of the nearby terminals turned and gave them all a stare. Williams held out an arm to him, an expansive gesture, as if he were about to embrace the fellow across the room. "My man!" he said. "Jay, *paisan'*, come join us." But Jay turned his back and concentrated on his game. "Look at him," Williams said admiringly. "He's *good*. Never saw anyone blow away so many bad guys. Never. Watch out around that corner! Ooh." Williams winced, then faced the group once more.

"You back already?" Hobie asked Chase.

"Just finished a 'round about'," Chase told him. "Goddard to Tsiolkovsky to Sky Dragon to SpaceLab to Europa. Mostly tugboating ram pods full of air and food and crap. I even had a layover at FreeFall SkyResort this time. Then, it's back to the Moon and I get my layover dirtside. That'll make Karen happy."

"Why?" said Olya. "Does your space travel worry her?"

"Nah. She just has this long list of chores waiting. Now I gotta cool my heels a couple days. A pod of Earthside nitrogen got delayed because of maintenance problems at the Antinsana Ram and everyone has to wait for the next launch window to roll around. Some genius got the bright idea to load the stuff on a ballistic ship and kick it over to Jo-burg, so they could lift it on *Valeri Chkalov*. So now me and the station help have to muck around with individual containers instead of just snatching a whole ram pod on the fly." A thoughtful look and a swallow of near-beer. "And it'll be just as bad at the other end, now I think of it. The *Shepard* can't actually *land* anywhere, so I gotta slip into the moon's 'roadstead' and offload into the *Hebe* G. and the other lighters." He shook his head. "I think there's someone, they pay him good money and he sits around all day thinking of ways to make my life harder."

Hobie saluted him with his fruit punch. "Must be the same guy handles my life."

Chase laughed. "Word up, my man."

Olya spoke up. "Khobie is being finished with parasols; but now Blackhall does not let him launch them." Olya always pronounced H with an aspiration, an accent Hobie found charming.

"A case of lawyer's feet," Williams explained. "What you need, *paisan'*," he told Hobie, "is an orbit where there's *nothing* to bump into your doohickeys."

"That's it!" said Chase.

"I think risk is just excuse," said Olya. Then, "What is 'it'?"

"Empty space," said Chase.

"Well," said Hobie. "Yes, it is. Mostly."

"Where is space empty? I mean *really* empty?"

"Is this a riddle?" asked Hobie.

"Past GEO, in cisLunar!"

"Of course!" Olya smacked her forehead. "Chase, you are genius!"

"Someone *will* let me in on this, right?" Hobie looked from one to the other.

"No, it's easy," Chase said, laying his cup on the table and leaning forward. "I'll take the parasols with me when I torch for the Moon and drop them off along the way."

"I don't know," said Hobie. "I'll have to reconfigure the built-in A/Ss and . . ."

"Fine. Come along and make the adjustments en route and we can drop them off on the way back."

Hobie ran his knuckles through his sandpaper hair. "I feel really stupid."

"We all feel that way now'n then," Chase admitted. "Some of us get more practice, is all."

"Do the rules allow you to take hitchhikers?"

Chase looked blank. "Rules? Me, if I'd operated by the rulebook, why . . ." And his eyes took on a thoughtful, distant gaze. ". . . I'd never have seen the Moon when the Moon was all there was to see."

Hobie expected more obstruction; so he was surprised when Rock not only offered no objection to the Moon trip, but even dropped a great deal of unsolicited help in Hobie's lap. Facilities that had been booked solid suddenly had free time. Technicians who had been too busy dropped what they were doing and gave a hand. Almost, it was too much help and Hobie nearly asked them to back off; but the parasols were quickly reprogrammed and validated on computer sims. The machine shop fabbed a spring-loaded launcher and timers to open the parasols once they were clear of the ship.

Perhaps the earlier obstruction hadn't been deliberate, after all, but only the hassled response of people already overloaded with their own tasks. Whatever the reason, Hobie's equipment was loaded courteously aboard *Shepard* just before *Chkalov* brought up the last of Chase's cargo.

"There she is." Chase pointed through the viewport in the Hub's cargo bay. "*LTV Alan Shepard.*"

Hobie had never seen a lunar transfer vessel up close, but he recognized the ungainly assemblage immediately. The linked pressure vessels, tubes, struts, translucent aerogel space-junk "bumpers," and other not-quite-random bits and pieces were arranged like a cube hammered together from scrapyard pieces.

Chase nudged Hobie with his elbow. "Here comes my copilot for the run, fresh off the *Chkalov*. Cadet training," he explained. "One of the thrills of holding a master's certificate is you get to watch bunnies screw with the controls. Hey, you! Sulbertson. Over here!"

Hobie saw a young man in the powder blue of the Space Academy hovering near the west end manlock. A brother, almost as dark as Hobie, but slender where Hobie was solid. Chase made the introductions. "I can hardly believe it," the lad said. "I'm going to the Moon."

Hobie could hardly believe it himself, though he maintained his cool. Going to the Moon excited him almost as much as the pending experiment. Chase could complain about the routine, but Big Mike's boy had never been farther from home than LEO, which was, after all, only three hundred miles away.

Granted, that was three hundred miles straight up . . .

The Moon was at once familiar and exotic. Hobie gazed from orbit at features and terrain that had once required heroism even to glimpse. The flat, dust-filled plains of the Sea of Tranquillity and the Ocean of Storms. The rugged uplands of Fra Mauro and the Taurus-Littrow Valley. The footprints of *Eagle* and *Falcon* and *Orion* and *Antares*. And later, during the Second Wave, of *Artemis I* and *Enterprise*. There, Artemis Mines snuggled into the regolith of the Smythe Sea, its plasma separation towers, magnetic catapult, and buried living quarters giving no sign of those first desperate days. And there, in Riccioli, Ned DuBois and Chase himself had landed an SSTO with barely enough fuel to lift off again. How dare Hobie, a mere sightseer, follow in their orbits?

The Backside was half in daylight and Hobie was startled at its very different face. No vast open *maria*, only a churned and pockmarked hemisphere of rock. *Like the front side of a shield*, he thought. And the comparison was apt. Everything that had struck Farside had been headed for Earth.

A flock of "lunar lighters" rose from Artemis and Selene, and Chase and his cadet copilot suited up and off-loaded deliveries while Hobie made his final readiness cheeks on the parasols. Halfway through the loading, the storm warning went off and Hobie took refuge in *Shepard*'s shielded center capsule, where he and Chase and Lonzo spent the next two hours becoming very friendly. When the flare surge was past, Chase checked everyone's dosimeter and taught Lonzo how to run the checklist for equipment damage from the high energy particles.

"All these storms do on Earth," Chase told the cadet, "is make honking big auroras and some static on long-range broadcasts. Even in LEO, below the Van Allens, you're not too bad off. But on the Moon or in a ship in cisLunar space, you'd best be careful. Wheezer Hottlemeyer thought he could ride one out in his spacesuit, and now he has a tan two inches deep."

Hobie suppressed a snicker over the ubiquitous Hottlemeyer. "Too bad I didn't run a superloop around the ship," he said.

Chase looked at him. "How come?"

"Create an artificial magfield. Deflect the particles."

Chase continued to look at him.

Hobie squirmed and dropped his eyes. "Well, how w-was I to know there'd be a storm this trip? They d-don't happen all that often."

"I'll tell Wheezer that, next time I see him."

"Oh, c-come off it, Chase. I just d-didn't think of that application." God-damn, he hated it when he stuttered. He had spent years breaking himself of that habit; but stress and embarrassment could bring it back in a moment.

"We're coming off a solar minimum," Chase said, "so, yeah, the big storms are rare for now. But the cycle is swinging up to a peak in '21, '22, so they won't do anything but get more common from here on out. Be real nice if we had something we could retrofit before then. Isn't that right, Lonzo?"

The cadet looked embarrassed at being caught between two old friends; but, what the hey, he'd be working out in the hail, so he nodded and said quietly, "Sounds good to me."

Hell, it sounded good to Hobie, too. A.V. would probably roll his eyes. Shielding the LTVs and the LEO/GEO "scooters" and tugs was certainly an application with more immediate profit potential than the parasol ships Hobie had envisioned.

Sometimes a man could be *too* far-sighted, and miss something right under his nose.

Shahrakh Shary had a gift for Hobie when he finally returned to LEO Station: a list of all the VHI installations and their locations. Hobie thanked him without mentioning the long delay in producing the list, but Rock himself admitted, with a deep and sincere blush, that Blackhall's recent game of mu-sical chairs had resulted in "misplacing" several installations.

"Topologically, we knew where everything was," he said, "but the moves had screwed up the correspondence between dataports and physical locations." Some techs had not completed their work orders. Some moves had been made on Blackhall's verbal OK without documented work orders. There had been data entry errors.

Hobie thought that was a bit slovenly and that an orbital industrial park was not a place where you wanted to lose track of things; but he also had to admit that for a facility this complex, some errors were inevitable.

But now that he had the list, Hobie could carry out the second half of his visit's purpose. His parasols were launched and the sooner he checked the other installations, the sooner he could return to Charli and thaw out the permafrost in her voice.

When Hobie entered Hub 4-D to examine a pharmaceutical experiment for Gaea Biosciences, he found Uncle Waldo parked right in front of it. Wouldn't you know it. Traffic jam. "Hey, Uncle," he said, looking directly into the mobile's optics, "gonna be long? I need to access a unit." He waited for the inevitable lag while the signal dropped Earthward and the reply bounced back.

Nothing. Hobie waited a little longer. Still nothing. Hobie felt the heat in his cheeks and set his teeth together. Damn it, was he some sort of pariah that no one would talk to him? "Hey . . ." He waved his hand in front of the optic, held it there to block the view.

One potato, two potato . . .

No complaint on the bounceback. Losing patience, Hobie shoved the module gently and it floated slowly down the length of the bay. Must be a derelict. Damned teepers, they left their dead bodies floating all over when they cut the connection. No manners. Hobie turned.

And the Baleen man was across the bay staring at him.

No, not at him; at the mobile now bobbing against the ring frame. Desherite's face was creased in thought and his right hand went to his chin, one long finger curled against his cheek.

That gesture!

Desherite turned and must have noticed Hobie's eyes grow round in recognition, because he spared a glance at his escort—Blackhall was talking on his cell phone and had his back turned to both of them—and made a small gesture with his hand. *Keep quiet.*

Hobie was too stunned to react. The tank was just over eight meters wide, but much of the internal volume was taken up by Blackhall's "Chinese jigsaw," so he and Desherite were only a few feet apart. The eyes were the wrong color; so was the hair, and the styling gave his head a subtly different shape. The scar on the cheek was a distraction. But now that he knew, Hobie could see the face behind the face. No question. It was Adam van Huyten.

No wonder he'd been avoiding Hobie! He didn't want anyone from VHI to know that he was still hand-in-glove with Klon-Am. A tremendous sadness overwhelmed Hobie. He had never wanted to believe the rumors. He opened his mouth to say something, he wasn't sure what. Something bitter; something about trust. But in that moment of hesitation, of searching for the right word, of feeling his throat tighten into a stammer, he closed his mouth. And a look of relief crossed Adam's face.

Of course, Hobie thought. *It's Blackhall he doesn't want to know.*

And that meant . . . what? That thieves fell out? Or that Adam was playing a different sort of game? Why had he come up in disguise? And how had he fooled the Facemaker at the spaceport boarding gate? That was supposed to be impossible. The bond Cerberus Security had posted remained uncollected after half a decade.

Too many questions. Confused, Hobie said nothing. Better to wait and see. If Adam couldn't be entirely trusted, he was still a man that Hobie had liked and admired for a number of years.

Blackhall folded his cell phone and turned piercing dark eyes on Hobie. "Naughty, naughty, you handsome devil," he drawled. "You oughtn't go shoving our equipment about like that, Dr. Hobart." Blackhall had a bland face and his lips pursed out as if perpetually amused. He spoke with a peculiar blend of mocking humor and self-deprecation. In a way, he was complement to the manic Rock Shary. "I've summoned our maintenance folk and they should be here shortly." He glanced at the derelict waldo and shook his head. "Blasted nuisance," Hobie heard him say.

Hobie had spent the next day doping a new slurry for what he hoped would be hobartium VI. He was proceeding across the response surface in incremental steps, a procedure known as evolutionary operations, or EVOP. It was not difficult work—a lab tech could have carried it out, once Hobie had set the desired parameters—but he no longer trusted the OMC techs to run his tests for him. About half the VHI packages he had checked had shown evidence of shortages. The material balances hadn't worked out. On the evidence, someone was skimming materials. He hated to dump that into Rock's lap, but he couldn't let it continue. Who knew how many other tenants were getting the same treatment? Bad enough to screw manufacturers out of materials bought and paid for; even worse to bias the results of scientific experiments.

Adam set a cup of fruit punch on the table in front of Hobie and sank into the seat opposite. "Hello," he said, extending his hand. "My name's David Desherite."

Hobie looked at the hand. Okay. If that was the way Adam wanted to play it . . . Adam had come up incognito for reasons of his own. This Baleen organization he was involved with really was looking for ziggy stere, and for some reason he had felt compelled to inspect the premises personally and anonymously. Whatever the reason for the disguise, Adam would want some assurance from Hobie that the whistle would not be blown. "Leland Hobart," he said, accepting the grip. "Call me Hobie." It didn't involve Hobie, and there was no reason to expect confidences from Adam.

"You don't look very happy," Adam said.

Hobie shrugged but said nothing about the suspected skimming. "Oh, the usual flubber," was all he said. VHI affairs were no longer Adam's business. Unless (though the idea hurt) the skimming *was* Adam's business. How far could he trust Adam? He didn't want to read too much into a name, but whales used baleen to skim krill from the ocean. Was Baleen skimming materials on LEO—unbeknownst even to OMC? That might be why he hadn't wanted Blackhall to know his identity. Hobie did not want to believe that of Adam.

"I'm leaving tomorrow," Adam said. "They tell me you'll be up for a while longer."

"I have some experiments running that I want to see through personally."

"Do you remember that derelict waldo we saw yesterday?"

Adam seemed to be zigzagging all over the conversational map. "Yes," said Hobie slowly, not certain where he was being led or if he wanted to go there.

"Olya Tsvetnikova—Do you know her? She's the—"

"Energia electrician on loan to the Consortium. Yes, I know her."

If Adam thought Hobie was being curt with him, he did not show it. "She told me that she sees waldos acting like that all the time. Then . . ." A snap of the fingers. ". . . they come back to life."

"I've noticed it, too. Teepers trolling deebies would look absent-minded."

Adam grinned. " 'Absent-minded.' I like that. Yes, if a teeper switched channels to check a deeby, the waldo's 'mind' would be absent; but . . ."

"But you don't think that's it?" And why would the waldos interest Adam? What was going on here?

"I don't know what it is," Adam confessed, with a gesture of frustration. "Olya said that Blackhall never called on her for repairs until yesterday. So was yesterday's unit more than just 'absent-mindedness'? Olya couldn't find a malf when she ran the diagnostics."

"Maybe Blackhall thought I damaged it when I shoved it out of the way."

"It wasn't that hard a shove." Adam ran a hand through his hair. "I have to leave tomorrow. I was only up here to check out loft rental and there's no reason to extend my visit; but I'd like you to do me a favor."

"Sure." Hobie was appalled at how easily that word slipped out. What was it about Adam that drew people in? He hadn't explained his motives or purpose or even what it was he wanted Hobie to do; and yet Hobie had agreed, just like that. Nevertheless, he felt an anticipatory tingle. Things used to *happen* when Adam was around. "If I can," he added lamely.

"Just keep an eye open for anything unusual."

"Relating to the waldos?"

"Relating to anything. I don't know what I'm looking for, so anything you notice might help. If you do see something you think is odd, call Poole sEcurity. They handle Baleen, and Poole is one of our partners."

"Jimmy Poole?"

Adam raised an eyebrow. "You know him?"

"Not well. We went to high school at the same time."

Adam cupped his chin. His forefinger stroked his cheek. "What can you tell me about him?"

Hobie shrugged. "Anything dealing with computers, 'He the Man,' like they used to say."

"I don't mean that. I mean, can he be trusted?"

And wasn't that a hell of a question to come from Adam van Huyten? Hobie had avoided broaching the subject of trust. He didn't want to fling accusations in case the rumors were just rumors. And if they weren't, he didn't want to know. "About as well as you can trust anybody." He skirted as close to an accusation as he cared to come. "I can't swear that everything he does is the Jenuine Bean, but when he puts his name down, he keeps it."

Adam nodded. "Good enough."

One question, at least, had been answered, Hobie thought later, after Adam had dropped Earthside. If Adam had hooked up with Jimmy Poole, there was no longer a mystery how he had fooled the Facemaker at the spaceport. Earned or not, Jimmy had a reputation for free range ethics; so Adam and Jimmy would make the perfect partners.

Though if they were engaged in extracurricular activities, what did that now make Hobie? An accomplice after the fact?

And if so, what were the facts?

Rotation Day came and the *Hubert Latham* docked. Hobie was dropping home.

Would Charli still be waiting for him? She had always stuck it out before; but the thrill of being married to a "real astronaut" wore off real fast in the face of the real thing. Hobie tried to imagine his feelings if Charli walked, and was disturbed to find relief among them.

Among those disembarking from *Latham* was a baldish white man with a ruddy beard who wore the sea green jumpsuit of Baleen, so whatever it was that Adam was up to, he must have decided to go ahead with it.

10.

Cheese and Crackers

Jimmy Poole studied himself in the mirror and he liked what he saw. *You've still got it*, he told the image that smirked back. Adam van Huyten had slipped the Desherite persona aboard LEO; and *that* had taken some pretty phat hacking. Jimmy finished brushing his teeth and spat into the sink. And it didn't hurt that someone as connected as a van Huyten owed him a debt of gratitude.

He tugged his pajama top off and let the bottoms drop to the floor. He turned sideways to the mirror. Definitely thinner, he thought. His skin fell in folds. His belly hung out like a flour sack. He had, for crying out loud, tits. But definitely thinner. A few miles on the stationary bike tonight; a few regattas on the rowing machine. But he never pushed it more than what his doctor told him. When it came to hardware, Jimmy always deferred to the experts.

A motion in the bedroom caught his eye. Tani had rolled over in her sleep. Unbound hair spread like a black fan across the silk pillowcase. Breasts rose and fell, dark nipples against the smooth tan of her skin. No blemish, as Jimmy knew from personal and painstaking exploration. Little Stevie had stretched her belly and it no longer lay flat; but then Tani had never had the sort of hard model's body that men were told to covet. It had always been soft and pleasant to lie against—like a pillow. Jimmy's eyes finally reached her secret place, half hidden by a fold of the sheet, where a small, dark fan echoed the spread of her hair upon the pillow. The saffron of the silk sheets was picked up somehow in the coloring of her skin, so that she seemed a dusky gold.

They had been living together for seven years, married for four. It was good to know that the sight of her still caught him short. Sometimes, when he remembered what a fumbling fool he had been that first night together, he was astonished to find her still in his bed.

He had, of course, come to attention. He couldn't help himself.

And Tani, that little tease, had a smile on her face.

Still asleep, my ass.

Jimmy returned to the bed and lay down beside her. The sheets were cool and smooth against his bare skin. Tani kept her eyes closed, but the smile was broader. Gently, he placed his hand between her legs, the way she had taught him. Tani tilted her head back and opened her eyes.

"What? No good-morning kiss?"

So he kissed her.

"Not *there*, silly . . ."

So he kissed her again.

They wrapped arms around each other, and her flesh felt feverish after the cool silk of the bed sheets. Her tongue found his mouth and forced its way in, urgent, probing and caressing. After that, for a time, rational thought ceased.

Jimmy felt the glow for the rest of the day—a contentment deep in his belly like the warmth from a smoldering hearth. His skin tingled with remembered touches, his mouth with the memory of kisses. The two of them entering each other, *becoming* each other. There was a yearning he felt when her presence occupied his thoughts—the sense that he was, in some way, incomplete when he was not joined to her; that he was only half a person.

The computer beeped at him, and he realized abruptly that his mind had wandered. He hit reset and the video started from the beginning. It was on days like this, when the smell of Tani lingered with him, that he felt the ultimate meaninglessness of his work. None of it was real, none of it mattered. Only touching mattered. Touching and ****ing Having relations, he meant. Monosyllables could never express what he and Tani did together.

If he never took on another client, he and Tani could live comfortably for the rest of their days. Walking-around money would never be a problem. He had assets squirreled away in places that even the squirrels had forgotten about.

Maybe that would be best. Wash his hands of everything and walk away. Forget Adam van Huyten and his plans within plans.

"Do you have a few minutes, Jimmy?"

Tani had entered his sanctum. She wore an open, suede vest over a low-cut, partly unbuttoned blouse and a short skirt that did little to cover her soft thighs. *Down, boy*, Jimmy told the eager and perky part of him. *Stand at ease, soldier*. Tani had her author's journal with her so—unless she had taken to writing erotica—her intentions must be professional. She kept the journal in a locked drawer in her office. Jimmy had never dared read it.

"A few minutes? Sure." Jimmy put his screen to sleep and spun his "star cruiser command chair" to face her. "Go ahead."

"Am I interrupting something important?" There was no second chair in Jimmy's sanctum, so she had wheeled her own high-back swivel from her office.

"Nothing is more important than you," he said, and he tingled to see her flush at the compliment. Next to being inside her, nothing pleased him more than pleasing her. "I was just reviewing a stack of RFPs. Decide which ones are interesting enough to handle personally and which to pass along to my subcontractors."

"What can you tell me about the Five Fingers?"

Jimmy went bland. "The who?"

"Don't play coy, Jimmy. I've seen stuff on the net. Passing comments. Like everyone is already supposed to know who they are. I just need some background detail for my novel. 'The illuminating detail.' Like Dunning says: 'Describe the thumb so well that the reader thinks he's seen the entire hand.' "

"The entire hand . . . But you only want to know about the Fingers . . ." He guffawed, wiped a teary eye with his sleeve. "Well . . ." He was reluctant to talk about the wild side, but the glow of Tani's love was still on him; and what the heck, it would make her happy. "They're supposed to be virtchuosos who are, well . . . especially skilled."

"Aren't all virtuosos skilled?"

Jimmy snorted. "No, virt*chuosos," he said, emphasizing the *tch*. "Amateurs surf; virtchuosos troll and dive. Fingering . . . Well, fingering means sticking your finger in to stir things up. Or sticking in your thumb to pull out a plum. Or running your fingers along the keyboard to play an arpeggio. It means . . . Well . . . an ultimate sort of virtchuosity."

"And there are supposed to be five of them?"

He coughed and shrugged. "Not. Everybody has a list; but you don't always find the same names on them. There might be, oh, ten or fifteen who make the cut."

Tani's pencil was flying. Jimmy wondered how she could reach the age of thirty-two and never hear about the Five Fingers. Didn't she have a life?

"Does Billie Whistle make the cut?"

Jimmy started to laugh, but then remembered what he had found lurking in the code of Baleen's operating system. "She's a virtchuoso, no question; maybe better than she thinks she is. But I wouldn't put her in the top five."

"Is this Billie good-looking?"

"She's gorgeous. If you like ladies with shaved scalps and wires running out of their heads . . ."

Tani grimaced. "I can't imagine why anyone would do that. It seems creepy."

"Has to do with dedicated loci in the brain. The sockets help position the interfaces for greater specificity of thought/command pairing. 'Kosher' cheeseheads wear ordinary induction caps and they manage to conduct most routine operations."

" 'Kosher'?"

"The caps look like beanies. You know I could review your draft and see if you've captured things right."

A quick shake of the head. "No critiques until it's done."

"What if I promise not to say anything."

"That's even worse."

Jimmy gave it up. Tani fretted constantly that her second novel would not measure up to her first. *Taj Mahal* had been a hit with critics and public alike; but its very success had become an obsession with her, and she had written and rewritten the new manuscript until she had rubbed the phosphors off her screen, and possibly all meaning from the words. After seven years, her publishers had grown impatient; and the steady stream of short fiction had done nothing to placate them. Yet the longer she took, Jimmy knew, the greater the expectations would grow. So, in a way, her constant polishing and fine-tuning was self-defeating.

"Maybe you should meet Whistle, then," he suggested. "More and more virtchuosi are cheesing it. If you knew what made them tick—" He gave a nod to her journal.

"That's an idea." Tani scribbled something. "I think there was a Tom Whistle two classes ahead of us at Witherspoon. Big basketball player . . . ?"

Jimmy shrugged. He hadn't known anyone back then, least of all an upper-class jock. Jimmy Poole had lived in his own pocket universe, ostracized for his intelligence. He used to have, he remembered, a crush on Styx, but he thought now that going into Roberta Carson would have been like making love to a pencil sharpener. He crossed his legs. "I don't remember."

Tani looked up from her book. "Who would you put on *your* list of Fingers?"

He flapped his arms and leaned back in his command chair. "Me "

Tani made an impatient sound. "I'm serious."

"Hey, I'm not saying I'm in a league by myself; but there aren't too many players who can suit up when I'm in the game." He laughed at a sudden memory. "Except once."

"Once?"

"I went head-to-head with the best." He rocked back and forth in his seat. A grin split his face. It had been a delicious hack altogether.

"And you won, of course."

Jimmy savored the confidence in her voice. "Well, I had to. The fix was in."

"I don't get it."

"If the best went against the best, who would it be?" He waited, and his grin faded a little into impatience at her continued puzzlement. "The best against the best," he repeated. "Jimmy Poole against . . . ?"

He could almost see her puzzle out the answer. ". . . against Jimmy Poole? But . . ." She shook her head. "How . . . ?"

"Do you remember the Skopje Rescue, back in seven?"

"Sure. You were a hero." She reached out and placed a hand on his knee.

Jimmy basked for a moment in the glow of that word, in the reverence he heard in her husky voice, while the sensation of her hand touching him traveled up his leg like imaginary fingers. There was nothing imaginary about the effect.

"Defusing the 'logic bomb' in the rescue ships' collision-avoidance software—"

"In real time," he reminded her. "The flock was already flying. Fractional orbits."

"But how was that the best against—"

"The best. Because who planted the bomb in the first place?"

She hesitated. "No one knows for sure. Some say old Cyrus Attwood was so afraid of the new world that it drove him mad. But nothing was ever proven. Do you mean Attwood . . . ?"

"That evil old fart? Not. But he knew enough to hire the best. He hired Crackman."

"But Crackman is . . ." Her eyes widened. "*You* planted the bomb? And then defused it?"

His grin threatened to tear his cheek muscles. "Aurora hired me to write the security software; then Attwood hired me to sabotage it. The best against the best. So I cut some cheese that would never go off. It needed—I forget—four or five ships in close proximity before it would scramble the collision avoidance system; and none of the traffic projections showed that kind of flight path density for the foreseeable lifetime of the software."

"But . . . At Skopje . . ."

"OK. Attwood had an ace palmed. He knew about the Emergency Response Team the Air Force was putting together and figured sooner or later there'd be a mass convergence of ballistic ships on some trouble spot—a flood, an earthquake, whatever. It just happened to be the UN rescue mission."

"That was . . . evil." Tani shook herself. "I can't think of any other word for it. Evil. To deliberately endanger not only the rescuers, but also the victims. It's hard to realize such people exist."

Jimmy pulled at his lip. "I used to think so, too. But now I think he was just sick." Jimmy being wise and judicious. *Nil nisi bonum.*

"But *you* did what he asked."

Jimmy scowled. "I screwed him. I planted a dud. Not my fault I didn't know about the ERT. If I had, I'd've picked some other way of diddling him."

"You could have refused . . ."

He shook his head. "Then he'd have hired someone else. Someone who would *not* have planted a dud. Someone whose trojan stallion I could *never* have gelded in time. I wouldn't even have known about it to intervene."

"So, you planned all along to . . . Oh, Jimmy!" Tani leaned forward. Wide, brown, doelike eyes engulfed him. "Jimmy, it was an awful chance to take!"

He had planned to forget it. He had hesitated to intervene for fear of exposing himself as Crackman. He had even entertained the notion of letting Fate play out when he learned Chase Coughlin was copiloting one of the rescue ships. He had not, he realized looking back, had the foresight and nobility he now ascribed to himself. He had taken up Attwood's offer for the sheer bravado of fulfilling two, mutually-contradictory contracts. But if Tani wanted to join him in the revised version, he would not shut her out. Reality was far too complicated.

"If they had found out what you did . . . If they misunderstood your motives for helping Attwood, then . . ."

Then S. James Poole would have been clapped into a righteous dungeon where they dribbled in sunlight on weekends and where they'd never—ever— give him net access. He placed his own hand atop hers. Partly to comfort her; partly to keep her hand on his thigh. There was a fierce light in her eye, but Jimmy was not sure if it was anger at the chance he had taken or something else.

"Promise me," Tani said, "that you'll never do anything like that again."

"I haven't . . ."

Her fingers tightened on his thigh. "Jimmy . . . ?" In the low voice that always meant storm flags.

"Sure," he said carefully. "I'll never do anything like that again."

"Good." If she noticed the equivocation, she gave no sign. She rubbed her hand up his leg and Jimmy shivered deliciously. "Now," she said, sitting back and taking on a more businesslike tone. "Tell me about the Fingers."

He wanted to say, they felt wonderful where they touched me, but he sensed the moment had passed. An odd moment, too. While her tongue had chastised, her hand had caressed.

"If you had to make a list of five fingers, who would you put on it?"

Jimmy sought insight from the acoustic tiles on the ceiling. A good question. He'd never given it much thought. A list implied a certain equality of accomplishment, so there never seemed any reason to compile one. "Well, Norris Bosworth, for one—calls himself SuperNerd, which is silly for a guy pushing forty. He works for a think tank called Utopian Research Associates. They do mostly social and economic analyses."

"Utopian Research Associates . . . Wasn't there a big fuss about them when we were kids?"

"Yeah, they had this big, honking deeby and they'd massaged it enough they could make all sorts of socioeconomic projections. Which reminds me of another name. Sarah Beaumont was involved with them. Nobody's heard from her since the nineties; so maybe she's dead and shouldn't be on the list. But she wrote the Beaumont Worm, and that alone puts her in the Hall of Fame. Then . . . Let's see . . ." Once he started thinking about it, several names came to mind. Second string, of course; but that was still damn good when there was only one slot on the varsity.

"Okay. There's a guy, calls himself Captain Cat. A freelancer, works the wild side. We think he's American, but nobody really knows. Then there's Chen Wahsi in Guangzhou. Government droid for the Three Cities, but maybe he runs a personal agenda under the table. There are four personae walking the net whose style resembles Chen's. Maybe one of them is him. Maybe all of them are. We call him Official Chen and Unofficial Chen."

"Should he count as one finger or two?" Tani asked with an impish grin.

"The U.S. government has a droid, too," he went on. "Calls himself Earp . . ."

"Like Wyatt Earp?"

Jimmy nodded. "Patrolling Dodge. Whoever he is, the government doesn't want us to know; but he's supposed to be town marshal of the global village. He roams the virtch, looking for evildoers, fighting for truth, justice, and the government way. Not exactly *creative* work, but very skilled, especially at counterhacking. Then, let's see . . . Pedro the Jouster—"

"Wait. That's six."

"No, it isn't. Beaumont's out of it. Even if she *is* still alive, she'd be pushing fifty, way too old for a good finger. So put Pedro the Jouster in for fifth position. The pinky finger. Like Earp's the middle finger?" Jimmy leaned his head back and laughed. "Middle finger. Oh, that's a good one . . ." He brushed the tears aside. "Pedro is Pete Rodriguez. He's got his own consulting firm down in San Juan and the virtual Plaza. Solid, honest work—or so they say."

"And those are the Five Fingers?"

Jimmy shook his head. "No. Those are five fingers. My personal list. Anyone else—*I'd* be on the list. Finger? Heck, I'm the opposable thumb, itself."

After Tani had gone, Jimmy turned back to his work with renewed confidence. There were five requests-for-proposal waiting in his in-basket. One was from Pegasus Aerospace; another, from DoD. Yeah, the world came to Jimmy Poole because he was the best. Whatever gray work Adam was up to, Jimmy could deal with it and come out clean. Cloning Baleen had been child's play. The facility he had contracted on Goddard would be blowing and doping before Red ever left the ground.

But there was a fly in the cheese. He had found it lurking in Baleen's operating system: a cute little daemon, crafted to enter Leo's system through the internal utility portals and, once there, lurk and learn and, eventually, download.

Very cute. Jimmy hadn't thought Billie capable of such fine work. People were just full of surprises.

But the fly meant that Adam van Huyten had planned to spy on LEO well before Jimmy had coaxed him into bonebagging; and that raised two difficulties. If he was already slicking a *virtual* spy aboard LEO, why had Adam agreed to go up *in corpora*? Simply because he needed Jimmy's troy and bagging had been a condition?

The second difficulty was that the fly was so clearly over on the wild side that, if it ever came to light, the fan would be stained deep umber for years to come. Jimmy was a Baleen, now, a partner. Would he be liable if the hack fooed?

Now there was a chilling thought. Given the choice between Jimmy Poole and Billie Whistle, the authorities would surely credit Jimmy with the authorship of the fly. What if Adam had lured Jimmy into Baleen precisely to set him up as the herbert in case the fly came unzipped?

He began to hum, and called up the first RFP from the cue. Whatever happened, he would handle it.

There was a small, neighborhood park a few blocks from Jimmy's house. It had swings, seesaws, a sandbox, even a jungle gym all padded up with foam around the bars. Jimmy remembered bare steel bars from his own childhood and wondered if kids today were more clumsy and ill-coordinated than in earlier generations. Usually, it was Rada who took Stevie out for walks; but every now and then, when the weather was right, Jimmy did the honors himself.

Right weather, to him, meant foggy or overcast. He loved it when the fog bank rolled over the hills from the coast and engulfed everything in wispy streamers and sound became close and muffled. He didn't dislike sunlight exactly, but he had sensitive skin and burned easily. Maybe his father had been right when he said, If you live like a mushroom, you'll grow into a mushroom.

Jim Poole had possessed the rugged, outdoor manner. Big, thick-armed (and, to the younger Jimmy, thick-headed), his dad had tanned a deep nut-brown, saving only the pale band around his forehead where the hard hat rested. He had tried constantly to pry Jimmy away from the books, the PC, the computer games. Let's play some ball. Let's shoot some hoops. He was an alien from another planet.

Maybe, if he had gone out with his dad more often, Jimmy would have developed tougher skin. Or maybe he would only have fried to a crisp. Certainly, the number of footballs successfully caught could be counted in single digits; and his hoop shots had gone near the basket only by wonderful chance. Watching Stevie in the sandbox from the wooden park bench, Jimmy wondered how he would embarrass the little dude when they were older. From what beloved activity would he drag the kid, saying, Let's cruise the net!

Stevie grabbed small handfulls of sand and tossed them laughing in the air. To what purpose? Exploring the properties of this strange material? Why did children like to play in the sand? Maybe it was true that humans were once tidewater apes, wading in the shallows and resting on the beach, and this was simply some atavistic longing for those languid days on Danakil Island.

He became aware that someone had sat beside him.

"Your housekeeper told me you'd come down here," Adam van Huyten said without preamble.

Jimmy turned and studied his visitor. He rubbed his palms against his pants legs. "What did you find out?" He fought to keep eagerness out of his voice.

An angry shrug. "Nothing!"

Jimmy slumped against the bench. After all that work crafting a persona for "Desherite," he deserved a fuller report than "Nothing." He noticed the tight set to Adam's jaw, the hard look in his eye. "Any problems with the persona?"

Van Huyten shook his head and Jimmy nodded in satisfaction. He hadn't expected any. The suture and guardian angel had been the solid muldoon. Had anything gone wrong, there would have been knocks on his door; or at least, strongly-worded questions. Still, he was just as glad this particular hack was over. It wasn't illegal for Adam to travel under false colors; but the authorities could be just as vague about the law as the perps. They often levied big fines and "settlements" on clearly legal acts, then sat back and dared you to fight it. Most people didn't even try, and such "settlements" had become a source of budget enhancement.

"Shary and Blackhall showed me everything a potential customer could expect to be shown," Adam told him, "but, dammit, I know when I'm being led around with a ring in my nose."

Jimmy wondered if Adam van Huyten might be just as skittish as his cheesehead. After all, he was planning a major hack—using Baleen and LEO and who knew what other pawns—and he must be getting twitchy as all hell about it. Seeing lurkers behind every curtain.

"How about Baleen?"

Adam gave him a quick look, as if just reminded that Jimmy's curiosity about the laager and Billie's unease about OMC management might be two separate issues. "I'm giving the go-ahead. There's no plausible reason for delay, and my partners are losing opportunity costs. But I'm still not comfortable. Until I know what LEO is up to, I don't know how secure Baleen's investment will be."

Not the investment, Jimmy suddenly realized, but the fly. Adam had agreed to bonebag because he was nervous about his fly getting unzipped. Most laagers were a classic crust defense, with all the guards on the input/output boundaries: an Iron Curtain, impossible to break through, but, doggy-fashion, penetrable from behind. LEO's system handled hundreds of tenants: handshakes, inputs, outputs, controls, exchanges. There had to be slipstreams in such a torrent of data, and a well-crafted fly might buzz through portals without attracting attention. But to be useful, a fly eventually had to download what it learned, and the download would have to cross the border. That was the vulnerable point. The guards along the old Iron Curtain had shot down a lot of would-be escapees.

But that was Adam's problem, not his.

Or was it? Adam might have a different agenda, but the whole reason Jimmy had sent him upstairs was to peek behind the curtain. And now Adam had come back empty-handed. (Or said he had, which from Jimmy's point of view was isomorphic.) So what next?

"Thanks for trying," he told Adam. He pushed himself to his feet and went to fetch Stevie, hoisting the kid to his shoulder. Adam followed him.

"Keep digging," Adam told him.

"What, are you running a tab? I asked you to do something for me. You hired me to do something for you. Both somethings are finished. Or was there something else?"

Adam extended a finger to Stevie and Stevie grabbed it and tugged. "Your son?"

"No, I just like to kidnap children from the park."

Adam gave him an icy stare. "Testy, are we?"

Actually, Jimmy had thought it a funny line; but sometimes other people had an odd sense of humor. He sighed. "Sorry," he said. "I'm just disappointed, is all."

"You're part of Baleen, now. If OMC screws us, they screw you. It's not just to satisfy your curiosity."

"It's more than just curiosity," Jimmy told him. "It's professional interest. I'm a security consultant and the LEO Laager is the best I've seen. I don't want to lose clients to whoever the author is, when he finally surfaces."

"So, you want to do a little reverse engineering? Fine. We still have a community of interest. What I want you to do is study the software for Baleen, and maybe have your 'friend' look at it, too."

Jimmy shifted Stevie to the other shoulder. That was as close as Adam would come to admitting there was a fly in the ointment and he wanted Crackman to ensure its survivability. But Jimmy didn't want to go there openly. They began walking toward the corner of the park, where there was a gap in the wood rail fence. "You know," Jimmy said carefully, "if you're worried about Baleen proprietary data getting snooped by OMC as it passed through the laager, you could write to an internal seedy and have Red Hawkins bonebag and fetch it." And *that* was as close as he would come to telling Adam that he had already snooped the system and knew there was something smelly in the cheese.

Adam gave no sign that he heard the subtext. "I'll mention that to Red and Shao. A simple mod to the equipment so only Red can access the internal drive . . ." He rubbed his cheek, then bobbed his head emphatically. "That was a good suggestion."

"You'll get my bill."

Adam started, then laughed. "There'll be a lot of bills coming due. That's my car over there. Need a ride?"

Jimmy shook his head. "My doctor tells me I should walk a mile each day."

Adam aimed his wand at the car, which beeped and started up. He paused with a hand on the latch. "There's something funny about the waldos. On LEO. I don't know what it means, but it was the only odd thing I saw up there. They seem to go dead sometimes and the staff shows no interest in fixing them."

Jimmy shrugged. "Sounds like an out-of-body experience to me."

"That's what Dr. Hobart said. He'll be dropping next month. Talk to him and see if he's learned anything more."

Jimmy kept any expression from showing. Hobie was in on this, too? Jimmie harbored no weenie for "The Doorman." In a school filled with cowards and tormentors, Hobie had been a bystander; and that did not merit a very high position on Jimmy's payback list.

*   *   *

The source of Billie Whistle's unease, when Jimmy finally diagnosed it, was a tremendous letdown. Not only did it have nothing to do with the craftsmanship of the LEO Laager, but was of such insignificance that Jimmy cursed the hours he had squandered viewing and re-viewing the DVD he had made of the visit.

The dejection must have shown in his posture, because Tani asked him about it over dinner that evening.

"I just hate wasting time," he told her. "I don't mind rolling over rocks to see what's underneath; but I do want to see *something* underneath."

The dining table was a little longer and wider than Jimmy found comfortable. He had grown up, as he liked to put it, in a kitchen-table sort of house. Everybody kicking and snacking and arguing around the old Formica. Formal dining rooms struck him as an affectation. All they did was add distance between you and the food; and they injected a note of stifling decorum. Jimmy always felt compelled to speak in complete sentences. *You don't do "rich" very well*, Tani had told him one time. Jimmy had taken it as a compliment and assumed she had meant it as one.

"So what was it?" Stassy had prepared a stroganoff—one way to ensure that Rada shunned the table—and Tani paused with her fork raised halfway. She did not have her notebook at hand. At a formal dining table? Never! But Jimmy assumed that whatever his answer, it would wriggle its way into the plot. Tani was smart enough not to use unalloyed real life in her writing. *Not well-scripted*, she often said with her impish smile. But the heart, the essence, the flavor, would find some use.

"Okay," Jimmy said, "picture this. Billie is telepresent, right? And this dude, Blackhall, is showing her the available sites and quoting prices and sh—stuff." (Formal dining room meant no bad words.) "So, we're in Hub-3, the one they call Rome, heading into Hub-2, where they've got some slots open. Through the lock, in the background, there are these two other waldos, right? So Billie's mobile passes through the lock and there's a moment of interference because of the magnetic bearings and the telecomm handoff to the next cell and, when the picture clears again, the two waldos are gone." Jimmy grinned. Even if it was something of no consequence, finding it out was a tribute to his perception. His grin faded at Tani's evident puzzlement.

"I don't get it," she said.

Jimmy suppressed a sigh. "Maybe you should look at it yourself. It's a subliminal thing. Something in the background changed. Whistle *saw* it, but didn't *notice* it, if you know what I mean, and that bothered her without her knowing why. If she had *seen* them move off, no problemo; but they moved off in that moment when the visuals went gray so her hindbrain was insisting that they had vanished into thin air."

Tani shook her head. "I'm not sure the mind really works that way."

Jimmy turned his lip out. "It's how *my* mind works. I do some of my best thinking when I'm thinking about something else."

A small smile showed her teeth. "You don't ever think about something else." She cut a stalk of broccoli. "So," she said casually, "what now?"

"A direct probe is definitely out," he said. "And van Huyten's end run came up dry. Maybe Hobie will come down with some astonishing evidence, but I won't hold my breath. So, the best bet is to work it was from the other end. Find out *who* built the laager. Get him involved in shop talk and he might let something slip."

But who? Jimmy didn't think his list of Fingers was definitive; but the more he thought about it, no one off the list had the skill. Unless there was a New Kid on the Block . . . But Jimmy thought he would have heard of that. So which of the Five could it be? SuperNerd wasn't into industrial security. Official Chen didn't care about anything outside the Guangdong Republic, and Unofficial Chen didn't care about anything outside of Chen, so the job wouldn't have interested him. Scratch two. The Captain walked the wild side and Leo was legit, so why hire a netwalker? That left Pedro or Earp. Jimmy thought he would ask the Jouster about it, but he didn't have high hopes. The smart money was on Earp. After all, it was the marshal's job to protect good cybercitizens like OMC. Problem was: no one knew Earp's URL.

And Earp liked it that way. Asking around might not be too smart. The government would want to know who wanted to know. And why.

The problem with contacting the Fingers, any of them, was that it meant surfacing Jimmy Poole and calling attention to his interest in Leo's cybersecurity.

So what if Leo was dark? Why should it matter to him? Wounded pride, because he couldn't peek wherever he wanted, whenever he wanted? Professional jealousy? That didn't matter any more. He'd done his thing; he'd made his splash. He could retire.

As for Baleen and their fly . . .

Adam van Huyten was playing some sort of game. Revenge. On who? His father, maybe. He was using Baleen for cover; as a tool. None of them suspected Desherite was anyone but, and other than Billie, did not even suspect there was a second agenda in play. Or, if they did, there was no hint in their private deebies.

Though, if Adam planned to sell Baleen down the river for some reason, Jimmy was on the boat; so it was just as well he had copied the process and sent it up to Goddard. Baleen had a damn fine product idea. It would be a shame to waste it as nothing more than a cover for something else.

These days, you never knew who you could trust.

11.

Common Sense

In the heart of autumn, with golden leaves heavy on the trees, and the rosebushes in the garden stark and barren, Harriet van Huyten, née Gorley, died. There was no parting scene, no last words. One night, she kissed her daughter on the cheek, smiled and closed her eyes in sleep and, when morning came, never again awoke.

For two years, Mariesa had been vaccinating herself against the event with doses of anticipated sorrow. Yet, when the time came at last, she was astonished at how empty was the chasm that suddenly opened in her life. She felt as if a stone wall against which she had butted her head for years had suddenly vanished. Though, to be fair, in the last few years a truce had descended—a sort of armed neutrality—as if mother and daughter had both sensed that the causes were long mooted.

After the funeral, there was a reception at Silverpond, and Mariesa threw herself into the preparations—arranging the flowers, selecting the guests, choosing the menu—until Armando politely told her to butt out so he could do his job. Yet the activity had been like a shield to her, and she retired to her room and threw herself onto her bed and lay thoughtless until the guests arrived.

Originally, she had intended a small, family affair. But Harriet had possessed an extensive social circle, and it would not do to neglect them. The servants, too, including the retirees like Sykes and Laurence and Mrs. Pontavecchio. And because Harriet had remembered them so fondly, she invited many of the men and women who had once visited as children. She even invited Barry.

They didn't all come, of course. Many sent their regrets with their condolences. Flowers arrived, and official notifications of charitable donations in Harriet's memory. The Rose Fanciers Association provided a bouquet arrangement of Harriet's Sterlings, and Mariesa nearly broke when it arrived. Ed Bullock sent a polite, formal note, observing the proprieties and social conventions. There was no hypocrisy to it—even enemies could feel a momentary pang of brotherhood when contemplating the Great Abyss.

Harriet's circle was as old as she was. They sat apart from the other guests, speculating morbidly on who would be next. The other guests were mainly

Mariesa's own circle; but funerals, they said, were for the living, and some people came less out of respect for Harriet than out of empathy for her daughter. Roberta brought Phil, who appeared thoughtful and subdued. Jimmy and Tani Poole brought their young son. Belinda brought memories, and Barry, an air of unfinished business.

And Adam brought a few moments of frosty silence.

"I wondered," Chris said stiffly when he spied his son across the room, "if he'd come."

"Chris," his wife, Marianne, replied. "You're both here. Talk with him."

Chris imitated a stone. His head barely shook. Marianne turned abruptly and walked away. Mariesa watched her go, wondering whether the woman had delivered a plea or an ultimatum. Marianne was deceptive. Retiring by nature in a family that liked to swagger, her quiet was often mistaken for complaisance, if one forgot the reputation of the Godwins for iron resolve.

Mariesa laid a hand on her cousin's arm. "Then, at least remember the time and place," she cautioned him. Chris gave her a sharp look, half angry, and she left him alone with his own misfortunes.

Roberta sat with Mariesa quietly for a time, on a chair against the wall under one of the dour portraits. She said nothing, mouthed no platitudes, nor even mentioned the death of her own mother years before. Only, when Mariesa thought she was strong enough to face her guests once more and started to rise, Roberta reached over and squeezed her hand with the spare eloquence of the poet.

Barry Fast had had the rare good sense not to bring a date. He was older than Mariesa by a few years, but he dyed his hair and had evidently taken hair replacement hormones so that, paradoxically, he looked older still. Mariesa found him talking with cousin Brittany and with Tracy, her old college roommate. He took her hand and said something common and soothing. He always did know the right words and the right gestures. Partly, it was affectation; partly, it was genuine feeling for others. It was the latter that had led him astray years ago. Genuine feelings. The utterly cynical never had a problem focusing on the main chance.

"You and Harriet never got along very well," she reminded him.

"No," he admitted with the sheepish grin that used to charm her, "but I think we reached a mutual respect." Then he told them an anecdote involving him and Harriet and a dinner party that soon had all of them reduced to tears of laughter, earning odd glances from more conventional mourners. And yet, thought Mariesa, this is the best way to remember her. So, she told a story about one of Harriet's countless attempts to attach her to the right man, and Brittany chimed in with a personal recollection of Harriet on hands and knees grubbing in the rose garden.

"I was only ten," she said, "and I thought she was a servant. I sent her on an errand. For a lollipop, I think."

Mariesa chuckled, as much at Brittany's self-revelation as at the picture of Harriet.

"But you know," Brittany added thoughtfully, "she ran that errand promptly and efficiently. I think she enjoyed helping people more than we gave her credit."

Mariesa, who remembered how Harriet had maneuvered her and Barry to the bench on top of Skunktown Mountain, silently agreed. Even when it went against her personal preferences. . . . She noticed Barry's glance out the rear windows and wondered if he was recalling the same sunset, the same hot passion.

Barry had proven, as always, the right medicine. Afterward, Mariesa mingled with the guests more easily and, following Barry's lead, reminded each of some encounter with her mother. As often as not, she heard some new anecdote in return, so that before long her mother seemed more alive than she had at any time during the past two years.

Business associates were rather less inclined to sentimental recollections. Dolores Pitchlynn approached Harriet's age herself. She had officially retired from Pegasus—chairman emeritus—but unofficially still pulled all the strings. An outdoorsman, she had acquired a rugged, weathered look decades ago and so seemed now as ageless as the rocks she climbed. Lately, she had become one of Chris's inner circle of advisors and Mariesa wondered if leaving Pegasus had been no more than the shedding of a chrysalis, effecting her emergence on a higher plane of existence. Mariesa asked her why she did not simply "vejj out" in retirement.

"Why keep climbing?" The older woman gave her a look that Mariesa found hard to fathom. "When climbing is all there's ever been, there comes a time when you can't stop. You've got to go for that next rung because there isn't anything else to do."

Privately, Mariesa pitied the woman. "I've found that I too miss the rough and tumble of running a—" she started to say, but Dolores interrupted.

"Mariesa," she said sharply, "running VHI was never more than a game with you. It was a way for you to chase your private demons. We're better off with Chris at the helm."

Mariesa, who remembered Dolores's enthusiasm for *Steel Rain*, opened her mouth to respond, but, remembering that this was her mother's funeral, kept quiet. Dolores had been with Prometheus from the start. She believed in the Goal. But she also believed in sandbagging her corporate rivals, like João Pessoa of Daedalus. The old woman must have had her first orgasm in many years when João and the Brazilians bought Daedalus out from VHI.

"Mind you," Dolores continued, "Chris was born rich, too. That's why he needs people like me to advise him. You don't know what it's like." She looked across the room and a shadow passed her dark, obsidian eyes. "You don't know what it's like."

Dolores's troubled mood struck a dissonant chord, and Mariesa brought their encounter to a hasty close. Dolores remembered the purpose of the gathering and tossed off a few words of condolence barely in time to avoid being boorish altogether. She had been rather better natured on her arrival, Mariesa recalled, but something had evidently altered her mood.

Belinda Karr hugged Mariesa briefly before sagging gratefully into a stuffed chair. The former Principal Teacher of VHI's Mentor Academies, now rector of independent Karr Academy, had been an athlete in her youth. The stocky build and the aura of strength and confidence were long familiar; the stout cane was not. Belinda reached out and Mariesa accepted the hand. "I don't suppose it's any secret," Belinda said, "that Harriet didn't care for me. But she was your mother and I have some appreciation for how you feel."

"Yes," Mariesa replied, "though I never understood why she took such a dislike to you."

Belinda looked at her, with eyes a little sad and wistful; then she shook her head. "Sometimes, Riesey, you can be remarkably obtuse."

"How are Karr Academies getting on? I'm not sure I should be talking to a competitor of Mentor." She smiled to show she was in jest, but it was a sore subject that Mariesa hesitated to touch. Like João Pessoa, Steve Matthias, and others, Belinda had left VHI in the wake of *Steel Rain* and the Donaldson scandals; but, unlike the Brazilians, she had been unable to take her company with her.

"Well enough," Belinda replied. "Onwuka and I keep in touch. No educator is ever a competitor of another." She spoke lightly, but Mariesa sensed a tincture of resentment. Belinda had *founded* Mentor, long before VHI had bought it and made education a part of the Fifty Year Plan. It had to be hard, letting go of something you had built yourself; and Mariesa did not begrudge Belinda any of the bitterness she might still feel.

"The schools are doing well, I believe."

"Well enough," Belinda answered. "Though it's hard these days to tell the difference between private, charter, and public. Remember how 'controversial' we were in the beginning?"

"In some quarters, 'controversial' was more damning than 'ineffective'."

"Yet, there was not a single aspect of our approach that had not been tried with astonishing success in one school or another, many of them public."

"No more challenges, then?"

Belinda shook her head. "There are always challenges. With each new class.

And even with the old. Onwuka keeps me up to date on the children I helped nurture when I ran Mentor. You know Jenny Ribbon started one of those new sisterhoods, don't you? The silver apples, they call themselves . . ."

" 'The silver apples of the moon,' " Mariesa quoted, " 'The golden apples of the sun.' "

"Yes." Belinda pursed her lips. "I'm not sure I approve of all their precepts, but it is past time that young women banded together for support and kept themselves—"

"Pure and holy?" said Mariesa.

"Kept themselves from being used by boys for masturbation," snapped Belinda. Instantly contrite, she added, "I'm sorry, Riesey. I know you weren't being sarcastic, but . . ." Mariesa laid a hand on her forearm and the other woman subsided into silence. "I should keep my own viewpoint out of it," she said at last. "I suppose you heard about Billie Whistle."

"The accident? Yes. Terrible." Was it Belinda's intent to distract her from her own sorrows by focusing her on the tragedies of others? Or was it simply Belinda's all-consuming interest in her charges?

"She landed on her feet, though . . ." A sudden, appalled hand masked Belinda's lips as the figure of speech struck home. "I mean . . . Some charity paid for her to train as an encephalographic computer operator. She's a partner now in a closely-held start-up venture. Baleen, I think she told me when we spoke last."

"Mariculture?" Mariesa guessed.

"It sounds like it. Whales. Plankton. Or is it krill? Whale baleen is a sort of sieve or filter for straining food out of seawater, isn't it?"

"She always had a talent for computer systems," Mariesa recalled.

"Talent," said Belinda, "but not interest. Her passion always was dancing." She shook her head and stared past Mariesa's shoulder. "That dream was broken with her body. I'm not sure that any other can ever quite take its place."

Mariesa circulated among her guests, exchanging handclasps, brief embraces, murmured words of varied depth of feeling. People turned, spoke, parted—and suddenly she was face-to-face with Adam. She hadn't been avoiding him, exactly. Only she didn't know what she had to say to the man who had sold out the dream she had built.

There was a moment of self-conscious silence. Adam was tall and lean. He had lost weight since she had last seen him. He had acquired a tan and a more hardened set of muscles over the last two years and did not look his forty-one years. Somewhere, she had heard that Adam had worked briefly for Gene Wilson, but was now relying on personal investments and his stipend from the Trust. He had always worn his hair long, but Mariesa was certain it was now a wig. And what did that betoken?

Then, Adam engulfed her hand in both of his. "I'm so sorry about Aunt

Harriet," he said in his deep, compelling voice. When he spoke, one *knew* he was well and truly sorry. Kathryn, his wife, a thin and sharp-faced woman with short-cropped hair, nodded and smiled sadly, keeping a talonlike grip on Adam's upper arm; as if he would otherwise float away like a child's balloon.

"She led a full life," Mariesa offered. Platitude Number 17, useful because it eliminated the need for thought.

"Yes." Adam shifted awkwardly, mimicking physically his search for something to say.

"Have you spoken to—"

Adam's face hardened into a duplicate of his father's. "No." They could have graced Rushmore, the two of them, immobile side by side. "He stopped listening to me long before we . . . parted company."

"Adam's father has behaved abom—" Kathryn's acerbic comment was cut short by Adam's gesture.

"This isn't the time or place for that." His eyes, catching the reflection of the overhead lights, glowed like coals. Mariesa, tracking his gaze, saw Chris on the other side of the ballroom in close conversation with Dolores, Khan Gagrat, and two other VHI officials.

That was me, once, Mariesa thought, watching her cousin conduct business. Every venue was a business venue, every gathering, an excuse to discuss affairs. She considered briefly the hours thus spent that she might have spent with Harriet instead. Yet, the quality of that hypothetical time was doubtful, given how often she and mother had been at loggerheads in those days. When she turned her attention back to Adam, she noted how the muscles bunched at the hinge of his jaw, as if he had made up his mind to bite through cable. *But my conflicts with Mother were never as knife-edged as this.* They had never involved the death of love.

Roberta had left Phil coated and bundled in the foyer with Armando and took Mariesa aside. Dressed in a long, black-hooded winter cape she looked like nothing so much as a monk. "Who is that fellow?" she asked, a slight inclination of the head serving as a pointer. Mariesa followed the glance.

"You mean Adam?"

"Your nephew."

"Second cousin, once removed."

Roberta laughed and shook her head. "Jesus, you're precise." She studied the man from the shadows of her hood. "He's a buff stud dude, that's for sure. He's the one who handed your space station over to Bullock, isn't he?"

"It wasn't really 'my' space station . . ."

"Don't give me that. Ownership has nothing to do with names on papers." She reflected silently for a while. "Any idea why he did it?"

"No."

"Ever ask him?"

"He's cut himself off. I started to say something earlier tonight, but he turned his back and walked off."

"Friendly son of a bitch."

Mariesa tightened the reins on her own temper. "*He* had no call to act offended."

"Where did he ever meet Jimmy Poole?"

Mariesa looked at the young woman. "I didn't know he had. Possibly here."

Roberta shook her head. "No, Jimmy caught his eye as soon as he walked in. Went over and introduced Tani. I didn't hear all they said, and I didn't want to look like I was lurking, but it sure sounded like they already knew each other."

Mariesa shrugged, not understanding the importance. "Perhaps Adam had some computer business with him."

"Could be. But whatever they were whispering about, it had Tani looking scared and fascinated at the same time. I only caught a few words. But one of them I thought I ought to pass along."

"What word was that."

" 'Revenge'."

Mariesa felt a shiver of fear. " 'Revenge'," she said. "Against whom?"

"Hey. I read the newsloads. Only common sense. Not too hard to guess who your *cousin* has weenie for, is it?"

"Revenge," Mariesa said again, watching Adam and Kathryn standing in stoic, silent isolation under the portrait of Conrad. She saw Norbert approach the pair, but whatever conversation he started petered out to an awkward parting. As soon as the social graces had been observed, Mariesa knew, Adam would leave and a great deal of the tension filling the house would loosen. Mariesa returned her attention to Roberta. "Why are you telling me?"

Roberta fastened her hood's golden draw cord and picked up her bag. "I've seen where revenge takes you; and there's nothing at the end of that road but emptiness and abandoned buildings. Been there; done that. And *you* know what the outcome was. No, the best revenge is to turn your back on the hurt and get on with things. Jimmy, he didn't used to pay close attention where the law drew lines, if you know what I mean. So, if your cousin is trying to involve him in some Hamlet ploy—" She shook her head. "I don't want to see Tani hurt. She thinks she's plugged, but she's just acoustic."

November was a month without color. The flowers had withdrawn for the winter; and the trees on the slopes of Skunktown Mountain had dropped their scarlet canopies and now stood naked, a thousand penciled fingers scratching at the sky. Above, a formation of geese cruised effortlessly south, their wings skulling the air in near unison. Another dark shape—a hawk—circled patiently while, below, squirrels and other scuttling things hustled among scattered nuts, spiriting them away in their cheeks and paws with an air of hassled urgency—one eye on the main chance, another on the fell swoop.

Mariesa's doctor had recommended brisk walks each day, as if hours grew on trees and could be squandered so. And yet, since relinquishing VHI, Mariesa had found those hours lying newly idle and, rather than let them drift past like the wind-blown leaves, had taken them and filled them with, if not genuine accomplishment, at least a sense of motion.

Silverpond was a large estate, but not indefinitely so. There were places where even a determined walker would not venture. The wetlands around the pond itself. The tangle of briars and stickerbushes along one margin of the meadow. The bridle paths which, while walkable, had too many reminders that horses used them. And so, if one were not to stride the same dreary round forever, one came at last to the path up Skunktown Mountain.

It was overgrown, of course. She hadn't used it for nine years. But the thought reminded her that she had been divorced rather longer than she had been married, so whatever wretched memories lay atop there, they surely possessed no more power to harm. And the view from the crest was superb; she had deprived herself of it for far too long.

It was a steeper climb than she remembered; or perhaps it was a younger woman who had once climbed it. She found a branch lying in the clutter, fallen from a tall hemlock. It was straight and as tall as her shoulder, so she used it as a walking staff. Her brisk walk whipsawed the grasses. Here and there, cocoons and chrysalises affixed to stalks and stems held promise for the coming spring.

When she reached the top, she was out of breath and her heart hammered in her chest. There was a bench there, built from thick wooden planks upon bricks believed to be relics of the forge that had given Skunktown Furnace its name. Such towns had dotted the Middle Atlantic in colonial days: Oxford Furnace, Durham Forge, any number of forgotten villages in the Pine Barrens. Why an ironmaster would ever build atop this ridge, she could not imagine; unless smiths, too, had a yen for lovely vistas while they worked. Nothing remained of the old works but a few courses of brick that peeked through the grasses.

Great-grandfather Conrad had built a gazebo to protect the bench and those who sat on it, though it was open latticework that, when the wind and rain did blow, would offer scant shelter. Mariesa saw that neglect had taken its toll: shingles were gone from the roof and wood-rot had spread from water seeping through the sun-cracked paint. The dried and brittle husks of monkey vines insinuated themselves among the latticework. Mariesa shook one of the newel posts on the steps and it wobbled like a drunkard. She stepped inside and sat on the bench, facing the charcoal-gray world below. Dry, crisp leaves broke beneath her feet.

Trees had grown up, partly blocking the view; yet, she could still see the line of birches at Old Coppice Road and the village of Hamm's Corners, looking like trees made of lichen and sticks, houses of paperboard and plastic. On the horizon, a dull smudge, North Orange loured.

The view on the back side was different. The trees there had never been properly opened out—van Huytens had always preferred to gaze over their own holdings—so the ramshackle houses of Skunktown Furnace, the pale ribbon of the Gray Horse Pike, the miniature tombstones of the cemetery on the far side of the highway, all of it was glimpsed through a moiré pattern of branches and twigs. During the summer, the foliage blocked that view entirely.

She had sat beside Barry on this very bench and he had handed her an envelope and in the photographs she had seen her husband huffing and grouping with a dull, mousy woman in a tangle of arms and legs and heaving buttocks. Cyrus Attwood had hoped to blackmail Barry into sabotaging Mariesa's plans; and Barry had thrown himself on his sword instead; because—as he had explained years later, when she was in a mood to hear him explain anything—he knew that if he did not, he would succumb sooner or later to the old devil's blandishments.

And there went several years of social climbing down the memory hole. It was a noble sacrifice on Barry's part, if you overlooked the grabbing and stroking in the eight by ten glossies.

Mariesa rubbed her hand across the rough wood of the bench. It had started here, too. (At least, it had ignited here. Who knew when it had started?) She had lain back on the hard planks while Barry tugged her pants down. And *that* for Harriet and all her connubial scheming. It had been awkward and uncomfortable, she remembered; but pleasurable, too. Not every entry in Barry's account was a debit.

Mariesa stretched out on the gazebo's bench and closed her eyes. It felt narrower than she recalled. Surely, she hadn't grown wider! The wind soughed through the trees and the loosened planks of the gazebo, and in its whispering she thought she caught an echo of his voice, husky with both trepidation and pent-up lust. Was it the memory of his touch on her lips and his weight upon her loins that sent a shiver through her, or was it the chill of the late autumn breeze? She would not choose. The photographs, she had flung into the dirt and trampled underfoot as she fled; but paper rots in the acid of rain and soil. Mice chew on it and the wind scatters it. Other things, far less material, survived.

"Yes." Her breath had become a word. *Yes. Oh, yes.*

Rattling branches brought her suddenly upright. Footsteps crunched. "Who's there?" she called. A furtive shape moved through the tangle of dogwood, spicebush, and witch hazel that littered the far slope of the ridge. "Come out. I can see you." The figure paused by a tall hemlock and Mariesa saw it was a child. "It's all right," she told the other. "I don't bite."

The snapping of dead branches underfoot; the rustle of parchment leaves . . . The young boy who appeared at the edge of the clearing could not have been more than ten. He was pale-complexioned with hair of straw, and he wore baggy canvas trousers and a warm jacket.

"You a'right, ma'am?" he finally asked. "I seen you lay down, an' I thought . . ."

"Quite all right," she assured the boy. "I was . . . resting." And remembering.

He began edging toward the brambles and Mariesa said, "Wait. What's your name?"

Hesitation; then, "Will," in a small voice.

"Don't worry, Will. You're not in any trouble. Come on out where I can see you. It's no fun talking to a stickerbush."

A laugh, quickly stifled, and the boy entered the clearing. "You really th' Moon Lady?"

Now it was Mariesa's turn to laugh. She hadn't known people still called her that: "Yes. That's me."

"They say kids come up here, sometimes they don' come down again 'cause you done have 'em 'rested."

"Now why would I do that?"

"'Cause yer rich."

"That comes from making investments, not from arresting young boys. Come on over here and sit on the bench with me."

The boy took a hesitant step. Then, as if that step had taken him over a cusp, he scampered across the clearing and up the gazebo steps. "Dick Miller! The Skunks, they never gonna believe me."

"And the Skunks are . . . ?"

"You know." Will made a gesture with his hand. "The kids, down t' the Furnace. 'S what we call ourselves."

"Not a very attractive name."

An eloquent shrug. "We ain't very attractive kids," he said with a grin. "But a skunk, you know, he don't mess with no one. Jus' minds his own skunky business. But no one messes with him, neither; because, you know . . ."

"Yes. I know. Do you come up here often, Will?"

The boy nodded. "Sometimes," he admitted.

"Why?"

"Oh, you know . . . The trees and flowers. And all kinds of animals. I seed a 'possum oncet, jus' like back home."

"Did you?"

"Yeah. And you know different flowers, they come out at different times, like spring or summer or fall? So ever time I come up here, it's a li'l differ'nt."

"Different. Yes. It is for me, too. Since the last time."

"You like plants and animals and stuff?"

"And stuff. Things bloom; then they fade. It's better to remember the blooms."

"You look kinda sad. How kin y' be sad when yer rich?"

She handed him a cliché: "Riches can't buy happiness."

"Hey, Maw says that, too! 'Cept, she always adds, 'But poor cain't buy nothin'.' "

Mariesa smiled. "What does your mama do?"

"She takes care o' me."

"And your dad?"

"Whatever he can. Paw says boys shouldn't like to look at flowers."

"Nonsense. Many great botanists have been men. Carver, Burbank . . ."

"What's a 'bot-tan-ist'?"

"A scientist who studies plants and learns how they grow and what they do."

The boy's eyes widened. "You mean, they's a *job* where people do that? They git *paid*?"

Mariesa wanted to say, Of course, but she saw in his face that there was no "of course" about it. What you saw ahead of you depended on how close the mountains were that bordered your life. Sometimes you had to climb to the top of one to see there were possibilities beyond.

The two of them sat in companionable silence while the afternoon sun sought the treeline. The circling hawk suddenly dived and swooped across the meadow; then beat its wings back toward the sky with something small clutched in its talons. Will whooped. "Got him!"

Mariesa looked at him. "Do you root for the hawks, then?"

"Naw. Hawks and mice, I figger they just do what they gotta do. One grabs; the other runs. Next time, maybe the mouse gets away. I'll cheer for him, too; 'cause I like it when . . . When . . ." He frowned, searching for the words his heart needed.

"When work is done well?" she supplied.

"Yeah. That's it. Grabbin' mice or running from hawks. Diggin' coal, like afore we come up north; or drivin' a truck, or cookin' dinner. That's what Paw says, anyways. Says, don't matter what you do, 's long as you do it the best you kin."

Zen from the Appalachian hollers. "For a sentiment like that, I'll forgive him his remarks on botany."

"Hunh?"

"Nothing. Will, you can come up here whenever you want and study your flowers and trees and . . . stuff."

"Well . . ." He seemed doubtful.

"The red maples are lovely," Mariesa told him with a sweep of her arm toward the empty canopy, "especially in the fall; but the hemlocks have a stateliness that—" She broke off. The boy was goggling at her. "What is it?"

"They got *names?*"

His voice was so full of surprise and discovery and awe and excitement that Mariesa nearly burst and she covered her face with her hands to contain herself.

"Why you crying, lady?"

"I'm not sure. I'm not sure."

Mariesa rubbed her eyes with her sleeve. She didn't notice exactly when he slipped away, leaving her alone with her memories on the hilltop; and when she listened carefully she could not be certain of his footsteps on the farther slope. It could have been the wind stirring the autumn leaves. A wraith, she wondered? Had there ever been such a boy?

Will, he called himself. The sun had passed its zenith and fell slowly toward the horizon. The air grew noticibly cooler. She had had a son once, almost, and had planned to name him William. He would have been nine by now, had he ever been born. A likely boy, she thought. Curiosity on two legs, looking to Mariesa to guide him.

But that was a world that never was.

She stood up and held her jacket tight around her throat. She had rested here long enough. There were still worlds that yet might be.

A warm spell had swept the December snows from the streets when Mariesa arrived at SkyWatch's Washington headquarters. John Inkling met her in the lobby and led her to the conference room. Mariesa noticed in passing how many cubicles were unoccupied and how harried the staff appeared. Granted, the government needed every dime to shore up the tottering Social Security system—the early cohorts of the Baby Boom had begun retiring in the last few years and hundreds of thousands of unsecured chickens were coming home to roost. Detweiler's Associates, the forecasting firm that VHI employed, had projected a major recession within the next five years. But surely a few dimes could have been shaken loose to help watch for that which might obliterate fund and retirees both and put paid to all obligations.

George Krishnarahman and Daryll Blessing were waiting in the conference room along with the senior staff. One pixwall was tiled with popper windows showing conference rooms at JPL and elsewhere. On the other wall, digital readouts and charts ringed a blank space. Mariesa glanced at it.

"No transmission yet?" Inkling shook his head.

"The command was sent; but no bounceback yet."

Mariesa found a clean mug and filled it with coffee from the urn on a back table and placed it aside on a coaster to cool. There were placemats and chairs all around the long conference table, but no one was sitting down, except Darryl Blessing, who appeared to be asleep. The buzz of anticipation filled the air. Gayle Foose was on the horn with Marshall, reviewing protocols for the datalinks. Cheng-I Yeh twisted a pen in his hands, around and around. Bernie Lefkowitz rocked to and fro with his hands clasped behind his back.

The wait dragged on and Mariesa chatted inconsequently with people in the same room or others a continent away. A series of digital images lined up on the data wall like cards from a blackjack dealer. Visitor Probes had been rendezvousing with their target asteroids since November and someone was using the idle time to review prior transmissions.

Finally, someone shouted, "Incoming!" Two of the older men flinched and glanced up, but everyone else turned expectantly toward the blank pixcreen. Snow and static filled the screen with bit-shot. Test images flickered by and the receiving systems shook hands and adjusted their parameters to suit the datastream. Street-jive handshake, they called it. A picture condensed out of the fuzz and clarified as the imaging A/S took hold.

It looks like a potato, Mariesa thought. An irregular, ovoid lump of dark and bright gray. Asteroid 2004AS. There were two bids on its name, one on its mineral rights. Mariesa noticed its steady motion, not one of the random tumbles that marked what she thought of as untampered asteroids. Her heart began to thud in her chest and she placed a hand over it.

The techies at JPL and SkyWatch called off numbers to each other. Range, albedo, apparent size, major and minor axes, velocity, orbital position, probable composition. The probe's angle of approach was from aft and sunward. Mariesa glanced at the dual time displays: time of transmission, time of receipt. It was strange to think that the probe was "already" a great many meters closer to the asteroid than the image showed.

"There!" Mariesa jolted at the cry and spilled her coffee. "There," said Cheng-I Yeh. He strode to the pixwall and pointed to a dark splotch at the tip of the asteroid. "It's another cave."

Excited chatter arose as the scientists and technicians argued the point. "Just a crater . . ." said one. "Same location as on Calhoun's Rock *and* on 2007KT . . ." ". . . a shadow." "Use some common sense . . ." "Could be a bit transmission problem . . ." ". . . a better angle so we can see how deep it is . . ."

Daryll Blessing pushed himself erect and leaned over the conference table, supporting himself on his two arms as he stared at the wall. One by one, the other voices fell silent as they waited for the old man to speak.

"Sample size?" he asked in a high pitched, quavering voice. Mariesa believed he kept himself alive by sheer will power, as if the thought that he would not be around for the resolution of the Visitor Question were intolerable.

"Uh . . ." Bernie Lefkowitz picked up a cliputer. "This is the eighth probe to arrive at its destination; six have downloaded data. We're still querying the other two."

"Plus the FarTrip expedition," Cheng-I Yeh added. "That makes seven as-teroids on which we have close-up information, and three of them have features resembling Mendes's Cave." He glanced at Lefkowitz, who nodded. "That's fifty percent," he added, "and there are five other probes still en route."

Blessing waved him off. "Of the four with no such feature—"

"We couldn't get a good look at the west end of 2010GD," Lefkowitz reminded him. "Wrong angle. And the probe ran out of compressed gas for the steering jets before we could move it into position."

Blessing scowled. He did not care to be interrupted. "Of the *three* asteroids which we are *certain* possess no 'cave,' how many are known Shifters?"

"Shifter" was SkyWatch's name for a near-earth asteroid whose appearance coincided with the loss of a "regular" asteroid, the working hypothesis being that they had shifted orbits.

"Umm." Lefkowitz did not need to consult the summary sheet, but he flipped through it anyhow. Nervous at being questioned by the Great Man, Mariesa suspected. "None. That we know of."

"And other than Calhoun's Rock . . ."

"Both the others are Shifters," Bernie confirmed.

Blessing bobbed his head. Nodding his acknowledgement or simply nodding off? "Well. Assuming Calhoun's Rock was wrecked by collision with the Head-rock before the modifications could be completed . . ."

"That's quite an assumption," said someone from JPL, "even for the likes of Daryll Blessing."

Blessing turned about to glower at the JPL screen. "Perhaps a little common sense is in order," he suggested. "I will ask to see the president . . ."

"Isn't that a little premature?"

"It's gone!"

Mariesa turned from the bickering among the scientists to the main pixwall and saw that the download from 2004AS had indeed ceased. " 'Faster, cheaper'," someone scoffed. "What a time for something to malf . . ."

Mariesa cut through the moans of disappointment. "Was anyone watching when the transmission was cut?"

Cheng-I Yeh said, "I was. There was a big flash of light, then nothing."

"Play it back," suggested Craig Purdy, telepresent from Goddard.

This time, they all saw it. The probe had maneuvered close to the west end of the asteroid in the interim. As the view came around the horizon, Mariesa could see from the shadows cast by the craft's strobe lights that the opening was indeed the entrance to a deep bore, as on Calhoun's Rock. Daryll had been premature, but correct. As the probe crested the lip, a bright flash, like a searchlight, wiped out all visuals. Then all telemetry shut down.

"Computer. Cheng-I. Time ratio 20:1, set. Replay from previous start point, replay."

This time, it all happened in slow motion. This time, they could see the brightness emerge from the borehole and engulf the view. "Did you see those readouts?" someone cried. ". . . achieve that range of temperature . . . ?" "If we'd installed a radiation meter on board, like I suggested . . ."

Blessing caught Mariesa's eye. He nodded toward the now-blank datawall. "It sensed our presence," he said. "And then it fired its engine."

"To change orbit," she said. Blessing nodded. "To hide?" she asked.

Blessing shrugged. "It may be programmed to avoid contact. The asteroid will fall behind the sun in another month. We may be able to make enough observations to calculate its new orbit before it reappears in the east."

"And if not?"

Blessing sighed. "If not, we will have lost a tremendous opportunity."

Mariesa shook her head and faced the blinking screen. "We'll find it," she announced. "Or it will find us."

12.

Cursors, Foiled Again

Thin and gangly, rather like an ostrich, Norris Bosworth wore oversized glasses that accentuated his eyes and gave him a lingering adolescent appearance despite a calendar age at the high end of the thirties. Rumor had it that he had his glasses specially fabricated with taped-over nose bridges and that he had personally kept the entire pocket-protector industry solvent. All part of the SuperNerd image.

Jimmy Poole popped a can of Jolt with his thumb as he studied the face on his pixwall. It displeased him when other virtchuosos played to the stereotypes. It was demeaning and it undermined respect—even if what he saw on the screen was no more than a morph, and the real Norris Bosworth could, so far as Jimmy knew, grace the cover of GQ.

And that was good to remember. Bosworth was one of the Five Fingers— he made just about everyone's short list—and what Jimmy saw was pretty much what Norris wanted him to see. *What you see*, he reminded himself, *is what you get*. But it might not be all there was to get.

Fair was fair. Jimmy sat in his Sanctum wearing nothing but boxer shorts and a day-old shave and presented Norris with the image of a slick business-droid—fashionably retro "overbreast" business jacket; hair slicked back bird-wing style. Jimmy was Naughty Ought and saw no reason to pretend otherwise. Let the bunnies prance in their baggy "mainstreet" rags and prattle about the Terrible Teens. Jimmy could still eat their lunch and ask for seconds.

But Bosworth was another fish fry entirely. Only slightly ahead of the curve—thirty-eight or thirty-nine to Jimmy's thirty-one—he carried much the same baggage Jimmy did. It would not do to think of him as less capable. Jimmy kept a wary eye on his input doid. It was powered down, but who knew what sort of stealthbot the other dude could slick through? Turn on the eye and see Jimmy *in the flesh!* Maybe he should've stuped up for this call? Nuts. If Bosworth wanted to peek, maybe Jimmy ought to peel off the shorts, too, and give him a real thrill. . . .

A beep from his number three auxiliary terminal told him that his own stealthbot had been deftly countered by Bosworth's defenses. Not that he and Norris were dueling; exactly; but it would have been rude not to try. Like two

181

cholos squeezing knuckles when they shook hands, just to see what kind of dude they were dealing with.

"You don't understand," Bosworth said, pushing his glasses up the bridge of his nose with a forefinger—a gesture a little too over-the-top, Jimmy thought. "I'm not a lone wolf, like you or Pedro. I'm part of an organization. And I don't walk the wild side, like Mighty Mouse, Crackman, or Captain Cat."

I only use my powers for the forces of Good, Jimmy ran the parody in his head. Virtuous as well as virtual, following the arbitrary dictates of a hypothetical god. Jimmy depended on reason and logic for his own code of conduct. Besides, if half the whispers were true, Utopian Research Associates had been data-hacking even before there was a Net, using human informers and moles instead of knowbots.

"This isn't a wild hack, SuperNerd," Jimmy responded. His voice would be mouthed by his screen morph while the Artificial Stupid supplied body language and lines of business. Another A/S would salt the transmission with his signature montages; and still a third would salt the transmission with assorted knowbots and other virtchlife—just in case one slipped through with the comm packets into the Nerd's system. Word was that the Associates' deeby was phat and sticking a straw in there would be a real coup. "The security laager around LEO Station is top weenie. Nothing goes in or out, except through the authorized ports. I wanted to shoptalk with the creator and thought maybe you had the mojo."

"The Associates are into social and economic projections," Bosworth reminded him, "not datacomm security. But it *is* a piece of work, isn't it?" There was a note that crept into Bosworth's voice. Admiration? Envy?

Jimmy grinned. Looks like ol' SuperNerd had been sniffing around the laager, too. "I know, but I figured it was worth a shot. You have any idea who did write it?"

SuperNerd went into thought-simulation mode, one virtual hand tugging at a virtual lip. "If it's legit, I would've guessed either you or the Jouster."

"Negatory on the Jouster. I already faced with him."

"There's Sokhrannost/E or Schildwache or Web Wardens. They sometimes do high-end custom work. The truly curious might even try worming into Orbital Management Corporation's MRP system and troll for P/Os—except that would be illegal."

Jimmy snorted. SuperNerd would have to take a lot more psychology courses before he would get Jimmy to play cat's paw for him. And OMC would have to be monumentally stupid to lay that kind of security on Leo Station and then leave the purchase orders and invoices sitting around in "plain site."

Still . . . "Big corporation" and "monumentally stupid" were not mutually exclusive. Lots of cubicle droids there, and they had a tendency to copy all sorts of things for all sorts of reasons, no matter what company policy said. Noodle the desktop drives in the purchasing department and who knew what would pop up? Jimmy placed the suggestion in the "maybe" file for Crackman to look at. "Have *you* poked it?" he asked.

"Do I look like a fool?" Bosworth shot back.

The obvious answer being "yes," Jimmy remained silent. So SuperNerd was afraid to touch the laager, too. Yeah. You got old, you got shy. Couldn't trust the old mojo any more. But why so curious, if datacomm security was off his orbit?

"Why?" Nerd responded petulantly when Jimmy asked. "Because Associate projections depend on getting reliable information on the current system state. Social Security is train-wrecking. We'd like to know if the rest of the economy can take the hit. But you system security droids have mucked things up. Data that used to be public or at least, uh, accessible is under crypt and key now. Our models are recursive, so if the domain space is fractal, input uncertainty can output divergent scenarios."

Smell *his* feet, Jimmy thought. People who threw jargon in your face should be tied in a sack and drowned. At birth.

Afterward, Jimmy crossed SuperNerd off his list of possible authors.

Well, he hadn't put much faith in Pedro or the Nerd as possibilities. Writing security for LEO didn't *feel* like their work. It was the wrong venue—like a tennis star throwing a forward pass. Earp was still the high-prob option. Jimmy was sussing the others only from a sense of thoroughness, and because it didn't pay to rely too heavily on deduction when you could actually survey the population. He leaned back in his chair and stretched until his joints popped.

The next part would be tricky. Like Poole sEcurity, Pedro and SuperNerd were open and accessible; but the other Fingers treasured privacy above all else. Earp, though he walked the line, owed much of his power to his anonymity; and Cat, who was over the edge, owed his very existence to it. Chen prowled both sides; so which one did you look for?

Unofficial Chen might actually be easier to contact than Official Chen. In theory, Chen was just as accessible as Pedro and the other straight-edgers, but traffic into and out of the Guangdong Republic was closely monitored—on the banks of the Potomac as well as the banks of the Pearl. And some of those nodes had nutcrackers that were phat stoopid: "unbreakable" code that went in came out with more scar tissue than Frankenstein's monster, and as often as not had been jekylled to turn on its master. The whisper on the Shadow-Web was that the CIA had a liquid q-bit supercomputer stashed in a coffee cup somewhere. *The Kraken*, it was supposed to be called. Prime-factor dark codes dissolved in quantum processing like so much sugar. Jimmy hoped some operator would get absent-minded and drink the coffee. . . .

Meanwhile, Official Chen sat behind the virtual picketwire with a bland smile and a language that never quite meant what you thought it meant. Poole sEcurity had dealt with him only twice—and both encounters had been official business, mother-henned by DoD and State.

But Unofficial Chen, if the rumors were true, walked large steps. He was Out There, like Bigfoot—never actually seen, but leaving tantalizing signs and glimpses. He was in the Net and on the Web and under the Lattice. He had, it was said, numbered accounts in Liechtenstein, the Caymans, and Montana. The Three Cities either countenanced his freelancing or, helpless to control it, turned a blind eye.

But how to make contact? Tracking down Unofficial Chen—or Earp, or Captain Cat—was not like calling up Bosworth or Rodriguez. And he couldn't exactly take out an ad in the personals. More to the point: How would they react to a contact?

Jimmy snagged his housecoat from the hook behind the door and wandered through the house. Today was Stassy's day off, so there was no one in the kitchen to stop him from rifling a hot dog from the magfridge. Wrapping his lips around it, he sucked on the tip for a while before biting it off. That always drove Stassy nuts when she caught him. You must cook it, she would say, you must cook it! But what the hell, it was just cylindrical bologna. You didn't cook bologna, right?

He stepped through the sliding glass doors onto the sun deck. The air was chilly and damp and he pulled the robe tighter. California winter, he thought, eyeing the dark clouds scudding across the distant headlands of the peninsula. Sometimes he missed the cold, honest snow of the east. Slushballs down the back of the neck. Icicle duels. The time he had worn the toes off his galoshes using them to brake his sled down Deadman's Hill. Santa ought to drive a damn sleigh, not dude up in rain gear.

He beat a tattoo on the wrought iron rail with his fingers. Maybe it was time to fold his hand and admit that his cowboy days were over. Tell Adam he was backing off. He had things that he cared about now.

On the other hand, yields on Baleen Number One *were* running ten points behind the clone Jimmy had set up on Goddard City. Red had gotten respectable figures for the start-up batches; but since handover to LEO the yields had hit a glass ceiling at a barely tolerable 75 percent. Whistle was adjusting her models to account for the real-world data; yet Flaco Mercado was reporting yields on Goddard in the low eighties—and the figures were still climbing as the equipment was debugged. So, was LEO a poor babysitter, or had Red fooed the installation?

Or had Adam made some sort of deal with the LEO folks?

And how did Jimmy point out the discrepancy without revealing his secret installation?

Keep digging . . . Jimmy sighed and rubbed his hands. It hadn't been an order, exactly; but it hadn't been a request, either. Yet, what duty did he owe Adam van Huyten? Wasn't his duty to Stevie and Tani? Come to that, given the man's track record, how far could he trust Adam? At the funeral at Silverpond, Adam had glared at another mourner across the room and went how

someone had done him dirt and deserved payback. Jimmy never wanted that
look turned in his direction. Tani, listening, had said nothing at the time; but
that evening in their hotel room by the Interstate, she had scribbled madly in
her notebook.

Sighing, Jimmy stood back from the rail and stuffed his hands in the pockets
of his robe. People. That was always the complication. If there weren't any
people, there wouldn't be any problems.

Jimmy re-entered the house and went in search of his wife. Tani had better
people instincts than he did; and, having now met Adam, she might have
useful input. No one could finger the web like S. James Poole; but humans had
a lot more unconstrained variables to consider. Tani had been studying the
human operating system all her life and knew more about the relevant architecture and commands.

He looked in the nursery first, but she wasn't there. Little Stevie was asleep
in his crib, surrounded by creatures of plush and velvet larger than he was. Did
they appear cuddly or frightening to the small child? A mobile of wooden birds
dangled over him. They rattled when Jimmy brushed them peeking into the
crib. Rada frowned and put a finger to her lips. Jimmy smiled and nodded and
pantomimed quiet motions. Whose kid did she think it was, anyway?

What was it about sleeping babies that made them so endearing, he wondered as he gazed at the serene face of his son. Was it that, having a template
almost completely blank, babies reflected whatever hopes their parents projected? Or was it only that they were incapable of guile or deceit? Could it be,
he thought as he turned away from the sleeping child, that they endeared
because they trusted openly and completely and without reservation and, being
therefore utterly vulnerable, evoked an urge to protect from the old and cynical?

Tani was hard at work and did not hear him enter her office. She sat with her
fingers hovering hawklike over her keyboard. Blocked, or just mousing after
the right word? Tani's approach to writing was like making a stained glass
window: each piece crafted and set individually into place before proceeding.
She couldn't move on to the next scene until she had gotten each word right.
To Jimmy, whose own writing style more resembled potting—throw a mass of
clay on the wheel, then shape it—Tani seemed slow and finicky. But then, he
had only written some technical papers. He'd never made the bestseller list.

Since she seemed to be having an out-of-body experience, Jimmy padded
softly to one side of the room, near the credenza, so as not to startle her.

Tani's office was very like her, and nearly the opposite of his own. Potpourri
bowls of dried flowers and herbs graced the room. Photographs of family and
friends hung on the walls and the shelves. Candles burned with various pleasant odors. The only concession to high tech was the word processor itself; but
even that was set in a decorative wooden cabinet of the new "coke" style. Her

wiring was held in place with twisties and plastic conduit. Jimmy's own equipment dangled nakedly—wires, junctions, switches, and all what-have-you
strung wherever they were not too much in the way.

Not that Tani was a neat-freak. There was hardcopy all over the place:
pinned to bulletin boards, taped to her cabinet doors, stuffed into manila folders fanned on a credenza behind her. One long sheet along the wall looked
like a timeline. He supposed that the rest of the stuff was character sketches,
background materials, and such.

Writing a novel, he thought, must be nearly as complex as writing code for
a large application program—with the background material and shared culture
of the readers acting like the operating system. The main differences were
plot—programs had to hang together logically—and the depth of characterization.

Idly, Jimmy picked up a folder from the credenza. The label was a character
name: Duncan Orb. The front flap was covered by a series of scribbled notes.
"Overweight." "Long-hair (dusty blond)." "Brown eyes." "Mid-twenties" was
crossed off and replaced by "25" and "Birthplace—Suburban NYC," by
"Westchester Co." Jimmy suspected these were reminders so she could describe
the character consistently throughout the book.

The first page inside the folder contained a single, handwritten paragraph.
"Duncan is totally absorbed by the unreality of his abstract world and completely divorced from all social norms. His redemption is the core of the book."

The folder was snatched from his hands!

Tani snapped at him. "Don't sneak up on me! I don't like people reading
things before they're finished. You know that!"

"I—" said Jimmy Poole. "You were—I mean—" He stopped on the verge
of stammering and said more calmly. "I didn't want to bother you."

"Well, you have!" Jimmy imagined tears in Tani's eyes.

"I'm sorry."

"You scared me! I didn't hear you come in and—"

"I wanted to talk with you about something," he said. "Maybe later, when
you're not so—"

Tani made an exasperated sound and dropped into her chair. "It wasn't going
well, anyway." Yes, Jimmy decided. Those *were* tears, held back by sheer will.
He edged toward the door.

"Then I *will* come back later," he said. "Those are the times when you
shouldn't quit. That's how it is for me when I'm stuck on a program. I just
duck my head down and keep going."

"If I did that, I'd write eighty-percent foo."

Jimmy shrugged. "Then, tomorrow, keep the other twenty percent and go
on from there. The important thing is to keep moving. Newton's Law. A body
in motion tends to remain in motion."

Tani said nothing, but sucked on her lower lip. When she turned to face her screen once more, Jimmy beat a hasty retreat. He knew it would do no good to tell Tani to relax. She probably saw as clearly as he did that her anxiety created its own positive feedback loop. But knowing it did not help address it. He thought his "keep on keeping on" advice would help, though. It was just like falling off a bicycle. You had to get right back on. Someday, if he ever did become stuck on a program, he would try it himself.

When Tani found him later, Jimmy had showered and dressed and was feeding Stevie in the kitchen. The rugrat was strapped into a high chair with more safety harnesses than an Indy driver, and wore a bib featuring Spacer Sam (the Rocket Man) in bright pastels, although from his vantage point, Stevie could not possibly see the cartoon hero. In addition to his sleeper and his bib, Stevie wore a colorful assortment of strained fruits and vegetables. The greatest concentration was around the mouth, but he had contrived to get some on his cheeks, forehead, in his hair, and even—Jimmy never saw how this was accomplished   in his left ear.

Rada sat nearby, looking displeased and conducting a non-conversation with Stassy. Rada did not think that feeding babies was a task that men did well, or that men ought to do at all. She had very strict notions of place and duty. Jimmy suspected it was her upbringing in Calcutta, in a land where, despite official abandonment, the caste system still informed who ought to do what. Rada was lighter-skinned than Tani, too; and from some of the glances Jimmy had intercepted, she no doubt thought it further evidence of the world turned upside down that a woman of her status should be working for one of Tani's. Rada even wore the caste mark on her forehead, something Jimmy had never seen Tani do. A mark that meant *nada* to the Africans, Irish, Chinese, Puerto Ricans, and all what-have-you that made up the American stewpot.

Stassy, in particular, was unimpressed with Rada's *quondam* rank in India. Her own father had been *nomenklatura*, the Soviet equivalent of the *brahmins*. Jimmy supposed it had always been that way. The sons of English lords had punched cattle on the plains beside emancipated slaves, and Talmudic scholars had pushed vending carts around the Lower East Side. Now, brahmins were babysitters and the daughters of privilege, cooks. Jimmy's own ancestors, the time he had tracked them down, were a long line of undistinguished yeoman farmers, sprinkled here and there with smugglers and poachers, one of whom had been hanged in Bristol in the 1740s. In a way, as Crackman, he had carried on his family's poaching traditions.

When Tani entered, Jimmy saw right off that things had gone better. She had that satiated look that runners have at the finish line when some final burst of speed had carried them past their hopes. She caught Jimmy's eye and smiled, and Jimmy beamed back and she walked right up to him and planted a big one right on his hips. *Later,* her tongue told him. Jimmy heard the faint cluck that escaped Rada's teeth and saw the wistful smile that passed briefly over Stassy's countenance, but it didn't matter to him what either one of them thought.

Afterward, they played with Stevie in the living room. Stevie sat upright with his legs spread, clapping his hands while Jimmy rolled a bright red ball toward him. The kid hadn't figured out that if he clapped his hands together at just the right time he would actually *catch* the fool thing. Perhaps he lacked the hand-eye coordination yet; or perhaps he just didn't see the point.

Tani sat on the long, wheat-colored sofa under the fabric painting of coppered autumn leaves and watched with a curious and cautious smile. "Should you trust Adam?" she said, repeating his question. "I can't say. I only met him that one time, at Mrs. van Huyten's funeral, but he certainly struck me as a man who bends everything toward the goal he's picked."

"Everything," Jimmy said.

"Including everyone who comes into his orbit. You're a tool. This Baleen is a tool. Hobie is a tool. There are probably others."

Jimmy didn't like to think of himself as a tool. "He's a persuasive man."

"I could see that. I wonder how many women he's persuaded. Put that *focus* of his between the sheets . . ."

Jimmy glanced up sharply, saw her impish grin. "That's not the issue."

"Not to you; but I was thinking of him as a character. You saw that wife of his. I wouldn't care to be on her shit list. She didn't have a hand on his arm; she had a grapple."

Jimmy grunted. Sure, Adam was a studly dude. Jimmy could see that. Men blushed with envy, and women let their tongues roll out and stood in line; but what did that have to do with anything? "Did *you* find him attractive?" he asked.

She didn't answer him. "I think Adam is so accustomed to getting his own way that he can't imagine anything else; and that invincible confidence is what draws everyone else along. It's all subconscious. He gives out signals—'here's a dude who knows what he's doing.' Since the rest of us don't, we tag along."

"I know what I'm doing," Jimmy said, but he was too aware of his doubts to put much punch in his voice. "Besides," he pointed out, "Adam doesn't always get what he wants, or he wouldn't be running a two-bit start-up like Baleen."

"Unless," Tani said thoughtfully, "that *is* what he always wanted. To be on his own, without his family's grease. Could be, his confidence demanded testing somewhere where the fix wasn't in."

Stevie hollered and Jimmy realized that he hadn't rolled the ball in a while and the kid was calling time on him. He pushed the sphere across the carpet and Stevie laughed and clapped his hands. This time, they came together with the ball in between and a look of immense surprise came over the child's face. "Are you describing Adam," Jimmy asked Tani, "or a character for your book?"

"Both maybe. I wish I had met him earlier." Tani pulled her legs up and tucked them under and crossed her arms. " 'Revenge,' he said. I can't believe anyone would hate his own father that much. Look, Jimmy, be careful. If there is a law between 'Ahab' van Huyten and his vengeance, he might not be too scrupulous about observing it. Don't get dragged down with him."

"I'm analyzing the teep his cheesehead made. Nothing illegal about that. They *hired* me to ride shotgun. And I'm looking for the author of the LEO security A/S because it's such a beautiful job I want to talk shop." He reached out and snagged the ball that Stevie had pushed back. Maybe the kid was catching on.

"If it's so legal, why are you so hesitant about contacting the other people on your list? Those Fingers."

Jimmy shrugged. "Legal isn't the issue. Manners is. Here you go, Stevie. Catch it! I'm thinking about using a condom."

Tani cocked her head. "What?"

Stevie didn't even try for it and the ball rolled right past him, forcing Jimmy to crawl after it. "You just like to see me run around, don't you, Small Person?" He squatted again on the rug and resumed the game. "Rodriguez and Bosworth are public," he told Tani. "They take calls. The others don't, except Official Chen—and there are other problems with him. If the Fingers don't want to be contacted, they might give me VD—a virtual disease—out of spite. I've got top-notch protection; but why take chances?"

"Oh. I thought you meant . . . How does a 'condom' work?"

Jimmy suddenly realized how she had misconstrued the term. He wiggled his eyebrows provocatively. "I'll show you. Later tonight." When Tani did not reject the proposition outright, his grin widened. "I'll set up a node somewhere else. Use a series of fronts to buy and install equipment. Nobody knows anybody else, so nothing can be traced anywhere. Shunt the bounceback through a decoupler. One-way info-channel. Packet the output as an audio squeal and listen with a parabolic mike five blocks away." He put on an exaggerated accent and twirled an imaginary mustache. "We haff our ways . . ."

Tani laughed and shook her head. "Who ever said, 'Appearances can be deceiving'?"

Jimmy nodded gravely. "In some venues, appearances are everything."

When Leland Hobart was angry he resembled nothing so much as the working face of a quarry just after a buried explosion and just before dropping a few hundred tons of rock. The look he gave Jimmy said the rock would drop on him and Jimmy did his best not to cringe back farther into his seat.

"I don't like being summoned like some kind of servant," Hobie said.

The two of them sat in sling-back chairs in Jimmy's library: a broad, open room with racks of μCDs and other media on one wall and a large paneless window of spun plastic on another. The woods were light and inlaid with parqueting that formed abstract patterns. A Gyricon screen and reader in the

severely functional style of the Naughty Oughts hung on a gooseneck that
could be pulled to almost any point in the room. It peeked now over Hobie's
shoulder like a kibitzing, cybernetic diplodocus. Spare, simple, and open compared to the ornate new "coke" style, the room already had an antique feel
to it.

"It wasn't a summons," Jimmy told him. And it wasn't, not really. Adam
had suggested he talk to Hobie, and Jimmy had sent Hobie plane tickets to
San Jose for the earliest date Jimmy had free. Two tickets, in fact. And a hotel
room in San Francisco for the weekend with the siggy of his choice. Jimmy
hadn't known if Dr. Hobart was married or not, but he figured everyone had
a significant other, even if the significance level might vary.

"Okay, a bribe, then."

"I thought you might enjoy a weekend by the Bay," Jimmy said. "Just you
and—what was her name? Charlene. Get away from the kids for a couple of
days." And that Charlene was a fox. If Jimmy had not already given his heart
away, he might have considered lending it to Charli Hobart for an hour.

Something of his lustful thoughts may have surfaced, because Hobie's face
condensed into a scowl. "Some weekend with Charli," he said.

"I'm sure she and Tani are having fun up in the city. Plenty of shopping
there. We'll take the maglev in and meet them later for dinner. Don't worry.
You'll have plenty of time together." He favored Hobie with a knowing leer,
but the chemist's smile back was more rueful than lusty.

"Yeah," he said. "Plenty of time." He shifted in the sling chair and continued
to ignore the drink that Stassy had placed on the side table by him. "Well, I
guess we both gotta do what Adam wants; so let's cut to the chase."

Jimmy bristled. "I don't 'gotta do' what Adam wants. I'm a contractor. I
pick and choose what I 'gotta' do."

For the first time since arriving, Hobie smiled. "Sure. I don't even work for
him at all; but we're both here. Go figure."

"He does have a hard time," Jimmy conceded, "hearing 'no'."

"No flubber," Hobie said. He picked up his drink at last and swirled it in
the glass. "You've got to understand," he said slowly, "that there's a problem
with Adam. He used to be my boss at Argonaut, and I liked him. Most of the
staff did. Oh, you sometimes heard moans from the upwardly mobile crowd
about needing the right family name to get ahead; but I was there to do science,
not manage a corporation. You hear what I'm saying? But Adam, he did something whack and Van Huyten Industries' controlling interest in Leo Station
suddenly became Klondike-American's, and there was OMC holding the management contract. So you see, the guy I liked turned out to be a traitor."

"Then, why are you here?"

Hobie shook his head. "Damn if I know. Because I still like him. He always
treated me okay." He looked up and caught Jimmy's eye. "Understand what
that means when a black man says it. He never made a big deal about my race;

and he didn't make a big deal about ignoring it, either. Never tried to show off how oh-so-tolerant he was. Dealing with him, I never felt I was just a black skin in a suit. So, yeah, maybe he did some other people dirt; but he never did me any, and that means something to me."

Jimmy nodded. The proverbial ace of spades would "pass" before Hobie did. With his build and demeanor, it was hard not to notice. "Any idea why he did it? The Klon-Am deal, I mean."

A rough shake of the head. "Grapevine said that he and his dad had gone at it a couple of times at board meetings, and he had one royal set-to with Pitchlynn, the old bat who used to run Pegasus, but that was way out of my league. Rumor was that he had signed over his share of stock in the LEO Consortium to a couple of Klon-Am front companies and, what with other alliances on the LEO board, it gave Bullock a swing vote on key issues. The board was already honked at VHI because Old Lady van Huyten let Donaldson put those kinetic weapons up there, which led to the *soyuski* attack that wrecked part of the Hub . . ." He looked off out the window with a doleful look on his face. "So Bullock eased two of the three VHI votes off the Board and eased himself on." Hobie put his drink down, still untouched. "High finance isn't my 'hood."

"Did you ever ask him about it?"

Hobie shook his head. "We don't move in the same circles. Never even saw him again until he came up to Leo that time. And the subject . . . No, I didn't mention it." He picked up the fruit nectar again, and this time, for a wonder, drank some of it. "It's a touchy subject. I didn't want to be unpleasant."

Jimmy grunted. "Yeah. 'Hi, Adam, sell out any friends lately?' could be a real conversation stopper."

Hobie's glare was momentary, replaced by a despondent grimace. He looked away. "I just hate that it went down the way it did."

"If it helps," Jimmy said, "his new venture is perfectly legitimate." (Okay, *mostly* legitimate. There was that fly, after all.) "I'm not at liberty to discuss what Baleen is producing, but it's an exciting product concept and one that really will benefit the world. Our problem is Leo. For a variety of reasons, Baleen is concerned about piracy and we've been looking into security arrangements on the station."

Hobie set his drink down again and leaned back in his chair, linking his fingers together over his chest. "You know what hurts? Adam didn't even tell me that much."

Jimmy shook his head hard. "Nothing personal. We're trying to keep things close to the vest. Adam told me you might have learned something while you were up there."

"He always was an optimist." Hobie stood, easing out of the sling chair far more gracefully than Jimmy had ever managed. He walked to the window, where pulled the curtain a little to one side and looked out over the driveway that curled down the hillside. "Why is he calling himself 'Desherite'?" he asked without turning.

Jimmy covered his ignorance with a smile. "Because he doesn't want his rep to influence anyone. Who would do business with a guy they didn't trust?"

Hobie turned. " 'Didn't trust' or 'couldn't trust'?"

"He may be trying to make a new start. Make amends." Actually, those were not bad guesses, and they certainly put a more benign aspect on Adam's deceptions.

"It's French, you know."

"French. What is?"

"Desherite. It means 'disinherited'."

Jimmy laughed. For a pampered rich dude, the guy had a fine, in-your-face style. For some odd reason, he suddenly felt much better about Adam and his plans. "So, what did you learn about LEO?"

Hobie turned away from the window and studied the room. He shook his head. "Why do you call this a library when there isn't a book anywhere in it?"

Jimmy shrugged and pointed to the modest rack of μCDs. "I have more books here than some universities. And that"—a gesture toward the Stupid Browser—"gets me all the rest." He let the silence that followed speak for his impatience.

"Okay," Hobie said. "Okay. But don't noise this around because right now it's just slander. I've told some people in confidence who need to investigate. If I'm wrong, it stays quiet." He glared at Jimmy from under lowering brows.

Or maybe he was smiling. It wasn't Hobie's fault that he had a countenance that sent people scurrying across the street. Jimmy had seen enough smiling villains to discount flashy dental work. "If it would make you feel better," Jimmy said, "I could tell you bombshells I've kept quiet for a decade or more—but telling secrets might not assure you that I can keep them."

Hobie laughed, and Jimmy discovered that the other man's face could indeed brighten. "Okay, Jimmy. I think management on LEO has been negligent."

Jimmy's first reaction was, *Is that all? That* was the slander? When had there ever been management that was not? He shifted his posture and assumed a look of interest. Surely there must be more . . .

"While I was up," Hobie continued, "I ran material balances and other checks on VHI packages. Production and research. The pure data experiments looked okay, but physical plants were coming up short about half the time. Maintenance records showed a lot of downtime, for repairs and refitting. They short-filled the raw materials on my pilot plant. I think there may be a mission specialist skimming raw materials. Maybe pocketing a little DSM now and then . . ."

"DSM?"

"Directionally-solidified metals. You can fabricate machine tools and bearings that last practically forever. Some of it grows in four-inch slugs." He held his fingers apart to show. "Fits a coverall pocket."

"Worth a lot?"

Hobie nodded. "Enough."

Jimmy pulled at his lower lip. Baleen's product was lightweight, but way too large to fit into anyone's pocket. The start-up catalog number was designed for industrial effluent pipes. As for the raws, if some Lightfinger Lou was running around picking pockets, he'd have a hard time with aerogel and biocanisters. Still, that sort of petty thievery might account for the difference in yield between the LEO and Goddard plants. "Adam said something about waldos misbehaving."

Hobie shook his head and returned to his seat, though he did not sit down. He picked up the nectar and finished it. "I couldn't figure anything there. Teepers check out of their mobiles and go deeby-diving all the time. I've done it myself. Granted, if I'm shelling good troy for a LEO teep, I want as much waldo-time as I can squeeze; but maybe other teepers have more money than they can spend."

Jimmy agreed. "That can be a problem." Which earned him an odd look from Hobie.

"It wasn't so much the trancendental meditation that puzzled me, though. Olya—that's the electrician who was up that rotation—she told me that she never gets a call to fix them; which to me means . . . it's not a malf, right? All except one time when I lost patience and shoved Maharishi Waldo out of my way. Olya got called in that one time, but she says she couldn't find anything wrong."

"Might not have been hardware," Jimmy suggested. "Might've been the cheese."

Hobie spread his hands. "Or Blackhall thought I shoved it harder than I did."

Jimmy checked his watch. "Or it might have been little green men from the asteroids. Well, we better get operational if we're going to match orbits with the wives." He tried to roll out of the chair and got tangled in the frame. Hobie gave him a hand up.

"Why don't you get regular chairs?" he asked.

Jimmy brushed himself off. "Psychology. This way, I keep being reminded to lose weight. I'm going to go look in on Stevie before we go. Do you want to meet him?"

Hobie hesitated just a moment, then said, "Yeah. Sure."

Inwardly, Jimmy shrugged. Some people just didn't care for kids.

Knowledge

When the chatter in the common room in Grissom dorm grew too much, Jacinta sought refuge on the cool grass of the quad, where she lay on her back gazing at the silent and comfortably distant stars. As she often did on these occasions, she amused herself by picking out planets and orbiting stations and imagining the launch vectors that would take her there. The LEO stations were fairly easy. Time the passage across so many degrees of arc and estimate orbital time. Since altitude and velocity were linked, the time to complete a full orbit ballparked the altitude; and, once you knew the altitude, launch on an easterly insertion would need . . .

"Which one is it, do you think?"

By act of will she kept from starting at the voice. "LEO Station," she said of the blinking orange light drifting against the background stars. She spoke with more confidence than she felt, but the appearance of uncertainty was an invitation to others to take control.

Yungduk Morrisey plopped on the grass beside her, sitting cross-legged, not quite in a lotus. "Isn't that where Captain Sulbertson went for his mooner?"

"On *Shepard*. Yeah, that's the place." She used the Voice of Polite Distance. Too much familiarity with the hormonally-challenged could imply invitations, as well.

"That is so bone," he said. "Wish it was me."

She turned her head and looked directly at him. A slim boy. A long, dusky face with just a hint of folding at the corners of the eyes. He had a habit of encountering her that exceeded the known bounds of probability.

He poked at the grass, looked back at the sky. "Always wanted to go out there, like Calhoun and the others. Wrestle with contrary machines; make them dance. How about you?"

It was not a personal question; yet, how could the answer be anything but personal. *I used to watch the birds through the window of my bedroom, wishing I could soar like them.* She'd been, what? Six or seven? And already the feelings of imprisonment had bound her. Escape. Soar. Fly away where her mother's sarcasm would fade into distant, animal barks. Share secret moments like that with a quasi-stranger?

"It's not a question of who's the master," Jacinta said. "The pilot must be-

come one with her machine." She wished he would go away and leave her to
contemplate the stars alone.

Telepathy failed. "I'm going for orbit," he laughed, "not satori."

The ground was warm, like a griddle lately shut off, yielding to the sky the
heat soaked up by day; but already she could feel the chill of desert night
creeping in.

"Cold?" asked Morrisey.

"No," she said, shivering.

"Funny how it can get so cold in a desert," he said.

It was not an original observation; not even the first time she had heard
him say it. She studied him covertly. Was he disappointed that she hadn't
asked him to warm her up? Would he dream about her tonight while he fondled
himself? Imagining that he had lain with her? *Why me?* There were dozens of
girls on campus prettier than she was and, for the most part, more willing.
Nancy Weed was drop-dead gorgeous; and Aodh Kelly made up in enthusiasm
what she lacked in looks.

"The Romans used to make iced cream in the Sahara," Morrisey went on.
"They'd put the jars at the bottoms of pits, keep 'em insulated during the day,
then expose them to the deep sky at night. A cloudless desert sky is a heat
sink."

"Thank you, 'Lou Penny,' " Jacinta said, voice thick with irony.

Morrisey clapped both hands over his chest. "Oh! That hurt!" He dropped
backward, mortally wounded.

Jacinta returned to her study of the heavens. She had wearied of his badi-
nage. "Morrisey," she sighed. "I came out here to be alone."

She heard nothing for a moment, then the sound of scuffing on grass and
gravel. She felt rather than saw him loom behind her. "I wouldn't worry so
much about achieving that particular goal," he said.

She wondered, when he was gone, what he had meant.

Nothing in excess, the recitative went. *Strength lies in the middle. Temperence in
all things.*

Jacinta knew how to have a good time. She enjoyed singing and even joined
the academy choir, where, if she did not contribute greatly to the quality of
sound, neither did she subtract much from it. She liked to swim, too; though
she timed her sessions to hours when few others were likely to use the pool,
and if boys showed up, she quickly found excuses to leave. Her swimsuit covered more than most, even given the circumspect fashions of the late teens;
but it still exposed more flesh than boys were entitled to see—and even where
it did cover, it relieved their pubescent imaginations of too much effort.

There were a handful of sisters in the corps of cadets and they sometimes
met informally in the refectory or the meditation room or even outdoors under

Ad Astra. There were two white roses (both from the southwest, of course), a star of the sea, a huntress, and others; but none of them were silver apples. Jacinta had known that her fledging would be lonely, but she found that she missed the routine of the North Orange Retreat. The morning meditation and recitative, the communal breakfast, the round of classes for the younger sisters, the counseling sessions and support groups. Quiet times tending the garden. Learning a craft. Community service in the neighborhood. There was a certain comfort in knowing how your day would be laid out and even a mystic unity when, once a month and regardless of the local hour, every silver apple on Earth recited the Fourteen Precepts at the same time. She wondered if the other cadet sisters felt the same sense of isolation, as if they were living in a strange and foreign land.

Like most of those who wore "Diana's Bow," Total Meredith was a master of martial arts, so the sisters would sometimes reserve the gym and work up a sweat laying into one another under her guidance. Unpledged girls sometimes joined them; but, while they were never made unwelcome, they seldom stayed more than a few sessions. Sisters often regarded the unpledged as holding themselves more cheaply than they ought, and perhaps these occasional companions sussed that—or, as Jacinta's Granna used to say, "picked up on the vibes."

The huntress was an exacting master. Tall and lean with a whipcord body, the third-year student reminded Jacinta of a greyhound trembling in her starting box. She had a habit of leaning forward when she was intent on something, and seemed perpetually on the verge of toppling over. Yet, her own graceful balance never failed her.

"You could be good," Total told her in the shower one time after an especially strenuous session.

"As what?" Jacinta said. "A punching bag?" She raised her arm to rinse the suds off and winced at the dull pain. They wore padding in the gym and pulled their blows, but they were not expert enough to avoid the occasional strike.

Total laughed and took Jacinta's arm, turning it so she could study the bruise. "You'll live," she decided. "No, I meant you have a natural talent for the Art."

"I've had a few lessons," Jacinta said. "The apples practice self-defense."

"Hunh." The smile on Meredith's face was lightly mocking. "There's a difference between self-defense and the Art." So saying, she drew in her breath and withdrew into the Turtle, her arms weaving slow motion patterns before her. The other sisters turned to watch. Total spun one-footed—on the wet tiles of the shower!—and came down with fingertips brushing gently down Jacinta's spine through the curve in the small of her back. Jacinta gasped at the touch and twisted to keep Total in view.

"I don't think you should be doing this . . ."

"The Art is a dance, an expression," Total said. "A celebration of the body." She struck a pose, displaying smooth muscles and curves, gleaming wet in the spray. Then her torso rose, dipped, and jackknifed and a mock kick toward Kiesha Ames's thigh drew high-pitched giggles from the white rose. The shower cascaded over Total, plastering her short, light blond hair against her head, so that she looked almost skull-like. Her lips were pulled back from her teeth. "What I mean, Sister Jacinta," she said as the concluded her moves, "is that you could be that good, too, if you put in more practice. You've got a good build, good balance." Total circled Jacinta, checking her out. A hand pressed against her shoulder and waist corrected her posture. "A little top-heavy," Total concluded, "but we could work on that."

Adrienne Coster pointedly turned her back, stepped out of the shower room, and bundled herself into a towel large enough to pass for a Roman toga. Total grinned at her. "She's right, sisters. We'll all turn to prunes if we don't finish up." She turned to Jacinta. "Would you mind scrubbing my back?" When Jacinta hesitated, she whispered, "Don't mind Sister Adrienne. You can't be body-shy like she is and live for days at a time on board an orbiter or an LTV or . . ." A wink and a nudge. "On board the *Ares*."

Jacinta took a brush and soap bar from a niche in the stall and rubbed it up and down the taller woman's back. "I need a stepladder," she said, and Total chuckled. After a moment, she said, "I don't think I want to go into the Art that deeply. I mean, it's fun, and all; but I like doing lots of different things. 'Nothing to excess. Strength stands in the middle.' "

"Not me," said Meredith, turning around and taking the brush from Jacinta's hand. "Your turn now." Jacinta turned her back and the other began gently rubbing her. "No, I'm 'total,' like my name. 'Straight out, all out, and all across the board.' Whatever I do, I give it everything I've got."

"Which came first," Jacinta asked, "the name or the attitude?"

Meredith laughed. "My parents were late Boomers, barely old enough for the tail end of the Sixties. My legal name is Totally Awesome. No flubber, charlie," she added as Jacinta turned halfway 'round in astonishment. "Don't even ask about my brother's name."

"I don't think you should dance in the shower," Jacinta said. "You could slip and fall and then Mr. Calhoun would expel you for terminal stupidity."

"Not 'Cat-Foot' Meredith. I've been doing that since I was a weenie, back home in Kansas."

"You're not in Kansas anymore, Total."

Meredith spanked her sharply on the buttock. "Do you want to know how original that one is?"

Jacinta grinned and rubbed the sting. "You mean, I wasn't the first to think of it?"

* * *

The whisper rushed through the academy. Have you heard? Have you heard? The Man! The Man is coming! Repeated on two hundred lips, the sussurrus became a breeze. You could positively hear it if you held still and listened—like a zephyr off the mountains. Ned DuBois, "Doo-Bwah," "The Man Who," dropping by to say hello to his old buddy, Cowboy Calhoun.

The Man Who first flew an SSTO to orbit.

The Man Who first refueled on-orbit.

The Man Who lassoed Gregor Levkin, the Human Moon.

The Man Who flight-tested the sabotaged *flocker* collision-avoidance software.

The Man Who flew the Skopje Rescue.

The Man Who planted the first lunar footprint in forty years.

DuBois had walked large steps. Where Calhoun had gone about his work with quiet competence and good-old-boy joking, DuBois had strutted with style and panache. He had that likable little-boy grin and endearing, can-do flamboyance that guaranteed news-bytes and magazine covers. Jacinta wondered, while she waited for the rumored arrival, whether the superintendent ever felt the slightest twinge of jealousy whenever his "ol' buddy" showed up.

The cadets stood a watch in four on the roads from Tehachapi and Edwards AFB. Each approaching car was scrutinized though telescopes or binoculars.

They should have watched the sky, of course. The jump jet from Edwards was settling onto the athletic field almost before the watchers were aware of its approach. It hurtled across the academy grounds, spilled its forward velocity in one great roar, and baffled over to its lifter fans so smoothly that there was barely a flutter in its attitude. The maneuver even had a name: the DuBois Skid, of course.

By the time she got to the landing site, Jacinta was a short girl in the back of a large crowd, so she climbed the embankment at the base of the admin building and stood on the retaining wall. It was farther away, but she could actually get a better view.

She gained her vantage point in time to see Calhoun and DuBois trade fives at the base of the jet's stairs. Then The Man Who turned and raised his hand to the assembled cadets, who, predictably, went wild, throwing caps and such in the air.

Calhoun was not tall, but he topped DuBois by several inches. DuBois had narrow hips and small feet. Solid in the upper body, though. Almost a dancer's body, Jacinta thought. He wore close-cropped hair and a steel glint in the eye. His brown flight coveralls bore the winged sun logo of Daedalus Aerospace, the Brazilian company that built and flew the first SSTOs back in the early Oughts.

DuBois was swallowed by the hand-shaking mob, which moved off like an amoeba that had engulfed its prey. Jacinta began to follow, but then thought she would hardly get an opportunity for a close encounter in that crush; and besides, the jump jet itself was worth her attention.

A half dozen other cadets thought so, too, and Jacinta was unsurprised to see Yungduk Morrisey lingering among them. They trooped around the plane, singly and in groups, pointing out features to one another. Jacinta contrived to keep the bulk of the 'chine between herself and Morrisey.

Pearl-white, with sleek lines that made it appear to be soaring even while settled into the soft earth of the soccer field. Lifter fans in nacelles, two per side, on a skirt that ran down the side of the fuselage and flared out to form the wings. Centerline jet with an intake faring like a shark's mouth. Looking inside, Jacinta could see the baffles that deflected the thrust from horizontal to vertical and back.

Standing underneath one of the nacelles she peered at the propeller blades hidden in the shadows. They looked almost like feathers. The blade surfaces consisted of thousands of microscopic MEMS—like Ursula's prosthetic arm. A microprocessor in the shaft sensed air turbulence and flexed the MEMS to compensate, so that the fiercely rotating "hushprops" made very little sound. She jumped, hoping to get a grip on the lower rim and pull herself up for a closer look, but just missed. A second leap and . . .

She managed a fingertip grip, swung, fell badly, and knocked the wind out of herself. She sat up on her haunches, gulping air.

"Jacinta, are you all right?" Now how did Morrisey manage that? Did he have some sort of radar?

She looked around. The other cadets had either drifted away or were on the other side of the plane. She could see Morrisey's feet coming around the tail. Solicitude, she didn't need; his, least of all. She ran forward and scampered up the door-stairs into the jet.

The passenger compartment was small—only four seats, and two had been folded down, presumably to accomodate packages of some sort. She crouched behind a seat and waited.

She heard him call her name twice more, then nothing. Shortly, she peeked out the side window by her hiding place and saw the backs of a couple of cadets crossing the athletic field to the campus. She couldn't tell if Yungduk was one of them. She waited a while longer, then tiptoed to the open door.

And Morrisey was waiting at the bottom of the stairs.

"You know, you could get in trouble for that. Sneaking aboard The Man's plane."

"Hey!" she said. "They need a crew . . . You have a jump jet license?"

"What? Where are you . . . Hey! You can't go in there!" He climbed the stairs and followed her onto the flight deck.

"We'll only be here a few minutes," Jacinta told him, "and we won't touch anything. I just want to see what it looks like. You ever fly a jumper?"

He shook his head. "Only on simulators."

She nodded. "Me, too." She lowered herself into the left-hand seat. It was still warm from DuBois.

Morrisey sighed. "Who made you captain?" he demanded as he settled for the right hand seat.

"I did." She studied the array of dials, gauges, switches, and knobs. She recognized the jet controls—she'd seen similar layouts at flying school—but the lifter controls confused her for a while.

Morrisey pointed. "Those switches must start the four fans. And those throttles must adjust rotation and pitch."

"Okay, but where are the readouts?"

"Heads-up on the windscreen? Or maybe virtched?" With computers and A/S, you could have on-demand gauging, which helped reduce visual clutter on the control panel.

Jacinta shook her head. "No way. Single point failure, common cause design. They wouldn't be so bump. All the *basic* readouts must be permanent. That way if the computer foos, you don't lose critical flubber. There. Those are the fan readouts. You've got a back-up set on your panel." Jacinta settled in, checked the reach. "Okay," she said. "where to?"

Yungduk thought for a moment. "Pope AFB, in North Carolina."

Jacinta found the radio beacon code book tucked between the seat and the center floor panel. "Any reason in particular?"

"Yeah. There's a restaurant just off the base that makes a killer kimchee."

Jacinta looked at him. "You grew up there," she guessed.

"Yeah. Dad was stationed in Korea and brought Mom home with him." He rubbed his hands together and licked his lips. "Kimchee . . . Now, that's down-home cookin'." He laughed, forcing a laugh from Jacinta. She ought to guard herself better than that; yet Yungduk was not utterly impossible to like.

They ran through a simulated take off. Ignition. Jet first, then rotors. Number one, okay. Number two . . . Check the indicators. Yungduk supplied the imagined sound of the propellers himself. When all four were up and humming Jacinta pulled back on the throttle. Did a jumper lift with all four rotors on even pitch, or should she kick the forward pair on high and take it up at an angle? Okay, rising . . . Watch the attitude bar. What was the ceiling on the lifters? Kick over to forward thrust . . . Now? Whoops. Where was the switch for that? Hand control? Foot pedal? She ducked her head under the console. There was an extra pedal there. You needed four hands and three feet to fly this thing . . .

Voices outside. She fell silent, listening, and grabbed Yungduk by the arm. Mr. Calhoun was coming. With Colonel DuBois.

Jacinta unbuckled quickly and she and Yungduk scampered for the air stairs. But—no. *They'll see us coming out.* They ran to the back of the plane and shut themselves into the small washroom there. Jacinta wasn't sure if sneaking on board someone's bird qualified as a stunt dumb enough to warrant expulsion, but she was not too keen on finding out, either. She'd just wait them out while DuBois showed the Mr. Calhoun his plane. She looked at Morrisey.

"Don't get any ideas," she told him. "You're just a kay-det. If they wanted you to have ideas, they'd've issued them."

"I wouldn't—" But she cut him off with a finger to her lips.

". . . not just another FarTrip," she heard DuBois say. "If what I heard was the straight skinny, we're talking multiple flights."

"And you say this probe found . . . Where was it?" That was Mr. Calhoun.

"Asteroid 2007KT. It has a Cave just like the Rock—Hi, Liz, come on in."

Another voice, one that Jacinta recognized as her instructor's, said, "Hello, Forrest. Hi, Dad. How was your flight?"

Jacinta missed the travelogue. Ensign *Duh Boyz* was *Doo Bwah's* daughter? And she never told anyone?

"Because, old son," she heard Calhoun say, "if there were a showier entrance possible, you'd've made it. Reminds me of that time Mariesa van Huyten brought all the big hats out to Fernando. Remember? That 'chine was noisier than a Baptist preacher with the Spirit on him.

"How 'bout a little flight before dinner," DuBois said. "The speechifying is afterwards, right?"

"Speech?" Calhoun affected surprise. "Ensign, did we schedule a speech of some sort? Shoot, Ned. Officially, we didn't even know you'd be droppin' in on us. Why would we inflict one of your speeches on the poor kids?" Despite the mockery, Calhoun had used (unwittingly, Jacinta was sure) the Voice of True Affection; and, quite suddenly, the two icons of space flight became for her two human beings.

"The cadets *have* been slacking lately," said Ensign Dubois. "They ought to be punished."

"Hmm. A speech by my good buddy? Doesn't the Constitution forbid that sort of thing? Cruel and unusual?"

"Well, Dad making a speech isn't *unusual* . . ."

"Go ahead," said DuBois, "pretend I'm not here."

"What are they going to—" Jacinta cut Yungduk's question off with a *hush*. "I think they're—"

She didn't have to guess. She could hear the rotors winding up. She turned to Yungduk. "We," she said, "are in deep kimchee."

The washroom was a tight fit for the two of them. It wasn't all that spacious for one. The jump jet rocked and lurched and threw them together often enough that Jacinta began to suspect Yunkduk of enjoying himself. She had to remind herself that it had been *her* idea to hide in here.

Ten minutes into the flight, the knob to the washroom rattled. "What the . . . Hey, Dad! Your head's locked up."

"Shoot," they heard Calhoun answer. "I been tellin' 'im that for years."

"Where's the T-wrench?"

Jacinta looked around the water closet, but Yungduk shook his head. "No, you couldn't even stuff Lou Penny in that supply bin, even with folding and tucking." Jacinta sighed, braced herself, and faced the door just as it opened.

Ensign Liz Dubois stood there. She regarded them for what seemed a long time with no change of expression beyond a widening of the eyes. Then she closed the door. Jacinta and Yungduk exchanged glances. The door opened again. Ensign Dubois shook her head.

"There goes the hallucination theory," she said. Something in her face trembled and Jacinta bit her lip against the anticipated out-chewing; until she realized the Ensign was trying to keep from bursting into laughter.

"It's not that funny," she told the instructor.

"No? You should see it from this side. What are the six parameters that define an orbit?"

Jacinta had to open and close her mouth several times before she found a voice. "Are you serious?"

"Gig one. Morrisey?"

"Uh . . ." Morrisey swallowed, saw no escape. "Argument of perigee, ω."

The ensign was serious. "Eccentricity," Jacinta said quickly. "e."

"Inclination, i."

"Semi-major axis, a."

"Longitude of the ascending node, Ω."

Jacinta hesitated and Yungduk looked at her.

"That's only five," said Dubois with an air of patience.

Jacinta took a breath. "Uh, the sixth parameter is t, time of perigee passage; but, ma'am, that doesn't define the *orbit*, only the ship's location along the orbit."

"So. Then why do we include it with the other five? Morrisey?"

"I didn't know there'd be a pop quiz, ma'am . . . Uh, because satellites can share the same orbit,' like pearls on a string, and t is used to evaluate safe spacing."

"Ma'am?" said Jacinta. "Can we come out now?"

Ensign Dubois grinned. "All right. Dismissed."

Jacinta and Yungduk scrambled out of the lavatory just as Ned DuBois made his appearance. "Lizzie, what the hell is going on back . . . ?" His lips pursed out when he saw the two students. "I'll be . . . Hey, Forrest! We got stowaways! Two of your bunnies were making it in the head."

Jacinta said, "We were not!" in the Voice of Truth, and The Man Who blinked and stepped back.

Calhoun spoke from the cockpit. "Matched set or mixed pair?"

"Mixed pair."

"Mixed pair. Hmm . . . Weed and Ruger, right?"

"No, boss," said Liz. "Rosario and Morrisey."

The plane dipped and banked, throwing them all to the side. When they had untangled themselves, they heard Calhoun's voice. "Sorry, folks. Liz, you sure about that? I mean . . . I can't imagine . . ."

Jacinta drew herself up. "Sir! We were not doing anything."

"I believe you," said Calhoun. "There are a lot more comfortable places on campus for that sort of thing. It's impossible to get it on in a closet that small, anyway."

"Well," said Ned DuBois, "actually, it isn't." Everyone looked at him. He shrugged, palms up.

As they trooped to the front of the plane, Jacinta asked her instructor why she spelled and pronounced her name differently, and Ensign Dubois answered, "I didn't want to be 'Ned DuBois's daughter' all my life."

"Then why not use another name entirely?"

Liz shrugged. "I didn't want to disown him, either."

When they reached the cockpit, Mr. Calhoun relinquished the controls to Colonel DuBois and joined them in the aisle. He rubbed his chin. "So. What were you two doing back there?"

"Hiding," said Morrisey. "I wanted to see the controls and talked Cadet Rosario into sneaking aboard with me. When we heard you coming . . ."

"Hah!" said DuBois from the cockpit. "So that's why the radio frequencies were reset. You two were running a dry sim."

Calhoun held up a hand. "Is that true, Rosario?"

"No, sir. I was the one who talked Cadet Morrisey into climbing in."

"Hmm. A novel form of finger-pointing. Question is, what do we do with stowaways?"

"Throw 'em out the door," suggested DuBois, "or their extra mass will use up our fuel."

Calhoun nodded slowly. "Those are the cold equations, all right." He pondered the issue for a moment, then glanced at Liz, who nodded. Calhoun wagged a finger at the two cadets. "We'll discuss this groundside. Meanwhile . . . There's something to be said for a couple of would-be pilots who'd rather see the inside of a 'chine than tag after some washed-up, has-been, hotshot."

"Hey," said DuBois, the injured innocent.

"So," the superintendent said, "the only question left is: Which of you wants to be first to take a turn at the yoke?"

It would have been unseemly to push and elbow her way into the cockpit, so she and Yungduk deferred to each other until Mr. Calhoun, with an exaggerated sigh, pulled an eagle from his pocket and called the toss. Lady Liberty faced up, and smiled on Jacinta.

Later, sitting in the back, Morrisey whispered to Jacinta. "Did you hear what they were saying before, about a new FarTrip?"

Jacinta nodded. "More'n one." She wondered what was up. Or was this one of those periodic rumors that fluttered through the spaceflight community? President Rutell was not an avid supporter of manned flight beyond the Moon, as witness the dithering on *Ares*; and even the unmanned Visitor probes were launched only thanks to pressure from Darryl Blessing and Mariesa van Huyten.

"Take a couple years to get 'em mounted, I guess," Morrisey said.

Jacinta smiled and settled into her seat. "Well, if they ever launch 'em, there's one has my name on it."

13.

Lame Excuses

Billie Whistle waited patiently for her visitor to compose herself. Tanuja Pandya, the famous author—and wife to the flamboyantly reclusive Jimmy Poole—was short and dumpy, dark-skinned, with a large, round nose. Well, Jimmy was no Adonis, either; so maybe they made the perfect couple. Billie noticed how Pandya's eyes kept straying to the laser cup on the stump of her right arm. That sort of reaction annoyed Billie, who felt that accidents of appearance should not matter, so she left the stump resting openly on the chair arm. Stray thoughts caused the microlasers to sparkle like Christmas lights.

"Surprised?" she asked the novelist with just a touch of cloying sweetness around the whetstoned edge of the words.

Pandya sipped from her teacup. (And why, in an apartment piped for coffee, had the woman asked for *tea*? To show Billie how helpless she was when events deviated from her set routines? Billie could have made the coffee herself; but she'd had to ask Pandya to reach the seldom-used tea bags.) "Startled," the author said, "but not surprised. After all, so many of you people are off the norm in one way or another."

" 'You people . . .' " Billie bounced the phrase back, a high lob that hung spinning in the air. She shifted her body slightly and raised her stump just so Pandya would know she knew what *off the norm* meant. Billie hadn't tried to put any sarcasm into the voice; though if it was there, she didn't care. And she was genuinely puzzled. Why was Pandya here? Was it really for the sake of research, as the novelist had claimed? Or was she running some subtle errand for Poole?

"The virtch is a major setting in my new novel," Pandya told her, "and I need to know more about the people who live there."

"Who 'live' there . . ." Billie suggested.

"Who make it their life. Thousands of people 'surf the net' or 'hit the web' or 'slalom the lattice.' They research projects, post to hobby boards, chat with soul-mates half a world away; and it no more *consumes* their life than the telephone or the television. But there are others who. . . ."

"Are 'off the norm.' "

If that embarrassed the Indo, it didn't show. Instead, she nodded as if Billie had simply agreed with her. "Psychologically and physically. The socially challenged. The immature. The disabled. Jimmy is hardly normal. Neither are most of the people he talks about. Captain Cat. Mighty Mouse. SuperNerd. It all sounds so . . ."

"Stupid?"

"No. Like some odd blend of adolescence and Machiavelli. There is such a delight in secrecy and manipulation and pranking that—"

"You have a strange interviewing technique. No wonder you never wrote a second book."

Kazang! That one hit home. Billie could see the hurt flash briefly in the other woman's eyes. "I only want to understand you people."

Billie shook her head. "No. You want to understand some template you've created in your head. You want to know why so many of 'us' are 'off the norm'? I'll tell you why! Because, *in there*—" She pointed with her stump at her telecom console, and something in her anger must have triggered the right synapses, because the system suddenly booted. "—in there, 'no one knows you're a dog.' No one can judge you on superficial appearances—on your gender or your skin or your age or whether you have the *normal* number of arms and legs! Because no one knows *anything* but what you tell them. It's a meeting of minds. Only your words are real; and nothing's real *but* your words, because you *are* your words; and your words are you! In there, I get respect and admiration and—yes—argument; *but I don't get pity!*"

"The flesh made word," Pandya said, and wrote something in the stupid notebook she carried.

Somehow, the silence that followed was not awkward. Billie had thrown it all at Pandya; and the writer had simply taken it in. She was not sorry she had said it; not even sorry Pandya had provoked it. She was done with being sorry. "And do you know what the funny part is?"

Pandya shook her head.

"I'm not really all that into it. Oh, I'm good. Even back in grade school everyone was saying how I should be a 'programmer.' And, of course, now, it's what I do. But my passion was always for dancing." And now, for the first time, Billie saw dismay on Pandya's face. "Yeah. Dancing. Ballet. Jazz. Ironic as all hell, isn't it?"

Pandya shifted in her chair. "I'm . . . distressed to hear that."

And it *was* distress, not pity; and for that, for a brief moment, she loved the other woman. "I'll get over it," she said gruffly.

"I never would."

"What do you know about it?"

"Very little." Pandya put her teacup aside. "I apologize. Your appearance did put me off and I spoke without thinking."

"Don't apologize. Not for that. Too many people think 'polite' means pretending not to notice." She raised her stump and saw a wince on the Indo's face; but her shame at the manipulation was only momentary. Pandya's apology had been too perfunctory and she ought to suffer at least a little.

After that, the interview was endurable. Billie explained as best she could about the electro-encephalitic interface and how it "read" synapses in the brain and translated them into electro-optical signals that could be transmitted to her equipment. "I can tutor the A/S to translate any arbitrary signal as a specific command," she said. "For example, I think the menu bar down by imagining the taste of chocolate."

Scribble, scribble, scribble. "Really?"

No, I lie like hell in interviews. Did Pandya know how insulting she was? Billie showed her teeth. "Really."

More scribbles. "The thought has no connection to the command . . . ?"

"No more than ringing bells has with hunger."

". . . Because when Jimmy uses verbal commands, he—"

"—Has to say things like 'Open' or 'Run.' " Billie shrugged. "That's just the way the software's been winkled. Keeps life easy for the meatware. But for F/F, it's the *system* that's being trained."

"I . . . see. Do you . . . become one with your system?"

"Ah. The mystic unity of mind and machine . . . I was wondering when you'd bring that bump up." Billie did not keep the sneer from her voice. She had been waiting for the question. It was always asked. "Pure spam. My macdonald—"

More scribble-scribble. "Your macdonald?"

Billie ran her left hand through the input jacks in her skull. "The induction cap. Encephalic Interface for Electronic Input/Output. An EIEI/O. It's a neural net. You can train it to respond to specific neuron sequences, but it's nothing more than a surgically-implanted channel wand. The microlasers on my cup and headband are like those sticks people used to point at their TVs and VCRs before voice commands became the In Thing." Only faster and more efficient, and she had a *lot* of links, which she demonstrated by thinking rapidly through her "carnival" sequence and turning on every appliance in sight.

The computer booted, the speakerphone beeped a number, the TV activated and uploaded an old movie, and the speakers poured out Tchaikovsky's *Pathetique* symphony. *Only a parlor trick,* she thought as she watched Pandya struggle between being impressed at the accomplishment and being appalled at the price paid for the ability. The notes of Tchaikovsky's horns swelled and ached and tore at Billie's gut. She had forgotten she'd been listening to it earlier. Before the melancholy brass could carry her away, Billie thought the player off and, in the sudden silence, Pandya turned to look at her.

"Does it work the other way?" Pandya asked.

"You mean, can I download straight to cortex?" Flatskulls always wanted to know that, too. Could she "play" the music into her mind? Did the data analyses come into her thoughts? Some people had a need for fables; to imagine something wonderfully impossible rather than something boringly real. So: scare stories about people *with computers attached to their brains!* having *unfair advantages!* Flatskulls didn't have enough brain to jack into or they'd know better.

"You can train a macdonald to respond to specific neuron sequences; but you can't work the trick the other way. That would mean conditioning the *brain* to respond to the computer's signals." And leave it there for Pandya to figure out the implications. Maybe someday they could work the "reverse macdonald" and she could "remember" data by "wondering" the question. But that way (if the rumors were true) lay crippling agnosia. *Scroll down a menu bar, and get a sudden, irresistible craving for chocolate . . .*

Of course, there were rumors. Experimental prosthetics. Limited purpose. She lifted her stump to show Pandya how her wheelchair worked and, briefly, considered the thought of having an arm again. Strangely enough, she wasn't sure she did; and she wasn't sure why she didn't.

She showed Pandya the disk drive on the left side of her wheelchair, where she could insert and remove disks with her "good" arm. "I *think* the WRITE TO command and *ponder* the option menu until I get REMOTE," she explained. "The VCSEL laser chips have receptors on them, too. I pick up the signal with my stump—" She illustrated it by pointing her arm at the cell on the hard drive. "—And the datastream gets shunted to the floppy in the chair. That's less awkward for me than reaching for the floppy slot on the hard drive."

For some reason, that seemed to intrigue the older woman. Pandya leaned forward. "How close do you have to be for it to work? Do you have to be in the same room?"

Billie frowned. "I don't know. I suppose line o' sight and inverse square are what matters."

"So you could be in a building across the street, say?"

"I guess so. Why?"

Pandya wrote something in her notebook. "I probably shouldn't say; but you're involved anyway. It's because of the job Jimmy did for Adam."

Billie shook her head. There was a *non sequitur* there. Who was Adam? But she didn't quite ask the question. Pandya thought she knew something. Confessing ignorance might only perpetuate that ignorance. "Which Adam?" she said, suggesting with her tone that there might be more than one.

"Van Huyten. Adam van Huyten, your boss."

An icicle formed in her heart. Where had this woman gotten the notion that Adam van Huyten was connected with Baleen? If Baleen had a "boss" it was David Desherite.

Unless . . .

Could Adam van Huyten be the source of David's money? Was that why he was so wary of drawing on it?

"Oh," she said with the air of recollection. "Yes. When Jimmy helped Mr. van Huyten to . . ."

". . . get aboard LEO Station. Yeah. I wasn't too happy with that. Jimmy says it was all legal, but I'm not so sure. Now he's trying to contact these Finger people . . ."

It was all coming at her too fast. What did the Five Fingers have to do with anything? And Pandya had implied that David *was* Adam van Huyten wearing a false persona. But why? Unless . . . And now the chill became fear, her microlasers sending out conflicting signals as her mind raced. But she kept her face composed; and if she hesitated too long in answering, her visitor did not appear to notice. Billie smiled and said the proper, meaningless words. The royal road to knowledge was a knowing look and a profound silence. Pandya obliged and filled in the blanks.

It helped that Pandya was worried about her husband's exposure in whatever game David (no, Adam!) was playing. She mentioned things that a properly cautious person might have withheld, as if she was not even aware that there might be a second game being played. Each word was another brick walling Billie into her tomb.

How she brought the visit to a close she could not remember afterward. But somehow she shepherded Pandya out the door and then sat, shaken and bewildered, among the equipment the Nameless Ones had bought for her. Adam van Huyten was planning some sort of revenge and Baleen was somehow his tool.

Not hard to identify his target. If Adam van Huyten had discovered who had fingered the stock transactions that made him the fall-guy, he'd come down hard with both feet.

The question was—did Jimmy know, too? Was that his work for David— for Adam? *He* was going to do to her what *she* had done to Adam. In that case, Pandya's visit was more ominous. Not a naïf, but a messenger delivering the Black Spot.

Billie had to know what Poole knew; and the only way she saw to get close enough was to cooperate in his scheme to contact the Fingers. A set-up? Maybe. And maybe the whole of Baleen was a set-up, so David could entice her onto the wild side—else why insert that fly into Baleen's software? Not to eavesdrop on Leo, but to expose Billie to the hammer of Justice.

A laugh broke her silence. It fell on her ears like the bark of a far-off dog. All the while they were building Baleen, she had secretly dreamed that someday David would fuck her.

And now it looked like he would.

For the first time in three years she needed a drink; and when she reached for the bottle under the sideboard where she kept refreshments for her guests, she used her right hand.

One moment of distraction like that, and the past spits in your face. Billie sat frozen, the stump of her arm stretched out seven inches shy of the bottle, and cried.

14.

Common Ground

Washington was too far south to get genuine winters, but made up for it by achieving near paralysis with even a rumor of snow or ice. Mariesa and Dr. Blessing stepped from the taxicab into a wretched blend of sleet and rain. The sidewalk was a motley of ice patches and water puddles, sitting, as the town itself so often did, on the fence. It was not yet clear which way the vote was going. Blessing gave her his arm for support, though Mariesa wasn't sure he was offering or accepting.

The rundown store front had graced the flyers of The People's Crusades for the better part of two decades, a defiant symbol of the Little Guy versus the System. Not for the Crusades was the marbled lobby or the brass fitting; rather, an old neighborhood grocery, converted into offices. It stood on a Washington side street facing a humdrum lower-middle-class neighborhood. The staff, too, affected a funky, retro-sixties, tie-dyed-and-jeans image, though only in Phil Albright's personal case was it an aboriginal look.

"It's amazing," Blessing said as they paused outside the entrance, "what they accomplish on a shoestring."

Mariesa said nothing. The Crusades was the largest operation in the advocacy industry, and handled an impressive cash flow. The Crusades took in donations and grants—from corporations and charitable foundations and government agencies; from the plaintiff's bar; from those who wanted to feel good without actually doing anything; from an army of dedicated youth marching door-to-door; from the sales of items as diverse as Appalachian handicrafts, solar power, litigation kits, and even souvenir bric-a-brac. And donations and grants were disbursed—to buy up and "bank" emission permits; to fund battered women's shelters; to supplement union strike funds, to establish nature reserves; to purchase stock (and hence, a voice) in key businesses—or any of dozens of causes that Mariesa regarded variously as vital, useful, prudent, quixotic, counterproductive, or wrong-headed. You could call the Crusades many things, but a shoestring operation it was not.

And if some of that cash flow stuck to Phil Albright? Well, what CEO did not enjoy the perks of his position? The Crusades ran an eight percent surplus, according to most estimates; and, being a not-for-profit, did not have to disburse that surplus to any owners. Doing well by doing good. To Phil's credit, though he lived higher than his publicity let on, he did not abuse that surplus as badly as some non-profits had. A small inheritance, unmentioned in his official biography, removed whatever temptation there might have been.

Inside the building, young men and women answered phones and sorted mail and trolled the net. It was an open room, no cubicles, and the amount of chatter and horseplay would have distressed most office managers. The receptionist tossed a blond pony tail and said, "Can I help you?" At least Mariesa assumed he was the receptionist. His battered, old, secondhand desk sat nearest to the door.

Daryll Blessing said, "We have an appointment with Phil."

The young man looked over his shoulder at a closed door, unimpressed with the implied first-name familiarity. Albright was always "Phil." It was part of the image. "He's meeting with the Cadre right now, but they oughta be done soon. Have a seat over there by the big table. There's a coffeepot in the back. Help yourself."

They found the coffeepot in a niche in the narrow hallway that must have led, at one time, to the grocery's stockroom. The niche contained a sink, coffeemaker, and microwave. A rack of mugs hung from a pegboard that was screwed none too sturdily into the wall. Daryll reached for a mug and hesitated and Mariesa said, "Don't bother looking. I doubt there is a Styrofoam cup anywhere in the building."

"But Styrofoam is recyclable."

"I'm sure they keep the mugs clean."

Actually, she was sure of no such thing. Several water-filled mugs sat in the sink and a laser-printed sign read: THERE'S NO MAID SERVICE HERE. CLEAN YOUR OWN CUPS. The second sentence had been underlined with a red marker and exclamation points added. Someone else had written in blue: *This means you!* But if dirty cups were a problem, how would posting a sign help? The root cause wasn't likely to be that people didn't know the rules.

Mariesa assumed that the mugs without names on them were communal property. She took one off the rack and rinsed it in hot water from the tap. Daryll said, "I don't really need any more caffeine today." Mariesa looked at him, swallowed a smile, and rehung the cup.

They sat at the "big table"—it was actually several smaller tables pushed together—and watched the television bolted to a swivel platform on the wall. It was tuned to C-SPAN, where the 115th Congress was trying to organize itself—as it had been for three solid weeks. A messier process than even the 114th. The tote board in the screen's footer registered the vote for Speaker. Every now and then, the tally for one or another of the five candidates would change as members made up their minds. Sometimes, the total would go down, evidencing second thoughts on someone's part. One of the passing Crusaders stopped to watch for a moment.

"What a *foo*," she offered. "This is the *seventh* round, and not *one* of those charlies will drop. Don't know *what* Osborne is thinking. He's going against his *own party*. No *way* can he win."

"I suppose," Mariesa said, "at some point, the party leaders will go into a back room and cut deals."

"'S long as it's not a *smoke-filled* back room." The line was delivered straight, so either the woman was serious or she played a killer hand of poker. "Get the house*keeping* out of the way so the *House* can get down to *business*."

"Some people feel that the longer the Congress stays tied in knots, the less harm it can do."

Mariesa had meant the comment humorously. While it was remarkable how little daily life was affected by the deadlock, the government did have legitimate and urgent business to conduct. But the Crusader gave her an appraising look, as if seeing her for the first time as something other than an ear. Perhaps she was unaccustomed to heterodox opinions—a common trap for those who chattered only among themselves. Mariesa had seen the same reaction at board meetings.

"Woulda been better," the Crusader said, "if *one* of the parties had a majority or even a honking big plurality."

"Even if it were the American Party?"

"I meant a *legitimate* party."

Mariesa turned to the television once more. "If McRobb is elected Speaker, it would be a disaster for the country."

"Hey," said the Crusader, who had finally heard orthodoxy, "no flubber on *that* one."

The Cadre meeting broke up soon after, and Roberta ushered them into Phil's office. The office was sparsely furnished, in keeping with the man's self-effacing image—a pair of battered vertical files, an old wooden desk, a cork board full of newspaper clippings. Fading "grip-and-grins" on the walls showed a younger Albright with Rubin, Alinksy, Nader, and others. Albright himself rose unsteadily from behind his big wooden desk to greet them, but both Mariesa and Daryll asked him to stay seated. They took two of the folding chairs that the Cadre had just abandoned and pulled them up close to the desk. Roberta Carson folded the other chairs and stacked them against the wall, then stood a little behind Phil. Ellis Harwood and Isaac Kohl, two other members of the inner circle, lingered.

"Mind if we stay, Phil?" Harwood asked. He was a big man, a footballer in his college days, and liked to say that he was living proof that not all progressives were wimps. Isaac Kohl, who oversaw EarthSafe Solar and other technology issues for the Crusades, was the argument for the affirmative. Where Harwood was Albright's age and wore a professor's tweed jacket and an open, tieless shirt from which emerged a tuft of whitened chest hair, Kohl, who was closer to Roberta's age, was thin and gawkish and wore thick glasses. The idea that hair graced any part of his body other than the top of his head seemed ludicrous, and even there it was growing debatable.

Phil looked to Daryll Blessing for an answer to Harwood's question. Mariesa glanced at Roberta, who nodded very slightly.

"No objections," Mariesa said. Daryll gave her a raised eyebrow, but said nothing.

Blessing cleared his throat and leaned forward on his cane. "Phil, what we're going to show you isn't common knowledge yet. Mariesa thought you ought to see them; but we'd appreciate it if you kept quiet until Deep Space makes an announcement." Daryll stared pointedly at the three Cadre members flanking Phil.

Phil looked at them a moment, then exchanged glances with Roberta. "Deep Space?" Isaac Kohl pursed his lips and his eyes flashed. Harwood folded his arms across his chest.

Daryll said, "Mariesa?" Mariesa reached down and snapped open her portfolio. She pulled out a folder. "These are downloads from the cameras on the first six Visitor Probes to reach their targets." She opened the folder and spread the pixures across the desk. Black and white, with pixel-noise in spots. Small worlds against the pitiless stars. Some bright, some dark and ragged. All of them scarred and pitted.

Phil bent over the pixures. He sorted through them, one at a time, passing them to Roberta, who passed them on to an eager Kohl and a more blasé Harwood. Four asteroids seemed normal. Two had enormous craters in one end. And inside the crater of one of them . . . Phil stopped and held a pixure up, closer to his face.

"Yes," said Mariesa. "That one. That was acquired just after Christmas."

Phil fumbled in his shirt pocket and perched a set of reading glasses on his nose. He squinted at the pixure, held it at an angle. "What is that?" Roberta leaned across his arm to look.

"An engine. We think."

Phil's head jerked up and he stared at her. "An engine!" Kohl whistled. "Kool beans!"

"There's to be a conference over the matter next week, at Deep Space in Brussels."

"An engine?" Phil asked again. Harwood took the pixure from his hands and studied it. He looked over the top edge at Mariesa.

"These pixures aren't morphed, are they?" he asked. Mariesa didn't bother to answer him.

"You can't really say it's an engine," Phil objected. "It's just a . . . a reflective area. Maybe a closer look . . . Remember the faces on Mars? One looked like a smiley face button." Phil laughed and Mariesa forced herself to chuckle with him. She was acutely aware of Roberta's gaze.

"Deep Space is taking the idea seriously," she said. "The probe that doided that pixure was destroyed but—"

"Destroyed!" Kohl interrupted. "How?"

Daryll Blessing coughed, a long, wet cough. He wiped his lips with a handkerchief. "An energy flux," he said. "When the probe maneuvered for a closer look at that shaft, something inside the shaft ignited, vaporizing the spacecraft. The last few telescopic observations before the asteroid passed behind the sun suggest it is now in a different orbit."

"A different orbit," said Roberta. She looked at Mariesa.

Blessing shrugged. "The asteroid is sunward of us, moving faster. It will reappear in the east next April as a morning star. We've projected the right ascension and declination for the original orbit and for the series of hasty observations last December; and Venus, the only gravity well with any say in the matter, is on this side of the sun. So—"

"So, in theory," Isaac Kohl interjected, "nothing natural should perturb the orbit in the meantime."

Blessing breathed heavily and rested his chin on his cane. "That's right, young man."

"Then," said Harwood, "we won't know for certain until next April, when we either will or won't see it at the 'appointed time and place.' "

"Or we see it," Mariesa suggested quietly, "coming directly toward us."

Blessing humphed. "Hardly likely, dear. The probabilities are that any new orbit will send it farther off."

"Only if the vector change was random." She and Blessing shared a gaze. The astronomer pursed his lips. His head bobbed.

"Yes. Well. We cannot afford to ignore that possibility." He turned to Albright. "You see how important it is," he said to the activist, "to keep track of these objects. While the chances of an impact are slim, they are not negligible; and, if nothing else, careful tracking can help dispel any . . ." Another moist cough. ". . . Any hysteria on the public's part."

Phil's glance flickered to Mariesa for a moment. "What do you expect me to do, Daryll?"

Kohl broke in. "Mount a Crusade," he said. "Oh, man. If one of those hit us, it would be the ultimate ecotastrophe." Roberta opened her mouth to speak, but Harwood held up his hand.

"And just what would we be crusading for, Ike? What exactly will we ask people to do?"

It was the astrophysicist who answered. "Donate," said Blessing, "to keep SkyWatch funded."

"I thought so. Phil, we talked about this last fall and gave it a pass."

Albright picked up the photographs once more and looked through them. "We have more information now."

Harwood spread his hands as if praying. "What do we have? One very ambiguous glimpse. One spacecraft that malfunctioned. Let's not go overboard, Phil. Don't get me wrong. I'm all in favor of science; and this particular case might have some . . ." In a droll tone. ". . . Practical spin-off; but we need to look at the proposal and decide who it helps and who it hurts."

The meeting closed a few minutes later with no more resolution than a promise to rethink the proposal. Mariesa told Daryll that she had some personal business with Phil that would not take long and asked him to wait for her outside. When the door shut, Phil looked a question at her.

"Personal business?"

Mariesa straightened her skirt, shifted on the uncomfortable folding chair, straightened her skirt again. "Yes." She retrieved her portfolio and placed it on her lap. "McRobb must not become Speaker."

Phil blinked rapidly at the odd change in topic. Roberta cocked her head, but waited, saying nothing.

"We're in agreement, there," Phil said. "But what do you propose doing about it?"

"The Democrats are split. That was inevitable after the unions went American—"

"Not all of them," Phil made the conventional demurral.

"No, not all. But 'imported goods and exported wages' was too good a campaign slogan. And when he talks about immigrants driving down 'decent, union wages' . . . Well, now even the Democrats are echoing that line."

Phil said, "That's why Osborne is bidding for the Speakership." He paused and lowered his brows. "I guess I can tell you. One confidence . . ." He indicated the Deep Space photographs. ". . . Invites another. Osborne is trying to keep the waverers inside the party by giving them a 'McRobb Lite' alternative. If he doesn't, and the old Gephart wing bolts . . . Well, the oldest political organization in the country will go into the dustbin of history."

"The Republicans," Mariesa told him, "have the same problem. The old Buchanan faction—"

"My heart bleeds for the Grand Old Party."

Mariesa shrugged. "My Republican friends would be just as happy to see them go; but then . . ."

"Oh. 'But then' McRobb has the votes he needs. I tell you, if I ordered a truckload of sons of bitches and McRobb was the only one delivered, I'd still sign off the bill of lading." Albright's mouth thinned into a line. "To think I've lived this long to see this happen. It's just as well I won't—" Roberta reached out and squeezed him on the shoulder. Phil stopped and leaned back in his chair. He reached up with his own hand and covered hers. "Just as well," he said.

"What is it you want?" Roberta asked Mariesa. "To break his heart?"

Mariesa locked eyes with the younger woman. "No. Only . . . looking for common ground. Civil rights Democrats, free-trade Republicans . . . and the

Liberty Party, if they act together, might keep enough moderates from stampeding to McRobb to elect a Speaker."

Phil looked up sharply. Then he sighed. "And if pigs had wings . . . Who could those three agree on? They don't exactly see eye-to-eye on the issues."

"Neither do a husband and wife," Mariesa said. "They learn to accommodate each other." *Or they do not.* She was suddenly acutely aware of her own divorce.

"Now, there's a *ménage a trois*," said Roberta. "Just holler 'government program' and they'll run three different ways."

Mariesa shrugged. "FDR's coalition of urban blacks and Southern segregationists was not particularly homogeneous. Nor were Lincoln's Republicans— or Gingrich's, for that matter. It's a matter, as I said, of interested parties finding common ground. They may not agree on everything they support, but they surely can agree on one thing they oppose."

"Meaning McRobb." Phil shook his head. "Can you build an alliance based on opposition to one thing?"

"Ask Hitler. He went up against one."

Albright blinked, then smiled. "Good point. Even if a coalition doesn't last, it can last long enough to burn McRobb's bacon." He turned. "What do you think, Robbie?"

Roberta spoke to Phil, but she kept her eyes on Mariesa. "I've been telling you for years, Phil. If we all stand together, who can knock us down? You can bring us together."

"Blaise won't like it. This coalition might not—hell, they *will* not—agree on his man as Speaker."

Roberta rubbed his shoulder. "He'd like McRobb a whole lot less. You can bring Blaise Rutell around, if any man can."

Albright swiveled in his chair and gazed at where a window might have been, if his office had had a window. He steepled his fingers under his chin and thought for a moment. "You're right. The Speaker's no autocrat, not like in Reed's day. There are the committee chairs. Ways and Means, especially. We could do some horse trading. Divvy up the committees in exchange for lining up behind . . . ?" He arched his brows in Mariesa's direction.

"Does it matter?"

Phil grunted. "Right. We're not the politicians. We just nudge them in the right direction. I take it your part will be to swing Liberty behind the deal. What about the Republicans?"

"We both know people there," Mariesa said. "You have an in with the Rockefeller faction and I know some of the Kaisich people."

A grin broke Albright's face. The first genuine smile Mariesa had seen in their last several meetings. "It might work," he said. "It just might work."

"But there's a price," Roberta said. She faced Mariesa squarely, though her hand never left Albright. "Isn't that right, Mariesa? You never do anything without prices paid."

Mariesa said nothing. She reached across the desk and gathered the pixures from the asteroid probes, straightened them against the desktop, and returned them to their folder. She inserted the folder into her portfolio and closed the snaps. Then she looked at Roberta.

"Oh. I should have guessed." She gave a careless shrug. "Well, we're halfway there; we might as well throw in." She took a step toward the door.

"There's one more thing," Mariesa said.

Roberta stopped and a flicker of annoyance crossed her face. "Another price?"

"No. Nothing to do with any of this. Only, I—" Mariesa paused for breath, surprised at the sudden gust of emotion that accompanied her resolve. "I have decided to dedicate Silverpond as a nature preserve for the children of North Orange and Berwick Township. The mansion is to be converted to a museum and learning center."

Roberta said, "What?" Albright cocked his head, and his eyes danced with interest.

"The van Huyten Trust has agreed to underwrite half the cost, the remainder to be covered by donations. I wish The People's Crusades to operate the center and to oversee field trips by the local schools. The only proviso is that the exhibits will focus on the flora and fauna found on the estate and address nothing political."

"Everything is political," Albright said.

Roberta said, "It's a tax write-off, right?"

"Of course, it's a tax write-off. And, no, Phil, not everything is political. It's just that children should grow up . . . knowing the names of the trees."

"A bribe, to make sure the Crusades backs your asteroid tracking, in case the anti-McRobb plan falls through."

"Oh. And one other proviso—"

Roberta smacked her palm. "I knew it!"

"There is a young boy named Will Sutherland, who lives in Skunktown Furnace. He is to have access to the reserve at any time and personal tutoring if he wants it."

Roberta followed her to the outer room, where Daryll Blessing, bundled in synthfur against the sleet, waited patiently in a chair, chatting with Harwood and others.

"Silverpond was where you grew up," Roberta said.

"Yes. And my father, too."

"You've lived there all your life."

"There is no one there now but me. It is past time for a change."

"Why are you giving it away?"

Roberta was so distraught that Mariesa wondered. "You used to come by, too. When you were young." There might be an irrational nodule of possessiveness there. Another landmark of her childhood swept away.

"It's not that. It's . . ." Roberta stopped, confused. "I don't understand."

"Perhaps it is my way of seeing that the house goes to you." Before Roberta could respond with more than an astonished look, Mariesa asked in a low voice, "Tell me, have you told him?" The question hung in the air a moment before Roberta placed a hand over her womb and shook her head in solemn silence.

"I haven't decided. He won't be around to raise it, you know. That would break his heart."

Mariesa laid a hand on Roberta's arm. "Have faith in the future, dear," she said. "If you don't, who will?"

The jump jet sped across white, trackless wastes, and Mariesa kept a deathgrip on the armrests the entire distance north from High Level. The lifter fan hushprops were eerily quiet and the flight passed with a sound much like a constant wind. The pilot seemed a part of his machine—head phones, dark, mirrored glasses, and a stony look of concentration robbed him of humanity. A gust of wind sprayed the windscreen with ice crystals scoured from the prairie below and the plane bucked slightly. Mariesa sucked in her breath.

Nikolai Cunningham, in the copilot's seat, turned to face her. "We're almost there."

Thank God. Flying was unnerving at any time. A winter flight into northern Alberta in a four-seater was something else. Inkling, seated on her left, seemed to enjoy himself. He gawked at the whiteness below, pointing out the frozen Hay River, the ice-ensheathed trees, the cozy farmsteads with blacktopped roads scraped clear. Mariesa glanced where he pointed, smiled in an ephemeral fashion, and kept her gaze locked otherwise straight ahead.

Until Inkling pointed out the ash.

The jumper banked as it passed over a band of dingy ice and snow. A layer of soot and soil had settled into it and it was melting already from the decreased albedo. The dark band curved away in both directions, a vast circle whose far side could not yet be seen. A little distance beyond, lay a second band of darkened snow. Concentric circles.

"Interesting," Inkling said in typical understatement.

A house passed below them. Miniature people hammered boards over shattered windows, nailed down loosened roof tiles. Father along, the ash became a continuous layer, as if brown snow had fallen from the sky. A stand of cottonwoods lay splayed upon the ground, with stripped branches pointing south. No longer a "stand." Nearby, a barn had collapsed and a fractured silo had spilled its store of winter feed. A high tension power line had been blown down and the pylons lay like toppled dominoes across Highway 35. South-bound cars from Steen River and Indian Cabins waited patiently at police barricades while heavy equipment shifted the wreckage off the roadway. An ATV had cut across the field alongside the road. The plane passed by. A few people—workmen, police, stranded motorists drinking coffee out of thermoses—looked up. A child waved. Then the scene was behind them. Mariesa didn't see if the ATV made it.

Cunningham pointed out the front windscreen. "There it is."

"May we circle before we land?" Mariesa asked. Her body shrieked to be on solid earth once more; but this particular earth was not so solid.

The pilot asked for clearance—the first words he had spoken the whole way up from High Level—and must have received it, because he banked sharply to the right and then began a long, slow circuit to the left. Mariesa had to crowd close to Inkling to see out his window.

It was not a large crater, as such things went. The bowl was a bare hundred meters across—most of the bolide had vaporized before impact, sending its shock wave through the air. Yet, the heat released had been enough to sublimate the snow and ice for a mile around and turn the permafrost temporarily into a boggy pit. Witnesses had reported a violet streak across the sky, where the very air had been ionized by the bolide's passage.

Work crews were erecting equipment around the site. Beds of railroad ties had been laid down on the softened earth. Work trailers for the scientists were connected by cables and snow-fences and linked by satellite dish to the outside world. Banks of floodlights ran off portable generators. Mariesa watched a pair of researchers squelching through the crater bottom, their boots sinking deep into the grasping mud. A helicopter carrying some sort of equipment on its undercarriage passed back and forth over the impact site.

"Well," said Inkling. "It's not as big as I expected."

Mariesa said nothing, but stared at the scene and the mud, still steaming as it released its heat to the winter air.

"It's not exactly what you've been shrieking about all these years, is it?" Solomon Dark, the president's deputy security advisor and *de jure* chairman of the Extraordinary Commission on Impacts, raised his brows and looked at Mariesa over the tops of his reading glasses, thus managing to look both surprised and supercilious at the same time.

Solomon Dark was a short man and vibrated with the intensity such men often cultivated. He was never seen but in the cutting edge of fashion: by the time his suits, ties, and shirts adorned store mannequins, he was wearing something else. His shoes gleamed like mirrors and his ties, always perfectly knotted, proclaimed his university. Not for him the rolled-up sleeve or the loosened collar. And yet, for all that, a practical man and not a dandy. An accomplished Arabist, fluent in Hebrew, Pahlavi, and Turkish besides, steeped in the history and cultures of the region, he was credited with having averted two major wars and a revolution. Not that those he saved loved him for it.

The high, swivel-backed chairs that circled the meeting room's long table were soft and comfortable, which was fortunate because the commissioners spent long hours sitting in them. At one end of the room, the Great Seal of the United States was embossed in the wood paneling. Beside it hung a banner with the coat of arms of Canada. The dark, highly-polished table was covered with reports and photographs. Larger pixures—of asteroids, craters, charts and graphs—were tacked to the walls.

The commission was small enough, Mariesa thought, to actually reach a conclusion; and expert enough to reach a valid one. It would not do for the president's advisors to ignore any but the highest quality advice.

Mariesa had no desire to sit on the commission herself. She had faith in Cunningham, Inkling, and the others; and what could she add to the deliberations but her own feelings of dread and urgency? Still, she took a lively interest in the proceedings and attended *vice* Inkling as the AAU representative whenever she was in Washington. Dark took her occasional attendance amiss, but politics meant more to men of his background than wringing decisions out of data.

"No, not exactly the great doom you've always predicted," the security advisor added for emphasis. Some of the other commissioners frowned; others looked patient as they gathered their personal belongings, stuffed their briefcases. The session was over and the commissioners were leaving for the day.

"You deal in diplomacy, Sol," Daryll Blessing said from the coatrack, where he wound a bright plaid scarf around his neck. "There's a parallel there."

Dark gave his vice-chairman a look of annoyance, as if he were not sure what Blessing was getting at. Mariesa thought he was more put out with Blessing for having given her the pass than he was with her for using it. The authorities had always treated heretics more harshly than infidels. "I'm sure you'll tell me what it is."

"Certainly. Two countries are at odds with each other. There is a danger of a major conflict, one that drags in the allies of both, and those allies include regional powers and even global players."

"Yes . . ."

"Then the war breaks out, and . . . it's a wet firecracker. Allies balk and read the fine print in their treaties. The global ally plays broker instead of backer. Now, tell me, Sol: Does the fact that the actual event was relatively minor mean there was no point in working to prevent the more catastrophic possibility?"

The other commissioners waited to see what the chairman would answer. If Mariesa caught the allusion to a tricky situation Dark had dealt with three years earlier, no doubt Dark did, too.

Solomon—surely a piquant name for a global negotiator and troubleshooter!—smiled. "Your analogy is faulty, Doctor. The outbreak was minor *because* of that groundwork. You can't say the Alberta strike was minor *because* of the hysteria about 'dinosaur killers.' "

Blessing shook his head. "I only meant that a minor event does not preclude the possibility of major events."

"Then you ought to have said what you meant instead of drawing a strained analogy."

Daryll flushed and tightened the cinch on his overcoat with greater force than needed. That was the problem, Mariesa thought, when men of facts confronted men of words. To Blessing, it only mattered whether a proposition was correct or not. To men like Dark, what mattered was who won. It was a dominance game, not a discovery game; a means of establishing who was the alpha male. (Or female. There were women who played that game, too.) Such men made use of rhetoric—the word play of definition, the raised voice, the semantic quibble—to privilege a favored position and put others in their place. To them, a fact was just another rhetorical device. Solomon Dark represented the president of the United States, and he was not about to let anyone forget it, least of all his vice-chairman. Mariesa wondered why Daryll, otherwise so intelligent, did not see that.

"Dr. Blessing is right, Solomon," Mariesa said. "We cannot afford to overlook the possibility."

It was the word "overlook" that caught Dark's attention and caused him first to pause, then to nod. All Dark needed was the proper stroking and the right words. "Possibility." "We." Words that danced tentatively around the issues, never pressing too hard; words inviting mutual understandings until consensus condensed out of the fog. That was, after all, how diplomacy and negotiations were conducted. That the question of Impact might not be diplomatic at all was as invisible to Dark's razor-sharp mind as the political issues were to Daryll Blessing.

As for herself, there were also "men of deeds," for whom neither facts nor words were paramount, but only accomplishments. This required her to be, to some extent, bilingual. She could see two intelligent men talk past each other because she understood, a little, how each perceived the situation.

"If I understood the technical people," Dark said, "the Canadian object was not one of those that you've been warning about. Not one of your allegedly-modified asteroids." *Technical people* was Dark's term for the world-renowned scientists invited onto the commission.

Mariesa understood both of Dark's messages. One, that the commission would never have been formed except for the noise she and Daryll had been making about the Visitors. And, two, that Dark would not allow the public to believe that the Alberta bolide was connected with the Visitors. Well, neither would Daryll and the other scientists. There was no evidence that it was. Yet, if a public misunderstanding would have accelerated off-world colonization or the building of a planetary defense, Mariesa herself might have happily kept her mouth shut and let the public construe what it would.

"At least," said Mariesa, "it wasn't one that we had previously identified."

"No alien materials were found in the tektites," said Cunningham. "Even the ones that fell near Hudson's Bay and Duluth."

"Any equipment would have vaporized with the rock itself. And might have been made from *in situ* materials, anyway." She held up a hand before Dark or the other skeptics could speak. "Yes, I know. Without *proof*, we can't assume it was modified; but we don't *know* it wasn't. There's a difference between innocence and lack of proof of guilt." In her heart, though, *she* was certain. The Alberta bolide had been a warning shot, an opening blow. That belief was irrational and surely grew from her own nightmares. Whatever evidence might have existed had become ionized gas and a rain of glass and iron.

"But 2004AS certainly was modified," Inkling spoke up. Dark gave him a blank-look.

"And the relevance of that information is . . . ?"

Inkling had remained seated at the table, studying one of the shots of the Alberta crater. He set it down now, and Mariesa could see impatience purse his lips. Professors these days were less accustomed to being questioned than they had been in Mariesa's youth. "Asteroid 2004AS fired its engines when our probe came too close. It altered its course just before passing behind the sun. We don't know its new orbit. It could be on an intercept."

Dark shook his head. "This commission was convened to study the Alberta bolide and recommend policy to the president and the prime minister. If we expand the scope of investigations, this might as well be a permanent committee." Questions of authorization and jurisdiction mattered a great deal to Solomon Dark.

"Perhaps," said Inkling, "it ought to be. Or this might be a very *temporary* committee."

It took a moment for Dark to get it. When he did, he laughed. "Point taken, professor. But you have to admit that you're speculating beyond the evidence. All you know about that other asteroid is that there was a bright flash, the probe ceased transmission, and the asteroid apparently shifted into a new orbit. Everything else is 'might be' and 'could be' and 'what if.'" Dark spread his hands and looked around the room at the commissioners. "Surely, there are other scenarios that could account for the actual observations? Even the technical people haven't consensus. So, we needn't tie ourselves down to a single possibility."

And there he was, preserving options rather than seeking truth. Well, in his line of work, options and face-saving and diplomatic whitewash were sometimes all that stood between people's homes and jack-booted conquerors.

Daryll Blessing clapped his hat down firmly on his head and turned to leave. The other scientists exchanged meaningful looks. Inkling only shook his head and picked up the digital photograph again. The exchange apparently over, the others resumed their activities. Mariesa went to the coatrack and retrieved her winter coat. Shortly, Solomon Dark joined her.

Fedoras were back in style. Dark's crown was perfectly creased and his brim snapped down with just the fashionable degree of panache. He said nothing to her beyond a simple nod, but dressed with the air of one waiting to listen.

"Surely," Mariesa said quietly after a moment, "you don't think there is no danger whatever."

Dark raised a brow. "When did I ever say that? I only said the evidence isn't certain."

"Very little is, in this world. A man may wave his fist in another man's face, and it is not *certain* he will throw a punch until he does. Yet, a prudent man may act without certainty . . . and save himself a bloody nose."

"Yes." Dark slapped his gloves against his hand, once, twice, while he thought. Then he buckled his overcoat and patted himself to ensure that the pleats hung properly. "But what's the prudent course here? How much"—he waved a hand in the general direction of the table—"is cold, hard fact, and how much hysteria?"

"The boy who cried wolf?" Mariesa suggested

Dark nodded and tugged his gloves on. "Exactly."

"Remember, in the end, the wolf did come."

15.

A Site 4 Sore Eyes

Official Chen smiled blandly from Jimmy's monitor screen. Of course, he said, Guangdong had an interest in LEO Station. Celestial Metals rented a loft on board and it was the duty of the Three Cities to ensure the adequacy of the playing field for its citizens. There had been that unpleasantness regarding employee theft uncovered by Dr. Hobart late last year, yes. Directionally solidified metals commanded a high price in the machine-tool industry, and even a few such crystals might pay back the risks of smuggling. Regrettable, but the management should have been alert to the temptation. Still, it was merely a nuisance: The sums were such as to tempt lower class workmen, men who had been seduced into runaway debt by the excesses of Late Capitalism.

Crocodile tears. Jimmy Poole knew that the Three Cities were nearly finished with their own orbital factory complex, so any deficiencies in LEO's management were of transient concern to them. Besides, comments on the greed of western entrepeneurs rang a little false coming from a spokesman for a country whose biggest export was billionaires.

But Jimmy made no comment. As far as Chen knew, Jimmy was "Tulio Gucci," a Lombard businessman sussing out joint-venture possibilities. If "Tulio" acted out of character, Chen might begin to ponder—and Jimmy was no such fool as to think any persona could withstand Chen's ponder. After all, he was 'facing Chen with a datalink that ran through a complex and ever-shifting relay of terminals, pseudo-terminals, and decoys, the shortest thread of which was twenty-seven nodes long. The proverbial ten-foot pole. Caution cost more, but always paid for itself.

He did ask Chen (as "Gucci" naturally would) whether Leo's security was adequate. A great deal of information would be squirted back and forth, what with the teeping and uploading and downloading and yadda-yadda. It wouldn't do if competitors could intercept or eavesdrop.

Chen's eternal smile broadened just a fraction and he assured Gucci that the Three Cities were entirely satisfied on that issue. What the smile meant, Jimmy was not sure; only it was not the smile of pride. Whatever else the query might have meant to the Guandongese official, he had not taken Leo's impenetrability as a compliment to his skill. So either Chen, too, was frustrated in his attempts to peek behind the screen, or the man who had woven the Silicon Curtain between the Guangdong Virtch and the rest of the net regarded the LEO Laager simply as business as usual.

What Unofficial Chen thought of all this ran as subtext. He had said that the Three Cities were satisfied, not that Chen Wahsi was.

For verisimilitude, Jimmy spent a few more minutes doing the dog-and-pony for a couple of proposals. They were pretty phat proposals, too; and if they had been the Jenuine Bean, Jimmy would have inserted some cash in the slot himself. But where Chen was concerned, to use a facade that was anything less than a viable business venture would have been more than imprudent.

Before logging off, Chen commented. "It has been a pleasure speaking with you, Signor Gucci. You are a careful man. I know of only five others with the ability to be so careful." And with that, he cut the connection.

Irritated, Jimmy wondered who Chen thought the other four were.

Strictly speaking, sending the construct "Tulio Gucci" to contact Chen Wahsi had violated federal law, even though the direct node was sited in Milano and came under more lenient EU rules. But then, Jimmy comforted himself, you couldn't get through the day without violating a federal law somehow or other.

Such thoughts put him in an edgy mood and he surfed the house restlessly. Poole sEcurity had a number of contracts hanging, but Jimmy could do those standing on his head. None of them promised the delicious joy of a deep hack, when you became the code and the code became you and you were as close to universal truth as meatware could get.

He came to the nursery, where Rada oversaw Stevie's playtime. Jimmy was surprised to see the older woman squatting on the floor with the kid and making silly noises. It seemed behavior beneath her dignity.

Perhaps it was. Rada glanced up, noticed him, and with a stern look sent him scuttling away.

Stassy was cleaning the kitchen, scrubbing bowls and utensils until they gleamed with an unnatural brightness. Jimmy, whose standards of kitchen sanitation had been satisfied when no obvious food particles clung to the spoons, did not see the point of such fanaticism; but he paused in the doorway to watch. He wondered if there was such a thing as "deep cleaning" and decided there was. Whatever the work was, there came a point when you and the work were one.

Stassy lifted one arm from the sink and brushed it across her forehead, leaving behind a soapy trail. "Can I get you somethink?" she asked.

Jimmy pulled out a chair and sat at the kitchen table. "Breaking." Stassy waited a moment longer before turning her back and addressing the pots and pans once more. Aluminum clattered; water gurgled and ran. Interesting, Jimmy thought, how noisy silence could be.

"Will Mrs. Poole be comink home soon?" Stassy asked.

"No," Jimmy said. "She and Billie Whistle are still researching for her novel."

Jimmy saw no reason to mention that Billie and Tani had just abandoned ten thousand dollars of anonymously-purchased computer and communications equipment in Milano and were even now flying back to the U.S.A. The whole idea of "secret" was that you didn't talk about it, not even to the cook. Jimmy wasn't sure why Tani had proposed Billie as a "human circuit breaker" or why Billie had agreed, but it was definitely a phat stoopid way to make sure nothing unpleasant swam upstream to diddle S. James Poole's hardware.

Yet, it was astonishing how much emptier the house seemed with only one resident missing.

Maybe he should just get out of the house. He didn't get out often enough. He could sit in his Sanctum and 'face the entire world, yet he had no very good notion of what lay around his own block. He left the kitchen.

He paused by the entry to Tani's office. The room looked unnaturally tidy at any time. Now, in her absence, it looked positively sterile. The loose scraps of memoranda had returned to their folders, and the folders were filed and locked away. Even the timeline was gone from its place on the wall. Jimmy supposed she had taken a scratch copy of the manuscript with her on her laptop. He smiled. He could not imagine her not working on the draft every spare moment.

Would she be sharing passages with her cheesehead companion high up over the Atlantic? Tani did not like showing her incomplete draft; but did that apply to everyone, or only to Jimmy? He stepped inside the office, ran his finger down the credenza where, so recently, character folders had lain in an orderly line. Had Tani really found it necessary to hide her materials from him? He rapped his knuckles against the wooden credenza top. Where was the trust in that?

And even if he did peek at the manuscript, what was the big deal?

Maybe she had used him as an armature for one of her characters and thought he would be offended by it. But he wasn't so herbie that he couldn't distinguish between the exploits of—who? Duncan Orb?—and S. James Poole. In fact, it might be a kick trying to mouse out the real events behind the fictional ones.

The smile on his face died before it had even a chance to form.

Yeah. A *lot* of people might try to mouse that out. He stared at the dead screen, as if by force of will he could access the hard drive beneath it. Everyone would assume that, being married to the infamous Jimmy Poole, Tani would have included some of his actual exploits. And some of those exploits that he had shared with Tani ought never see the light of day, let alone the glare of publicity that would surround Tanuja Pandya's second novel.

She couldn't be so four-oh-four, could she? If she *had* used real-life escapades, she would have altered them, just like she altered Jimmy to create Duncan.

But a cyberwaif like Tani might not realize how carefully the digerati could read between her lines.

Or she might not care.

If the notion of her possible indiscretion had killed his smile, that of her possible betrayal froze his heart. *Something that will make the book stand out and grab people around the balls, so they sit up and notice,* she had said that day when they had interfaced on the grassy lawn. Yeah, and what better book-hype could there possibly be than the novel that unmasked Crackman!

Her fear of failure was so great that the anxiety itself was a barrier to completing the book. But how desperate did you have to be to burn seven years of life on the altar of success?

He didn't want to believe it. And yet it made a plausible scenario—one that would eat at him unless he put it to rest. He pressed the stud on Tani's hard-drive and the system began booting. Just a peek, he told himself, just to ease his mind.

The screen demanded a password. He tried three obvious codes and got kicked off. Another piece of evidence? Why use a non-trivial password on an off-line system that only Jimmy could ever possibly look at? Who was she guarding against?

He could use his own system to mouse in. Run a cable down the hall from the Sanctum. He had lock-picks that could slide into Tani's system slicker than Don Juan into a lonely lady. He ought to do it, for both their sakes. He had to know if he could trust her.

Tani stopped by the house a few days later. She and Billie had set up another remote node, in an empty San Antonio storefront this time, and Jimmy had downloaded a persona to troll the net for signs of Earp. Jimmy named the construct "Morgan" as a way of signalling friendly intent, but you never could tell. Best to keep Earp at arm's length, too. Tani had left Billie in a hotel room overlooking the site and had flown home for the weekend.

Jimmy had never seen Tani so up. She very nearly straddled him right there in the foyer before he could shut the door. They spent that entire evening in client-server mode, and Jimmy's bandwidth expanded so much that he thought that never again would plugging in be as sweet and satisfying.

He knew where she was coming from, too. Pulling off a killer hack fueled the need for decompression, and many a time, pre-Tani, Jimmy had saluted the flagpole after some especially tricky piece of work; so he didn't point out to Tani that what she and Billie had done in Milano was not exactly cake-walking on the wild side. It was perfectly legal. (Okay, not *perfectly*; but, barring a State Department reg or two, contacting Official Chen was not a hanging offense.) Still, if the romp had brought Tani home horny, Jimmy would be the last to complain.

And yet Jimmy felt a part of him holding back. For the first time he could remember, he "had sex" with Tani instead of "making love" to her. All the while Tani rocked beneath him, hot and sweaty and eager; touching, probing, caressing; hands and heels and tongues and hips; words gasped and whispered, exclamations and demands—all that while, some portion of Jimmy Poole sat far back in his mind and wondered whether someone so dear and open could munge their whole life together in return for a hit novel. He had to know, or he would never feel comfortable in her arms again. And he loved those arms too much to give them up easily.

Trust everyone, but cut the cards.

Good advice, and apposite, given the venue; namely, a "brodyazhka" in the Sargasso Sea. The site had been pixeled to resemble an old time Mississippi riverboat, complete with red velvet and green felt, gamblers and dancing girls, beaver hats and hoop skirts, and a large, dripping paddlewheel turning outside the windows. The string band played "Oh, Dem Golden Slippers" and "Hot Time in the Old Town" while imagos around a felt table flipped virtual cards at one another. Like other brodyazhki, the *Dixie Belle* was never anywhere very long and never anywhere very particular. Workbots constantly disassembled and reassembled it to new edresses, so it tended to drift through the virtch at random in the form of scattered bits lurking in the hash of other programs. It was, in a manner of speaking, a virtual site—a metajoke that appealed to a certain sense of humor. Like the Hole in the Wall or the Catacombs or the original Hobo Jungle, it was a place where the Wild Bunch could hang out. Everyone craved the company of their own kind, and the Bunch was no different.

Six imagos circled the table, though only four were active. The other two algored on automatic. The imagos were done up as Old West gamblers: Doc Holliday, Maverick, Calamity Jane . . . It was easier to slip inside a standard player than to create your own—and less likely to leave a signature.

("This is incredibly juvenile,") Tani said. Her lurker imago was a dance hall gal whose improbably large breasts threatened to pop from the top of her corset. ("Development arrested in High Puberty.") She was read-only from San Antonio and her audio was a dedicated side line straight to Jimmy's earplug, so none of the others in the room could hear her. Which was just as well. Jimmy hadn't come to dis anyone. The game was poker, but Jimmy was angling for Cat-fish. His construct, Morgan had been trolling for Earp for a week without success while Billie gamely stood watch over the San Antonio link, so Jimmy had decided to hunt for the Cat while they waited. Two birds, one stone.

"You were the one who wanted to piggyback," Jimmy said over the two-way. "Don't distract me. This is serious weenie."

Doc Holliday had the deal and the deck flashed in his hands. Cards defied the laws of aerodynamics and curled and swooped acrobatically to land in front of the imagos. ". . . pulled a salami on Southwest Bell," Holliday said. "Slagged the sys before they twigged . . ." No one actually played cards here. The gestures and motions, conducted by the A/S, were just for atmosphere.

"I think we woulda heard about that one, Mouse," said Maverick. Whoever was wearing the Doc Holliday claimed to be Mighty Mouse, but without tags who could say for sure? Billie Whistle thought Jimmy was pretending to be the long-inactive Crackman, so the others might be equally bogus. You never knew. (And the idea of Crackman pretending to be Jimmy pretending to be Crackman was just too stoopid for words.) Maverick claimed to be Doctor Doom and John Wesley Hardin called himself The Eel. Second rankers, all of them—except maybe Doom, who aspired to greatness—but they might have a line on Captain Cat.

Still, anyone who could find their way to the *Dixie Belle* and stay on board while it shot the rapids of disassembly-reassembly had to be one bean dude with a cheesebox. Topologically, the sea was a set of measure zero that approached perfect density in the continuum of the net; so that, while it wasn't anywhere in particular, it was everywhere in general. Access was through a bewildering variety of trapdoors, conduits, hyperlinks, and shunts. That manhole cover on the streets of Virtual Brooklyn—it's not just for show. Lift it and drop down. That mirror in the Sleeping Beauty kidsite—you *can* jump through the looking glass, sometimes. Follow the Yellow Brick Road *in the other direction*—it doesn't lead to Kansas. Not all the dead ends in the Minotaur gamesite are dead ends. You just have to know when to click your heels and push on through to the other side. So it was like they said; if that *wasn't* Mighty Mouse across the table, it ought to be.

"Hey," said Mouse. "The best hacks are the ones that *don't* make the newsgroups."

"Word," said Eel. "If the mundanes know you did it, you didn't do it well."

Crackman threw in his agreement. It had taken some effort—and Tani's coaching on the sideline—to steer the chatter to this topic. "It's fun to noodle it out, though. Like that DEFCON hack three years ago that made it look as if all the missiles in Dakota had been retargeted on the Pentagon. Wasn't too hard to peg the Midnight Rambler for that one. It had his style."

"Fingerprints," said Mouse. "He botched it. That's why no one's seen him rambling for the last two and a half years, midnight or not. Phone company has him locked away."

"It's a shame when the best work has to be anonymous."

"Stupid, to prank the P-gon," said Eel. "So what, he didn't really retarget? The Establishment doesn't have a sense of humor."

("Not about the targeting of nuclear missiles, anyway,") Tani suggested.

"What have you been up to, Crackman?" said Doom. "Haven't seen you around here in a while." A friendly question, delivered casually, but with an edge. Although Jimmy had lurked a few times in the past few years, "Crackman" had not sat down at the poker table in a very long time. Long enough that the others regarded him with a certain righteous suspicion. Hackers who reappeared after long absences had a disheartening likelihood of having been bit-flipped. As often as not, they had become Earp's deputies.

Crackman chuckled. "Mouse said the best work is anonymous; but I go a step farther. You guys think it's bean to banana peel a system. Watch it fall on its butt for laughs. I say it's better to pick its pocket; or—better yet—to sting it, so the mark never even knows its been conned."

"That's so boozhy," said Mouse. "Ars gratia artis, I say."

"Ars gratia pecuniæ," Jimmy retorted.

("Boozhy?") asked Tani.

("Bourgeois,") Jimmy told her. ("Mouse thinks you should hack for the artistic satisfaction, not to get rich.")

("And you believe . . . ?")

("In getting rich artistically. The axes are independent; you can score on both. Now be quiet.")

"What I'd like to know," said Doom, "is who wrote the Piccadilly Circus."

Jimmy wanted to kiss him for the lead-in. "Or the Erie Canal," he suggested.

"Small potatoes," said Mouse.

"But very bean," said Doom. "Crackman is right. It doesn't have to be grandiose to be good work. I liked the Canal's use of compression to keep the architecture slender."

"Clowns in a car," sneered Mouse. "The effect was almost comical when the logic realized."

("I don't believe this. Art critics!")

("Quiet.")

("Billie wants to listen in. I'm giving her the helmet.")

("Fine.") Whistle at least knew enough not to bother him. "And what about the LEO Laager? Phat stoopid."

"Straight edge," said Doom.

"Mainstreet charlie," said Eel.

"Yeah, but stupy. You got the mojo for it, Mouse?" Privately, Jimmy did not think Mouse had the beans for anything half as phat as the LEO Laager, but let's put melons under his arms. Mouse knew someone who knew someone. Three degrees of separation; and in the tight, close world of the wild side, closer to two.

The Doc Holliday imago stuck its tongue out which meant Mouse was channeling to manipulate the image, so Jimmy launched a grapple toward the access gate but Mouse was fast and the gate slammed before the grapple could hook into his system, all in the time it took him to say, "I don't do boozhy."

Jimmy's meta screen showed four other code strings. Each different, but each designed to suss out the portal and locate Mouse's origin node. He grinned. No flubber on us, as the kids said today. And it would have been an insult not to try, an implication that Mouse's system was not worth plundering.

His grin froze.

Four other strings?

He checked the two algored imagos. Hickok was still imitating a vice president. Calamity Jane was . . .

. . . wearing a cameo choker, a stocking garter, and a bawdy smile.

The silence was profound and admiring. Chat rooms on the wild side did not announce newcomers; but it was a bean dude who could walk in, manipulate his imago, and start trolling with no one twigging.

"Outstanding," said Doom.

"Applause," said Eel.

Jimmy wondered how long the other had been lurking. Not too long, he thought. Not with Crackman and Doom both in the room. "Admiration," he said, and he did not entirely mean the subtlety of the entrance. Skin texture on standard imagos was pretty wax; Calamity Jane's skin looked . . . good enough to touch. He made a bet with himself that the texture was not monet, and at the fine level there would be tiny hairs and goosebumps. Jimmy sucked on his teeth. Mouse liked to scroll on about art? *This* was art. The nipples were excellent; and, while the tight curls on the head still had the laminated look, those at the other end were definitely Brillo.

Ars gratia pecuniæ. If the newcomer had solved the Brillo problem, he stood to rake mucho troy. No more bad hair days on the net. No more video snips to mosaic human-looking hair.

("I suppose everyone's brains have downloaded to their gonads by now . . . ?")

It took Jimmy a moment to place the voice as Billie Whistle's. Jimmy checked the dance hall gal that hovered over Maverick's shoulder. Whistle wouldn't be stupid enough to enter the room herself, would she? She was supposed to stay in the read-only channel, but she had the mojo to houdini the safeties. She just didn't have the mojo to do it and still keep the channel clean.

And what did she mean by downloading to gonads, anyway? It would take more than virtual skin to fluster Jimmy Poole. He was the breast in the business. There was opportunity here. The newcomer's access gate had to have major babewidth to accommodate so much activity. He pulled up a second grapple. A bird in the hand was worth a hand in the bush. His finger hovered over the return button; but . . .

("Where's the access port?") he asked. Code flowed and spread across his number three screen.

Billie's response was dry. ("Where do you think?")

Jimmy scanned the imago again and, when he saw the pattern, swallowed hard. ("There?")

But by then, Calamity Jane had crossed her legs, blocking access to the hyperlink button.

("You guys sure know how to have fun.") That was Tani, again. Jimmy supposed Whistle had given her back the headset.

("Tell Whistle to stay on-line. I want her to study that morph. I want to know how it's done.")

("*I* can do that, and I don't need a modem.") Faintly, Jimmy heard the sound of laughter. He was glad his team was getting a good laugh out of this.

". . . honor of welcoming?" Jimmy caught the tail end of Doom's question.

Calamity Jane smiled—and purred.

"Captain Cat!" That was Eel. There was an awe in the voice that Jimmy had not heard when he introduced himself as Crackman. Well, the Cracker's best hacks were probably ancient history to the kid. Still, Jimmy felt a momentary irritation. It wasn't as though S. James Poole had gotten started by poking reeds into trays of mud . . . !

"My public," the Cat said, all coquette.

"*If* you're Captain Cat," Jimmy challenged.

"Ah, the famous Crackman. How are you, old timer?"

"Cat—if you are the Cat—you've been walking the wild side as long as Mouse or me."

"Sure, but I still have all my hair . . ."

Jimmy ran a hand through his thinning locks. A lucky guess? Or did Cat know something about Crackman? It was important not to react to the sally. "What brings you to the *Dixie Belle?*"

"Whispers and rumors. I keep hearing buzz about the LEO Laager."

"Like . . . there's a hole in it?" Jimmy put eager curiosity into Crackman's voice. This was the sort of intelligence the Wild Bunch yearned for; information bartered on the blackest of markets. Keys and crypts; secret trapdoors; passwords known or guessed. Doom and the others gave attentive silence.

Cat laughed. "Not. What do you think it is, the defensive shields for the Death Star? One lucky potshot and the whole thing slags?"

"Then, what's the buzz?"

"It's just that everybody and her grandmother is noodling at it. The straight-edge crowd—Bosworth, Poole, Rodriguez—"

"Poole isn't that straight, from what I hear," said Mouse, "and if half what they say about Utopian Research is true, Bosworth—"

"Mouse, do you want to hear what I came to say? Be a good boy, now." Calamity Jane shifted in its seat and displayed a favorable amount of skin. Jimmy made his own adjustments.

("Déjà vu,") whispered Billie Whistle. ("Who does she remind me of?")

"We're listening," said Doom.

The deal had passed to Calamity Jane, but Cat made no effort to coordinate his morph with the motions of the deck; so the cards floated and peeled off the deck by themselves. "Okay. Like I said, the edgers are oohing and aahing and asking each other if they were the ones who did the job. Daedalus, Boeing, VHI, Wilson, and some of the other tenants and players have done the 'wet paint' test. A Lombard suit named Gucci was asking, too; and a start-up called Baleen even lifted a bonebag to suss things out. And something very reminiscent of Unofficial Chen poked at it with a stick about a year ago—and triggered a cruise missive on the backtrace."

"You think it got him?" asked Mouse.

"Chen? Get real, honey-butt. But the logic bomb did go off somewhere in the Guangdong Virtch, so *someone* paid for the indiscretion." Calamity Jane smirked. "The Three Cities probably sent Official Chen to track the culprit down."

Chuckles all around at that, but Jimmy was getting impatient. "Then who did write the code, Cat? You?"

"There's too much curiosity out there, and I'm a cat; so here's the word: As far as I know, Earp wrote up the security for LEO—but I was a subcontractor on the project."

"Dude," said Doom. "You going straight-edge on us?"

"Or just going buddy-buddy with Earp?" Mouse asked with more angle on the cut.

"That's why I'm here." And now there was an edge to Cat's voice, too. "Inquiring minds will want to know; and they might wonder where I stand. My subcontract—through the usual facades, of course—was a wild hack strictly for Klon-Am. Officially, Earp doesn't know—though I suspect some troy changed hands and he closed his eyes on purpose. Far as I know, he never even ran the final validation tests, which would have shown the links to my subroutine. But the bottom line, honey, is—I have *not* been seduced by the bright side of the force."

("Karl Wincock!") Billie almost shouted in his ear.

("Quiet!")

("But Cat's imago . . .")

("I noticed, okay? Keep your panties on. One thing at a time.")

"That doesn't make sense, Cat," Jimmy said. "Klon-Am is legit. Why would they hire a netwalker to diddle themselves?"

"Maybe they're in civil war," suggested Eel. "Remember VHI a couple years ago?"

"What was the hack?" asked Jimmy.

"Part of the fee was that I keep my mouth shut."

"And Boy Scouts always keep their word," Mouse suggested.

Calamity Jane picked up an ace of spades and it morphed into a bowie knife. "Careful, Mouse. Remember I'm a cat." With a flash, the knife bobbited the Doc Holliday. The imago didn't react, of course, but Mighty Mouse squeaked, and even Jimmy winced at what Calamity Jane threw into the betting pot. "But if the price is that my friends don't trust me any more, I'll show my cards. If you can figure out why they wanted this off the books, you're a sharper dude than I am. All it was, was a subroutine to run virtual displays on the teep channels, so the managers could show visitors schematics, outside POVs, and other things the tenants' waldos aren't equipped for. BFD."

"Yeah," said Doom. "BFD."

("Bail!") Billie Whistle was a shout in his headphones. ("Look out the windows!")

Jimmy did, and saw that the virtual riverboat was churning its way implausibly up a virtual San Antonio Riverwalk. Lifelike figures on both banks waved, some with all their fingers. Jimmy released the deadman switch just as the whole scene went monet. He heard Mouse shout, "Incoming!" and then the virtch went black.

It was only later, while pondering the fate of the *Dixie Belle* that Billie Whistle saw the light.

There had been no time in the meantime. Someone very heavy had stomped hard on a safe house. You didn't dally, virtually or actually, when shit that heavy came down, or you'd get what Eleazar Avaram got. The equipment had been installed in an empty, ground-level storefront across College Street from the hotel. It was a simple matter for Billie to handshake from the fourth floor balcony using her I/R laser, wipe everything they hadn't recorded on sterilized floppies in her chair, and—just for fun—activate a squirtback virus. Billie didn't think anyone with the mojo to raster the *Dixie Belle* would be 404 enough to 'face a strange port without a condom, but you never could tell. Billie picked up the phone and dialed a number.

Pandya had packed swiftly while Billie poisoned the well. There was no reason to suppose the electronic trail could be traced to this room. You could mouse that drive until the numbers wore off the bits and never know the I/R link was even there. Not only was the drive passive—the app for the link was in Billie's chair—but the channel was analog. And even if you knew the data was being squirted over an analog I/R I/O, you would have to physically inspect the equipment to see where it was aimed, because the damned portal was set *manually*.

But she still wished Pandya would move her fat little butt.

The phone answered and a voice said, "Yeah?" Billie said, "It's all yours." The voice hung up without even a thank you.

Pandya snapped both suitcases shut and looked up. "Ready."

About fucking time.

"Did you tell the—uh—street people they could—"

"Yes. Let's move. Did you do the automatic checkout?"

Pandya made an oops and turned on the television. "Express checkout," she told the screen. Billie rolled her eyes and turned her chair to face the window again. It was a bright day, something San Antonio had a surplus of. *Send a few to Milwaukee*, Billie thought. Wisconsin was beautiful when sheathed in ice and snow, but it was *cold*. She ought to move out. Find somewhere warmer.

"Who do you think it was?" Pandya asked. "That stomped the riverboat, I mean."

Billie turned. "I've crossed Elvis off my list, but otherwise it's wide open."

"You don't think it was that Captain Cat?"

"What would be the point? Cat was afraid that if the others learned she had worked with Earp, they would think she'd been jekylled. A brodyazhka getting slagged right after she shows up won't exactly hype her *bona fides*. You done yet?"

Pandya turned off the set. "We're out of here."

La Mansion del Rio was modeled on a Spanish plan, with the rooms opening on open-air balcony walkways. Billie and Pandya crossed on the third floor. The Indo could not stop chattering, speculating on this or that aspect of the hack. She practically *bounced*. Billie fridged, playing the professional, but she felt the need for decompression herself. Maybe a cool brew in the airport lounge . . . She liked to watch the other travelers trying not to eyeball the crip. Below them, a fountain bubbled in a courtyard of broad, leafy plants enclosed by a stone wall.

A beat-up old '11 Chevy pulled up in front of the storefront across College Street, where the node had been installed. Three young men piled out, grinning and fiving. Billie winced at the value of the equipment doomed for the fence; but the boys had guarded the site and it was payoff time. Her lips curled back from her teeth. Probably the first time those skillets ever boosted anything where they had the bills of sale in their pockets.

Billie watched the computer go into the trunk of the old Chevy. *Mission accomplished. Sort of.*

"Do you think it was Earp?" Pandya asked as she held the door to the west wing open for Billie. "I think it was Earp. I think he left a hook in Captain Cat that time they worked together and Cat didn't know it, and Earp followed the line to the safe house—"

Billie braked her chair in front of the elevator door and swung to face Pandya. *Out of the mouths of babes . . .*

"I *told* Jimmy not to walk on the wild side again," the woman yadda-yadda'd. "What if Earp had caught him there! He could have . . . How does it work? You send knowbots into all the open portals and when they come back home they have the edresses of whoever was logged on. Even lurkers. Is that how it works?"

The elevator door opened and a pudgy, dough-faced man stepped out. His face was red and the skin on the forehead and nose was peeling. *Too long in the oven.* Billie thought. He almost bumped into her and looked down in surprise. Billie gave him a bright smile and waited until he looked away. She and Pandya entered the elevator and the door closed them in.

"Why do you do that?" Pandya asked.

"Yeah, that's how it works. Grapples."

"Flaunt your . . . condition. Try to embarrass people."

Billie nodded. "I think you're right about Earp."

Pandya pressed the button for the lobby floor. "All right." The elevator jerked and began a slow descent. "It doesn't do any good to be angry all the time. I was angry at Azim and his friends for years because of what they did to my father, but Baba never got any better because of it."

"He never got better at all." Billie saw the flinch and gave Pandya another of her razor smiles. She'd been saving the comment because she knew that sooner or later the woman would bring up her past. "See? I read your book, too, just like everyone else in the country." Though how anyone could use their family's tragedy as a lever to fame and fortune Billie did not know. What kind of soul did it take to cash in on your father's shooting?

"But—" Pandya seemed genuinely puzzled, as if she couldn't understand how her amateur counseling could fail. Well, others more professional than she had failed, too. The elevator creaked to a stop and the door opened on a carpeted interior hallway. "What do you know about it?" The all-purpose line that cut off further discussion.

Except, Pandya wouldn't go there. "I know this much," she said. "That tourist geek back there was *not* the drunk who flipped the median and smashed your car."

Some people could not accept the fact that they did not run your life.

They went down the ramp in silence into the covered carport. Across the way, by the door that led to the lobby and the pool and the meeting rooms, a bell captain leaned on his podium. There were no cabs waiting in the turna-round, but the bell captain could whistle one in for them.

If they could get his attention. He and the bellboy with him were absorbed in something across the street. Grins and elbow jabs traded both ways.

Crossing the red-painted concrete, Billie saw that two San Antonio police cars had pulled up by the old Chevy. The bell captain had evidently played civic duty and called in what looked like a boost in progress. The three skillets were surrounded by the forces of law and order, one of whom was reading the bills of sale that Billie had, through several intermediaries, passed to them. The cop did not look happy. The three skillets stood in confident poses. Their tight, short trousers and high, white socks . . . Their gimme caps turned defi-antly forward, with the bills shading their eyes . . . Everything about them said "banger." Yet, there was the title to the property, made over by the dummy corporation that had purchased it. Billie bit her lip to keep from grinning. It was the least she could do for the "salvage crew."

A man in civilian clothes stepped out of the building where the node had been set up and blinked against the light. He was an older man, about fifty, with steel-gray hair and the graveyard look of iron purpose. He barked some-thing at the police supervisor, who handed him the bills of sale. The gaunt man looked at them for a heartbeat before shoving them back in the cop's hands. A quick step took him to the trunk of the car, from which he pulled a piece of apparatus.

Pandya said, "Isn't that . . ."

"Yeah," said Billie. "The I/R link. But it's stupid. No memory; and no way now to know where it was aimed." Her heart began to thud. It had been a narrow thing, but they were well away.

The gaunt man frowned over the I/R link and turned it on its gimbals. Billie could almost feel his frustration. It rolled off him like a scent. Billie grinned. *I bet he's kicking himself right now for that bit of bravado in the virtch.* Then he stepped to the storefront window and crouched with the instrument in his hand, holding it at table height.

And that crouch . . .

He sighted along the barrel, turned it first one way, then another, left, right, up, down, checking its span. He scowled in frustration at an office building two blocks off, then shook his head.

And that crouch . . .

He stepped back outside and called the sergeant over with a jerk of his arm. He pointed to the top floor of a building peeking from the Riverwalk, then to the facade of La Mansion del Rio, where his fingertip traced out a rectangle. Windows within the compass of the I/R link.

That crouch . . .

"Tani," Billie said through clenched teeth, "don't look worried or in a hurry and don't ask any questions; but we're going through the lobby and down onto the Riverwalk. We'll cross over at the next accessible bridge and hail a cab on another block. Smile at the freaking bell captain."

They passed through a door held open for them by the uniformed young man. The lobby staff, determinably friendly, insisted on greeting them and holding doors. *I didn't want this. I didn't want to be noticed.* Tani had checked in alone under a phony name. They had checked out by remote. But . . . a cheesehead in a wheelchair? Too easy to remember. She wore a cowboy hat, but it might be noticed that her head was shaved. With her good hand, she grabbed at Tani's wrist, and the Indian woman, surprised, glanced at her.

> *The Lord will guard you from all evil; he will guard your life.*
> *The Lord will guard your coming and your going.*
> *Both now and forever.*

The old prayer came to mind unbidden—flotsam from her childhood. If there was an Elohim. She didn't believe there was; not since the accident that had taken her mother and her family and half her body and left the drunk in the other car bruised but whole. Yet, she and Pandya could use some guarding for their going now, and the words brought a strange comfort in the midst of panic, as if the eye of a storm had passed across her soul.

Past the restaurant and down the ramp to the flagstoned Riverwalk. It was crowded with *turistas* and, here, relatively narrow. They turned right, toward the Holiday Inn on St. Mary's. Tani stopped the chair for a moment and leaned over, adjusting the blanket around Billie's leg.

"What is it?" she asked in a low voice; and she had fridged well enough in the crunch that Billie graced her with an answer.

"I think that was Earp. In person."

"Who, the thin dude? Death warmed over?"

"Yeah. Him."

"But—Why do you think—?"

"Except when I met him, he was calling himself Tyler Crayle."

And the man had arranged her training and surveyed her apartment and, when it came to setting up the cabinets to be accessible, he had crouched down and tested the reach himself; and Billie had thought, at the time, that it was the kindest gesture she had seen in her life.

Billie was ice, but her mind spun furiously. How had Earp traced the node to the storefront on College Avenue? There must be a register of nodes and locations somewhere. Illegal under the Cybernet Privacy Act, but who policed the police? Poole should have winkled the topology. *Better yet, we should have moved the equipment each day.*

She and Tani waited inside the lobby of the Holiday Inn for the airport van to leave. Billie kept a watch on the front doors and estimated how long it would take her to roll out and be lifted into the van. Crayle wouldn't be sweeping the area yet—likely, he hadn't pinned down the hotel room—but her heart slammed against her ribs each time someone walked past the doors.

Had Poole and David arranged for her to be arrested here? Was that why Crayle had made a physical swoop? Yet, Crayle was as guilty as she of slicking Adam van Huyten—moreso, since he had instigated the whole thing—so he was unlikely to be David's ally in this.

She cast a careful glance at Tanuja Pandya who, with her tracy pressed to her lips, was reporting in agitated whispers to her husband. Was she Poole's instrument? A Judas Goat to lure Billie into a trap as part of Adam's revenge? Yet, Pandya herself seemed frightened. Eyes round as a federal dollar. Breath coming short. Sweat beading forehead and lip. Quick glances. But excited, too, as the thrill hit; her lips curled in a rictus.

No. Would Poole risk his own wife in a wild-side hack just to sucker Billie into a trap? He'd have to have pretty serious flubber against her for that kind of chill because, if Earp netted Tani Pandya along with Billie Whistle, the skein would lead unmistakably to his own sacrosanct portals.

She nudged Tani. "They're ready to board the shuttle." Tani said good-bye and (Billie almost gagged) kissed the tracy's input grill. Together with a perfectly coiffed business droid who seemed to have a cell phone physically implanted to his head, they crossed the—empty!—sidewalk, where Tani and the driver helped her into the van. The businessman made a face as he ostentatiously squeezed past her into an empty seat.

"Why did Earp raid the site?" Tani whispered, as the van pulled out. "We weren't doing anything illegal, were we? It's not illegal to visit a cracker hangout. It's not even illegal to pretend to be Crackman."

Privately, Billie wasn't entirely sure that Jimmy's Crackman act was a masquerade. "Earp might not care," she said. " 'Illegal' hasn't mattered to the government for more than twenty years. Do you know how many laws there are? No, no one does. There's no single place that even lists them all. And all those ambiguous terms, open to after-the-fact reinterpretation . . . ? Don't worry. If they want you, they got you. The only safe thing is to avoid being noticed in the first place."

Tani looked troubled. "That's a very cynical attitude."

"I lost *my* naïveté a long time ago."

The van turned a corner—away from La Mansion del Rio—and stopped at a light. Tani leaned close and whispered again. "Do you think he'll be able to identify us?"

"What it is," Billie said. "Look, Earp won't have any trouble identifying the room we were hacking from. Checking out right after the brodyazhka got stomped won't strike him as coincidence. So Earp gets the room number, but the registration leads nowhere. 'Maria Delgado' don't exist and by now Jimmy's purged that identity from the net. Unless he set us up." Ooh, that earned her a glare—but one that was half alarm. Interesting. Did Pandya have some reason to distrust her husband? "But what about tossing the room itself? Are there fingerprints? DNA? Eyewitnesses? The desk clerk saw you when you checked in. Was it the same one that saw us when we scorched the bricks? Did she notice the flight bags in my undercarriage? If so, that links 'Delgado' with someone in a wheelchair. To anyone but Crayle, that means diddly; but Crayle helped me get started and he might put two and two together . . ." Billie faded out. She was beginning to scare herself. "And if he gets us, he gets Jimmy."

"I'd never implicate him!" Righteousness personified sat stiffly in her seat. The driver glanced briefly in their direction, though the businessman was too deeply immersed in the latest deal to notice. If the van flipped over in a ditch, he'd just say, "Call you back."

"Duh?" Billie told her. "If Earp nabs *you*, he won't exactly assume you were working for Pedro the Jouster. And me, I'd sing like Xena Calloway at the Met."

"You wouldn't!"

"What do I owe Poole. Or 'Adam van Huyten'?"

"It's all *me*, isn't it?"

"It always is. Some of us are just more honest."

Pandya turned away and crossed her arms. Her lips pressed together and she stared out the side window of the van. Tani's tracy beeped and they both jumped. The businessman turned, scowled at the interruption, and spoke a little more loudly into his own instrument. Billie and Tani stared at each other. A fox in a trap, Billie had once heard, would chew off his own leg to escape. She and Tani were in this together. It made no sense to chew each other up. Tani glanced at the caller ID and sighed.

"It's Jimmy."

Not until that moment did Billie admit to herself that she had half-expected Earp to reach out and touch them. Given the speed with which he had swooped on the node, it would not have surprised her. Yet, *Morgan* had been trolling for a week, so Earp could have been backtracking all along and just assumed, because the analog link was digitally invisible, that San Antonio was the terminal node.

Pandya spoke low and listened carefully, then, logging off, sat with her lower lip between her teeth.

"Well?" said Billie.

Tani looked at her. "Jimmy says this is a private hack on Earp's part. He freaked when Cat revealed how he accepted bribes. If Internal Affairs catches on, he's meat; so Jimmy figures he can't call openly on government resources. He doesn't think that Earp will have the airport interdicted."

"But . . ." Billie had very definitely heard a 'but' in that sentence.

"But we won't take chances. 'Jennifer Trail' and 'Maria Delgado' disappear. When we get off this van . . ." Pandya glanced at the driver, lowered her head and voice, "We go inside the terminal, go down to Arrivals, and catch a different van to the Fairfield Inn on the 410 Loop. You still have the credit cards 'Andrea' and 'Jasmin' used in Milan last month? Jimmy set up some tickets on an *incoming* flight that will make it look like 'Andrea' and 'Jasmin' just arrived from Toronto. We lie low tonight. Tomorrow morning, someone comes to the hotel and picks us up, and we fly out on a private jet."

"Someone."

Tani shrugged. "He didn't say who."

Billie had a momentary flash of David Desherite riding to the rescue, lifting her up in his arms and carrying her off where they could . . .

But romance movies were no more real than westerns, and "David" was as likely to have helped sell her out as to save her. Billie wondered what she would do if Adam van Huyten did knock on their door in the morning, all smiles and handshakes and come-with-me.

Would she go with him?

And who else might come knocking in the meantime?

16.

What U See Is All U Get

The racquetball caught Hobie square on the right temple, causing him to see bright flashes and knocking clear out of his head any thoughts he might have been pondering. He clapped a hand to his forehead. "Ah!" he said and danced a few steps. His racquet dangled and bobbed from his wrist strap.

Otul Ganesh clapped time. "You the Master of Cool," he said and danced a few steps himself, his sneakers squeaking on the gleaming hardwood of the racquetball court. "He so cool . . . He so cool . . . " Otul spun with surprising grace, stopping with his arm outstretched pointing to Hobie. "He's *electric!*"

Hobie rubbed his temple. "That hurt!"

"My singing? I've heard worse." Otul scampered to retrieve the wayward ball.

"So have I," said Hobie, "but when the fight was over, the cats left." He flipped his racquet back into his grip. "Besides, I meant the ball hitting me in the head."

Otul picked up the ball and inspected it. "No damage," he said. He bounced the ball with his racquet as he crossed the court. "You must keep your mind on the game," he suggested helpfully.

"I was *thinking*," Hobie said.

"See? Now that was your first mistake. You can't think about these things. You have to move without 'paralysis of analysis.' Besides," he added, "the equations of motion are indetermine. The domain space is chaotically fractal." He hit the ball straight up, then caught it in his hand on the drop.

"I wasn't thinking about the *game*," Hobie said. He winced at the stinging sensation in his temple. He'd have a black-and-blue mark for sure. Good thing on his complexion it didn't show.

Otul dribbled the ball off the court. "That was your *second* mistake." He waved toward the windows, where spectators and the players awaiting their reservations sat. "The girls are here."

Great. Just in time to see him whacked like a cow at a slaughterhouse. Hobie waved to Charli and Peggy.

"You have to *feel* the game," Otul went on. "Think with your *body*, not your mind. You must *become* the racquet; you must *be* the ball."

"Thanks. I don't have a personal trainer."

Otul grinned. "Zen and the art of racquetball."

Hobie wiped the sweat off his face. "I thought you were Muslim."

"I'm a Turkish Muslim. That's like a European Christian. It's part of who I am, *Allaha tes ekkür*; but life has a mundane side, too. Yin and yang. Separate but complementary. Besides, Zen Islam has intriguing possibilities."

Hobie grunted. He was never sure when Otul was pulling his leg or not. When it came to the inner life, many people cloaked their beliefs in humor. Better to laugh together than expose yourself to the mockery of unbelievers. Hobie no longer took his mother's church entirely seriously, yet if you cut off your roots, you withered and died, and then where were you? He wondered if there could be such a thing as a hard-shell Zen Baptist. He crouched forward on the balls of his feet, waiting for Otul's serve.

"I was thinking about LEO," he said.

Otul balked his serve. He looked over his shoulder. "I thought that was all settled, Cool-man. OMC fired the tech who was skimming your materials and dell'Bosco put a reprimand in Shary's file for not being on top of things."

"Yeah, fired the guy just in time for Christmas. You gotta love a company that does that."

Otul shrugged. "He should have thought of that when he started boosting earths and precious metals from you and the other tenants. The Three Cities wanted the whole management team fired for shorting Tien Jinshu on their DSM crystals."

"The Three Cities don't like any arrangement where they don't call the shots. Once Celestial Circle is operational, they'll break their leases faster than you can say 'Guangzhou, Hong Kong, and Macao'."

Otul banged a hard shot off the wall and forced Hobie to run for it. They volleyed back and forth until Hobie missed an easy one. Otul went to the bench and swished some electrolyte in his mouth while Hobie retrieved the ball. "Okay," said Otul. "So here it is, March, and you're still noodling over it. I know you're like a dog with a bone when you have a problem, Hobe, but . . . where's the problem?"

"Uncle Waldo."

"The waldos?"

"Yeah. I'm missing something. I know it. Adam thought it was odd, so many modules going into 'Zen' meditation. I'm positive Rock was trying to tell me something, too, when I was up there, something he couldn't come right out with; but damn if I can figure out what."

"Have you talked with . . ." Otul looked over his shoulder at the waiting area. He lowered his voice and leaned closer to Hobie. ". . . With Adam . . . since you've been back?" Hobie glanced at the waiting area, too, and saw A.V. Deshpande and Chris van Huyten, togged up for racquetball, chatting with Charli and Peg.

"Big powwow at the lab," Hobie remembered. "A.V. must've invited The Man to the club for a workout. Jeez. That guy's, what? Sixty-something. Looks in good shape, though."

"And here you are, half his age and building flubber. Which, at the moment, you are not burning off."

Hobie took the ball from Otul and bounced it on the floor. "Yeah, I talked with him," Hobie said, after a moment. "Adam. Told him I drew a blank." He shook his head. "I can't help feeling I let him down."

"You don't work for him any more," Otul reminded him.

Hobie shook his head and whacked a serve. "Tell him."

Normally, when Big Mike Hobart celebrated his birthday, it was a small family affair. He booked rez at the Culinary Renaissance and the five of them—Big Mike, Mom, Aunt Justinia, Charli and Hobie—chowed down on the finest food in central New Jersey. It was the sort of place where jackets were required and you were expected to admire the presentation of the meal. A large, well-done steak covered with "sautéed fungus" usually satisfied Big Mike's dining aspirations; but once a year, as he put it, he liked to "eat elegant."

But 2017 was not a normal year. The summer would mark the tenth anniversary of the Skopje Rescue. Ceremonies were planned; reunions were in the works. Websters and news-readers trolled for soundbites and interviews. As senior surviving American peacekeeper, Sergeant-Major Michael T. Hobart, USMC (ret.) was in constant demand and he had "eaten elegant" so many times already this year, he was heartily sick of it and longed for something plain. Which is why, despite the chill of mid-March, he pulled on his wool jacket, fired up the grill in the backyard, and performed serious arson on dead cows. It was also why the "small family dinner" grew to include the reunion committee: Azim Thomas, Odumegwu Azikiwe, and Bjorn Johansson had been among the UN peacekeepers trapped with Big Mike at Skopje Airport. Johansson was the only white at the table and tried doggedly to look as if he was not acutely aware of that fact. Having been in the complementary situation himself many times, Hobie felt some empathy for the man.

There were the usual over-the-hill jokes, but under the circumstances it was inevitable that the table talk focused on long-ago hardships and heroics. Aunt Justinia chattered about the cousins and tried to get her brother talking about other topics, but Azim or Big Mike or the others would mention a name or say, "Remember when . . ." and there would be nods or smiles or thoughtful silences. Hobie grew unaccountably jealous of Azim, his one-time classmate, who in this one regard at least, seemed to share a special and secret closeness to Big Mike. Charli, whose tolerance for family get-togethers was marginal at best, did not even try to keep the boredom from her face.

When the steaks had been reduced to gristle and fat and the dishes carted to the kitchen, Mike Hobart sipped from his glass of red wine and then filled it and his friends' glasses with the last of the bottle. He rose and his face took on a distant look, as if seeing things not present.

He raised his glass. "Gentlemen. Absent friends."

The Swede, the Nigerian, and Azim rose like a shot and repeated the toast. The four of them drained their glasses while Hobie and the others watched in silence. It was not a large table, but Hobie suddenly felt as if there were two dining parties separated by time and space, and that he was as distant from his own father as he was from the son he would never have. Big Mike, the gentle, laughing giant who had tossed young Hobie in the air, was momentarily a stranger.

Azim didn't see it that way when the two of them spoke later. He and Hobie stood on the patio and watched the darkening sky. Azim was not a man who invited confidences—taciturn, lean as a whippet, with a dangerous look to him, the banger turned hero—yet it seemed to Hobie that he might be one who could understand. Hadn't he lived for eight years behind a false name, daring no close attachments to anyone?

"It ain't that, Hobe," Azim told him. "It's all of us gots places where no one else goes. The four of us, back there, we went through some heavy shit together. Skopje was bank. No one who wasn't there can ever be there, know what I'm saying? And everyone who *was* there will *always* be there. But when you go chemistry, the Sergeant-Major, he can't go with you, neither; but he proud to watch you go. I know. He tol' me." Azim shook his head. "Shit. An' all through school, I thought if dumb was bricks, you'd be a housing project."

Azim was right—and who would ever have dreamed Azim could be right about the human heart? Every man was many things. Son, chemist, otter, husband . . . and others might not see more than two or three of that host, or befriend more than one.

Yet Hobie could not shake the feeling that while he lived surrounded by others—Charli, Big Mike, Mom, Otul and the rest of the lab, Adam van Huyten—he was somehow desperately alone.

A pinpoint of light, rising perversely in the west, climbed the night sky against the grain of the ecliptic. Now there was a lonely sight! Coasting across the heavens, so far off that it was not even a ship passing in the night. "Which one is that?" Azim asked, so Hobie knew he was watching the habitat's solitary progress, too.

"Goddard City, maybe. Meat's on that one."

"Never knew that Meat," Azim said. "Never knew any of the white kids. Shit, bused in from Eastport, I never knew no one 'cept Zipper and Jo-jo, and I didn't even know them. Jo-jo got no brains, and Zipper, he didn't got no heart, so where did that leave me? Hobie, you bitchin' you gots only three-quarters your dad? Hell, I never been seein' mine."

"That Zipper," said Hobie. "He was bad." He didn't address the emptiness he heard behind Azim's gruff words. Never know your dad? Hobie could imagine Josephson effects and Coulomb interaction and interlayer binding energy; but he could not conceive of life without Big Mike in it. Some things lay beyond imagination.

Azim grunted. "Ol' Zip. Yeah. He sketch, no two ways." Azim cupped his hands and blew on them, rubbed them together. "Could do Jo-jo's thinking for him; but I never could do nothing for Zipper."

Hobie remembered that. The robbery and shootout at Pandya's In-and-Out and Azim running off ahead of an accessory charge. Next to that, Hobie's worries seemed damn small potatoes. "Thanks for the perspective," he said, to Azim's evident puzzlement. Well, putting things in perspective had not been his intent, but he had done it anyway and Hobie was grateful.

Charli was at the patio door. "We're going now," she said.

"Be right there. Gotta tell the folks good-bye." But Charli had not waited for his reply. "Gotta go," he told Azim.

Azim shook his head. "Whipped."

"What do you know about it?"

When Azim grinned, he could look like a skull. "Not much, bro', but I know when the postage too high."

"Charli's okay. She just doesn't like driving at night and we gotta catch a flight back to Houston in the morning."

Azim shook his head. "She wouldn't rub two words together for me."

On the way back to the hotel, Charli asked him what he and Azim had been talking about and Hobie told her that Azim had shown him pictures of his two girls, who were seven and five, and how the oldest one was taking ballet. Which was all true, even if that had been earlier in the evening, and it shut Charli's mouth good for the rest of the drive.

The reception area of Goldberg/Nigro Webstering was so "today" it was yesterday. The passion for the ornate that had only been a ripple when the office was modeled was the flood-tide of fashion now and Goldberg/Nigro was often featured in magazines as "a pioneer of the coke style." Hobie entered a world of fluted wooden columns, wainscoting, and elaborately patterned wallpaper in black and gold. The waiting chairs had plush seat cushions and carved feet. No two chairs were exactly alike, evoking the days of one-off craftsmanship. Lazy fans on the ceiling turned steadily. Large brass pots burst with sprays of flowers and green, leafy plants. Woodcuts in the eighteenth century style, matted in heavy frames, decorated the walls. A barometer hinted at rain to come. Why, great-grandfather, time-warped into this lobby, might feel that nothing had changed in a hundred years.

Until he looked closer. The temperature was far too cool and dry, given the muggy weather outside, than a ceiling fan could account for. The barometer was digital with solid state sensors and skip-optic processing that uplinked to the Weather Service deeby halfway across the continent. The old-style prints depicted not fox chases, but maglev trains, space vessels, and fractal cyberscapes. The chairs—though this might not have been obvious even to his keen, carpenter's eye—had been cut, turned, routed, and finished on flexible A/S universal jigs for which switching the tooling and patterns for one-off production meant no more than toggling the software.

The plants might have disturbed the old guy at some deep level, though without a DNA analysis he couldn't have said why.

It was more than packaging the modern into the less-threatening guise of a bygone and supposedly simpler era. (Simpler? Hobie wondered what Jubal Hobart would have said about that.) It was the rococo extravagance of cyberspace seeping into the outside world. Even the openly modern equipment, like the computer consoles, had been "coked."

Everyone thought the future would look like the Jetsons, Hobie thought, but it was looking more and more like the Victorians.

"Good afternoon, Doctor Hobart." The receptionist, in keeping with the trend, was human. "Should I tell Charli you're here?"

"Never mind," Hobie said. "I know the way."

"They're in the lab," she cautioned him.

"I'll be quiet."

Hobie made his way into the main office area. At one time, Goldberg/Nigro had been almost entirely teep. Charli had worked a node out of a guest bedroom at home fitted out with terminals, scanners, modems, goggs and helmet, gloves and body stocking, and all the rest of a webster's paraphernalia. She still spent four days out of five there; but Goldberg, the elfin little guy with the Vandyke who was "chief nerd," thought face time was important for unit cohesion. Could be he was right, too. Could be, too, some of the droids had been goofin' instead of teepin'. Charli had told Hobie that one of her coworkers had been caught sending an A/S construct to all the meetings; though, having sat through enough meetings himself, Hobie thought that an innovation on a par with the invention of fire, and just ahead of the wheel.

The "lab" was, almost literally, a rubber room. Inside, Peggy Ganesh, clad in a close-fitting MEMS body stocking and wearing the boots, gloves, and goggs of a webster, appeared to be performing a weird and ritualistic dance. She looked like some sort of bug-eyed monster beetle.

A very sexy monster beetle. A silver nude in mittens and combat boots. *Very jolly*, Hobie thought as he paused at one of the view windows to watch. *Otul, you lucky dude.*

A familiar poke in the small of the back . . . "Hey, Charli," he said without turning. "Ready to blow this joint?"

"In a few. Peg's dancing alpha."

Hobie grunted. "That's what I thought."

Charli stepped to his side and watched the antics with him. "It's not nearly so strange looking when you're Inside. That's where Brett and the others are—

lurking while Peg checks things out." Her hand indicated four men and women wearing goggs.

"She's checking a new web site?"

"It's not on the web, yet. It's still in rehearsals."

"And you call it 'dancing'?"

Charli nodded to the figure bending and twisting inside the lab. "What would you call it?"

"A seizure?" A light went on in his head. "Oh! 'Dancing alpha.' You mean she's lab testing the alpha version!"

Charli looked at him. "What did you think I meant?"

Hobie lowered his voice. "Now what did I say wrong?"

Charli folded her arms. "You know."

Since he quite certainly did not know, Hobie thought the extra penalty was piling on. But he also knew that to probe further would only turn an irritation into an offense. Silence, he decided, was the best reply.

"No, no, no!" Hobie turned and saw it was one of the gogged websters who had spoken. Judging from the long granny dress and the short stature, it was Maria Nigro, the artistic side of Goldberg/Nigro. "Brett, that cupboard is *so* monet."

"Oops. Didn't think anyone would get close enough to notice." A slim man, even shorter than his partner, Goldberg wore only wraparound cybershades, the latest style in goggs. He flipped them up and his fingers flew over the keyboard, striking the last key with a pianist's flourish. "Granulation's fixed. Hey, Doc," he said, noticing Hobie. "Didn't see you come in. People? We got unsecured ears in the vicinity. Loose lips shrink tips. No offense, Doc; but this is proprietary."

Hobie pantomimed key-locking his lips. "You should see some of the stuff I work with."

Goldberg grinned. "Yeah. Peggy? We're disabling your interface so we can rerun the module from the point where the player enters the banquet hall, but before Banquo's ghost appears. Take a rest and watch along with everybody else."

"I'll get my coat," Charli said to Hobie. "Back in a sec."

Hobie nodded. Peggy's form-fitting body mesh was designed to respond to the movement of the wearer. Micro-electro-mechanical sensors detected deflections in the sharkskin-weave material and replicated the movement in the virtch imago. Hobie had never worn one, but he surmised they were hot and uncomfortable from the way Peggy shifted and tugged at various parts of her body now that she was off-line. She ran her hands across her torso, straightening out folds and kinks in the fabric. *Ow!* Definitely scary.

Hobie stepped away from the window. If Charli planned to dance alpha at home some time, Hobie definitely planned to take the day off . . .

But she probably wouldn't, he decided. There was a *reason* the lab was padded. Wouldn't do to go knocking lamps over as you moved around an invisible room.

And Charli *had* explained this to him once. That was why she was jack frost on him a minute ago. *You never listen when I talk about my work.*

Okay, so some things tended to slip his mind. He hadn't known there'd be a pop quiz. He returned to the window to see what Peggy was doing.

Peggy wasn't doing anything. Just standing hipshot with her arms folded and head cocked.

Well, duh. He'd heard Goldberg say they were replaying the last scenario. Peggy was just watching the replay on her own goggs.

A guy in maintenance coveralls had entered the room through the backdoor and was adjusting something on the wall. A thermostat, Hobie guessed. Peggy had probably complained over her link.

Finished, the man stopped in front of Peggy on his way out and gave her the up-and-down with his eyeballs. He kissed his fingertips at her and circled around to check the view from the back. Peggy no more reacted to his presence than Uncle Waldo had to Hobie that time on LEO. The guy had started to make another, much more explicit motion when he saw Hobie watching. He flushed a deep red and hurried out the door he had entered.

Know how you feel, dude.

Be a hell of a thing, though, if Peggy had exited the system at the wrong moment. Of course, she hadn't known the mechanic was miming the jolly with her because she was virtching.

Charli was at his side, tugging at his arm. "Let's go," she said. "You can slobber over Peg some other time."

"Virtching!" Hobie said as realization dawned. "Virtching, not teeping!"

Goldberg and Nigro, huddled around a terminal, looked up at his exclamation. Charli frowned at him. "What are you talking about?" she demanded.

"Virtching," he said, more softly this time, "not teeping." Suddenly, he whooped and, grabbing his wife around the waist, lifted her clear of the floor. "You're a genius, Charli," he told her. "I really should pay more attention to your work."

Charli, startled at first and even now surely uncertain at the cause of this sudden adulation, smiled at him from on high.

The insight blossoming so unexpectedly after nearly four months of fruitless vexation threatened to burst Hobie asunder if he didn't share it immediately. Maybe that suppressed energy communicated itself to Charli on the way home. Or maybe it was the way he grinned or stroked her thigh or chattered endlessly about something important to do as soon as they got there. Certainly, Charli formed her own opinion about what that vital activity was, because when Hobie finished putting the car away and entered the family room from the garage, he found a shoe right by the door and, a step away, the other shoe.

Draped over the railing by the steps up to the kitchen, her blouse. The slacks, teasingly, placed on a chair, like someone sitting. The bra dangled on the pantry doorknob. Hobie was no woodsman, but this was not a hard trail to follow; nor was there much mystery about the quarry at its end. When he reached the soft, plush carpeting of the living room, he found pretty much what he expected to find.

Hobie sensed that wait-a-minute-while-I-call-Adam might not be the optimum conversational opener; and in fact, the sight of her drove all thoughts of Adam from his mind. There was no denying that he had a sweet tooth, and dark chocolate was his favorite. Semisweet. The unexpectedness of this particular Easter basket made it all the more tasty.

Afterward, while Charli showered, Hobie called Adam on his office terminal and got a voice mail menu, instead. Frustrated—making a recording wasn't as satisfying as announcing a discovery—he recited his conclusions and disconnected. He sat with his hands steepled for another minute or two, then shook his head and punched up Jimmy Poole's number. If Jimmy was working for Adam, this might actually be the best move.

The screen showed the Poole sEcurity logo with touch squares for a variety of options, none of which were germane to Hobie's call. He chose <Speak to One of Our Representatives>, figuring getting a human on-screen was half the battle.

He lost the battle.

He saw right away that Our Representative was a screen morph fronting for an Artificial Stupid. It was an especially good morph, but Charli had taught Hobie what cues to look for. Sometimes, when he was feeling particularly irritable and he could guess at the envelope of the A/S's knowledge base, he delighted in giving such constructs responses calculated to push them into do-loops and error messages. "Kirking the system," it was called. At the moment, however, he wanted access to the Poole-man and had no patience for the flubber. Figuring there had to be a keyword search engine in the A/S, Hobie leaned toward his doid to make sure his face appeared clearly on the other end and said distinctly, "LEO Station."

Whatever weenie Jimmy carried for LEO, Hobie wasn't sure. Something to do with the security system being better than it should have been. Hobie didn't see the problem, himself—after all, why settle for second best?—but he felt an obligation to Adam to finish the game.

The screen flipped and there was Jimmy—but a pasty-faced, nervous-looking Jimmy. When he saw Hobie, he slumped in obvious relief. "It's you."

Hobie wondering who he had been expecting. Not a pleasant call, to judge by his expression. "I think I figured out why the LEO waldos were acting so funny. Their minds were somewhere else."

Relief flashed to annoyance. "We already knew that. Look, there's some heavy shit going down and—"

"No, I mean the teepers were virtching. The reason they didn't see me—and why Chan Fulin nearly ran me down—was that they were viewing the virtch world, not the bone world."

Jimmy nodded impatiently. "Okay. That fits with some other information I just got. But it doesn't explain why adding that capability needed a netwalker and it sure as hell doesn't explain what's going down right now." Jimmy reached out to disconnect. "I'd love to chat, Hobie—and thanks for the datum—but I got troubles to deal with. My advice to you is—let it go."

Hobie almost asked what was going down, but from the hassled and frightened look he saw in Jimmy's eyes, he figured he might be better off not knowing. After the screen went black, he settled into his chair and stared at the bent crowbar mounted to the wall above his workstation.

"Don't everyone jump up and down thanking me," he muttered.

Only two reasons he could see for teepers cruising the virtch. The first was because they wanted to see something virtchuous. The other was to prevent them from seeing something real. If there was funny-bunny going on, the smart money was on door number two.

But it made no sense that Hobie could see. He had been bonebag on LEO and so had Adam and a half dozen other researchers and specialists. Whatever Uncle Waldo was kept from seeing, Hobie and the bonebags had full view.

His earlier exuberance slowly dissipated, leaving him with the gnawing feeling that he had gotten only half the answer. Let it go, Jimmy had said. Something bad was going down. Yet, if he had hold only of the back end of a snake, he had better grasp the other half right quick or it could double back and bite him.

17.

Geeks Baring Gifts

Jimmy Poole's equipment had been teased before. It had been spammed, noodled, ticked and jived. Poole sEcurity was a major Attractive Nuisance in the virtch and passersby always tried to peek over the walls. He had just cut the connection with Hobie when beetles began to scratch at his firewall. Some were charmingly forthright, running down thousands of permutations of likely passwords; but they were distractions for more subtle daemons that tried to latch onto incoming message packets. Jimmy's sentry A/Ss stomped on all of them, though many had tough carapaces—minifirewalls of their own—and resisted the counterviruses for entire nanoseconds before Seraphim could pass them on to Doc Scalpel for the autopsy.

Some of the squashed beetles were zombies and sprang to life as soon as they sensed the rewrite, only to bounce off the walls. Jimmy wasn't herbie enough to keep his morgue on a drive accessible to the rest of his system. Lurking Rollo overwrote the zombie addresses completely with a bit barrage. A tragic loss, for Jimmy dearly wanted to know how his attacker winkled that particular hack. Jimmy knew four ways to craft a zombie, but the morgue was warded against them, so there must be a fifth way.

Doc Scalpel autopsied the other beetles and came up dry. Jimmy hadn't expected a return address, so he was not disappointed; but he cloned one carcass, gave it *dataflocker* and released it back into the wild. If any of the attacking virtch-life did go home to mama, his jekylled zombie would flock with it.

Since his automatic defenses seemed to be handling the obvious channels, Jimmy turned his personal attention to the less obvious. He threw a trace out looking for the entry portal and found most of them were accessing his public interfaces. E-mail to Poole sEcurity was crawling with lice. *Item the first: Whoever was orchestrating this* knew *he was attacking Jimmy Poole. Item the second: The attacker was one bean dude with the cheese.*

A New Kid on the Block out to make his rep? Everyone had to prove himself; and how better to do that than by calling out a top gun? Yet the order of battle—beetles and zombies and weasels—was too sophisticated to be an up-and-coming code-slinger. The smart money said a Finger was poking him in the eye. But which one?

Automata began to clog the portals and Jimmy hosed them out. A patrol 'bot from the Internet Users' Protective Co-op, attracted by the hubbub, began bit-flipping the attackers from behind; but a lurking randomizer shot it full of holes and turned it to junk code.

That was serious weenie. The Co-op took its policing very seriously. Assaulting cop code was not just bad netiquette, but was certain to bring out the big guns, maybe even the Center for Computer Disease Control. Just in case the Co-op didn't know their 'bot had been rastered, Jimmy dropped them an E-mail.

It wasn't exactly a call for help. Jimmy Poole didn't need anyone's help.

There must have been a weasel among the beetles, because Jimmy's number three drive went down without warning. Something had piggybacked successfully on an inbound packet. Probably folded code with the virus built up *after* delivery from an anagram buried in innocuous E-mail. At any rate, number three was slag. The cutoffs were automatic, but Jimmy did a physical power down, just in case. Two of his favorite personas were trapped in the drive when the code-tight doors pinched off the portals. Whoever the attacker was, Jimmy vowed he would pay for that.

The zombies in the morgue grew too numerous for Lurking Rollo to handle and Jimmy shut that drive down himself and erased it—along with the working copies of Rollo and Doc Scalpel. Then, considering the situation, he did something he had not done in seven years.

Jimmy Poole went off-line.

It was like being castrated. Or at least what he imagined castration felt like. A tremendous longing; an aching absence. A feeling that he was cut off, bereft of his tools. He sat in his command chair uncertain of his next move.

Where, he thought ironically, *is Earp when you really need him.*

This game was getting far too chancy. It might be time to cut his losses, throw Adam to the wolves, and make a deal.

But that depended on why Earp (if it was Earp) had attacked. It might be no more than a simple slap upside the head, or whatever they did when you tried to call the authorities when the authorities weren't taking calls. But the timing argued against that option. The salami had to do with Cat spilling the beans. Jimmy was convinced of that. But if it did, *then Earp had matched Jimmy to Crackman* as one of those on-board the *Belle.*

Jimmy rebooted his master processor, but with the net connections disabled. Time for a post-mortem. He'd know what moves were possible once he knew how the dance had gone. Jimmy glanced at the chronometer. Five minutes? The core war had lasted an entire five minutes? That could make the record books, if anyone kept record books on that sort of thing.

He was deep in the code when the phone rang. It had been so long since he had gotten any calls except over the net that for a moment he did not recognize the chimes; and then he had to dig through printouts and other detritus to find the wrist-strap tracy.

One comforting bit of information was that the *telephone* interface for Poole sEcurities was still nestled snugly in the arms of Pacific Bell. But then the cracker with the nuts to slag the Mother would be one herbie dude. No one crossed the phone company, not even Earp. The phone lines were the air they all breathed.

From a safe house on the phone company's patch, he could thumb his nose at Earp; but dammit, Jimmy Poole didn't run to anyone for protection. He was Poole sEcurity, for crying out loud. If he couldn't sEcure himself, he might as well pack it in and sign on as Earp's stooge.

The call came from Tani, who told him about Tyler Crayle and the raid on the San Antonio node. Jimmy felt the cold clear to the bone. He had never expected physical action. Events in the real world never seemed quite real, and it bothered him to be reminded that things happened that were virtchually invisible. Jimmy had walked the wild side with panache for many years, and had skated along the edge for this hack. Dropping into a cracker hangout wasn't illegal, per se; neither was claiming to be the notorious Crackman. Yet, the whole might be suggestive to Earp, who was quite able to add 1 + 1 and get 10. Tani could have been arrested—as a material witness, if not an accomplice.

The next call was from SuperNerd.

He almost wished he could see the Nerd's face, because his voice was so high-pitched that Jimmy had a hard time understanding him. That was the problem with tracies. Poor sound and no visuals. Might as well be in the dark ages. But Jimmy's pee-phone was built into his net access processor, which had received the brunt of the attack, and there might be lurkers slicked into that drive just waiting for a reboot.

"It wasn't you," SuperNerd said. "Tell me it wasn't you."

"It wasn't me," Jimmy said, always ready to humor the other Finger.

"Then who was it?"

"Elvis is my guess. Look, Bosworth, I'm real busy right now. Usually, Guess the Topic is my favorite word game, but some other time, okay?"

"Wait."

Jimmy hesitated at the plaintive tone he heard in Bosworth's voice. "I'm waiting."

"You got slagged, too, didn't you?"

Jimmy made a silence while he digested that datum. If the Nerd spoke sooth, the slagger had *not* singled Jimmy out, which while a snub of sorts might also be good news. The most likely reason for a *personal* attack was that Earp had sussed him on the *Dixie Belle*, and that would be triple-plus ungood. An attack on Jimmy Poole *and* SuperNerd argued a broader rationale.

Unless the Nerd was secretly Mighty Mouse . . .

"Not slagged," he replied. "I'm way too stone for that; but I did get one heck of a sleet storm."

"Yeah, me, too. Just one question: Who and why?"

"That's two questions," Jimmy pointed out. "But if you made a list of all the people who could even *think* about slagging Jimmy Poole and Norris Bosworth both, how many names could *you* put on it?"

"Chen, Earp. Cat. Maybe Pedro. Doc Doom. The Krazy Kossack. No more than ten."

Jimmy scowled at his tracy. How many fingers did Bosworth have on his hand? "My money's on Earp," he said. "I'd bet a federal dollar that half the dudes you just named got slagged this afternoon."

"Why do you say that?" He could hear the note in Bosworth's voice: the knowledge that there was knowledge and that Jimmy Poole possessed it.

"Because Earp's been seduced by the Dark Side," Jimmy told him. "He played enabler to a wildside hack by Captain Cat and he's spooked that if the skinny leaks he loses his government pension. Now he's slamming everyone he thinks might know."

The more he thought about it, the more sense that made to Jimmy. Yeah, try to wipe any drives that might have the incriminating data; and that could mean everyone who had been nosing into the LEO Laager. The Truth might be Out There and the whole slag attack a byzantine plot involving thousands of improbably tight-lipped conspirators and their alien allies, but always bet on the high-prob scenario. He hesitated a few moments, weighing in his mind all that he knew of Bosworth and Utopian Research Associates.

True safety lay only in secrecy. Working alone, you could rely on your own mojo, and not expose your soft underbelly to the skills and motives of others. You could improvise. The one thing you could not do was watch your own back.

I can still winkle this. Some fancy footwork. Some pseudo evidence planted in yesterday. (He could create and backdate records in hotels or shopping malls proving *beyond a shadow of doubt* that Tani had been nowhere near San Antonio.) If he brought Bosworth into the game, the Nerd would want to know the score; and that was the rub.

And yet . . .

If Option one was throw in your hand, option two was stand and fight.

He had tried the safe and careful way, tickling his way coyly around the edges of LEO—sending a bonebag up to LEO, chatting up the Fingers—and all it had gotten him was a sleet storm, two trashed drives, and Tani on the run in San Antonio.

(The airport was probably safe. Earp couldn't move that fast, could he? And yet, if he had heard Tani right, Earp-Crayle would know Billie Whistle by sight; so all he really had to do was hang out at the airport on general principles and the fruit would drop into his lap like an eager intern. How hard could it be to flash his badge at the airline people and ask if anyone booked an outbound flight real sudden?

The smart thing would be to blow the Whistle; but a) Whistle would blow her own whistle; b) "David Desherite" might take that amiss and come down hard with a hammer the size of the van Huyten Trust; c) Tani would never go along with it; and . . .

And d). No matter how hard he squirmed and clung to logic and reason and the iron law of self-preservation, it was *wrong* to hang an ally out in the wind.

So he told Bosworth everything he could safely tell him. About his attempts to suss out the author of the LEO Laager, and how Norris's own curiosity, like Jimmy's, had surely marked him for a later slag attack. About the suspicions of "some tenants and would-be tenants" aboard LEO. (And how many of them had been slagged? Wilson? VHI? Boeing?) About the destruction of the *Dixie Belle* and the San Antonio Swoop. He said nothing about Baleen or Argonaut; nor did he say why he was aboard a notorious cracker hangout. Lurking, was all he said, hoping to find the Cat.

Bosworth seized on a detail. "Tyler Crayle?" the tinny voice on the wrist-strap asked. "Tyler Crayle isn't Earp; take my word on that. Crayle's strictly non-virtchuous; doesn't walk the net at all. But . . . You better tell your wife and her friend to go to ground, stat. You know the drill. Hide them with some digital razzle. I'll have a couple of our guys fly down there in a private jet and pull them out real time. No tickets; no record."

A fist clutched Jimmy around the throat. Had that been fear in SuperNerd's tinny voice? He looked at the clock. The ride to the San Antonio airport was a long one, he remembered. Tani wouldn't be there yet. He could still call before she got there.

"What's the urgency?" he asked Bosworth as casually as he could.

But Bosworth was a clam. "That information costs," was all he said, "and it's a price you don't want to pay."

It was a long night and a sleepless one. He wanted to call the hotel, just to assure himself that Tani was all right, but Bosworth was right. By now Earp would have a cat sitting on the fibrop fence, waiting for *any* communication between a Finger and San Antonio. He might not know who he was up against, but he knew the minimum cut set. Better to wait in quiet agony than make a hasty move that could draw attention.

Jimmy roamed the house at three A.M., moving aimlessly from room to room. For a while, he stood in Stevie's nursery, watching the small person in the crib breathe softly in and out in the glow of the night light. Later, he went to Tani's office, where he sat in her high-backed chair in front of her terminal. He didn't turn the lights on, but the quarter moon shining through the parted curtains brought everything out. He studied the locked drawers and cabinets, the password-protected hard drive. A little red light blinked on the console, showing it was active.

Finding the password had been an hour's work; crafting a context-sensitive search engine to hunt for indiscretions in Tani's manuscript had taken a while longer. He ran his fingers up and down the carved filigree of the cabinet door. The search was complete; the A/S had signalled itself ready to download, but Jimmy hadn't gotten around to reading it before the sleet hit the fan.

He thought about the assault on his own system; the rage and violation he had felt as he watched his drives penetrated. Then he reached around to the back of Tani's drive and disconnected the fibrop he had attached there. He twisted the cable in his fingers and the jack writhed like a serpent's head. It *was* a serpent, in an odd way. It had sunk its poisoned fangs deep.

Jimmy began coiling it up and unplugged it from the wall port where it connected to his home intranet. Tani's locked files and drawers had mocked him no less than had the LEO Laager, and as with Leo, he had imagined all sorts of secrets behind them. He turned off the drive and his ferret, deprived of its umbilical expired unread.

If he was going to start trusting people, he might as well start with Tani.

Jimmy's knees turned to water as he watched Tani scramble out of the backseat of a gleaming white limo and run up the driveway into his arms. "I'm so glad to see you," he said. "I was so worried." And Tani was chattering away. "It was so exciting. I'm so high! Oh, Jimmy!" There were kisses and caresses, and who knew what else there might have been if Billie Whistle had not forced them out of her way so she could roll past them into the house.

The liveried driver brought the suitcases in, then returned with another box. "What's that?" Jimmy asked.

"I don't know," Tani said. "They brought it with them."

"They" were the couple who had pulled Tani and Billie from the airport hotel: a man and a woman, both in their fifties. He was short and stocky, with swarthy skin. His shock of unruly hair gleamed a dull, brownish red when the light hit it just right. His companion was black with a high forehead and broad smile. Jimmy and Gloria. No last names.

"Hey," said the man with a well-worn smile. "A pair of Jimmies. Better just call me Red." He made himself instantly at home, unerringly picking out Jimmy's favorite chair for his own. He propped his feet up on the stool and smiled; but his eyes swiftly scanned the room, missing nothing. Behind him, Billie Whistle stared into the crackling fireplace.

"We're friends of Norris," said Gloria. "We've come to help."

"She did," said Red. "I've got another op. Isn't that right, Walt?"

The driver smiled lopsidedly and without humor. "It's always nice to meet old friends," he said cryptically. "Gloria, where do you want this set up?" Together, the newcomers had carried several boxes into Jimmy's house.

"Wait a minute," said Jimmy.

"We don't know who you are," Tani said. She flushed and looked at her shoes. "I mean, that was good of you to get us out of San Antonio, but . . ."

"No buts, girlfriend," Gloria drawled. "If Tyler Crayle had gotten to you—"

Walt, the driver, made a zipper across his lips. "Shaddap," he explained.

Billie looked up from the dancing flames. "Crayle seemed like a good man when he helped set up my apartment."

Red shook his head, smiled, but did not elaborate. Walt had opened the boxes and Jimmy saw a microwave laser and rectenna and other gear. Jimmy looked sharply at Red, but the stocky man laughed and wagged a thumb at his companion. "Not me. Her."

"We're going to give you a secure channel," Gloria said, "deeply encrypted— that's this black box here. Don't even think about opening it. It self-destructs, and you wouldn't like the way it does it. The laser beam is tuned to a rectenna on the roof of a receiving building in San Jose. We *are* high enough, aren't we, Walt?"

"I checked the satellite topo deeby before we left. Toldja not to worry."

"Who's worried? The devil is in the details. Jimmy, where do you want this? I mean the laser and receiver go on the roof, but the rest of it we need to integrate into your system."

Integrate into his system . . . What kind of herbie did SuperNerd think he was, to give him this chance to plant a backdoor into Jimmy's system? The two of them might be working together on this hack, but Jimmy wasn't about to throw caution entirely to the winds. Trust was all well and good. Stupidity was another order entirely. "I'll have to set that up," Jimmy temporized. "Poole sEcurity has a lot of proprietary client information. I can't give you access to those drives."

"We'll need a jukebox and a tree." Gloria suggested. "Two teras. Espresso-compatible, with heavy metal and excellence."

In fact, he could set up an entire dedicated system. It wasn't like his credit card had a limit or anything. He could buy virgin whatever this Gloria needed. No reason to let anyone inside his privates, where maybe the ghosts of ancient files could still be sifted from the substrate. "Hardware is easy," Jimmy said. "If I have to, I can have units delivered by this afternoon."

"Make sure it's remote operable," Billie Whistle said. When Jimmy looked at her, she returned an angry shrug and a defiant stare. "Obviously, I can't go home to my own set, yet. Not 'til we know it's clear."

No one had ever touched Jimmy's equipment but Jimmy. To give Gloria *and* Billie Whistle even this much access seemed almost obscene. Jimmy swallowed and sought Tani's hand. She squeezed him. "All right," he wheezed. Then, more forcefully, "Let's make it happen."

"What we're going to do," Gloria explained once she and Jimmy were settled in the Sanctum, "is build up a 'no-see-um.' The maestro I'm giving you will disperse a copy of your processor across a couple of hundred public-access drives, coordinate the cross-talk so it acts like a single unit, and shift the scene using the Buffalo Shuffle."

"Like a miniature brodyazhka," Jimmy said. "I know how to do that."

Gloria set the "goat-case" on the console and gave him a flat look. "You want an upload—or just a pencil and a blank sheet of paper?"

Jimmy blinked. "What'd I do?"

Gloria opened the goat-case and pulled a ROM pin from the foam holdfast. "I don't care what you know how to do. This is no time for ego games. We can't tolerate the sort of rowdiness that went down last night, especially from the man who's supposed to keep order in the first place. So we've got to deal with his problem—or neutralize him." She favored Jimmy with a careful scrutiny. "I know the wildsiders don't like it, but the net's a safer and more reliable venue because of Earp and his deputies. So a lot of us want to know: Is this a correctable aberration, or is he permanently damaged? I'd hate to see ten years of attaboys trashed because of one awshit." She inserted the first gig pin.

Evil Overlord—Jimmy's new dedicated system—asked for a command override to accept the input. Gloria moved the chair—it was Tani's writing chair—so Jimmy could reach the panel. Jimmy hesitated. He became aware of Gloria's knowing look, her slight smile. He flushed and reached out to tickle the keys. Gloria looked away, as netiquette required.

Overlord accepted the input. But into a segregated partition where Jimmy's wardens could check out the new system.

"Earp slagged the *Belle*," he pointed out, without implying that he had been aboard. "What makes this no-see-um safe?"

Gloria shook her head as she took over the installation. "The *Belle* was a Known Place. What good is a crack house if the crackers can't find it? The public key was Out There. Your no-see-um doesn't have a public key."

Jimmy tugged his lip as he watched commands flash and scroll at Gloria's fingertips. "Okay, but where Earp is concerned, I can't depend on stealth. I need armor and countermeasures, too."

Gloria tossed her head. "The laser that Walt and Red are installing on your roof? It's a squealer and it code dances using a read-only black box synchronized

with a twin at the receiving end. Cesium clocks. You'd have to physically open
the device to find the dance card—and opening it would be unwise. The boxes
use encryptions so deep, they've got trilobite fossils."

Jimmy was impressed despite himself. "And you put this all together since
last night?"

Gloria snorted. "No. It's eighty-percent off-the-shelf. *Our* shelves, but
still . . . All I did was mate the standard modules, reconfigure the architecture,
and add a little customization."

It was still phat stoopid, considering she had done it overnight on a red-eye
jet flight to pluck Tani out of San Antone. Jimmy studied the black woman
from the corner of the eye. "Who are you?" he asked as casually as he could.

Gloria's finger paused over the keyboard. Then she hit return and scrolled
down. Evil Overlord began to integrate its new ghostly twin. "Sometimes, I
ask myself that question."

"It's just that I don't know any virtchuosos named Gloria. I mean, I've never
heard of you, and you're too good for me never to have hear of you."

Gloria smiled wistfully. "Maybe you have." She nodded toward the screen.
"Will you be going out as 'Jimmy Poole'?"

Wariness returned like a comfortable old blanket. Sadly, Jimmy realized how
badly his years of waltzing the wild side had affected him. The price of the
thrill was the loneliness of paranoia.

Of course, like they said, even paranoids had enemies. "Who else would I
go out as?"

A shrug. "Sometimes people use other names on-line. For privacy. And
other reasons."

Duh? "You don't walk under your regular persona." Mentally, he ran down
the list of virtchuosos he knew only by their *noms de virtch*, but the list was
too long by far. Reach out and touch someone; but you never really knew who
you'd touched. NMissi. nitemar. Wesomniman. Come2Reven. Major oz.
RowrBasil. Our Coach. What did he know of any of them? They could be as
innocent as they seemed; or they could be a top-secret, sinister cabal in league
with the Illuminati and the phone company.

Jimmy grinned. Paranoia could also be vastly entertaining, as long as you
didn't take it *too* seriously . . .

Red and Walt returned from the roof. "All set," the stocky man announced.
"Clear line of sight, and we verified the handshake with Frank Chu and Helen
at the other end. We ran the fibrop through a window to a dataport in the
guest bedroom . . ." He turned to Jimmy. "Your wife showed us where. If you
want a more permanent installation, you'll need a carpenter and an opticri-
cian." He looked around for another chair, saw none, and leaned against the
door jamb.

Walt said, "We better get going."

Red grunted. "You done here, Gloria?"

"In a minute."

"I figure, cousin Tyler hitting Poole's rig was a CYA op, not an attempted deletion. Benny Ruiz is no whack. I got a different puzzle."

Walt, the driver, said, "Shaddap."

Jimmy said, "CIA op?"

"CYA. Cover Your Aperture. A gray op. He wants to erase his footprints. I don't see it as wet work. If we make nice-nice and stroke him a little, he crawls back in his hole."

"Shaddap some more," suggested Walt.

Gloria focused on the screen. "What's the puzzle, Red?"

Red's eyes lingered snakelike on Jimmy while he answered. "In all the years that we've followed cousin Tyler's stellar career, have we ever known him to do an altruistic deed?"

Gloria logged off and turned away from the screen. "No . . ." she said slowly.

The stocky man glanced briefly over his shoulder before his eyes again challenged Jimmy. "Me, neither."

Jimmy had the distinct impression that Red was trying to tell him something that he did not want to come right out and say. A warning or an accusation? Jimmy suspected that Red was a man whose suspicions were easily aroused. Yet what would make him suspicious of S. James Poole, aside from general principles?

The notion puzzled him for some time after the trio had left and he noodled his way through the new architecture he had been given. Then, stretching his back in an idle moment, he glanced out of his Sanctum and saw Billie Whistle dozing in her powerchair near the fire, and realized what Red had been looking at over his shoulder.

Tyler Crayle had showered Billie Whistle with generosity—phat equipment and cheesehead training—and Tyler Crayle never did anything from the goodness of his heart.

Temperance

The sign on the entry read UNCLE JOHN'S SWIMMIN' HOLE but the man who spun the wheel lock didn't look old enough to be anyone's uncle. "Stay on the platform, please. No horseplay. That tank is forty feet deep." John Sedgwick was in his thirties, but looked younger. Dark-haired, tanned, a former OTV engineer—tow-truck repairman, he liked to say. Except his "tow trucks" had been orbital transfer vehicles pulling disabled satellites in for repair.

Jacinta scampered past him, clenching her robe tight around her. "Uncle John," they said, had an appreciative eye for beauty, but Jacinta refused to play *objet d'art*. Inside, a broad platform encircled the bouyancy tank, which was a hundred feet on each side. Light flickered green off the surface of the water, casting dancing moiré patterns across the walls and the swimsuits of the other cadets. Echoes bounced in curious, flat tones. Overhead, a ten ton crane rested on its rails. Smaller jib cranes rose storklike on each side of the tank. A rack of neutral bouyancy suits lined one of the walls. The cadets looked at the suits, at each other.

Uncle John was flanked by two "pinned" cadets, Total Meredith and Nathan Caldwell, who would take turns babysitting. Total winked at Jacinta and made the thumbs-up sign. Sedgwick clapped his hands together, a sharp sound in the chamber. "First time in the barrel, right?" He collected nods. "And everyone's passed the physical gates for this." More nods, though it hadn't exactly been a question. They didn't leave that sort of thing to chance. No one casually wandered into tank training. Lou Penny was still stuck at Gate 3 and would probably not "get wet" until the next group formed up.

"All right, listen up." Sedgwick assumed the pose of a young man who had inexplicably become a wise old head. "This is just a familiarization dive, but that doesn't mean you're allowed to be stupid. Our training tank is only half the size of NASA's NBL at Houston, but it's still plenty big. That's three million gallons of water in there, recycled every day, and held at thirty degrees—which sounds God-damned cold, except it's Celsius, so we're talking just under body temperature." He waited out the few chuckles this elicited with the air of one who has used the line more than once before. Jacinta listened carefully to the briefing. She had experience on SCUBA gear, but this was different. Cadets would be lowered into the tank by one of the cranes, breathing oxygen-enriched NITROX through umbilicals. Descent and ascent would be by slow stages. Even at forty feet, depth precautions were wise.

Jacinta went down with the third dive, along with Kenn Rowley, Yungduk Morrisey, and Karyl Krzyzanowkski, known to all as "Kadet Konsonant." Caldwell rode the elevator platform with them. Jacinta didn't think she needed a babysitter, but Uncle John played by the rules. "I never had anyone drown on me yet," Uncle John explained, "not even Wheezer Hottlemeyer—and he tried awful hard."

Jacinta could feel the liquid through her membrane. It was as if a sea creature had wrapped its clammy hand around her body. Water seeped in around the edges of her face mask. Everything took on a greenish tinge and sounds became dull thunks. Halfway down, her wet suit powered up and the heads-up on her face mask displayed depth, NITROX flow, and more info than she wanted to know. Who needed GPS—given that she was on an umbilical and couldn't hardly get lost inside a barrel?

On training dives, they would be fitted out in bouyancy suits with lead weights and floats of ultra-high molecular density polyethylene. Neutral bouyancy was supposed to simulate ziggy. It didn't, quite—there was water drag, among other things—so some things in "neu-boy" were easier and some were harder than in ziggy. But this was as close to the real thing as bunnies were going to get.

Caldwell took them on a guided tour. He repeated the safety precautions Uncle John had given on the platform, but made sure they paid attention by asking snap question over the radio link. Jacinta tried to move about without overtly swimming. "Staying in character," actors called it. You couldn't move in space by stroking your arms or scissoring your legs, so why start bad habits? That was why only Caldwell's wet suit had flippers.

One portion of the tank was fashioned from the dorsal aeroshell of an older model Daedalus Plank, running from abaft Bulkhead Seven to just forward of the fuel tank modules. Jacinta wondered if it had been salvaged from *Bessie Coleman*, Forrest Calhoun's own "Queen Bessie." Somehow, that would have been fitting.

Later, when the cadets had their "legs," they would practice different procedures and motions, from routine tool handling to removal, repair, and replacement. The aeroshell featured a manlock and a cargo lock, outside-mounted sensors and instruments, oxygen and hydrogen refueling ports, beamed power rectenna. All sorts of objects that an otter might have to deal with in ziggy. For now, they were invited to inspect the set-up under their babysitter's watchful eye.

Okay. If you imagined the floor of the tank was the forward pressure wall of the fuel train, it was perfectly legitimate to spring off toward the dorsal manlock. She had just replaced the meteor-damaged Number Fourteen Aft Fibrop

Connector (Subassembly #FHD 08Y82043/14), restoring fault tolerance to the fuel initiator controls. Good job, Rosario, her imaginary captain told her. Now, get back on board so we can de-orbit.

Aye-aye, Captain. Did civilian orbiter crews use naval etiquette? And where did aye-aye come from anyway? An aye for an aye?

As she reached the personnel lock, she grabbed the handle and gave it a sharp tug, expecting it to spin open.

Oops.

Either the door was locked—and was space really a place where you wanted to forget your keys?—or it had enough resistance that Newton's action-reaction came into play. Instead of the handle turning, *she* turned, in the opposite direction. Water drag stopped her when she was upside down. She tried to stay in character and not right herself by swimming.

Okay, smartass, how *do* you do it? She sighed. Or tried to.

Her facemask flashed bright red letters across her line of sight. *NITROX flow constricted*.

"Hey!" she said.

"Hold on, Rosario," Caldwell said over the comm link. "Your umbilical's tangled on the lock handle." One of the figures on the bottom of the tank pushed off in her direction.

Suddenly, before Caldwell could reach her, unfamiliar hands were on her buttocks. She twisted away from the unwelcome fingers, kicked out by instinct, and connected with whomever was behind her. But the motion pushed her away from the aeroshell.

NITROX flow blocked.

To hell with versimulitude. Jacinta flailed with her arms. Suddenly, her head was snapped to the side, as the slack in the umbilical gave out. It lifted her facemask and the warm water flooded inside, invaded her nose and gasping mouth.

To clear your face mask, blow out the inside with air . . .

She reached for the SCUBA hose before she remembered she was on umbilical, and the umbilical was blocked. Nevertheless, she had automatically lifted her face mask and detached the hose—just in time for Morrisey, who was untangling the line from the handle, to yank it from her grip.

The kink relieved, the hose spewed NITROX into the water, surrounding Jacinta with a mass of bubbles as it squirted out of reach. The water churned. Spume swirled around her, disorienting her, blocking her sight.

Air. Fast. She'd had no chance to take a deep breath before losing her NITROX. But . . . Can't chase the writhing hose. Go for the top. *But which way was up?* The bubbles blinked and glittered like living jewels, surrounding her with a writhing, pearly featurelessness. She was lost. There! Light! Top of the tank or worklights on the bottom?

No time for debate. Go for the light.

Lungs burning, she scissored her legs and kicked blindly through the swirling bubbles, grabbing handfuls of water and thrusting them behind her.

Out of the bubbles! She was headed . . . not quite up. She changed angle. She could see anxious faces, blurred and wavy, on the roof of the world. Almost there.

But her body betrayed her. Inches from the surface—or was it feet, or was it fathoms?—she gasped for air that wasn't there. Water filled her lungs and she coughed to expel it, then sucked in more. Her throat closed up to block the incoming water and her body imploded with the demand for air.

Everything receded. The top of the tank became a distant circle of light rimmed by an utter blackness, darker than any she had ever known, as if she were at the far end of a long, long tunnel. The water's warmth enveloped her. Floating was so peaceful, so calm. Exertion was pointless; the floundering and splashing of her arms, foolish. The black at the edges of the tunnel crept in on her, like the forest around a fading campfire. The light shrank to a small disc, then to a pinpoint. She ought to strive for the light, she knew. All her friends were there. And Soren. He had noticed her. *Hey, worth noticing.* She could hear his voice. *We're all in the same boat—I mean, plane.*

Except they hadn't been. They should have been, but God hadn't kept proper count, so three of them had slipped through His fingers in that fiery crash. That was why Ursula had been so out of place. She hadn't belonged here any more than Jacinta or Lonzo. All three of them were on overtime and the universe was calling in debts.

She was lifted up on angels' wings and carried toward the light, which grew ever more brilliant before snuffing out into nothing.

Weight crushed her, squeezing her flat. Ribs protested. Then soft lips pressed against hers, filling her up with the spirit. She welcomed those lips; yearned for them. The pressure again, then once more the hungry lips, and again, and again, until . . .

. . . she coughed, and vomited water onto the deck.

This time, it was blessed, cool air that streamed into her. She retched again, spewing more water. A hand seized her face and turned it and, once more, those lips pressed against hers, only this time with tenderness. Jacinta's heart turned over—oh, yes!—and then she stiffened and *shoved.*

"Morrisey!" Her voice croaked like a frog.

But it was Total Meredith who had been giving her the mouth-to-mouth. The senior cadet knelt back now on her calves, her hands hanging limp at her sides. Her face spoke relief—and apprehension. "Morrisey ran off," she said.

"Total saved your life," Kenn Rowley said.

"But it was Yungduk," said Krzyzanowkski, "who carried her up and pushed her onto the mat."

Rowley snorted. "Yeah. After he yanked the air hose out of her hands in the first place."

"He was just trying to untangle it—"

"As you were," said Uncle John quietly, and the two bickering cadets fell silent. He squatted next to Jacinta. "Glad you came back," he said. "Wouldn't want my record spoiled."

It was a flip comment, the sort of line men tossed off to show they hadn't really been afraid. But the words couldn't hide the instructor's fear. In courtesy, Jacinta looked away from him. Her chest ached beside the breastbone, as if desperate fists had punched her there, hard.

"Rosario, we need to put you in the hyperbaric chamber. You came up from depth awfully fast."

She looked at the gleaming white cylinder against the east wall. "Yeah. Well," she croaked. "I was in a hurry." Show him that others could flip brave words. Even banalities were better than contemplating your own extinction.

"You up to walking," Uncle John said, "or should we bring out the stretcher?" Jacinta glanced at Total, who was squatting, looking down at the flooring. She raised her head and, when Jacinta reached out an arm, rose and helped her to her feet. The other cadets and ensigns applauded.

A fine gesture, though somewhat marred when Jacinta's knees betrayed her. She staggered, steadied herself on Total, and stood straight-once more. Amazing what people will do to earn the applause of their peers. Total put an arm around her to steady her and help her to the chamber. She gave Jacinta a surreptitious squeeze. Encouragement, Jacinta was sure, nothing more. But the press of the sister's lips lingered in her memory—soft and urgent, blowing the life back into her.

The clinic poked and prodded and thumped and scanned her, head to toe, and concluded, reluctantly, that, except for being dead longer than was healthy, she was in the pink. It must have offended their professional code. They made her stay a few days for observation—although Jacinta didn't see that anyone spent much time actually observing her.

She received a steady train of visitors. Uncle John, all grave and fussy; and Calhoun, who expressed his relief and good wishes and questioned her minutely about what had happened. Their visits were almost ceremonial. You expected that they would pop in; duty compelled them. But Ensign Matusek dropped by, too. She accused Jacinta of malingering to avoid the obstacle course, but her voice and posture belied the words. And Ensign Dubois brought a problem set "so you have more interesting math to do than counting the ceiling tiles." Sister Adrienne came and prayed over her and Jacinta didn't see that it did much harm, and afterward they discovered a mutual fascination with live theater. Lou Penny came by because he wanted to know "what was it like to be dead?" Jacinta told him that finding out would be easy enough and offered to help.

Most of the Grissom Hall cadets stopped in—Rowley, Carr, Bucktail Smith, Vincent, people she hardly knew. It could hardly be friendship; so maybe it was (literally) morbid curiosity, and Schimmelpfennig was the only one honest enough to say so out loud.

Had she been dead? It was an odd thought, considering that she ought to have been dead back in March when the commuter jet went down. Maybe it was her time to go—as her mother used to say every time she fell ill. God was calling her and she hadn't answered. Twice, now. Would He keep calling? A strange and cruel God, that; but maybe He thought He was doing her a Divine Favor. Chuck the Valley of Tears business and go straight for the Beatific Vision thing. You'll thank Us afterward. It was paradox enough to test her faith, had she any faith to test, and she wondered whether similar thoughts had ever plagued Sister Ursula. Who am *I*, why am *I* so special, that I should live while others died? And the answer that echoed off the walls of an empty, careless universe was: You are nothing; freak chance saved you, not any merit on your part. You didn't *deserve* to live; it just turned out that way. And that thought was intolerable. No wonder Ursula's unexpected reappearance last fall had upset her so.

Yungduk Morrisey never showed up, and of all the people who had ever wanted to see her in bed, she would have thought he'd be the first in line.

Total came, too; but Jacinta was expecting that. They chatted of this and that; how the huntresses emphasized physical culture—hiking, camping, rock climbing—and the silver apples went for reading voices and attitudes and Ursula's doves were charlie for contemplation, but all of it planted the seed of self-reliance and nurtured it. "All sisters under the skin," was how Total put it, and Jacinta laughed and asked if Total knew where the line came from, which she didn't, but the irony was too delicious not to share, so she told her about the Colonel's lady and Judy O'Grady. They discussed Lou Penny's conceit and Bucktail Smith's earnestness and the vagaries of Ensign Matusek. In the end, they had defined a topic by a sort of verbal intaglio. Talking of everything but, they had sketched its boundaries. Finally, it was Jacinta who jumped into the void.

"Thanks," she said. "For saving my life, I mean."

Total shrugged, looked down at her hands clasped between her knees. "Yeah. Well. We're all trained in that sort of thing. I was closest."

"Rowley told me you shoved him aside."

"There wasn't time for dithering. I was so . . . scared."

"*You* were scared?" Jacinta laughed. "That's funny. I was the one drowning, but I felt calm—and peaceful."

"Dying is easy. Watching someone else die is hard."

"So." Jacinta plucked at the sheets.

"Yeah."

"Total?" Without looking up.

"What?"

"How long have you wanted to kiss me?"

The answer was long enough in coming that Jacinta looked up. Meredith rose from the chair and walked to the window, to stare for a while at the blank rear facade of Gagarin Hall. Jacinta saw how her hands clenched and unclenched behind her back. Finally, she spoke without turning, "Was it unwelcome?"

"Compared to what, being dead?"

As a joke, it fell flatter than the test flight of the V. A. *Lebedev*. Total turned around, but stayed by the window. "I'm sorry," she said. "But I was so happy when you came back . . ."

"Don't worry about it."

"You thought I was Morrisey."

And why should that bother Total more than it did Jacinta? Yet so her voice and posture proclaimed. "Did I? I was having a nightmare."

"Look . . ." Total picked up her computer pouch. "I gotta go practice sims. I've got a mooner coming up next week and I don't want to embarrass myself too bad in front of Captain Feathershaft . . ." She took a few steps toward the door, paused, and looked back over her shoulder. "Whenever you're ready. You know."

Jacinta nodded mechanically and, when the sister had gone, she lay back in the bed and counted ceiling tiles.

And now it comes, Jacinta thought as she sat in the chair across the desk from Superintendent Calhoun. Expulsion for terminal stupidity. About as terminal as you could get without actually being carried out on your back. Calhoun fussed on his desk for a moment, closed some computer files, balled his hands together and looked straight at her.

I wasn't cut out for this, anyway, she told herself. Space pilot. Right: Dream all you want about soaring, but reality trumps dreams. Atmospheric flying was bad enough, but in space your first mistake could be your last. You had to have that sure touch, the instinct to do the right thing even when you didn't know what to do.

"They tell me," said Mr. Calhoun, "that you got a complete upcheck from the doc. The question now is, do you feel up to resuming your studies?"

Jacinta had thought the question would be whether she'd be *allowed* to resume her studies. She fought to keep the surprise from showing in her face but it was a battle she must have lost, because Mr. Calhoun cocked his head. "What is it?" he asked.

"You mean, I'm not being expelled?"

"Not yet. Maybe next week. You planning something bonehead?"

"I thought . . . I already had." Confusion, and this time she didn't try to hide it. Sometimes that was the best way to ask questions when you didn't yet know what the questions were.

"Ah." Mr. Calhoun leaned back in his chair and its MEMS structure shifted to accommodate his new posture. "Rosario, what you did isn't in the same league with what Kitmann did. You didn't *plan* to do it. In fact, you did things almost right."

"The 'almost' part can kill you."

Calhoun nodded. "So it can. It almost killed me, on FarTrip."

"I thought . . . The skinny says it was Krasnarov who bumped."

Calhoun looked a long way off. "Depends," he said, "on what you think the mistakes were. But, yeah," focusing on her once more, "that goes with the territory. A good buddy of mine, Bat DaSilva, he had an engine malf light on a ballistic run a couple years ago, but it wasn't steady-like. It came on, winked off, came back on . . . So he figured it was the light that was malfing, not the engine. He gyroed bass-ackward, hit the main burn for de-orbit . . . and the engine blew." Calhoun shook his head. "Damn bad luck. Stuck him in orbit— and the blow had taken heat and light out with it. By the time the Emergency Response Team could scram and match orbits, it was too late. Rough on Bobbi and the kids, but the point is this: You do your best, and sometimes the best just isn't good enough." He turned his seat and contemplated a bookshelf where two shot-glasses sat mouth-down. Five others sat upright beside them.

Jacinta sat quietly through the narrative. This certainly wasn't the stuff of dreams. She had often imagined herself grappling with some emergency, always pulling it out before it foo'ed. But reality didn't always cooperate with the imagination. I think I can, the Little Engine had said, but Life didn't care what you thought. If a pilot as bone as "Batman" daSilva could foo, what bump stunt might little Jacinta pull?

Facing her, Mr. Calhoun folded his hands and leaned across his desk. "But the fact that you weren't stupid on purpose," he said in a sterner voice, "doesn't mean you weren't stupid. Why the hell did you kick cadet Morrisey when he came to help you get untangled?"

Jacinta sat up. "Because I felt his hands on me where they didn't belong, and I was taught to defend myself." And what Voice was that? The Voice of Defensiveness? There was no such Voice in the canon.

"So," Calhoun said. "He was trying to help you get purchase. You'd better learn fast the difference between a helping hand and the other sort. If you don't . . ."

He left the warning unspoken, but he might as well have shouted it in her ear.

"If you had kicked him away because of some I-can-handle-it-myself fixation, you would have been out faster than you could say gee-that-was-really-stupid. But you were only thoughtless and careless and ignorant, and those we can deal with. We can teach you to think and to care and we can lead you to knowledge; but stupid goes down to the bone. Do you understand, cadet Rosario?"

Jacinta could feel herself flush. "Yes, sir." She wanted to run away, far from laughter and pity.

"I wonder." He rubbed one hand with the other. "All right. Your progress is adequate and your instructors give you an upcheck. So you're on probation as of now. Do you understand what that means?"

"Yes, sir. No more screw-ups."

Calhoun studied her for a while; then he sighed and said, "Dismissed."

Back in Grissom Hall, Jacinta's room was that of a stranger. A log book lay open on the desk where she had been working and Jacinta scread the last few screens. Problems worked. Projects accomplished. Occasional notes in a shorthand code she'd invented years ago when she learned to hide her heart. Who was the person who had written this? Someone who had died.

And if Jacinta Rosario had died, it was only fitting that her dreams died with her.

There was a spray of flowers in a vase on the desk. Jacinta picked it up and breathed the cloying fragrances. The petals were broad and fleshy: bright yellows and reds, surrounded by a cloud of tiny, white blooms. She looked for a card but found none, and set the vase up on the bookshelf. Then she lay down on the bed with her hands behind her head and tried to think of nothing.

She must have been successful because the next thing she knew the room had grown dim and shouts and cheers came from the athletic field behind the dorm. Dusk formed dim shapes and outlines not quite deep enough to be called shadows. Did that one there look like a head of curled hair?

For a while, she stared at the flowers in the vase; then, rising, she went to the window and watched, not the toiling scrimmage in the dusk but the brilliant pinpoints just peeking through the distant sky.

When the darkness was complete, with only a pale sliver of moon to cast its cold light, and the ball field had grown silent and deserted, Jacinta made her way down the hallway and through the lounge to the men's wing. Morrisey's room was third from the end. His door stood open and light and laughing voices spilled from inside it. Jacinta hesitated short of the doorway.

". . . stupid recital tomorrow," she heard Lou Penny say. "What's poetry got to do with space?"

"You're supposed to get a college education out of this, kay-det," Morrisey explained in a *faux*-Matusek voice. "And that means 'coot 'n' kultchah,' not just skill sets. That's why we make you read great books, not just great equations."

"I never thought of any equation as particularly great," Konsonant's voice said.

"How about $F = g(mM)/d^2$?" That was Lou.

"Good," said the K judiciously, "but not great."

"No one's more boring than the charlie who only talks shop," Morrisey replied. "On long flights in cramped ships, knowing how to curl up with a good book might even be a survival skill."

"A good book?" Lou Penny's laugh was geese flying north. "I thought you wanted to curl up with Rosario."

"Weeth Yah-seen-ta," said Konsonant with an exaggerated accent. "I don't know why you keep that pixure on your desk."

"The triumph of hope over reality," Penny said. "Doncha know she's a lizard, duckling? She rides out of Meredith's stable."

"That's enough—"

Jacinta backed down the hallway and stood near the lounge entrance while she gathered her composure. She unclenched fists she hadn't been aware of balling and sagged back against the doorway. *How dare they define who she was!* It wasn't their job—or Total's! She crossed her arms over her chest, her hands splayed, and she sucked in a long, slow breath as she called on her Inner Strength. Then she turned and strode down the hall where she rapped on Morrisey's open door.

Morrisey was lying on a rumpled bed, while Krzyzanowski had straddled the desk chair, and Lou Penny squatted in the reading chair by the window. They turned and looked at her and Morrisey's complexion grew darker.

"Hi," Jacinta said, forcing sprightliness into her voice, "I need to borrow Yung-duk's brain for a while. I promise to give it back." She stepped into the room and the others shuffled to give her space. A glance took in a pixure pinned to the wall above the desk: a group shot of the academy choir and there she was, front and left with the sopranos. By some accident, those immediately around her were Anglos, enough contrast that she stood out. Her hair was cut short, otter-wise; and her complexion and high cheekbones must have been computer-enhanced, because she actually looked halfway pretty. And yet, something in her expression seemed withdrawn, a tinge of sadness behind the smile.

Jacinta turned her back to the pixure, confused. So expert at reading others, she found her own image an alien script. "I've been out of the training loop for a couple of days," Jacinta said to Morrisey, "and I need to catch up. They tell me 'You the Man' for this problem set."

"Well," said Morrisey, "it's only differentials . . ."

Krzyzanowski waved his arms in the air. " 'Only differentials,' he says."

Lou Penny leapt to his feet. "Been there, done that. Welcome to it." He and Konsonant scampered for the door. In the doorway, Penny turned and wagged his eyebrows. "Maybe I should leave open the door . . . ?"

"Close it," said Jacinta without looking his way. "I don't want any interruptions."

When they were alone, Morrisey rolled off the bed and took the chair that Konsonant had vacated. He activated his terminal and called up the problem deeby, flipped open his log book, all without looking her in the eye. "We started into radial burns while you were in the clinic," he said without pre-amble. "You already got through the posigrade and retrograde burns, right?" Jacinta moved to his side and bent over to see the screen display better: a schematic Earth with a not-to-scale ship in circular orbit.

"Okay," said Morrisey. "You rotate on your gyros, like . . . so. When your engines are aimed at Earth-center, you light the torch. The ship begins to move *up*—but keeps going forward, too." He turned his head. "The burn point on your initial, circular orbit becomes the ninety degree true anomaly on your new, elliptical orbit."

"So far, so good," said Jacinta, leaning closer. "What if you're already in an elliptical orbit?" She used the Voice of Intimacy in Private.

Morrisey didn't know voices, but that didn't stop them from working. He squirmed in his seat. "Then a radial burn . . . Uh . . . A radial burn can be used to 'spill' your radial velocity and circularize your orbit; but *only* if you burn at the ninety or two-seventy degree true anomalies. Anywhere else, and your . . . and your burn only fixes a perigee or an apogee for a new ellipse." He took a sudden deep breath. "Jacinta . . . Can I ask you something?"

"Sure."

He seemed frozen in place, afraid to move. "You're pressing your, uh, your breast against my arm . . ."

"And your point would be . . . ?" She occupied his space, moving inside the Schwartzchild radius of the lips. They drew closer, their lips brushed. Morrisey pulled away, as if burned. "You didn't come here to talk ellipses, did you?"

"No."

"I don't get it," he said.

"You will, if you time your burns right."

His flush deepened. "I mean, here all semester you've been running away faster than anyone could chase you; and now—"

She kept her hands stiffly by her side. "Do you want to touch them?"

Slowly, his hand approached and she steeled herself for the alien touch. Then, convulsively, his arms circled her waist and pulled her onto his lap. He buried his face in the open V of her blouse. She stiffened involuntarily; then willed herself to relax.

"Jacinta," he whispered. "I'm so sorry." She could feel his lips move against her. "I didn't mean to—I almost killed you—"

"Hush." She grabbed the back of his head and held him against her. "You saved me, too." Just a few minutes, she told herself. This will be over in a few minutes. She sat up straight.

"Should I take my blouse off now?" she asked him.

Oddly, Morrisey drew back and took a shaky breath. "This isn't you, Jacinta," he said.

"Jacinta died," she told him distantly. "And was born again."

"Is that what this is all about? A thank you?"

"Would you rather get a Hallmark card?"

He flushed. "No, but . . ."

"Shouldn't you get your reward? You saved my life."

He shook his head. "So did Meredith. Did she get a reward, too?"

Jacinta jumped off his lap, giving his chair a quarter turn. "Why don't you want it? I thought all boys wanted it."

Morrisey closed his eyes. "If you only knew . . . But the Jacinta I dream about isn't cheap."

He could have slapped her in the face; it would have been kinder. Jacinta began tucking in her blouse. "I guess I was wrong."

"Not wrong. Just—"

"Total kissed me."

Morrisey was silent. "I see," he said after a dozen heartbeats. "And . . . ?"

"I had nothing to compare it to."

"And I'm supposed to be the control sample?"

"No. It's just that . . . No one's ever kissed me before . . . And I have to know if . . ." Of a sudden, she didn't know what to do with her arms. They flapped uselessly, crossed, uncrossed. She said, "I'll go now."

"Wait." Morrisey rose and came to her. "I'll kiss you, if that's what you want." He took her in his arms and pressed his lips against hers. She kept her teeth closed and waited it out. Her hands rested briefly on his shoulders, but fled immediately and she held her arms out like the wings of a bird ready for flight. Finally, Morrisey released her and stepped back.

"Is that," she asked, "what it's supposed to feel like?"

"Depends," he answered, "on which side of the kiss you're on." He turned away, pressed a fist into his palm. "It's like everything else, Jacinta. The whole thing is a lot easier when you *want* to do it. I don't need a reward for pulling you out of the tank. I'd've done the same for Lou Penny or Karyl the Konsonant. Except maybe I wouldn't kiss them afterward."

"Yungduk . . ."

"Look, don't get me wrong. I want to jolly with you so bad it hurts. I think about you all the time." He dropped his eyes. "I really like you; and I think maybe I could . . . well, love you . . . if I could get past your walls and learn to know you. So, I want my old Jacinta back, with her reserve and respect and temperance—" He grinned suddenly. "Only, maybe not so much temperance."

Jacinta fumbled with the door latch, fighting the tears. What would her sisters say if they knew? Scolding voices echoed in her mind. Stand on the rampart, sister! Your body is a temple! Repel the assault! Yet some boys came as pilgrims, not invaders. She had enough self-possession left to compose her features before leaving the room, lest she set tongues wagging, and she even managed to turn in the doorway and, for the benefit of any nearby ears, thank Morrisey for his "help with that problem."

"Don't worry," he answered. "And, what I gave you? It's a loan, not a gift. When you're ready, you can give it back."

Leaving the dorm, Jacinta fell in with a group of cadets who planned to graze the munch together in Titov Hall. Coster invited Jacinta to join them, and Jacinta didn't say no and didn't say yes; but as they crossed the commons, she lagged behind, until, by incremental steps, she had detached herself from the group and found herself alone under the desert stars, watching the laughing cadets pass under the bright lamps at the dorm's entrance. She didn't belong with them. She didn't belong with anyone.

Jacinta sat in the shadow of *Ad Astra* and tried not to cry in frustration. Maybe she wasn't cut out to be an otter. Her eyes traced the graceful curve of the sculpture, from the black, bubbled cloud of iron at the base up along the arc to where it turned red to represent the flame of a rising ship. Often when she studied it, her heart rose with it, imagining herself in the stylized ship at the apex. Today, however, she could not shake the feeling that she had been left behind, looking up while others soared.

Maybe that was the way it was going to be; the way it was meant to be. Maybe her mother had been right that day when Jacinta had blurted out her love of spaceflight. *Learn your limits, girl, before you smash into them.*

Whatever it took to make a pilot—the cool ability to function when everything went wrong—she didn't have it. Her stupid behavior in the tank had proved that. And the even stupider behavior just now with Morrisey. Mr. Calhoun and the others, they didn't realize it yet; but they would. The physical part . . . well, she had mastered that. She could climb like a monkey and contort like the Inja Rubbah Man. And the mental part . . . diffy-Q would always be a mystery to her, but she grasped the principles—which meant she knew *what* to do—and you could teach a machine the donkey work. And she certainly had the desire. It had been all she'd ever dreamed of since the night she stayed up late under her blankets with the radio turned down low, listening to tense reports of Ned DuBois's historic flight.

So what was missing? That innate confidence that Sulberston, and Meredith, and Colonel Nieves radiated. It was not enough to *know*. You had to know you knew. You had to be bone.

She should heigh back to North Orange while there was still time to do so gracefully; back to Mother Ellen and the comfortable routines of the Retreat—study and recital and the care-absorbing task. She had known peace there, and respect. She had been gone less than a year, and yet already it seemed an alien world. She didn't know if she fit there any more.

As for home . . . Childhood had been neglect punctuated by shouts—

expected to do for herself; upbraided when she could not figure out what was wanted of her. Dressing herself in the morning; finding her own meals in a kitchen too often barren. Her mother, primped like a harlot—dissing herself, though she couldn't see it—stepping out with her friends, too young herself to comprehend that motherhood might possibly impact her social life. And, clueless to the end, stunned and tear-riven when her daughter walked out of the house at thirteen.

I never belonged there, either.

And where did that leave? Nowhere. Maybe that was what the Universe was trying to tell her.

"Hello."

Jacinta looked up and saw an older woman standing nearby. A mundane, by her dress. Dark, baggy blouse and skirt and plain shoes. Long hair hanging down just past the shoulders. Certainly not a cadet. Hair like that in ziggy was more trouble than it was worth. "Hi," Jacinta answered in the Voice of Polite Distance.

The stranger looked at her oddly. It had grown dark and the woman's dark clothing caused her to fade, wraithlike, into the gloaming. Only her face—pale and with a perpetually doleful countenance—gleamed in the moonless evening. "Do you like sculpture?" she asked with a vague gesture toward the arc that soared above them both.

I like solitude. But this woman had done nothing to her, and Jacinta bit back the reply that nearly tumbled forth. "It's . . ." Which was it—awe-inspiring or depressing? "I take it you do," was all she said.

The woman looked a little sad. "I once knew the man who created this. I thought I would pay my respects."

Jacinta pointed. "All the cadets, they wonder what that golden thing is at the tip. Even with 'noccs, you can't really see because of the angle and the filigree around it."

The woman shook her head. "Sorry. He never told me. This is the first I've seen it. A space ship, would be my guess."

Jacinta shrugged. "I suppose so."

The woman extended a hand. "I'm Roberta Carson. I'm singing some poetry here tomorrow."

That explained the dark, baggy dress and the subdued, inward-directed smile. The consciously-affected "soulfulness" of the poet. Jacinta held the hand just long enough to indicate politeness. No pumping, no squeezing. Women had never had to prove weaponlessness. "I've heard about you," she said. "You were one of the Prague Fourteen that hung on the banks of the Vltava back in the Naughty Oughts, drinking bad coffee and discussing Serious Thoughts."

A momentarily pleased expression cracked the solemnity for a moment. "'I see a great city, the prophetess said/Whose glory will touch the stars.' Not many remember today." She gestured toward *Ad Astra.* "Vaclav was one of us.

But . . ." Another quirky grin. "Mostly, we drank beer, not coffee. The New Art is mellow, not jittery."

"I guess he's dead, the sculptor, the way you're talking."

Carson didn't answer for a while. She only gazed wistfully at the statue. Some chemical, pocketed in the sacs and capillaries of the aerogel, was phosphorescent, so the "vapor trail" glowed ever so faintly in the dark. "Oh, Vaclav," Jacinta heard her say. "We were so young." Then, as if suspecting she had been overheard, she turned suddenly brisk. "Unfortunately, beer wasn't all we drank, and Vaclav had a problem knowing when to stop. Well, he's stopped now." Carson sat on one of billows. "You haven't told me your name."

"Jacinta Rosario." The words came reluctantly, as if telling her name gave the poet power.

"And you're a space cadet?"

"Just cadet, ma'am. At least, for the time being. What did you mean, about *singing* poetry?" Not that she cared, but even meaningless chitter with a stranger was better than silence and her own thoughts. She pulled her knees up and rested her chin on them.

Carson studied her for a moment before answering. "Oh, some folk songs I've been collecting. 'The Goddard City Dockhandlers' Song.' 'The Orbital Willies,' 'Vyecherni Zvezda,' 'The Leaving of LEO,' 'Estrada Brilhantina,' and lots of others. They may not be the most technically-polished verses ever composed, but they're certainly among the most genuine. Written by orbital workers themselves. I thought the audience here would enjoy them."

"Otters make up songs? I didn't think they'd have the time."

Carson shrugged. "There's an islander named Delight Jackson who's pretty prolific. A few others. It seems wherever people go and whatever they do, they make songs about it—even in orbit. Which is why," she added with an inscutable smile, "people who think they need to plan every detail of the future should just relax and let the future happen."

Jacinta cocked her head. The advice might have been aimed at her, but Carson had to be talking about someone else. "Sounds bone. I guess maybe I'll go to your recital tomorrow."

"You don't sound very enthusiastic." Carson wasn't offended; her voice was that of curiosity, making a statement to ask a question. But it wasn't a question she had earned the answer to.

"Sorry," Jacinta said. "It's not you."

"What's his name?"

Startled, Jacinta lifted her head from her knees.

"Is he a real herbie?"

"A what?"

"A herbie. You know. A bozo, a creep, a—"

"No," she admitted. "In fact, he's a bone charlie. There's no flubber on him." Carson laughed and Jacinta said, "What?" in a sharp tone.

"Nothing. I just suddenly felt a generation older. There's someone else, then."

"No!" And that negatory snapped like a bullwhip, so that Carson flinched. "You know, you're not half as smart as you think you are," Jacinta said. "Your generation, all you did was party down and jolly your crotch and give each other diseases and babies. You were worse than the Boomers. Things are different now. Not every problem can be solved by true love."

"No . . . But hate and indifference don't have a very good track record, either.

"You used to call yourself 'Styx,' didn't you?"

A brief smile, like the glimmer of sun of a sheen of ice. "A blast from the past," said the poet. "I haven't been Styx in years." Her stance, to Jacinta's practiced eye, announced both wariness and weariness.

"You wrote 'The Good Little Soldiers' and the rest . . . You were all against the space enterprise."

"Yes. I was angry about some of the means, so I wound up attacking the ends."

"Attacking the future."

But Carson was not to be baited. She shook her head and her dark eyes bored into Jacinta. Not angry, not hostile. Only penetrating, like drill bits. "Space is *a* future," the poet said. "It's not *the* future. There'll be more voices than one in the choir when tomorrow finally sings." She paused and leaned forward. "You don't have to answer, but what did you mean when you said you were only a cadet for the time being?"

"You're right. I don't have to answer."

Carson said nothing, but before the silence could grow offensive turned her gaze skyward and said in an entirely different voice, "Anything familiar up there now?"

Jacinta followed her pointing finger toward the star-swallowed western sky, where a faint glow marked where the sun had gone. The coloring had deepened from iron blue to indigo and the stars were gleaming pricks of fire. Pegasus flew out of the sunset on diamond wings. "Depends," she told the woman, "on what you're familiar with."

"Oh . . ." A vague gesture. "Planets."

"Okay. You see the four stars there in the southwest that make a sort of box? That's the body of Pegasus. Scheat—that's Beta Peg's name—is the lower right corner. Draw a line through the brighter star in the lower left corner. Markab, that one's called. Keep going in a straight line until you reach a small red dot. That's Mars. That's where the *Ares* is supposed to go in a few years."

"And you want more than anything to go there on it."

It was a statement, not a guess. Jacinta composed her face, wrung all longing from it. There was an old folks' song that went *You can't always get what you want* . . . Maybe that was maturity, maybe that was the wisdom that went with the white locks and the liver spots and the pounding back-beat. The knowledge that separated the adult from the child. If so, it was no wonder that tonight she felt so old, so old.

"The bright white one below Mars, that's Venus playing at Evening Star. Neptune is there, too; but you can't see it by eye and—shoot—it'll be a long, long time before anyone heads out that way."

"I see." Carson nodded. "You seem to know your way around up there."

Jacinta shrugged. "Navigation. The J-2000 coordinates are okay for Earth orbit; but if you're planning any longer trips, you gotta know the landmarks."

Carson turned around and pointed to the eastern sky. Her arm, from where Jacinta sat, aimed up and along the arc of *Ad Astra*. "And what's coming up in the east?"

Jacinta shook her head. "The other planets are all off stage. Saturn's behind the sun. There's nothing in the east."

Carson folded her arms and squinted toward the horizon.

"Funny. Isn't tomorrow off that way?"

Jacinta shivered in the evening chill. Her eyes sought out the locus for tomorrow's sunrise. January was fading and the sun was marching north. Come March, and . . . "Jesus," she said. "I bet the damn thing's pointing to the equinox!"

"Ah, yes," Carson said. "That touch would be just like Vaclav."

Jacinta contemplated the stars slowly wheeling up the sky. Sometimes, indeed, life and death were nothing but chance. Chance had saved her from fire and air, but not from water. She had been pried from the grips of water by the love and concern of others. And how did you pay back a debt like that? Not with a strained kiss or an awkward and unmeant offer.

A bright streak of light shot from behind the Tehachapi Mountains. Distant thunder rumbled toward her. A night lift out of Edwards, she thought. You took your planar windows when they opened. Jacinta slid off the pedestal and brushed herself off. "I better be going now, ma'am. I'm way behind on radial burns and there's this guy I need to—"

"Be with?"

"No, ma'am. Bury."

She didn't explain to the poet who Soren had been or what it all meant. She wasn't sure herself what it all meant, only that it did mean something. And if a godless universe supplied no meaning, then people would have to do that themselves. Of one thing now she was certain. You didn't pay debts back at all. You paid them forward.

Later, in her room, Jacinta read *The Precepts of Mother Smythe*, as she did every evening. They had served her well through all the years of pain; yet now they seemed facile and strained. Perhaps that was because they had been addressed to a young woman who had drowned. *Nothing to excess*, read the Second Precept. *Virtue stands in the middle. Temperance in all things.*

She studied the words for a while. None of it was Morrisey's fault. He had never done anything to her but prefer her company; and if they were going to start hanging people for that . . . well, they might as well hang her, too. Soren had gone down in the commuter plane and would not come back no matter how long she waited. Jacinta picked up her stylus and added: . . . *including temperance itself*. She felt vaguely as if she had done sacrilege.

. . . *that thing I gave you . . . When you're ready, give it back.* It had taken her a while to figure out what Morrisey meant.

He meant the kiss.

18.

Codefight at the OK Core

Jimmy prepared for the meeting of the Fingers with grave solemnity. "Don't worry," he told Tani. "A meeting of the Fingers is a snap. Get it?" In case she didn't, he snapped his fingers, but Tani didn't smile.

"Be careful, Jimmy," she said. "Earp is government. Even if he's crossed the line himself, he can still swing a big club."

Jimmy ducked his head. "I know, but . . ."

"But what?"

"But he went after *you*." Jimmy turned away before Tani could say anything and picked up his virtch hat. Billie Whistle, parked in a corner of the Sanctum, paused while inserting the probes of her macdonald. Jimmy could not read her gaze—bleak, sad, empty. "Would you rather have me sit this out?" Jimmy asked Tani without turning.

"Just be careful," she said again.

Jimmy's lips split in his trademark grin. Whistle did not respond—had the woman ever smiled in her life?—so he turned the teeth onto his wife. "I always am. SuperNerd set up an entire mainframe for this and Unofficial Chen and I spent all week laying down the security. We left the peripherals and some partitions open—deliberately—but the core is as safe a laager as cheese can ever be." His gut was a ball of ice. Yet, beneath the chill of fear, he felt a calm certainty, as if shaking fury had been frozen into a solid, impenetrable block. He had taken chances before. He had walked the wild side as Crackman, and more often than not had done so with a glow of pleasure.

There was no pleasure in this hack; only a knife-edged necessity. Earp was fully capable of giving the finger back and had resources to draw on that Jimmy could not dream of. Earp could, in spite of all the precautions that Jimmy and Chen and SuperNerd could mobilize, mouse his way through secret portals, lie doggo in deebies, plant flies that would sit quiescent for months until, wariness ebbing, a moment's relaxation opened the barn doors and all the trojan horses in creation galloped forth. He might even finger Crackman himself, if he once turned his cybernetic stare in Jimmy's direction.

Jimmy settled the virtch hat comfortably on his head and wriggled his hands into the data gloves. He had walked the net for fun and profit; he had fingered

deebies to test himself and prove his own cleverness. Now, he was going Out
There because it was the right thing to do.

"Ready, Billie?"

The cheesehead blinked and the monitors he had assigned to her booted
and scrolled. "The interfaces are a little different from what I'm used to. Some
of my commands may mistranslate."

"Deal with it," Jimmy said.

Billie Whistle—his sidekick, his tail-gunner, the virtchuoso who would
watch his back while he dealt with Earp—and who had taken favors from
Tyler Crayle (for what? for what?)—donned a pair of eyescreens. She touched
the side panel and her eyes slowly faded behind opaque discs. "Ready-freddie,"
she said.

Jimmy could think of nothing to say except a phrase that scumbag Chase
Coughlin used to use. "Let's make it happen." He took a deep breath and a
last look at Tani and phased over his own goggles.

The room went black.

The room went light.

It was a barroom in dark wood and bright chrome. Art deco planters gleamed
with lacquer. Styling was all smooth curves and abrupt angles. The morphs
were slick-haired, center-parted men in tuxedos and wing collars, and women
sporting low-waisted tube dresses, long-knotted ropes of pearls, and cloche
caps. Behind the bar, a brawny bald man algored on polishing glasses. It was
Speakeasy, a commercial chat room in Virtual Chicago where the Fingers had
agreed to meet.

A liveried boy wearing a chin-strap pillbox cap and bearing a silver salver
algored across the room. "S. James Poole and guest have entered the Speakeasy," he announced. Jimmy datagloved the salver and plucked the message.
"Check the perimeter," he told Billie. They had already agreed on her anonymity. If Crayle knew about Billie Whistle so might Earp.

Jimmy's other reason for leaving her out of the direct loop was that he did
not yet understand where she stood. According to Tani, Whistle had been
genuinely disturbed when Crayle showed up in San Antonio; but when Jimmy
had asked her about the man, she had only repeated her earlier story about
how she got started as an encephalic operator. Jimmy sensed there was more
to it—that Billie was deliberately concealing something—but he didn't know
what it was.

The message on the salver was a list of those already present. It was a potent
list. He expected the digital paper to burst into flames from the mojo and
scorch his dataglove.

Norris Bosworth. Pedro Rodriguez. Wang Wei. Andreas Bauer of Schildwache AG. Irenia Markovna of Sokhrannost/E. Even Doctor Doom. Jimmy
was surprised that Bosworth had invited a wildsider; and even more surprised

that Doom had accepted. As he read, the page boy announced the entry of
Kendrick Ogylvie of Web Wardens and "Oog the Morph" from the Internet
Users' Protective Co-op.

"Where's Chen?" Billie whispered in his ear—a disembodied voice since
Billie was not enmorphed in any of the imagos.

Jimmy gloved an elderly Chinese mandarin sitting alone at a cocktail table.
It was like Chen to bring his own imago with him—and to enter the room
without registering on any of the sensors. Naturally, the virtchuosi had their
own private portals scattered around the net, but Chen didn't have to remind
everyone of that. "Perimeter secured?" he asked Billie.

"Just the usual virtch-life that home in on any active node," she told him.
"What's with Wang?"

"He's top weenie. He pioneered the use of inverse trig functions in deep
encryption schemes."

"Old Wang's Sine. I know that. What I meant was, isn't he supposed to be
one of Unofficial Chen's footprints?"

"That was the rumor." Yet here were Chen and Wang together. It was like
Superman showing up at Clark Kent's birthday party. Chen couldn't be cholo
enough to handle two imagos in the same room. No one could do that. One
imago would have to algore while the other was active. Or else they'd play
Pete and Re-Pete. Trying to watch both, Jimmy noticed that Chen and Wang
were not actually together, and that it was in fact impossible to view them
both from the same vantage point. Clever use of the observer effect. And come
to think of it, Superman used to pull stunts like that.

Jimmy occupied a standard morph sitting on a bar stool and saw no need to
shift his point-of-view. The bartender poured him a virtual drink—Jimmy had
no clue what it was—and his imago went through the motions of casual,
sophisticated drinking. He wondered why Bosworth had invited the white-
bread dudes from the big software security companies. Surely, Earp hadn't
slagged them, too! He would have heard about that. Maybe they were just
concerned netizens. After all, Web Wardens and the rest were no more white
bread on the surface than Poole sEcurity or Rodriguez Consultants. They were
just more . . . corporate.

Perhaps a little too corporate. They weren't sure they believed the accusations against Earp, "the man who brought law and order to the net."

"Take the word of an outlaw hacker?" said Ogylvie in scandalized tones.
"Where is this 'Captain Cat'?"

"Off-line," said Doom. "To all our loss. She's gone to Kuala Lumpur to
pursue other interests."

"No loss at all, I'd say. I'd kiss the whole lot of you gone."

Doom chuckled. "You wouldn't be half as good as you are without our 'lot.' "

"Wot's that mean?"

"Your security software would have more holes than Swiss cheese if you didn't have us out there probing all the time. Think of us as freelance beta testers."

Markovna chuckled. "A public service? That is what you are?" Even Oog the Morph expressed skepticism.

"That's not the issue," Jimmy said. "Cat inserted code into LEO's software, and Earp failed to do a retest afterward. Doesn't that sound odd?"

"So says Cat," the Web Warden insisted.

"And then, right after Cat spilled the beans, everybody who ever, uh, showed curiosity about LEO's security, their systems got attacked."

"Mine wasn't," Ogylvie said.

"All right," Jimmy amended. "Anyone with beans."

"No flames," said SuperNerd before the Web Warden could answer. "Answering that question is why we're here. It wasn't my imagination that the Associates' deeby was assaulted. Or Poole or Rodriguez."

"There were unpleasantries in the Guangdong Virtch," Chen allowed. Wang, when Jimmy turned his head, was already nodding agreement.

"And a couple of Co-op antibodies were neutralized," said Oog the Morph. "But that doesn't mean it was Earp that did it." Oog was an odd fish. Strictly brown shoe, but he liked to come on as sneakers. The Co-op projected an image of on-the-edge netwalkers—as kick as a tie-dyed, jean-faded, granola-munching Northwester; but they were, after all, only hired guns working for a membership that included everyone from AOL to *The New York Times*. On the net, though, image was often all that mattered.

SuperNerd indicated the wildsider. "Doom? Did you bring what I asked for?"

"Cat gave me her complete file on the LEO hack. Ready to accept download?"

"From an outlaw hacker?" said Ogylvie. "Do I look stupid?"

Jimmy held his tongue. So did everyone else, so the silence did for an answer. SuperNerd said, "The download is to a safe core that we've set up. If you feel that you can't examine the files there without risking infiltration, you don't have to come with us."

A slap in the interface, Jimmy thought. Everyone present, save Doom, sold computer security—encryptions, firewalls, code dancers, and the like—to refuse was to admit they didn't have the mojo to shield themselves, and how would that look when the others inevitably leaked the word? There was more grumbling, but in the end, they all accepted the hyperlink from SuperNerd.

Before jumping, Jimmy glanced at Chen's imago, and the old mandarin was no longer there. Had he winkled the hyperlink from Bosworth's pocket? Or had he gone to lurk mode? In either case, the record said that Chen had never entered the room and now it would show that he had never left.

The safe core was not virtched. Neither Bosworth nor Jimmy had seen any reason to dress the set. Consequently, Doom's download was text-only: a series of E-mails between Cat (acting as Creative 4 Play, a gaming and simulation contractor) and Vittorio dell'Bosco of Orbital Management Corporation. Ordinary business snooze, unless you knew C4P had roots on the wild side.

"Ogylvie's not here," Billie reported after making the rounds.

Jimmy toggled SuperNerd and passed the skinny.

<Oops> posted the Nerd. <I musta given him a hyperlink to an access port on the LEO Laager.>

<Hoping he'll get slagged?>

<Earp's getting twitchy. Maybe Ogylvie'll take a more personal interest afterwards. You ready to ride?>

Jimmy saluted and he and Billie slipped out of the safe house using an escape hatch he had written into the firewall. An "Elisa" A/S would simulate his presence while he was gone—an easier hack to pull off in text-only mode than in the virtch, where he'd have to leave a convincing algore.

"Earp swam upstream as far as the San Antonio node," Jimmy said to Billie, "where he lost the skein because you were acting as circuit-breaker. The *Belle* is disintegrated, and you hosed the equipment in San Antonio, so let's start checking the intermediate nodes in the relay and see if he left a footprint. Do you have the code from the Riverwalk scenes he projected? Good. Let's cruise."

Every save rewrote a file to whatever addresses were available, and those were not always the same ones each time. Deletes only pulled the flags from the addresses, leaving the bin contents untouched until another file used the address. So the fragmented ghosts of old files could sometimes be found lurking in stripped addresses. Jimmy had half a dozen file recover programs in his ammo belt, primed with the video Earp had used in his premature taunting. The A/S would comb the drives and copy any partial matches. Some of them might contain headers and routing information.

The first node back from the trashed brodyazhka was a public library in Memphis. The system there was clean; but when Jimmy checked the dates, he found the whole system had been refreshed the day after the *Belle* went down. "Must have got fallout from the bit bomb," Billie suggested.

Jimmy agreed. There'd be no footprints there.

The penultimate node was on the campus of the University of Michigan. They found a partial footprint, but it was mostly overwritten by later users. Jimmy had laid his skein through high-traffic nodes for that very reason. Documents and apps would use and reuse the address bins, erasing his own footprints. Now he almost wished he hadn't been so forethoughtful, because the activity brushed out Earp's tracks, as well.

Normally, a tracker could never have followed the skein without the escort daemon's log of the nodes and relays the bit packets had bounced through. But, having laid out the skein themselves, Jimmy and Billie knew the rocks already, so it was only a matter of following their own backtrail.

The Florida Motor Vehicle Department computer contained a few more traces, including a doppelganger—a duplicate ghost file. Billie harvested the bits and patched them together on a second drive. If they recovered enough fragments, they might be able to reconstruct the whole.

The first trace of a log showed up on a usegroup server on the fifth node. By stroke of luck the group's server had gone down for unrelated reasons within a day or so of Jimmy and Earp passing through, and so there had been minimal overwriting. Billie took the addresses, full and partial, and checked them against the Registry in Washington. For once, Jimmy was glad of the Legitimate Net-Users Licensing Act. A popper window in the corner of his goggles tracked the status of the search. One of them might be revealing.

On the seventh node, Earp had left a lurker. While Jimmy studied the ground for footprints, the lurker tossed a randomizer at his search program, overwriting the addresses Jimmy occupied with random digits. But Jimmy's program was running Bojangles, which code-danced his software from address to address at irregular and unpredictable intervals, so the bit-bomb missed and Jimmy was able to fire a toggle that stripped the endpoint from one of the lurker's do loops and it went into contemplative nirvana. "Where the hell were you, Billie?" Jimmy demanded, perhaps a little ticked at the close call. "You were supposed to be watching for ambushes."

"I went after the sidekick," she said calmly. "It copied your daemon and ducked for a portal, but Lasso disabled its <execute>."

"Oh." Jimmy fumbled for the right words. "Uh, thanks. Good work."

"Yeah, well, he gets you, he gets me. Oh, this is beautiful! Paydirt!"

"What'd you get?"

"A perfect copy of the sidekick's bounceback. We know where it was taking the news. I'll check the nodes against the Registry and against the footprint we've already got."

"Great. This may be easier than we thought."

"Yeah," said Billie, suddenly cautious. "Maybe too easy."

"Meaning?"

"Maybe we should go back to the core with what we've got?"

"We don't know what we've got. Earp may no more be at the end of this trail than I was at the end of the trail he followed from the *Dixie Belle*."

"And it could be a trap. If it is, the others should know, in case we get knocked off-line."

Jimmy thought it over. A month ago, he would have laughed at the notion that S. James Poole could get knocked off-line. "All right," he said. "Duck back—you know the trapdoor—and see what the Nerd has to say. I'll check this routing."

Jimmy studied the list. Some of those nodes could be restricted government deebies. At least, if he were Earp, that was how he would hide his footprints. He pulled his lip and considered his options. Following Earp across a government deeby without the right password would be like stepping on a land mine. One possibility was to find where Earp had come out again and take up the search from there; but that was tricky, and following Earp up this stream, he lacked the benefit of knowing the routing ahead of time.

If Jimmy couldn't stick his head inside, maybe he could make Earp come out.

The popper screen blinked. Billie's Registry search had confirmed that Earp had ducked into a Department of Commerce database. That wasn't as bad as Justice or Defense. In fact, it was a blatant invitation. Of all the cabinet posts, only Education's deebies were easier to mouse into.

A grin creased his face. Yeah, like Billie had said, way too easy to punch the Tar Baby.

He called up Bloodhound, removed the ID tag, and let it sniff the router. "Go find it, boy," he said. He left a Kamera in some unused bins, pulled out of the host, and de-fogged his goggs.

"One potato, two potato," he counted. "Hey, Billie," he called across the room. "Don't go back out there until I tell you." The cheesehead flipped up her goggles and studied him; then she nodded.

"Pop the cherry on a virgin drive for me," Jimmy said. "I'm about to land a fish and I don't want it stinking up my primary." Whatever he hooked could be infested.

Billie booted up one of the auxiliary drives. "Number five."

Jimmy set up the macro, hit return, yanked Kamera into number five, and bailed out.

Kamera was toast, but Jimmy ran a file recovery and got 74 percent. It was enough. "Looks like Bloodhound flushed a rabbit," he remarked.

"Yeah," Billie agreed, "a two-hundred-pound carnivorous rabbit. Anything useful on the snapshot?"

"Yup." Jimmy displayed the router that Kamera had captured from the bush-wacker.

Billie whistled. "Straight-on honky handshake. No intermediate nodes?"

"Should we go in?"

"Use Periscope," she suggested.

"And Earp follows the conduit right back. What if we both go in. He won't be expecting two of us. Rush the portal, you go odd and I'll go even."

"It's a virtched node," Billie pointed out. "Check the extension."

"You want an imago? I've got a library."

"No. Set up a couple extras to algore. We all go in together: you, me, the algores. Only we go in as text-only, without imagos. We duck and lie doggo in the code while Earp rasters the morphs. Then we just lurk there and suss until we can sneak out."

Jimmy grinned. "You've got a twisted mind. I like that."

He got no grin back. "Yeah. Goes with the body." And she flipped down her goggles.

*   *   *

<We were beginning to wonder> SuperNerd posted when Jimmy and Billie returned to the core. <Thought you'd been knocked off-line.>

Jimmy didn't dignify that with a response. <Did Ogylvie ever show up?>

<Negatory. Markovna called up Web Wardens' HQ in Leeds and they are definitely hosed. I think LEO cruised them when Ogylvie stumbled into the unauthorized portal. They don't know whether to blame LEO for lashing out or me for tricking them into it.>

<Have any of the others come back?>

<Doom pulled a wild side on Klon-Am's purchasing that confirmed the contract with Earp. It shows C4P as a subcontractor.>

If Doom could be trusted. If this whole affair was not just something Cat and Doom had cooked up between them to whipsaw the straight-edge crowd. Jimmy, with a foot in both camps, could see the appeal of such a romp. <I'd like to look at his evidence.>

<Chen already has,> SuperNerd told him. <He ghosted with Doom and Doom never twigged. What did you and Faithful Companion come up with?>

Jimmy uploaded the router fragments he had found in Earp's footprints, plus those of the bushwackers they had encountered. <I've flagged the ones the Registry shows as government nodes. These others. . . . They don't show up on the Registry at all.>

<Top secret?>

<Dunno. All I know is, I'm not sticking my mojo in there.>

<Too bad there's no way to match nodes with physical location. . . . >

<Yeah>, posted Jimmy. <Too bad. <Fe>>.

<So.> The new post was accompanied by an ideogram, but no other identifier. Either Chen or Wang, unless Wang was Chen. <He seeks to cover his tracks by wading through nodes where we dare not follow.>

Jimmy noticed that Chen had not said <can not follow>. A man after his own heart.

Markovna: <Is this something that might be attempted through foreign conduits? Entry might be possible through diplomatic databases.>

Chen: <Firewalls separating outland nodes from American government nodes are very thick. Ratholes few and known to fewer. Considering what Earp wrote for LEO, imagine what he has written for his masters.>

Billie: <Heavy action around the perimeter. I mean *heavy*. I peeked into the vestibule partition we left open and nearly lost my Buffalo Shuffle.>

"Are you okay?" Jimmy asked off-line across the room.

"Limping," Billie replied. "My persona isn't shifting addresses fast enough to suit. I'm going to dismount and pull a fresh copy."

Jimmy phased back into the deeby through his trapdoor.

And it was virtched out like an Old West movie set.

A long, dusty street lined with saloons and hitching posts. At the far end, a clapboard church. In the foreground, an empty corral and a taxidermy shop. Tumbleweed danced across the rutted street.

Uh-oh.

Jimmy went to lurk mode. This host was supposed to be secure. He and Chen had noodled it, yet Earp had managed to insert a scenario. Question was: Did Jimmy want to play? An imago was a more specific locus than pure code and made it easier to draw a bead on portals and addresses. "Billie," he said off-line, "Earp's in town. Walk softly when you re-enter." He flipped up his goggles and studied his monitors. One showed a view of the virtch. Others showed active nodes and addresses. Where were Nerd and the others? Jimmy had ducked out only for a moment. Earp couldn't have erased the other Fingers in such a short time. The white bread dudes, sure. They were lunch. But not Bosworth or Rodriguez. Maybe not even Doom. Certainly not Chen.

There were no imagos on the street and his monitor did not show any elsewhere in the core. (Was the entire core virtched? Yes. Dude! That work was the Jenuine Bean and Jimmy wouldn't mind shaking hands with Earp someday, except he'd have to count his fingers afterward and maybe check the gold fillings in his teeth.) For all he knew the others had bailed out as soon as Earp took control of the server's housekeeper, leaving Jimmy to face the marshal alone.

Or they could be lying doggo, like he was.

"Billie, call up Bosworth—on the telephone. Black code encryption. Find out where he's hiding." It suddenly occured to Jimmy that communicating off-line might give him an advantage over Earp. As far as he knew, he was the only one out there with a sidekick; unless Bosworth was working with that Gloria woman. She had the righteous bean.

He flipped his visor back in place and once more floated ghostlike in the streets of Virtual Dodge. (Or Tombstone, or whatever vanity Earp had used.) From a side street, four imagos came walking, all of them dressed in long dusters and wearing floppy, broad-brimmed hats. Their boots kicked up small clouds from the dirt; their spurs jingled. Good Kai enhancements, Jimmy thought. Excellent work. He watched long enough to be sure that all four morphs were independently operated.

Earp had brought deputies.

Pay no attention to the armament. The shotgun. The rifle. The belted six-shooters. There was no reason why a morph's motions should echo a command entry on Earp's keyboard. He could launch a bit-bomb or spray a virus without ever touching his virtual shotgun. That was the trap some amateur, would-be wildsiders fell into. They forgot that the virtch cues were only to help coordinate game players sharing a commons. They forgot that unmorphed commands were only poor game netiquette and not forbidden by the Natural Law. They had seen too many bad "cyberspace" movies.

Although. . . . If Earp's deputies were remote-sited, he might indeed have to use his imago to communicate with them. Could be, only Jimmy and Billie were situated where they could coordinate their moves off-line. Though for all Jimmy knew, Earp operated out of an office with a staff of hundreds sitting in their cubicles waiting to do his bidding.

"Well, well," Earp said. "Looks like the rats have run back to their holes."

"Billie, check to see if any outgoing packets from the Earp-morph addresses get echoed by incoming packets to the deputies. Don't try to read 'em. I just want to know how the posse is coordinating. I'll see if I can find the others."

"Here's SuperNerd's location." Billie handed him a slip of paper. "I talked to him on the phone. You want a headset and a conference call?"

"Do it." He checked the locus Billie had given him. The Nerd was evidently embedded in a pile of hay just inside the livery stable.

When Jimmy turned his attention back to the virtch, he had to bite his tongue to keep from laughing. The clapboard church in the background had changed to a pagoda. So, Chen was on-site, too. Jimmy hoped no one would point it out to Earp. There was an art to this sort of thing. The longer Earp went without noticing, the better the effect would be when he finally twigged. For Chen to call attention to it would be *tres gauche*.

A standard algore in a modern business suit stepped out of the saloon into the street. An entry port in the saloon, Jimmy thought. That would force an imago to exit the saloon in order to access Main Street addresses. Jimmy— and presumably Chen—with their own private trapdoors, could enter or depart the server at almost any address.

"This is a confidential meeting of legitimate business interests," the morph said. Jimmy rolled his eyes. Had to be one of the white breads. *Had* to be. No one else could be so clueless.

Earp lifted a lip. " 'Legitimate' and 'business' don't fit too well in the same sentence, Herr Bauer. A meeting of business interests is *ipso facto* a conspiracy against the *public* interest. And considering your line of work, against the national interest, as well. Encryption and security prevents law enforcement from monitoring the activities of terrorists and organized criminals."

"It is all legal, by international treaty," the Schildwache man protested. Jimmy bit down hard on his tongue. Every message packet that passed between Earp and Bauer was another opportunity for Earp to stick a straw into Schild-wache's deebies. The commercial security firms weren't herbies (though they didn't measure up to the custom work from Poole sEcurity or Rodriguez Con-sultants); but their firewalls could be 99 percent reliable and Earp could slick them on the 1 percent.

"Billie," he said off-line, "you got a copy of the contract that Doom boosted from Klon-Am's deeby? I want to lay it onto the next message packet out of a deputy." He called up SuperGlue from his Bag o' Tricks, inserted it into the file, and then set the assembly in an address that the deputy's packets had been using. The next burst from the game site to the deputy that bounced to Earp would contain a copy of his contract. Not that Earp didn't know the contents, but he would get the message anyway. Jimmy told SuperNerd over the telephone what was going down.

Jimmy didn't have long to wait. Earp's imago froze, always a sure sign that the bonebag at the other end was engaged.

If only momentarily. "I see there has been a breach of the Computer Security Act," Earp said.

Bauer didn't know what Earp was talking about. Ghostly laughter wafted through Virtual Dodge. Chen, Jimmy thought; it had his style. Earp and his deputies looked around at the sound. The problem with using a morph interface was that visual inputs were restricted by the imago's putative field of view. That went into the heavy metal, the underlying conventions of the virtch software. Short of rewriting the basic packet-handling protocols from scratch, this was one command that was always echoed by the imago. Jimmy much preferred the omniscient point of view of an unmorphed presence. In fact, he much preferred eyeballing monitors to wearing virtch hats and goggs.

Searching for the origin of the laughter, Earp at last noticed the pagoda. Although the morph's expression did not change—the hacker had to command that to happen—Jimmy thought he heard testiness, and a touch of wariness, in Earp's next comment. "I see the conspiracy extends further than I had suspected."

"What conspiracy?" asked Irenia Markovna, also appearing in the virtch. She, at least, had taken the trouble to enmorph herself properly—as a schoolmarm wearing a poke bonnet. "Last week someone staged highly skilled attacks on some of the net's most talented citizens and the Co-op called a meeting to discuss what we could do to protect ourselves."

"A vigilance committee," Earp sneered. "If there was outlaw activity, you should have called in the Law."

"Well," said Oog the Morph, who enmorphed as a sheriff, "there was a little difficulty there, you see, because the suspicion was aimed at, uh, you."

If that announcement surprised the town marshal, his morph gave no sign; but Jimmy didn't think surprise was in it. At least the man didn't put hand to breast and say, "Who? Li'l ol' me?" Instead, he asked flatly, "Why? Seems to me a slag attack would be more in the line of Mighty Mouse or Crackman."

Jimmy bristled at being compared to a weenie like the Mouse, but he held his peace. No point in complicating the discussion. Billie tapped him on the arm.

"Poole. I backtracked one of Earp's deps. Guess who?"

"No games, Whistle."

"Think slimy and twisted."

"The Eel!"

"None other. He's the one on the far right, duded up as Doc Holliday. Don't know if he's bit-flipped or if he was always a fink. His routing daemon was completely unguarded. I don't know how he's survived as long as he has on the wild side."

Jimmy wondered whether: a) the portal had been as open as Billie thought and the information at the other end as reliable as it seemed or b) Eel was under duress and had left the channel open so that a stone charlie would winkle his way "behind" the posse. He touched the stud on the telephone and told Bosworth what Billie had found.

"Pass me the address," the Nerd said. "I'll let Doom handle it."

But Doom had other ideas. "Why'd we think you did it, Earp? Because you've gone rogue, that's why." And the Doctor enmorphed as a gunfighter. *Bad move, Doom,* Jimmy thought. *You're playing into Earp's paradigm.* "You took bribes from Klon-Am to look the other way while Cat gamed their system."

"Is that true?" asked one of the deputies.

"Now here's a case of the pot calling the kettle black." The Earp imago brushed its dust-coat away from its holster, a move certainly intended as a warning. "Why should Klon-Am hire a wildsider to game their own system?"

That was a question Jimmy had been asking himself ever since Cat had made her somewhat dramatic appearance and, if he was not mistaken, there was a note of puzzlement in Earp's own voice.

Billie heard it, too. "He knows he was bribed to ignore Cat's work, but he's damned if he knows why."

"Something funny about Cat's virtch module. Something that would have come out if Earp had run his final software validation tests."

"Does it matter why, you sunuvabitch?" Doom asked. "You drove a classy lady right off the net."

The sheriff, the schoolmarm, and the eastern dude exchanged looks that said, "and good riddance, too," and their imagos edged away from the gunfighter as they shifted their addresses. If Earp aimed a bit-bomb at Doom, it could randomize their own files. But they were also concerned about Earp. When the Law went bad, everyone suffered. Competitors could offer bribes or campaign contributions in return for selective enforcement of laws. Jimmy knew of three "American content" laws that he could invoke that would shut Pedro right out of the high end of the U.S. security market—if he made enough "campaign contributions" down in Washington.

"If you did orchestrate the slag attack against Rodriguez, Poole, and the others . . ." Bauer said.

Jimmy inserted a message packet of his own into the system. <And send Crayle out to harass people . . . >

"Eel?" cried Doom, who must have just gotten Bosworth's E-mail about the deputy's identity. "Eel, you God-damned traitor!"

Earp said, "Who the hell is Crayle?"

And Eel went for his randomizer.

An amateur when you got down to the bone, Eel telegraphed his move with his morph. The imago grabbed its bitshooter. But this was no virtch-game, where the players shared a consensus reality and a set of rules. The move was enough to signal the others what was coming down.

"Heavy action outside the firewall, boss," Billie said.

Jimmy didn't even stop to think. His fingers flew over the keyboard, calling up auxiliary programs he'd had already in position. He partitioned the core and raised an interior firewall. Chen said, "I attend to the gates," and displayed a string of code numbers in the clouds. Jimmy flipped his goggs up and examined the map. Replicating code was emerging from several of the I/O nodes, searching for the gates to the other processors. Jimmy was safe for the moment; even if Earp found his gate, the virus would only slag the virtual system Gloria had set up.

If "Gloria" had told him the truth. It had not escaped Jimmy's notice that SuperNerd had stage-managed the entire confrontation so far without ever appearing, posting, or even being mentioned by the others. Oog the Morph probably did believe that he had organized the meeting himself.

"Copy that file," he told Billie. The code that Earp was scattergunning might have genetic relations to the code that Doc Scalpel had analyzed before its untimely demise. If it did, they would have additional proof.

One potato, two potato. Jimmy launched a countervirus that selectively randomized the code strings that enabled the attackers to replicate. He saw the eastern dude go algore, then vanish, which could mean that the core war had entered Schildwache's system or only that Bauer had broken the connection.

"Here," said Billie, "I copied Eel's I/O when I sussed his portal. Feed him this and he'll get a replay of what he saw five minutes ago." Code scrolled up on number four monitor and Jimmy copied it to the gate that Eel's packets were using. An evil trick. Eel would hesitate in puzzlement just long enough for . . .

Doom to send a bit-bomb down the portal.

Eel was slag, and Jimmy couldn't say he didn't deserve it.

Chen was still holding the "eastern" gates against incoming virtch-life. SuperNerd's location in the haystack had become known somehow and replicators were gnawing away at his interior firewalls. He was not counterattacking, Jimmy noticed. *Doesn't want to get Earp really mad . . .* The weenie. It hadn't been *his* wife who'd had to run from San Antonio . . .

Markovna had vanished; but Oog the Morph had gamely called in the posse—automata that cruised the virtch for the Co-op.

Okay, Earp, Jimmy telepathed, *you stone to take on the local sheriff?*

The answer was apparently: Yes. Jimmy took a deep breath. With Earp distracted by Doom, Chen *and* SuperNerd, Jimmy would never have a better chance. He booted up another drive. "Billie, feed me the address where the bushwhacker came from." Whistle looked at him, said nothing, and the code appeared on the new monitor.

"Keep an eye on Dodge," he told his sidekick. "Feed in a couple of A/S morphs through the phantom system to keep things confused. In fact, to really confuse him, have some of our morphs attack Doom or SuperNerd, but give them a heads up first. *Don't* try that on Chen. We don't have a sideline to warn him. Then realize 'Jimmy Poole' as the 'rich banker' morph. I want Earp to think I'm in Dodge the whole time." Without waiting for Billie, he turned to the fresh system.

Jimmy signed on as <Crackman>.

And he was in Earp's system.

Oh, man! This would be a hack to brag on, if he ever dared brag on it. If he didn't get clapped in a dark place. And yet, if the law went bad on you, what else was there? Tani would understand. He hesitated only a moment before releasing the Beaumont Worms he had prepared. Each worm had a search engine in its head that would hunt down files containing keywords like "LEO" or "Crayle" or "San Antonio" or "Captain Cat." The remaining segments were flypaper that would pick up copies of those files, flee for an I/O port, and download the files into randomly selected nodes on the internet. The worms' tails would kick dirt over the burial spot and E-mail the URL to half a dozen interested parties, from Chen to Oog, plus a few red herrings.

He also placed some shadows in the folders, giving them file names similar to those already there. If Earp did anything after the codefight, he would consult files and contact people connected with the LEO Laager, the *Dixie Belle* and the slag attack on respected netizens. Jimmy's files would lurk for a while then play me-and-my-shadow with Earp. They would mouse into whatever files Earp consulted, browse his E-mail whenever he did—and cache whatever skinny they found into outgoing mail packets that would clone off on the second rock and bounce to a node at Berkeley that Jimmy had already selected.

Jimmy logged off Earp's system, shut down the system he'd been using, and sagged back into his command chair. He glanced at the clock. Two minutes? He hadn't meant to linger so long. That was more than enough time for Earp's internal defenses to notice the intrusion and identify the source.

"Any sign over in Dodge that Earp noticed?"

Billie shook her head. "I think he's too focused," Billie said, "He slagged Doom. Then Oog and Chen got the two deputies. Oog's threatening a class action suit. Should we log off?"

Jimmy shook his head. The real fight was over. If the evidence they needed was anywhere on Earp's system, Jimmy's worms would finger it out, even if they had to lurk for days by juke box addresses waiting for an entry. Whatever went down in Virtual Dodge was irrelevant now that it had served its purpose as a distraction.

"Tell the Nerd the end run looked successful," Jimmy said. "We'll keep the codefight going for a little while longer. Earp might wonder if we suddenly quit for no reason. Then I'll holler truce and point out it was the two wildsiders—Eel and Doom—that started it, and we'll come to some accommodation."

And now, Jimmy thought as he prepared to face the marshall *in propria persona*, there would be only the waiting. Waiting for the worms to report. Waiting for the shadow messages.

Waiting to see if Earp traced Crackman's hack to S. James Poole.

19.

Achilles, in His Tent

Rain ran in sheets down the window, turning the scene outside into a blur of greens and browns that resembled a failed painting more than it did a landscape. The brook that wound gently past the edge of the property had become a churning torrent, fat with the mountain snows. The runoff waters had created a temporary pond in a low spot in the lawn. Eager flowers turned their mouths skyward for the welcome moisture. Spring had come, and with it the promise of renewal. It was the time of year when gods returned from the dead.

Adam van Huyten watched the downpour, half-wishing for the thunder and lightning that marked the storms of summer. Something at any rate more dramatic than this persistent, gentle soaking. He thought again of his father's arid southwestern home and how it reflected the man himself. Bone-dry sand and rock; prickly cactus, infested with lizards and snakes and scorpions; nights as cold as death. Striking the sash with his fist, Adam turned to face the pixcreen once more. "You're absolutely certain?" he asked.

Red Hawkins tugged his beard. "Yeah, I'm sure. Thought at first maybe this sheila had things mixed up when she said Goddard instead o' LEO; but I asked around some, and—yeah—there's a second plant running up there. Eddie Mercado's the operator."

Adam spoke between stiff lips, holding the anger within him. "Do you know who he's working for?"

Hawkins shook his head. "Me an' Chico go way back. Can't say we're mates, exactly; but we done some things together. He tightened right up, an' said it was confidential work. Well, I didn't tell him nothin' myself, not without your say-so. So I asked Nigel Long, who does 'goods inward' on Goddard, and he says Mercado's been getting biocanisters from Wincock Pharms."

"Wincock!"

"Yah. Wincock's always said how he coulda done this himself, if he'd only happened to think of aerogel filters and zero-gee manufacturing and rounded up the coin to do it . . . But, you ask me, the strumpet doesn't have what it takes to set up another operation on the Q.T. And I don't just mean the cash."

"You think Jimmy Poole is behind it." It was a statement, not a question.

He didn't need confirmation from Hawkins. He'd had his doubts about Poole from the first. Still, the betrayal stung. It seemed as if every person he had ever given his trust to had thrown it in the nearest dungheap. "I appreciate your calling, Red."

"Every ounce I got is sunk in Baleen," the Australian told him. "If that brumby highjacks the scene, I'm up the bleeding creek, aren't I?"

Adam assured him of prompt action and broke the connection. Afterward, he paced his study, contemplating his options. It was a small room, almost claustrophobic; not a room for pacing. The walls were lined with dark wood cabinets with racks of floppies and seedies, meticulously labeled and ordered. In the interstices between cabinets: a pixcreen that (when not portraying anxious callers) imaged a fractal seascape; a self-contained workstation and another with net access; a set of pixures showing Adam aboard SpaceLab; another, of Kathryn and himself doting over a younger Bryce and Melanie; and a third—before which Adam paused—that was a montage of the Baleen partners.

He held it for a moment in his hand. Save in the lying facade of the virtch, the six of them had never actually been together in the same place at the same time. He had gleaned the images from news deebies and blended them into a group pose. He had even added Poole, after the geek had come on board with financing. The imaging effort was not entirely successful: The bodies were in the right proportions to one another but the eyes were not all looking in the same direction. Maybe there had been a portent in that. He let go and the picture swung to and fro on its hook, before settling at an angle.

He could hear the rain sheeting against the roof and wall, a steady sound, almost like a hiss. Abruptly, he turned and left the room and, passing through the adjacent family room, stepped out onto the porch through the glass and wood doors.

The rain here was more honest, the sound more vivid. He could smell the dank, moist rocks and earth and feel the drifting mist that passed under the overhanging roof. The rock face of the mountain behind the house had turned from gray to shining black; and water beaded on the sealed redwood planking of the porch. A rivulet twisted down the sheer mountainside to a culvert that carried it away from the house. To left and right, distance vanished behind water-gray curtains that whorled and danced in the flurries that played off the mountainside.

A screen door slapped shut behind him and he heard boots strike the planking. "Hello, Kathryn." He spoke without turning. "Just enjoying the weather."

"Who called?"

"One of the Baleens. There may be some problems in that quarter."

"Does that matter any more? They've served your purpose. The equipment's on board."

She had stepped to his side and he draped his right arm around her. She was dressed for riding, he saw. Khakis, knee-boots with spurs. The bush jacket hung open on a flannel blouse. "I want Baleen to succeed," he said.

"Cares should stay closer to home. Baleen isn't the most likeable bunch."

"They . . . have their points."

Her arm snaked around his waist. "I'm sure they do," she said dryly. "Underneath."

"Oh, Billie Whistle is—"

"A bitch."

Adam raised his eyebrows. Kathryn was almost as tall as he was and they stood eye-to-eye. Actually, Billie struck him as a woman with a buried hurt, angry and defensive at the way fate had crushed her. "Hawkins," he suggested.

"Coarse and common."

"Guang."

"*Weird!* And Poole is sneaky, and Wincock likes boys."

"Really?"

"A woman can tell."

"And what about 'Desherite'?"

"Mm. Dangerous." She stroked him with her hand and he pulled her against him.

"Doesn't look like much of a day for horses," he suggested.

"I was hoping it would blow over."

He stuck his head outside the roofing and gauged the sky. "Give it another half hour." He imagined the smell of a newly wet meadow, with the memory of rain lingering in the air; the energy of a fractious horse between his legs. "I'll join you."

"We could go freestyling." She pointed at the rock face with her quirt. "Hands and feet."

"In the rain?"

"How long has it been since you went up without ropes and pitons?"

"You're serious!"

Kathryn's face was narrow and sharp, like a logger's wedge. Her eyes glittered like diamonds—hard and beautiful at the same time. "Of course!"

"Bryce is coming home for spring break. You wouldn't want him to find his parents' mangled bodies at the base of No Foolin' Peak."

"Always solicitous of others' sensibilities . . . Or is it fear?"

He never knew where she drew the line. The Colorado high country was very near his wife's idea' of heaven on earth. Skydiving. Rock climbing. Double-black ski trails in the winter. Kayaking down whitewater in the spring. Safe enough when you knew what you were doing and followed the rules; but sometimes she grew bored with the rules, and Adam would hold his heart in his hands until she had come to herself again. "Brave isn't a subset of stupid," he said.

"You're no fun." And Adam relaxed, because that meant she'd been kidding, after all.

"Why don't we wait until"—a sudden gust of wind blew the downpour across the porch and in an instant he and Kathryn were drenched—"The rain passes," he finished lamely.

Kathryn laughed. "You're soaking."

He plucked at her shirt. "You, too."

They stood close in silence, he fingering her blouse, while the rain hissed and spattered and gurgled down the spouts and dribbled from the edges of the eaves. The glint in Kathryn's eyes changed in some indefinable fashion and her lips curled a little at the ends. Adam pressed with his hand, found what he sought, and Kathryn did not brush him away. She unfastened buttons.

"Mother always said to get out of wet clothes as quick as you can."

"Your mother was a lewd woman." Adam tightened his grip and Kathryn sucked in her breath. "I could wring the water out, if you want," he said.

She seized him down below. "You man enough to try it?" Her other arm hooked his neck and pulled his face into hers for a kiss so hard their teeth clacked together. Her quirt's handle dug into his back. He slid his hand inside her unfastened blouse, felt the warm, yielding flesh—and squeezed, hard. Kathryn yelped and slapped him sharply across the shoulders with her quirt. Her mouth ground against his like a hungry cat, devouring him, catching his lips and tongue briefly between her teeth. Laughing, she shoved him away and ran. He vaulted the railing and caught her on the grassy lawn.

The rain soaked through their clothing, plastering it to their bodies. He could see Kathryn's every contour molded in cloth. She stood a little hunched over, like a panther crouched to leap, her breath coming in short gasps, steaming just a bit in the cool air. Her short-cropped hair looked like paint, and had changed from a dusty blond to sodden, dark brown. He had never desired anyone half so much as he desired Kathryn at that moment.

He told her so afterward. After they had lain in the wet grass and the mud and the pouring rain—he, pushing her into the ground with urgent thrusts; she, kicking and scratching and biting. You are, he said when they parted, more sensuous as a "drowned rat" than other women are primped with makeup and thousand-dollar gowns. She laughed and spread her arms to the sky and let the rain shower rinse her clean. God, she said. Oh, God, I love you.

Exhausted now, Adam sat on the steps leading up to the deck and watched the rain run off her. Was this the same woman who stole dinner parties and benefits with the elegant perfection of her dresses and jewelry; with long, white gloves, diamond brooch; makeup, and a haughty look? *And she wrestles in the mud and rain with her husband.* Love with Kathryn was never less than an athletic contest. Never tender and soft and gentle; and certainly never a tepid conjugal obligation scheduled for birthdays, anniversaries and alternate

Wednesdays. Absently, Adam fingered the welt her spur had raised on his leg. Sliding through the forties as he was, how long could he keep up the pace? All he knew was that he never felt as intensely as this when he was with other women. That mechanic on LEO . . . That had been nothing more than an hour's relaxation; nothing of the oneness that he experienced with Kathryn.

The rain had ended at last, and the fierce, high-country sunlight sliced through the fading wrack of cloud. Kathryn had gathered up the ruined clothes and tossed them on the deck before straddling his lap and linking her arms behind his head. "An ounce for your thoughts, lover."

"Just comparing you to other women."

The contact of her lips and of her nipples on his chest was feather-light—inside his space, but not quite touching. "Favorably, I hope. Which ones?"

Sometimes she asked him to describe those encounters. He ran his fingers down her bare spine and she writhed. "It doesn't matter," he said. "They aren't even in the same league with you."

She was close enough that he could feel her lips move when she spoke. "They'd better not be."

His hands settled on her waist, just above the swell of her hips. "We ought to get dressed. If Bryce comes up today instead of—"

"How does he imagine he was conceived? Under a cabbage leaf?"

"Children are prudes where their parents are concerned. Did you ever see your parents doing it?"

She shuddered. "God forbid! What are you going to do about Baleen?"

"Hmm? Oh, I'll check into Poole's activities. I have connections on Goddard that owe me favors. If it turns out he's screwing us, I'll screw him to the wall."

"Mmm. Me first." She brushed him with her lips. "But, lover," in a harder voice, "don't let salvaging Baleen distract you from the main objective."

"Don't worry, honey. Everyone will get what they deserve."

"God, you're phat nasty. They say that's the worst fate you could wish on anyone—that they get what they deserve."

"Uh-hunh." He could feel the rays baking his skin, drying him. He rubbed his wife's body to speed the drying and smelled the rich, earthiness of her flesh. "And what is it you deserve?" he asked her.

"This," she said, seizing her reward.

Wally Jenks favored jeans and cowboy boots and a checked flannel shirt. He drank beer out of long-neck bottles and danced the Texas two-step; but that aw-shucks, shit-kicking image went with top-flight law school credentials and a long career as a federal prosecutor. Retired to private practice now, he sat in Adam's lounger with one leg propped up, and took notes on a cliputer resting on his knee. A bottle of Coors stood on the table beside him. The pixwall provided a real-time view of a high meadow two miles distant. Cupped between two mountains dark with Douglas fir, the meadow was bright green from the recent rains and was speckled with Parry primrose. The music was Richard Strauss, though—"Ein Heldenleben"—and Adam sipped cognac.

"I agree," said Jenks, "that the evidence is suggestive; though I would never go into court with it. I won't even ask how you came by some of it—"

Adam turned away from the vista and faced the lawyer. "A Deep Throat."

"Maybe. But none of it supports your main contention; and there's no law against being duped, anyway."

Adam flushed. "I wasn't 'duped.'"

Jenks held up a hand. "You don't need to tell me again. I believe you. I believed you from the start."

Adam turned away to refresh his drink. "That's more than others did," he muttered. But he wondered if it were true. Lawyers were hired guns and they believed what they were paid to believe. Jenks and he went back a lot of years on a lot of deals, but the man might not even care about the truth. Was that friendship? To believe the lies, but stand fast regardless? Or would friends refuse to credit the lies at all? Who beyond Kathryn believed in Adam van Huyten?

You're feeling self-pity again, he warned himself. And he *had* been stupid, regardless what he had just said to Jenks. "It was a wild side job," Adam said. "It had to be."

"Fine," said Jenks. "I've told you before. Find out who and get him to testify. That's how you crack white-collar conspiracies. Someone has to turn over."

Adam snorted. "The hacker hasn't been born yet that would turn in one of his own."

Kathryn entered the living room. "Excuse me, Adam. Hello, Wally, you gorgeous stud-muffin. Adam, Jimmy Poole is returning your call."

Adam rose and Jenks rose with him. "Excuse me," Adam said. "I've been waiting for this."

"There you go," Jenks said. "You could ask Poole. They say he knows the wild side." Jenks started to follow him to his private office. "Do you want me to listen in?"

"Wait here with me," Kathryn said in a mock-sultry voice, "and we'll do the dirty on the rug."

From the flush and covert glance, Adam judged that Jenks had jollied with Kathryn more than a few times. He laughed. Everyone needed a hobby. "You and Kathryn play nice," he told the lawyer. "I may want to ask you a question or two, afterward." He let Wally wonder what sort of questions he would ask.

In the office, Adam connected the hard drive that he used only for 'facing with Poole. Not that he didn't trust Poole, but he didn't trust anyone much, these days.

Certainly not the flamboyant, disembodied head that appeared on his pix-creen.

"There were two of them," Poole said without preamble. "Earp wrote the main program, then looked the other way while Captain Cat did an add-on. But crossing the line made Earp skittish so he hooked the Cat, and then slagged the *Belle* when it looked like inquiring minds were getting too close—"

Bell? Cat? Adam felt as if he had just tuned into the middle of a conversation. He held a hand up, halting the torrent of words. "What the devil are you talking about?"

"The LEO Laager." The face seemed both eager and impatient, waiting for some sort of kudos. "I found out who wrote it."

"That was your jones, not mine. It doesn't matter to me who wrote it."

But he might as well not have spoken. Poole's words flowed uninterrupted. "Billie was working an analog link on a daisy chain when Earp slagged the chat room. He followed the digital skein back to San Antonio, which he thought was the home site, because the IR link was transparent to digerati. He couldn't resist a little victory dance, but his timing was off and Tani and Billie bailed before Crayle made the scene—"

Adam stiffened. Was Billie Whistle working with Poole, too? His voice came out hard as ice on a high country lake. "Let's try this once more. Did you rope one of my people into an illegal hack?" He leaned closer to the screen. "Is she in on Brass Balls, too?"

The screen blinked, and now Poole smiled. "So, you know about Brass Balls?"

Did he just "go live" or did he just start using an imago? Adam shrugged in irritation over the juvenile games the virtchuosi sometimes played. "Brass Balls, PLC," he said. "Tenanted aboard Goddard Free Port, and making baleen."

Poole nodded. "Uh-hunh. How deep did you dig?"

That smug look. It had to be Poole-in-the-flesh. No screen morph could bring off a smirk that good. "Deep enough," he admitted, "to learn that it was installed two months before our own facility; that it has a full-time operator on board; and that it was chartered in Great Britain as 'a wholly-owned subsidiary of Baleen Partners.'" Adam braced both fists on the desk. "Setting up a pirate operation, I can understand; but assigning it to us, I don't."

"You're forgetting something, van Huyten."

"What?"

"I'm not the one who screws my partners."

Adam's eyes narrowed. "And that means what?"

"What do you think? Your fixation on LEO made rotten business sense. Had to be personal weenie. You thought something wasn't right on LEO, but you were willing to risk Baleen by putting it aboard. Well, I wasn't. Just because I have money to burn doesn't mean I like watching the smoke curl up."

Adam stood, backing away from the screen a step. "I personally assessed the situation on board LEO, if you remember."

"Oh, I remember. It's how you roped me into this game. But if you suspected something, you should have told the rest of us. You and me, we're phat; but the others aren't. I didn't want you to hang them out to dry because of some crusade against your dad."

"You think I was trying to screw Baleen?"

"Why not? You screwed VHI, didn't you?"

Adam tasted bile. "Everybody knows the answer, but nobody ever asks the question." That was the worst part, he decided. The loss of faith.

Poole sucked on his lip, staring at him. Adam could see the circuits firing behind the eyes. "All right," Poole said after a moment. "I'll ask. Did you?"

Adam didn't ask him what he meant. "No."

Poole nodded. "Okay," he said.

Adam was irritated at the flash of gratitude he felt. Why should he care what S. James Poole thought? "Don't you want to know what really happened between me and Klon-Am?"

Poole shrugged. "If you didn't sell out, they must have picked your pocket. I can think of five ways to slick those shares away from you . . ."

"I was looking for promising start-ups in the environmental engineering field—"

"Like Baleen."

"Only this was earlier. Pitchlynn put me on to a couple of leads. I investigated. They looked good. I signed over some stock—and so did Pitchlynn— to help capitalize them. The deal was, we would get the stock back after they were up and running. Then, magically, the start-ups turned into wholly owned subsidiaries of Klon-Am and the loan was an outright sale—with payment in my accounts well above the stock's market value."

Poole cocked his head. "Okay. Six ways."

Adam's fingernails bit hard into his palm. "Does it matter how it was done?" He recalled words bitter from his father's lips, though not half so bitter spoken as heard. Being stupid was one thing. Being doubted was another.

"Sometimes virtchuosi develop a style. They use the same algorithms and subroutines. So how it was done might give you a clue. Or not. My guess is they brought in a one-shot charlie. So you and this Pitchlynn took a bath—"

"Pitchlynn was a Judas Goat. She got her shares back after the takeover and kept a board seat when O & P and Ruger AG lost theirs. I've analyzed the voting within LEO since then. Pegasus *never* votes against Klon-Am on any issue where Klon-Am interests are involved and Pegasus holds the balance."

"Okay," said Poole with an impatient cough. "You have weenie for Pitchlynn and Bullock. So, why stick it back in after you got bobbited once already? Why put Baleen on LEO? I'd think you'd stay as far away from Klon-Am as possible."

Adam closed his eyes and blew his breath out his long, thin nose. If you wanted trust, you had to show trust; and he had spent the last few years out of that particular market. Yet, hadn't Poole shown, in a strange, roundabout way, that he could be trusted? "Is this line secure?" he asked.

He was answered with silence, rolling eyes, and a flashing placard that read: POOLE SECURITY CONSULTANTS.

"Fine," he said between his teeth. Though it was the cocksure that often made the biggest blunders. Adam himself was living proof of that. He lowered himself into his desk chair and turned it to face the screen. "I didn't suspect Klon-Am of anything specific, beyond what they had done to me. But a man's character is seamless. If he screws one person on one thing, you can bet that he's screwing others. So, I decided to go fishing.

"Now, Bullock is not a big believer in the orbital trade. He fought my aunt every chance he got, until Wilson and the other players sat on him. So why'd he slick his way onto the LEO board? He bought—and conned—enough stock that, with Pitchlynn's help, his was the swing vote. The rest of the board was angry with Aunt Mariesa over the Steel Rain fiasco, and Bullock parlayed that resentment into a contract to operate the station for five years. A man like that doesn't buy himself a five year contract in a market he thinks has no future. He must be out to maximize profits *muy pronto*; and that means that— somewhere—he is cutting corners. I find out where—I got him by the short curlies."

"Dude," said Poole.

"That's why I had to put Baleen aboard LEO. Embedded in Baleen's oper- ating software is a fly that—" He hesitated; considered Poole. "I don't want to implicate a third party."

Poole made rolling, get-on-with-it motions with his hands. ". . . That Billie Whistle wrote for you," he supplied.

"I'm not confirming that," Adam insisted.

"Good for you. Do you want me to guess what the fly is supposed to do? Infiltrate LEO's system, mouse around the deebies, then download the skinny. You figured that since the tenant intallations have to handshake with the station's system all the time, security couldn't be so tight *inside* the firewall. Right?"

"Right. And that's why they couldn't suspect that Desherite was anyone but who he seemed to be. They'd be very shy of anything 'Adam van Huyten' wanted to place on board. But, when you told me about how phat the security system was, I had to chance a personal look. Billie designed her fly to encrypt its download into Baleen's regular telemetry. I talked to the system techs, told them how concerned Baleen was about datacomm security—proprietary issues and all that—and they told me . . . maybe more than they thought. Enough to convince me that it was safer to send Red up to retrieve disks during pre- ventive maintenance visits than it was to put contraband in the download." Adam looked at him. "I'm going to bring them down. Bullock and Pitchlynn, both."

"And your father?" asked Poole.

Adam shook his head. "That's between me and him." *And Dad didn't have to believe the maliciousness so readily. All my life I looked up to him: stern, upright, as firm and dependable and unchanging as a rock; only, amid shifting currents, to discover that rocks could be a hazard, as well.*

A van Huyten, and son of the chairman, with the path made smooth before him . . . He'd been too cocksure and, because of that, too oblivious to the ambitions of others. The smiling circle of presidential faces around the board table and at the management retreats . . . Sharpening their knives for each other; but most of all for him. Take down the last van Huyten, and the path of ambition would be free of obstacles. Pitchlynn, he was sure of. Had he ever brought a proposal before the executive committee that she hadn't poked full of holes? Always "helpful." Always an "improvement." Always making him look inept in front of his father. Wilcox had not been a friend, nor Tottenham at Morpheus Plastics; but Pitchlynn had laid for him at every turn.

Adam felt suddenly older than his years. There was a spot on the wall where Kathryn had taken down his father's pixure. He had never hung anything else there.

Afterward, Adam told Jenks what had happened and Jenks ran a hand through his thinning hair and said, "I thought you told me one time that this Whistle woman was set up by some charitable institution."

"Sure. It was the . . . Oh."

"Yeah." Jenks tilted his beer bottle and drank. "So where's this Crayle come in that Poole mentioned? Why did he arrange Whistle's training and equipment? And what was the quid for that quo?"

Bryce van Huyten was a likely young man. He had the family's height, the strong jaw, the gray eyes. Perhaps he was a shade more convivial than other van Huytens, but that was partly youth, and he otherwise exuded the earnestness of his generation. It was typical of him that he spent spring break with his parents while his sister, only a few years older, decamped for the beaches along the Baja. University had stolen him, and Adam saw him now only in glimpses. All the in-betweens had been excised, so that each time he visited he seemed a different person. Just now, Bryce was taken up by philosophy and, with all the easy judgement of the young, held forth at dinners on the insights and oversights of Spinoza and Hume and Whitehead. He misunderstood, in Adam's judgement, the nature and intent of the *Principia* and certainly overestimated the importance of Gödel's Theorem outside formal systems; but Adam held his peace and savored the fact of the conversation itself. At that age, he remembered, he had avoided his parents as often as he could and his conversation had consisted largely of grunts, monosyllables, and the always-useful "whatever."

He and Kathryn shuttled Bryce around the state, packing a year's experience into a week. Mesa Verde. The Black Canyon. Dinosaur Monument. They camped in Arapahoe Forest and Kathryn took Bryce up a modest face with rope and piton. When the family returned to Denver and Bryce introduced them with a proprietary air to a bright, young California girl who had flown out for the last week of break, Adam did not refuse his request for time away on his own. It would be, he thought, the last time his son would ever visit. At the next iteration, it would be the man his son had become. Adam felt both the pain and pride of that and Kathryn, he supposed, felt the same, with perhaps the greater intensity of a mother.

All the way up I-70 through the Eisenhower Tunnel, Kathryn sat with a melancholy look staring out the van's side window and brushing it from time to time with a knuckle. In the back, aluminum tent poles and climbing gear rattled in their bags. Adam wondered if his own youthful disinclination to associate with his parents had been the first, thin wedge driven between Christiaan and himself.

He ventured as much to Kathryn, who turned from her study of the window with stark disapproval on her face. "Don't go hunting ways to blame yourself for *his* behavior," she warned him. "You can't spend your whole life begging for his approval."

"I'm done with that."

"Are you?"

He did not glance at her. The highway wound steeply down the mountain's western slope and required attention. The shoulder on the left dropped off sheer into a broad meadow and sluggish, meandering waters. On the right, the shoulder rose just as steeply into mountainsides punctuated by runaway-truck ramps that angled sharply upward through deep pits of sand.

Jimmy Poole watched Stevie pull himself to his feet against the edge of the sofa. The kid's frown was almost comically intense. Jimmy put aside the flatscreen he had been screading and told the chair to tilt more upright, so he could see better. "Whatcha up to, Stevie?" His son looked at him as if to say, Hey, can't you see I'm busy?

With great care, Stevie released his hold on the sofa cushion and stood, arms hovering as if he poised on the edge of a great abyss. Why the kid had this obsession with unsupported standing was hard to fathom. No one had told him, Now look, Stevie, you've got to learn to stand. Was it an instinct, a gene-wired drive? Or was it only that Stevie saw everyone else—Mommy, Daddy, Rada, Stassy—all walking on two legs and figured, hey, it was the hip thing to do.

Jimmy grunted and picked up the flatscreen again. The downloads and snippets from Earp's system were dribbling in at last and, with them, no whisper that Earp had twigged. *That was the problem with a really bean hack,* Jimmy mused. *You could never talk about it afterward.*

He inserted a file with his stylus and the affinity diagram on his comppad jostled like people on a crowded elevator making room for a new entrant. He ought to do this on his pixwall, he thought. Comppads were nice, but their screens were too small to scread the total topology. But today was Rada's day off and he had promised Tani that he would watch Stevie. Not that he minded. Tani couldn't write amidst distractions; Jimmy could. *The Man with Two Brains!* One occupied with organizing the goods on Earp; the other occupied with monitoring the Small Person.

Said Person gave a squeal at that moment and Jimmy glanced his way in time to see the kid walk across the room.

Well, it was sort of walking. It looked more like Stevie was stumbling forward—each step a temporary expedient to prevent a fall. Soft, pudgy arms waved like a tightrope walker's. Across Stevie's features, a look very like astonishment, fear, and excitement bundled into one. Jimmy dropped his comppad and clambered from his recliner to put himself in Stevie's path.

"Come to daddy," he said. He spoke with his arms and his smile. Stevie grinned single-toothed and staggered into his father's embrace. No explorer ever reached Everest's peak to greater acclaim. Jimmy reveled in Stevie's triumph, overwhelmed by nameless thoughts that threatened tears. More of those hard-wired instincts, he supposed.

Jimmy awoke in the middle of the night. A notion, half-formed and fuzzy around the edges, nagged at him. He pulled on a pair of shorts, in case Stassy or Rada felt the need for a late-night snack, and made his way to the Sanctum. Used to be, he'd do his midnight rambling in the altogether, sit before his monitors nudely enthroned, clicking his mouse or pulling his joystick. Now, decorum ruled.

He called up the record of Whistle's teep from last year and ran it up to the point where Whistle was just entering the interlock to Hub-4. Okay, there were the two waldos in the background. He selected the view, cropping the peripheral foreground of the 3-4 Interlock mechanism, and saved it to a region on his pixwall.

Then he ran the teep forward. Billie's waldo entered Hub-4, turned slightly and . . . Freeze that! Jimmy took the second view and put it on the pixwall next to the first. He adjusted the scaling and the angle until both displayed the same POV. Now, overlay . . .

The two scenes converged toward the center of the pixwall, and Jimmy spun in his command chair to watch. Oh, yes! Oh, yes, baby! His pulse hammered. With his left hand, he activated the joystick on the chair arm and set it to "nudge." Gently, now. The two views were lying almost atop each other. Up a hair. To the left. Just right. Insert. Oh, beautiful. It felt so good.

"Computer," he said. "Overlay. Congruence. Degree. Calculate." He used the vocoder, because he needed both hands for his joysticks.

"Congruence, eighty-seven percent," the A/S told him.

"Congruent region. Mask. Discrepancy. Color-code. Execute mask. Execute color-code."

Most of the overlaid graphic faded to gray-line. That was where the two overlaid scenes agreed. Where they disagreed, the discrepancy was highlighted in Day-Glo orange or green. Jimmy knew a spasm of pleasure. Most excellent!

There were the two waldos. Seen from the interlock, but gone once Billie had entered Hub-4. But also highlighted were three manufacturing or experimental self-contained units that had vanished also. Barely visible—only the edges or corners had been visible from the lock—but the SCUs were definitely there in one view, gone in the next. The two waldos might have moved faster than they should have, but either Blackhall reconfigured Hub-4 in a New York minute, or . . .

"Or the second view," Adam said, "is a recording." Unshaven, tangle-haired, eyes bleary with interrupted sleep, harsh words regarding three in the morning; but interest had sharpened his features. He scowled, and one finger curled across his cheek.

"A simulation, more likely," Jimmy judged. "I think they make the switch when the waldo passes through the interlock. I checked something with Hobie"—who hadn't been too thrilled at the wake-up call, either—"which I passed along to Chen." Chen, at least, had been awake. It was daytime in Guangzhou. "Chen dug up a snippet from one of his guys back last September. The waldo's heading through an empty interlock; then, presto, next moment, there's Hobie right in front of him. Almost ran into him. While they're in the manufacturing bays, teepers see only what OMC wants them to see. *That's* what Cat's module was for, and *that's* why it was a wildside job. Only question is: Why?" Jimmy scratched himself. Adam was 'facing with a morph, all duded up phat. Jimmy never real-timed his physical self and he wondered why a rich boy like Adam came to the screen in the middle of the night looking like someone woken up in the middle of the night. Put it in the pot with his penchant for face time, riding mass transit, environmental remediation, and other whack notions. Either Adam had a deep conservative streak, or he was way ahead of his time.

Adam shook his head slowly, as if rolling thoughts back and forth inside. Jimmy watched his features soften, then turn hard and settle into a thin line. "When you told me that there was a virtch module in the laager—and Dr. Hobart said that it looked like a lot of waldos were virtching, not teeping—I was like so-what. It even seemed like a useful add-on. Yet, OMC hired a netwalker—and corrupted Earp—to implant it; and then never said boo about the feature in any of their advertising. So, either the module hadn't worked. . . ."

"Unlikely," said Poole, "if Cat did the job."

"Or the teepers aren't supposed to know about it. When Doctor Hobart was up in October, he told me the station was chock-full and Blackhall had doubled up in some bays."

"That was a few months after Billie's teep," Jimmy pointed out. "Blackhall showed her an empty bay where Baleen could go, but warned her they were going fast."

Adam smacked himself on the head. "Of course, he showed her an empty slot. *That's why they used a sim.* Hobie saw the facility in October and it was full-up. We lifted Baleen in November. *So where did they install it?* You know what I think? I think they yanked something out, just so they could show the empty slot to 'David' and Red could hook up Baleen."

"But what about the installation they pulled out? Wouldn't the owners get . . . ? Oh!"

"Right. Low yields—like Red's been getting lately. Like Dr. Hobart was getting. Groundside, we think the plant is running full time, but it's only running part time—sharing space with another plant. They run the equipment balls-to-the-walls to make up as much of the difference as they can. Disguise some of the shortfall as maintenance breakdowns. Smuggle out the unused raws—or maybe pirate them for their own processes—so the material balances come out right."

"That's got to be a last resort," Poole said. "Easier to double up *research* modules. I bet a lot of groundside scientists are getting *really good* data from their orbital experiments. All OMC has to do is install the equipment long enough to get some genuine data, run the data through a simulator to get the distribution parameters; then remove the equipment and feed the researcher simulator data from then on." He thought about it a moment, then grinned; though he had to remember to tell his morph to follow suit. "If they're smart," Jimmy said, "they'll throw in random spikes, just so the researcher has a few anomalies to toss out again. But why take such crazy risks?"

"Because demand outran supply and Leo ran out of ziggy stere. Klon-Am must be renting the same volume two or three times over, to maximize their up-front earnings."

"Well, duh," said Jimmy. "Then you add another quartet of spokes . . . ?"

Adam shook his head. "That's outside the box for Bullock. He thinks the orbital trade is a temporary bubble, so he's not about to sink capital into additional facilities, even if Boeing and the other partners were willing."

"Yeah. And what about the partners?" Jimmy made notes on his sidescreen for Mr. Stockman, his A/S trader. (First A/S to get a seat on the Exchange, and no one had twigged yet. Which said something either about Jimmy's skill at constructing an A/S, or about stock trading.) *Dump Klon-Am.* He waited to see if he ought to dump anyone else. If Matsushita, Boeing, Deutsches Bundesbank and the other backers were in on this . . .

Adam tugged his lip. "The others don't know," he decided. "OMC has the operating contract. The Boeing or Energia people on board wouldn't get involved in sales calls or visiting teepers. All their bonebags would notice would be a lot of plant engineering activity." He smiled through carnivore's teeth. "It sounds right," he said with righteous joy. "It sounds like just the sort of cheap-jack stunt that Bullock would pull. When potential customers outstrip your capacity, you expand capacity. That's the whole point of market signals. But Bullock doesn't believe in markets. He believes in allocations and agreements and 'rationalizing the economy.' And so now he's done something monumentally stupid. And I've got him by the short curlies."

After Adam had logged off, Jimmy swung back and forth in his command chair, pondering his options. Tani, awakened by his absence from her bed, stuck her head in the Sanctum and asked sleepy questions, but Jimmy put her off and, after a moment or two, she retreated.

Short term thinking. Bullock didn't believe in the future. It had probably started as an act of desperation. Unable to fill contracts, but unwilling to decline them, he had taken a shortcut—or one of his managers had—and now everyone was stuck with the tar baby.

He recalled Mr. Stockman and ordered sells on Pegasus, Boeing, Energia, and the other partners in the LEO Consortium. Adam was on the warpath, and those dudes were standing too close to ground zero. Bullock wasn't the only one thinking short term, or who might, through inside-the-box thinking, do something monumentally stupid.

20.

Where You Gonna Run to, Sinner Man, All on That Day?

It might be that surrounding your life with things of beauty served only to highlight how ugly that life had become. Billie Whistle favored fine music and sculpture of the New Art and paintings of any period. With no furniture clutter for someone permanently imprisoned in a wheel chair ("assistive mobile device," was a weenie-word) her rooms resembled nothing so much as they did a museum. And yet, the graceful carvings and colorful daubs accomplished little more than to remind her of her own foolish dealings and how justice—in the form of Adam van Huyten—seemed to be catching up to her, at last. There were entire days following her return from San Jose when she failed to emerge from an alcoholic stupor.

Poole had given her a clean bill. No one was watching her apartment, according to his paid snoop, and no one was cracking her cheesebox. So either Crayle hadn't made the connection between the hastily-evacuated hotel room and Billie Whistle, or the mysterious Red had taken care of him. *You're safe*, the Poole-man had told her. The thought stuck her as unbearably funny and she laughed out loud in the emptiness of her room. Safe from Crayle, maybe; but what about David?

The rum was sweet, almost sickening. She threw up twice during the weekend—or maybe it was three times—when her tortured system could take no more. The purges left her shaking and feeling terribly cold; but a fresh bottle could warm her up nicely. You just had to learn how to pace yourself. Control, that was the key. You could get as stoopid as you wanted, as long as you were in control.

The electro-encephalitic interface picked up her brain activity and translated signals into commands; but she was giving the poor, dear Artificial Stupid a rough time of it, because she couldn't think straight to save her life. Equipment booted and shut down at random. Maybe she should have deactivated the interface, but she became engrossed in the light show the flickering equipment provided and afterward forgot about it.

She had lived with being half a woman with half a life for several years now. Half a woman, because while all the definitional organs were present and accounted for and in good working order, the accessories were somewhat lacking. She could, in a foul-enough mood, repel even herself with her appearance, let alone the parade of imaginary lovers her dreams created.

And half a life because, while she had a past, she had very little in the way of future.

In the past, there had been a family; and a good one, too. She had thought her mom a nag and her father remote and her little sister a pest, and not until she had lost them all had she imagined what she could lose.

In the past, there had been dancing. She could remember her first day at the barre. Had she been six? Five? The weenie barre was just right and she had learned to cross her legs and lift her arm and turn about without looking like a clumsy, ill-coordinated child. In the mirror she had seen herself, rail-thin in pink leotards, flanked by a dozen other weenies driven to the dance by everything from passion to pushy parents. In the mirror, the plain dance hall had become an elaborate set and herself a regal presence garbed in graceful ballet or hard-edged jazz costumes. Afterward, waiting for Mommy to fetch her, she had watched the grownups—teenagers, actually; but what did she know at that age? And it seemed to her that she had never seen anything so beautiful as those smooth and elegant older dancers. The girls in gorgeous costumes had floated across the floor as delicate as flowers; and the boys—there were a few—were as handsome and lithe and supple as she imagined the lover-princes in the stories. Years later . . .

Billie upended the bottle and swallowed fire. Look, what was the point of mixing it with anything? Mixed drinks were just pretense; water and ice, only a way to dilute the inevitable. Her computer comm screen activated and it seemed to be the face of Jimmy Poole goggling at her.

"Up your nose, Poole-man," she said, and giggled.

Years later, she had been one of the older girls herself, practicing for the annual recital. Working through a pass with Damon Rubin, her lungs pumping, and her legs flexing and leaping; Damon's hands upon her body—here, and here—lifting her, touching her, so the sweat was not wholly that of exertion. Descending from the lift, she had noticed one of Ms. Holland's baby class staring at her with the same round-eyed awe that she herself had once worn. She had almost missed her mark, but she had treasured that look ever since.

"I don't understand," the image said. The Poole-lucination.

"Don' haffta," she giggled. "Whu cares . . . ? Only kine' act anyone ev'r done me . . ." Did she mean Crayle, when he stooped to help her install her equipment? Or the small child whose eyes had praised her grace?

"Damn it, don't quit on me. You got a job to do!"

Poole's voice snapped like a whip, and Billie turned away so she did not have to look at him. The tubes and wires got all tangled, and the gown parted up her back creating a chill draft. She shook her head, feeling dizzy and slightly nauseous from the antiseptic smell. She buried her face in the pillow. "Lemme alone," she said.

"Not yet."

"Fuck you."

"Is that an offer?"

Billie rolled over and found that she was lying flat in a hospital bed, surrounded by incomprehensible equipment and walls painted in hatefully bright colors. Her eyes sought out Poole, brought him into focus. "What if it is?"

Poole shrugged and pointed across the room. "Take it up with Tani. She handles all my bookings."

Turning her head set off another wave of vertigo. When it had settled, Tanuja Pandya was sitting on the other side of her bed. "What are you doing here?"

"You went on a bender," said Poole in voiceover. Pandya, shaking her head slightly, said nothing. Billie glared at her, daring her to speak.

"What, you trying to get inside my head?" she asked the other woman.

Pandya said softly, "That's not a place I want to go just now."

"What do you know about it?"

"Nothing, if you choose not to tell me."

Billie sighed and a snappy comeback wafted unspoken from her tongue with the gust of her breath. She turned her head away and closed her eyes. "Go away." The bed was a boat, carried on waves that rose and fell. When she held herself very still, she could feel the bed slowly rotating.

She opened her eyes and it was dark in the room. The only light came from control panels and readouts and glowing computer screens. She stared at one where colored bars grew and shrank across the screen. Red, blue, orange, green . . .

"It's for your medication." Pandya's voice. "There's an implant—a MEMS remote—that monitors your blood chemistry continuously and the A/S unit dribbles in the right proportions of each medicine. One of them—they told me it was the red bar—is a designer molecule that cleans up the alcohol. Breaks it up, or prevents it from binding, or something, until the body flushes it out."

Billie turned. "What, weren't you taking notes during the lecture?"

Pandya's solemn face grew long. "You know, if I started first thing in the morning and spent the whole day feeling sorry for you, it wouldn't be a drop to how sorry you feel for yourself."

"You don't care about me. You don't care about anyone, not even that kid of yours; because if you did, you wouldn't be here. You wouldn't spend a single moment away from him if you could help it—because you never know when there might never again be another moment."

Pandya reached out and took Billie's arm to straighten some of the tubing. "You loved your family very much, didn't you?"

Mind your own business was Billie's automatic thought, but she held her tongue and, when she finally spoke, she said only, "I didn't love them all that well, when I had the chance." She tried not to look at Pandya while she said that, but somehow their eyes locked for just a moment.

"You almost died."

"Damn. Can't do nothing right." She squeezed all the flippancy she could into her voice, though her stomach seemed to drop five feet. No more? Extinguished? Never ending blackness? She began to shake and Pandya pulled the covers up over her.

"Were you *trying* to kill yourself?"

"Just can't keep out of other people's lives, can you?"

"Because if you were, there are more efficient ways than drinking yourself stoopid."

Billie hesitated. "That's chill, charlie." she said. But Pandya's answer had been like a slap in the face and, after a moment of silence, she said, "No, I wasn't; but I wouldn't have minded. Not then."

"But, now?"

"Now, I'm not drunk. Damn, what are the chemicals in that dribble tank? They should have them in bars and give them out at parties. No more hangovers . . . Party hearty, then flush and, ka-zow!" Billie laughed. "What else do they have in that cocktail? Feel-good juice? Because I feel . . ."

"That's the first time I've heard you laugh," Pandya said, "where it didn't have an edge to it."

"Yeah." The silence grew longer and more profound. At last, Billie said, "I guess I should thank you. You came and got me?"

"We called the Milwaukee emergency squad from California."

"I guess I'm lucky you called and saw what happened."

Pandya gave her a funny look. "You called us," she said.

"Did I? I *must* have been drunk. I was stinking fried. My interface was switching things on and off all weekend."

"Have it your way."

Pandya had not released her arm. Instead, the squeeze grew tighter. And then, as if the squeeze forced the words out, Billie blurted out, "Adam's going to screw me over."

The writer cocked her head and frowned. Billie could just see her consider and reject one meaning of "screw" before asking, "Why do you say that?"

"Why is it," Billie asked, "why is it that no one can do a kind act for me and have it be just that? Crayle . . . I was so far down I had to look up to see shoelaces, and he helped me. He pulled me out of the foo and he set me on my feet and he, and he, he crouched down and tested all the furnishings just to make sure I could use them. And all he wanted was I should walk the wild side for him."

"And did you?"

"And Adam. He brought something good into the world, and I helped him do it. I trolled the net for him and found Wincock and Guang and the rest; but Adam made it all happen. He organized us, brought Karl's microbes and Shao-ping's aerogel and Hawkins's ziggy and my own virtchuosity together, and created something exciting that will clean up some of the poison we've been spewing. But the whole thing was a sham; just a way to set me up."

Pandya frowned. "Jimmy talked to Adam last night. They've cracked LEO, they think. Jimmy ran the file for me later and Adam . . ." She shook her head. "Billie, I've never seen a man so intense, so fixated. He's determined to bring down Bullock and Pitchlynn . . . and maybe even his own father. Why do you think it was to set *you* up?"

"Because he had me write a fly into Baleen's software that would infiltrate LEO Station's system from the inside."

"He was scrounging for evidence against OMC—"

"A fly like that is illegal. When he reveals what I did—"

"Why would he do that?"

Those colored bars on her monitors were flapping like flags in the breeze. A machine beeped and Billie felt a sudden lassitude overtake her. "Because," she murmured. And Pandya had to lean close to hear the slurred words. Billie found herself whispering in her ear. "Because the wild job I did for Crayle . . . Tha's how they slicked Adam's stock away from him."

"He told Jimmy he'd been conned, but he didn't know how. But he never said anything in public."

"Too proud," Billie said through lips that barely moved. "Too proud."

"Have you told Adam?"

Billie drifted further away from the insistent voice. "Cou'n't do that . . . No . . ."

"Why not?"

"Because . . ." Because as long as she didn't see the hate in his eyes, she could create illusions and live inside them. She could pretend the world was different than it was, as long as she did not engage it.

Billie saw the surprise in Adam's face when he opened the door to his mountain retreat and found her sitting in her power chair on his front porch. His glance took in the special ADA rental van, the climbing wheels on her chair, and nodded slightly, as if in approval. "So. You know."

"Obviously, or I wouldn't be here." Adam's house was built from logs and had a rustic, rough-hewn appearance. Behind the building, No Foolin' Peak was a sheer wall of gray rock. The spring wind blew cool and dry. How was it possible to sweat in air like this?

"How long have you known?" he asked.

"That 'David' was Adam? Since February."

"Poole told you."

"No, his wife let it slip. Are you going to invite me in?"

He shook himself and held the door open for her. "I'm sorry. I was just shocked to see you here."

"Yeah, I bet you are." She rolled past him into the foyer and, at his nod, turned right into the front parlor.

Accustomed as she was to the openness of her own place, she thought the parlor curiously cluttered. A barrier of chairs and sofas blocked the walls; tables and lamps impeded movement. The decor surprised her: New Art rather than the "rustic/western" she had expected, or even the current rage: "coke." A large representational painting of a well set up nude woman ironing clothing. Another of a crowd of people waiting at a ballistic port—every face individually rendered; every face telling a story. The walls were inlaid with woods of various colors. Here and there, shelves were inset: not in regular stacks, but seemingly at random. Books and μCD racks shared the niches. Somehow, Billie had envisioned a different environment; as if a man obsessed could not also be a man with taste.

"You look like hell," he said.

"Fair enough. I've been there. Just got back."

He looked disturbed. "Can I get you anything?"

"You're being gracious."

His eyes narrowed. "Is there some reason I shouldn't be?"

"I'd like *Gorbachev, at Sea*."

If he was surprised to hear her ask for music rather than a drink, it showed only in the tilt of an eyebrow. He went to a wall panel and pressed buttons, consulted a menu screen, and pressed more buttons. A moment later, the ominous strains of the Overture in G-minor wafted through the speakers. Just a whisper of clarinets, at first, but growing.

"It's the St. Petersburg version," he explained. "I don't have a personal copy, so I uploaded one from the net. I didn't know you were an opera lover."

"Only the modern ones," she said. "You can have *Aïda* and all those other overblown pageants."

"How about a wine, then, to go with the music. Mmm. I don't have any Odessa wines. Maybe a vodka, to stay in theme."

Billie shuddered. "No, thanks," she said. "I've used up my quota." Van Huyten didn't ask her what she meant, for which she was grateful. It had been difficult enough for her to come here, even with Tani's support. He offered her a glass of spring water ("From our very own glacier, out in back") which she accepted, using the delay to cover her silence. She had no idea how she would begin.

The baritone had begun the aria, "V stranye slyepikh," and Billie listened to the rolling, rushing notes "as turbulent as Dnepr in his flood . . ."

At Volgi da Dona, f shirokikh styepyakh
At Volgi da Dona, gudyat pravada . . .

In Adam's face, she sought the outlines of David Desherite, the man she had thought she had known. And, yes, there was that same frown of concentration as he listened to the music, as if the baritone were somehow on trial.

"I tried to contact you last week," Adam said after the music had played awhile, "about the marketing plan. We've got enough baleen in cold storage now, and inquiries are starting to come in . . ."

"I was . . . indisposed."

"We ought to get moving. Pick a good marketing firm to subcontract. 'There is a tide . . .' and all that. Did Poole tell you about the second plant he set up in Goddard? Financed the whole thing himself, in case something went wrong on Leo."

Billie took up the challenge. "He told me it was because he didn't trust you."

Van Huyten turned away from the music. "And that's why you're here. To see if you can." It didn't even sound like a question.

"Can I?"

"You knew I wanted to eavesdrop on LEO. You wrote the fly for me."

"I didn't know why."

"You never asked. When did 'why' become important?"

"When I realized how exposed I was."

"Worried about the legal implications?" Van Huyten considered his glass, and set it aside on an end table. "You knew all that before. If the legal aspect worried you, why did you do it?"

"Because I would have done anything for David."

That startled him. He paused and regarded her, peeling away her skin, laying her desires bare. "Anything for David," he said finally. "But not for Adam? Why not?"

"Because Adam might have different motives than David for enticing me into an illegal act."

He pointed his wand at the control panel and the sound of the opera damped. He turned and faced her fully. Billie tried to read his eyes, but leaning forward as he was, they had disappeared into dark pools beneath his brows. "Why do you say that?"

Billie's heart hammered and she took a deep breath. She wasn't in any physical danger, she reminded herself. If that had been Adam's plan, he would have acted long ago; he would never have woven this elaborate Baleen deception to ensnare her. "I think you know."

"Suppose you tell me." And now, she could hear hardness in his voice. Iron in his words.

She tilted her chin up. "Revenge," she said. "For what I did."

His brows lowered. "What was that? Something you and Poole cooked up?"

Billie activated her chair and turned toward the door. "I'm not into playing games." But van Huyten had risen from his chair and blocked her way. He placed his hands on her chairs arms, holding her.

"Neither am I," he said.

Billie began to tremble. She had come here to make her peace, to seek a truce. Instead, it was growing into a contest of wills. Adam was mocking her. "You want me to grovel? All right, if that's what it takes to call you off. I'm sorry I did it. I was desperate, scraping by on assistance and disability, but I didn't have to take their offer. Only, it was a way out of the barrel. And they offered all this phat equipment. And . . ."

She had begun to cry. Adam took her by the shoulders and shook her—not gently, but not very hard, either. "What on earth are you raving about?"

"SiteMasters and Tincture Tech. They wanted me to—"

"Wait!" He stepped back. "The consulting firm that studied prospective plant sites for environmental impact and the—"

"—company that sold detection kits for trace contaminants. Yes."

"That was *you?*"

"It was a way out. The fee was enough to—"

"Stop!" Van Huyten ran a hand through his hair and strode away from her. He faced the pixwall with the live panorama of some remote valley, then turned abruptly and looked at her. Behind him, trees swayed gently in the high country wind. "That was *you?*" he said again. "*You* set up the false fronts for Klon-Am? *You* altered the contracts from a loan to a sale?"

The surprise in his voice rocked her. "You didn't know? I thought—" Her own words strangled her. He hadn't known. He had gone looking for a phat freelance virtchuoso to troll for opportunities; and the gods had conspired that he find her. And now, she had told him everything. Her eyes grew hot and wet. "You must hate me now."

"You learned who I was in February," he insisted. "Why didn't you come to me then?"

"Why?" She almost shouted. "I was afraid, that's why!"

"Afraid? How long were we working together? How could you be afraid of someone you knew so well?"

"I knew a screen morph that called himself David Desherite. Once or twice, I met the man that used the morph. Who on earth was it that I 'knew so well'? Tani said you were 'out for revenge.' Why shouldn't I have been afraid?"

"If someone hits me in the head, I don't spend three years plotting revenge on the hammer."

Billie rubbed her face with her good hand, but that only spread the tears. "Oh, God," she said. "Oh, God. Please don't hate me."

Adam came to her and placed his hand on her shoulder. "I don't hate you. I don't think God does, either."

"There is no God," she said, gulping. "How can there be a God?" Not one that marked every sparrow's fall. Unless he only watched, and didn't try to catch them.

"Well, if God doesn't exist, then obviously He can't hate you."

She laughed into her sobs. "That's . . . really stupid."

He rubbed her shoulders. "Bullock used your talent and your desperation to get something of mine that he wanted. We should be on the same side here."

"I didn't think you would be hurt. You were rich. Even afterward, you were still rich."

He stopped rubbing. "It wasn't the loss of money that hurt." He began to withdraw his hand, but Billie reached up and grabbed it with her left.

"No. Don't stop. No one's touched me for three and a half years. I'd forgotten what being touched felt like."

"I want you to talk to my lawyer. With your testimony, we can . . ."

"I'd be confessing to a crime. I couldn't . . ."

His hands stroked her shoulders, sending a shiver down her spine. How often had she dreamed of this? How often had she dreamed of more?

"I'm the injured party," he said. "I won't bring suit against you."

Billie could hear the eager tension in his voice; feel the trembling in his hands. "But I never dealt with Bullock; only with Tyler Crayle, and Crayle works for Earp."

Adam shook his head. "Earp's files have nothing about Crayle. Poole and I figure he was consulting for Klon-Am, not Earp. That might even give us leverage with Earp. The deal with Cat was unethical, but what Bullock, Crayle, and Pitchlynn did to me was illegal. Tie Earp to Crayle over the laager and he just might get mad enough to help stomp Bullock."

She closed her eyes. "That feels good." His fingers worked the muscles of her neck. She brushed another tear away. When he hesitated, she said, "Yes, you can go there." She couldn't see his face, but his hands found her and strokes became caresses. "It would only be my word."

"There are people who need to hear you say things. I want to watch while you tell him." Billie closed her eyes and tilted her head back. She was not surprised when, a moment later, she felt his lips on hers.

He thinks if he fondles me enough, I'll do what he wants. That I am so desperate for affection that a little kissing and squeezing will persuade me. God, he was a calculating SOB. And yet . . . And yet, it wasn't as though she was opposed to the idea. She had dreamed about it often enough. And his tongue was very convincing. "Yes," she said, when they parted for breath.

She meant that she had agreed to make the deposition he had asked for; but he took it that she had agreed to something else entirely. When she realized that—when he plucked her bodily from her chair and carried her in his arms into another room—she saw no reason to correct his error. Perhaps it was a calculated act on his part, but she was not above arithmetic herself.

But, calculated or not, she detected no shudder of revulsion when he un-

veiled her mangled limbs. The finger he ran along her scar was sympathetic—
and it tickled. He spent sufficient time exploring her, preparing her, height-
ening her awareness, that she trembled in expectation. When, finally, he was
with her and they moved together as one, she began to cry again.

He had been silent throughout, addressing her with the same fierce intensity
as he did any of the tasks he had handled for Baleen. But his breath came
faster, and she could feel his heartbeat shift gears. He moved in her like a
leashed tiger, as if he could burst her open like a soap bubble. When her tears
came, he brushed them with his hand. "You *are* beautiful when you smile, you
know," he told her. "I never understood why you didn't."

But that brought up memories better unremembered. "I don't need your
pity," she said.

"You've never had that."

They lay together for a while, talking of nothing consequential. Then, he
began to dress her.

"Freak show's over, I guess." Billie didn't know why she said that. It simply
came out. Adam paused with her blouse half-buttoned.

"Only if you want it to be." A button came unfastened. She brushed his
hand away.

"I won't be your lover."

"I know that."

"And what about your wife?"

"A little late to ask about her, isn't it? Kathryn and I have an understanding.
We can eat lunch out, as long as we come home for dinner."

"That's . . . a rather cold-blooded arrangement."

"It's also none of your concern."

Billie accepted that. She even accepted his dressing her without lashing out
at him. Kindness was not always condescension; and if what she and Adam
had shared had fallen far, far short of love, it had also risen well past pity. At
first, when they returned to the parlor, she would not quite meet his eyes.
Adam spoke lightly and easily—sex was something he and his wife freelanced
for sport—while Billie worked through her own uncertainties. Her relationship
with Adam had altered irrevocably, but in what fashion she did not yet know.

That he had jollied her for his own purposes—hey, he didn't have anything
else on his calendar and going into a gimp might be kinky and maybe she'd
be more likely to go along with his plans—that sort of took the edge off; but
that he had jollied her at all meant something. It meant that she was not
entirely dead.

"There are new prosthetics," he suggested. "Still experimental, but they use
a neural-laser interface like you already have to activate micro-electro-
mechanical structures that act like muscle fibers."

She pretended that she had never heard of the experiments. It was easier
to train your interface to do things like "bend knee" or "flex ankle" if that was

what the neural pattern used to do anyway; but the reverse process—flex the MEMS and read the feedback and yes, that was the sensation of a bent knee or a sprained ankle, and that was what heat/tickle/pain felt like—she was afraid of that. "It must be hideously expensive."

"It is," Adam admitted. He did not come out and say he would pay for it. She did not come out and ask him to.

Kathryn returned from Dillon and found them in the parlor listening to the final aria, when Gorbachev, released from the dacha in which he had been held prisoner, finds that all the world outside had changed. Adam had been telling her a story over the singing and she was laughing at the punch line. Billie grinned and said, "Hi, you must be Kathryn."

The tall, hawklike woman studied her wordlessly, then stepped to the chair in which Adam sat and slapped him across the face. She turned to Billie.

"You are not welcome here."

"Bone," Billie responded and added, provocatively, "I got what I came for." She activated her chair and rolled past a bewildered Adam. "I'll have that market plan we talked about by the end of the week. Let me know when you need that testimony." She meant her own testimony about Crayle and the set-up. Adam, rubbing his cheek, nodded. Billie turned to Kathryn. "And, thank you. I might not have known, otherwise."

Billie left the rancho smiling. Adam might not know why Kathryn had reacted as she had, but Billie did. An open marriage, setting wide limits to each other's pleasures . . . But no one is more intolerant than the tolerant, once their limits have been reached. Kathryn would abide Adam's every dalliance—except when done from genuine care.

Justice

Jacinta straddled the platform atop the scaling tower, one leg dangling over each side. "C'mon," she hollered to the bunnies swinging and struggling on the climbing ropes. "Up and over! Up and over!" Yungduk, clipped to a safety line at the other end of the wall, clapped his hands rhythmically. It was a new crop of bunnies, freshly sprung from the spring rains. A boy, pale and slightly overweight, huffed his cheeks out on the number two rope. Jacinta leaned over. "Let's go, deTrobriand. A one-armed girl can make it over!"

The newboo gasped. The sun, even in March, had kissed him. Glowing red on brow and nose tip, whitening, about to peel. His sweat was basting juice. "Bump," he said. "Space got no gravity."

Jacinta threw back her head and laughed. She cupped her hands around her mouth and hollered, "Hey, Matusek! Fresh meat!" The ensign instructor made a fist and pumped it three times. "Three gigs, deTrobriand," Jacinta relayed the news, "until you can explain to the Ensign why what you just said was too stupid for words."

DeTrobriand muttered something and Jacinta said, "What was that, de-Trobriand?"

"I said, 'Yes, cadet sergeant!' "

He hadn't said that. Jacinta had heard "macho girl" within the mumble, but she let it go. The new bunny crop did not seem very promising to Jacinta. Surely, her own cohort hadn't been this callow a year ago! Though she wasn't about to pass that observation along to Matusek. The Ensign probably had a different spin on things.

A spindly little critter, all arms and legs, scampered up number five rope and rappelled down the other side with barely a pause. Yungduk watched him down. He shook his head. "Some people, you wish they would sweat, just a little."

Jacinta grunted. "Hope Cutler prepped his brain as well as he prepped his bod. Otherwise, he'll sweat plenty in diffy-Q." She checked out the next wave on the ropes. "Stall out on number three. Give him a lift down, Duk."

"On my way." Yungduk dropped down the ascent wall on the safety line. After he had rescued the bunny and returned to the catbird seat, he asked Jacinta if she had gotten the billet for her training flight yet.

"Nine July," she told him with a grin that felt near to split her head. "Supercargo on RS-75, *Charlie Rolls*, a FedEx ship under pilot-captain Kilbride. Phoenix to Aomori with a stopover at Goddard City. They dump off packages for other ballistic routes, pick up anything waiting for the Far East, and deorbit. 'When it absolutely, positively has to be there in an hour,' " she quoted. "How about you?"

He made a face. "Tourist flight. *Sasebo Maru* in June, out of Aomori for LEO."

"Bone! I only get a fractional orbit."

"Yeah, but you get to watch a docking," Yungduk said wistfully. "I get to babysit sightseers. Just a 'circle tour.' They're not even booked into FreeFall Resort. Would *you* pay fifteen kilobucks just to go around the Earth for half a dozen orbits?"

"In a New York minute. If I ever had fifteen kilobucks," she added.

Yungduk shaded his eyes—noble scout peering into the distance—and Jacinta had to admit to herself that he did look bone when he struck a pose like that. "Bunny run's over," he said. "Matusek's calling us down." He waved acknowledgement. "Bunch of us are going into Tehachapi Friday to lighten the load. Celebrate Year One. Interested?"

"Sure. Who all's going?"

He grinned. "So far, you and me."

Laughing, she followed him down. She was halfway down the wall when she remembered that that would also be the anniversary of the plane crash on the Grapevine. She faltered for only a moment, suspended between earth and sky, staring at nothing in particular, then finished her descent; but she wasn't laughing when she reached the ground.

Cadet captain Alonzo Sulbertson was packing when Jacinta came calling in Titov Hall the next day. He had just about bareboned the place, she saw. Pictures and posters had been dewalled; books boxed and shipped. Ebooks and deebies racked and secured. She watched him fold shirts and lay them out precisely in his suitcase.

"Need a micrometer?" she asked. "I think you set one out of place."

Sulbertson looked up, positioned a shirt just so, and grinned.

"All ready for your midship year?" she asked.

Sulbertson dropped into his desk chair and propped his legs up on the bed. "Gave it some thought, 'Cinta. Maybe I ought to stay on. Who'll make sure you keep your room tidy?"

Jacinta squatted cross-legged on his reading chair. "Dunno. Haven't seen the promotion list, yet. Hope it's not Coster. She's more anal than you are. They posted the training flights, though."

"I saw." Sulbertson nodded. "You got Kilbride."

"Yeah, a parcel postman." She whirled a big deal finger in the air.

"Look closer. Kilbride was one of the original members of the Emergency Response Team. Flew an unarmed Plank into Skopje. You stone for that?"

Jacinta was impressed despite herself. "I'd like to think so . . . Hey! How 'bout you? Have a midship assignment, yet?"

"I'll be 'prenticing on the *Jacqueline Cochran,*" he said, and Jacinta could hear how he tried to keep the pride from showing.

She whistled. "High-V work. That is so bone! Didn't know *Yeager* and *Cochran* took middies."

Sulbertson shrugged. "Chang-Diaz drive is . . . different," he admitted. "Maybe they want to train people from scratch."

Nuclear reactions in a magnetic bottle . . . Granted, you got one hell of a specific impulse through the wind hole, but if the bottle went . . . She wondered if Lonzo had felt any hesitation accepting the billet. The two *Yeager*-class OTVs were still X-ships, but middies had to take what was offered or go to the bottom of the list. Or did they rig the lists to match middies with their ships? "Hope I pull a berth there, too," she said in the Voice of Confidence, "when it's my turn." She wasn't sure she did, but it was a top assignment and you had to *act* like you wanted it; and you didn't dare say no if they called your bluff.

Sulbertson's lips curled into a lazy smile. "I don't hear you doing that thing with your voice so much these days."

Jacinta unfolded from the lotus and leaned forward. "I'm still a silver apple," she told him. And why did that come out so defensively? Because she had been annotating her copy of the *Precepts* with her own personal observations? Because with each gloss the distance grew between her and the Retreat? But she was still an apple. She was.

"You just don't shove it in people's faces like you used to," Sulbertson observed.

"Hey, Lonzo . . ." Total Meredith, spiffed in U.S. Space Ops black, leaned through the doorway. "Noëlle's hosting a buster at oh-nineteen for the new mid—Oh, hi, Jacinta." She looked from one to the other. "'Rupting?"

Sulbertson waved a hand. "Nah." He tossed his chin, indicating the new uniform. "Commission came through, I see."

"Street, isn't it." Total posed and turned a slow pirouette. Tight-fitting coveralls that flattered her figure and matched perfectly the jet of her hair and brows. Silver trim flashed; ensign pips gleamed on her shoulders. Jacinta had to admit she was bone charlie. "Lonzo, I'll see you tonight. 'Cinta . . . Maybe our orbits will match someday." Her eyes trapped Jacinta and held her until Jacinta nodded, "Yeah. Someday." Then, a quick smile that might have been friendly or merely predatory, and she was gone.

"Bone," Jacinta said.

"Yeah. Too bad she ain't broadcasting on my frequency."

"No, I meant she'll get to fly those high-performance 'chines AFSO has."

"Sure, but how much flight time will she rack? It's not every day they call out the ERT. That's why most of us put in for research or commercial work. More hours behind the yoke. Pay's better, too." Sulbertson settled back and linked hands behind his head. "Now, what did you come here about? You didn't just drop in."

Jacinta tried to gauge him. There were no micrometers for the psyche; and Lonzo had always been particularly difficult to take a bearing on. His easy, quiet manner bordered on the Sphinx. More than once, Jacinta had imagined him a panther, languid on a tree branch, but capable of instant, decisive action. Sometimes, she had even wondered if, when the time came to share herself, it might be better done with a man of Sulbertson's intensity than with the Sorens and Yungduks of the world.

Just now, though . . . "I need your help. After you leave next week, there'll be only one of us left here. And . . . I want to do something for the others."

Sulbertson didn't ask her what she meant. His obsidian eyes regarded her, revealed nothing. "What do you remember about them?" he asked after a soft silence. "The others."

"Well, Ursula wrote me—" But Sulbertson cut her off.

"No, I'll grant that you know Ursula. I hear from her, too, time to time. I meant the three who didn't make it."

"Who died." Jacinta noticed him flinch at the blunt word. Yeah, what was it Total had said to her that time? Dying was the easy part. Surviving was harder. "Not too much," she admitted. "We didn't klatsch all that long . . ."

"Remember their names?"

"Soren, Marta, Jason . . ." When Sulbertson said nothing further, she continued. "Soren was shoog. The Little Boy. Clever, playful. He liked having fun."

Sulbertson nodded and looked off. "I remember him saying, 'If you can't have a good time, what's the point?' " He gave her a sharp glance. "Do you think Soren would have snuck on board DuBois's plane?"

Jacinta laughed. "He'd've been up the ladder before The Man was down."

A white grin against his dark face. "Yeah. *He* would have. I was surprised that *you* did. I remember you crushed on him right off."

Resentment stirred; honesty quenched it. "I never admitted that, even to myself." There, the words were out now, poor, helpless things struggling on the table. And what did they say about her?

"He was hurt, a little, when you blew him off," Sulbertson continued. "But he was rubber. He bounced. Told the rest of us you were just shy." Then, in a more serious tone, "I don't think he ever knew you'd done it on purpose."

Jacinta felt the blood rush to her cheeks and looked down at the nondescript carpet. "I was alone. I was trying to be careful."

"Being too careful can seem uncaring. What about Marta Molnar? The Hungarian girl."

"I barely spoke with her. She seemed lonely. The Waif. Out of place. Like she didn't belong."

"And so most in need of a friendly voice? Never mind. What's done is done. We all feel out of place, time to time. I guess I don't need to ask your impression of Jason."

"Macho-man," she said. "Swaggering, absolutely sure of himself, and gung ho about everything."

Sulbertson grunted. "Those aren't necessarily bad traits, you know. And not," giving her a curious, lopsided grin, "necessarily masculine."

Jacinta wasn't sure what he meant. "It doesn't matter," she said. "They might have been God's Chosen or they might have crawled out from under rocks. The thing is, they never had the chance. And do you know the worst part?"

Sulbertson straightened. "I'm curious what you think that is."

"The worst part is, I missed that plane *because I screwed up.* If I had done everything *right,* I'd be dead now, too." Jacinta stood and walked across his room where she stared, not out the window at the bright March afternoon, but at the bare cement cinderblocks that made the blank wall. "We'd both be."

"It's a hell of a thing," Sulbertson admitted, "to owe your survival to a lapse of attention."

Jacinta turned her head. "We're training here to do everything right."

"And so?"

"And so, I want to do something wrong. For them."

"It won't bring them back."

"I know that. Do you want to help me do something really stupid?"

They met on the commons at five in the morning, still dark enough for cover, but with a blush of false dawn along the crests of the eastern hills. Impossibly starred, the desert night lay crisp and clear above her. A few high horsetails were pale riders against the jewelled backdrop. The moon brooded at three-quarters, with Saturn trailing below and to the right. Farther up the ecliptic, Jupiter gleamed white just above Spica. Jacinta traced a line between the two and followed it down toward the horizon. There. Just to the right of that peak. She marked it in her mind.

Yungduk Morrisey coughed and shifted his stance, drawing her attention. He glanced nervously about, one hand running up and down the coil of rope hanging on his shoulder. Alonzo Sulbertson might have been a statue. He partook something of the night, in his complexion, in his stillness; so that sometimes Jacinta had to look twice to be sure he was there. Never a question, never an objection. Just a nod of the head. Yungduk had worried and fretted, raised objections and cautions. So, who was the truer friend?

"Let's get it on," Jacinta said, striding toward the base of *Ad Astra*.

"You could get in big trouble for this," Yungduk said. "Superman expelled Wilcox last December after he got stuck halfway up."

"I won't get stuck," Jacinta told him. "You with me on this?"

Yungduk sighed and unshipped his rope. He clipped the end to Jacinta's belt harness. "I won't let you down."

Jacinta smiled and placed a hand on his shoulder. "But that's your job. If I slip off, you let me down with the rope."

Yungduk studied the faerie arc, glowing faintly in the fading night. "Too high to throw a grapple, or you could climb straight up."

"That wouldn't be right." She turned to the silent Sulbertson. "Isn't that right, Lonzo?"

The middie shrugged. "I'm not sure 'right' enters into it." He laid his own rope out and stood with the clip in his hand. "Whenever you're ready, Rosario."

Jacinta pulled a pair of heavy gloves from her belt and tugged them on. Then she approached the bubbled mass that formed the base of the statue. Yungduk trailed behind her, while Lonzo positioned himself on the other side.

There were plenty of footholds here, in the undulating iron of the base. It was not unusual during the day to find cadets hunkered on various easy-to-reach roosts, reading, studying, or simply vejjing. Jacinta had scouted her route carefully the day before.

First, she clambered to the other side, where Lonzo handed her the clip for her other safety line, then her helmet with the attached night-goggles. "First part's the hardest," he told her in a low voice.

Jacinta turned and studied the nearly vertical column of smoked iron, rising nearly fifty feet before curving east. The artist had captured the turbulence of the plume in curls and flares and streamers. Surely, there would be handholds a plenty on the way up.

Sooner begun, sooner done. Jacinta positioned her night-vision goggles and stepped up to the base of the pillar. It towered above her, its faint phosphorescent glow gathered and amplified by the goggs into a pillar of fire. She reached up, found a hold, and began her ascent.

She had two shorter cables on her harness. Six feet up the column, she found a streamer of aerogel curled almost into a circle, and clipped the first cable to it. She tested it with her full weight. Nothing bent. She hadn't expected it to—aerogel was among the strongest materials made—but you never assumed.

Five feet later, she found another likely curl for the second line, attached it, then climbed down and disconnected the first and let it snake into its take-up reel. It made for slow climbing, but it also meant that she could never fall much more than her own body length.

The column plumed and twisted like a beanstalk. There was no shortage of cracks and holes and protrusions to give her footing. Life narrowed, focused tightly on the launch plume of *Ad Astra*. *This* projection; *that* recess. Foot goes *there*. She reached for a cup and, night goggles or no, was deceived. It was only a chance shadow. She found no purchase, slipped, and swung down and backward on her safety line. For a moment, she seemed to be soaring through the empty air itself before she came up, hard, against the iron aerogel.

The impact drove the breath from her and she spent a few moments sucking it back. An anxious voice from below asked if she was all right. She waved Yungduk to silence. "I'm fine," she stage-whispered. "Don't wake up the dorms."

She wasn't entirely fine. She'd have one nice collection of bruises come morning. Taking stock, she found nothing worse. It was always the little things that tripped you up. When your actions became automatic. She gripped her safety line to climb back and noticed she was dangling out of plumb. She had not fallen *down* the column, but *away* from it.

She was on the arc now. Not quite parallel to the ground, but no longer vertical. Somehow, she had managed to work her way to the side and had nearly slipped off. She pulled herself back onto the contrail and luxuriated for a moment in straddling it. She felt as if she could stand up and walk the rest of the way.

Of course, that wouldn't be bone; it'd be bump. Even with Yungduk and Lonzo holding the safety ropes and using the arc itself as a pulley to belay a fall, it would not only spoil the grandeur of the gesture, but it would be a foolish chance that she didn't need to take.

The arc was curiously foreshortened. The plume grew sharply narrower as it went forward. From the ground, it looked as if it were still climbing, an artifice of the designer. "Cute," Jacinta murmured.

Carefully, Jacinta crept forward on her hands and knees. On the ground, Yungduk and Lonzo tracked her, playing out enough slack that the ropes did not pull on her, but holding tight in case she did slip and fall. Soon, the sculpture had narrowed enough that she had to straddle it. With the curls and plumes and other irregularities, that was decidedly uncomfortable.

Only when she had neared the tip did she dare to glance at her watch. After six? She'd been climbing for over an hour. *Time flies when you're having fun.* Regulation sunrise was pegged at oh-six-fifty-five, and the sky behind the mountains was already brightening into sheets of red and pearl. *De facto* sunrise would lag by a minute or two, because of the ragged horizon.

"Can you see it yet?" Yungduk whispered from below.

"A little farther," she told him. Lonzo said nothing. Perhaps he was incurious.

Breezes, awakened by the coming sun, coasted down from the Tehachapi Mountains and whipped the gypsum of the high desert. Alkaline dust tickled Jacinta's nose. The arc swayed a little, but not much. It was too slender, had too many holes, to offer much wind resistance. Jacinta clipped both her safety cables to the span and inched forward on her belly.

At the tip, the aerogel swelled into a ball that teasingly enveloped the figure there. A flare here; a curl there. From no angle could you get a full view of the golden ship.

Except, she saw, from over top.

Her gasp was lost in the birdsong that greeted the coming dawn.

Not a space ship, after all, but a woman, like a figurehead on an old sailing ship. She was slim and nude, of shining gold, attached to the towering plume by the merest toe tips, as if she had just now dived forward into the sun. Arms were stretched out before her, hands reaching. Wings sprouted and flared from her back, lending her grace and motion. Her face, upturned toward the morning.

Jacinta brushed tears off her cheeks. To find such an exquisite figure here, in this place, in that pose, fully visible only to someone who had done what she had done . . . There was an unexpected beauty in it that transcended the mere craftsmanship of the casting itself. When she pulled the camera disc from her pocket and aimed it at the soaring woman, Jacinta found her hand trembling.

The face, she thought, looked a lot like that poet, Roberta Carson. Odd, to think of the somber, older woman in the deliberately side-street clothing as having once been young and naked with her lips curled back in yearning before an artist's camera.

She shuttered the disc without taking a digital image. She was cheating Yungduk and Lonzo, she knew. Giving them a graphic was part of the deal. She hesitated only a moment longer before dropping the camera and letting a calculated *damn* escape her lips.

The other part of the deal, the one she had made not with Sulbertson so much as with others, she could carry out. Opening her shirt pocket, she unfolded a utility knife and looked for a reasonably flat surface. But when she tried scratching letters into the aerogel, the blade made hardly a mark.

She found a plate near the foot of the statuette, apparently of softer metal, because there was something scratched into it. A plaque, hidden away also? She turned her goggs on it and saw that several sets of initials had been scratched there. Most of them she didn't recognize; but "NN"? Surely Noëlle Nieves, the outgoing cadet colonel, hadn't crawled up here her bunny year . . . And what about that "AS"? Jacinta looked down from her perch at the shadowy figure holding her safety rope. Alonzo Sulbertson had been remarkably incurious about what was affixed to the tip of *Ad Astra*.

Okay, so she never imagined that, in the ten years the academy had been in existence, she would be the first to successfully scale the arc . . .

It was awkward, but she managed to scratch the letters into the plate.

Instead of her own initials, she wrote, *For those who fell along the way.*

Afterward, she sat and waited.

Only a few stars were left—the bright ones that could brazen it out for a short while. There was Altair, above and a few degrees left of the peak at which the woman seemed to be aimed. And above that, near the top of its nightly arc, Vega.

Our destination. In a sense. The Earth, the Sun, the Moon, the whole kit and kaboodle were heighing off in that direction. She turned her face toward Vega and willed herself to feel the motion, as if she were on the bow of a ship, cutting through the waves of the æther at twelve miles per second. *Another 450,000 years and we'll be there.* She laughed at the thought.

Maybe the arc of *Ad Astra* ought to be aimed at Vega, instead.

A brilliant diamond rose above the hills, ten degrees left of the notch. Venus. Morning Star. Jacinta sighed.

First things first.

Ten minutes later, dawn poured through the notch in the hills and turned the golden woman to brilliant flame.

Forrest Calhoun wasn't omniscient or anything; but he did a damn good imitation of it. Somehow, he was standing by the base of *Ad Astra* when Jacinta slid down the safety rope to land at Yungduk's feet. She had already clipped the ends of the two ropes together, and now she and Yungduk and Lonzo hauled until they had pulled the second rope over the arc. The loose end came coiling down like an attacking snake and the cadets scattered, laughing, to get out from under, and that what how Jacinta found herself face-to-face with the superintendent.

"Good morning, Mr. Calhoun," she said brightly, coming to a sharp salute. She stifled a giggle. Not at all *de rigeur.* And then, because she refused to believe in coincidences, "What are you doing here?"

"The usual answer," Mr. Calhoun replied, "is that everybody gotta be somewhere."

Yungduk had come up beside her, coiling a rope but pausing long enough to squeeze her arm. She couldn't see Lonzo, but felt his presence behind her. She refused to acknowledge the trembling within her.

"You knew I'd be climbing that thing, sir. Didn't you?"

Calhoun nodded, once.

"How'd you—" Suspicion struck like a knife. She whirled and looked at Sulbertson, whose expression didn't change from its perpetual languor. He shook his head briefly. "Not me." A simple glance at Yungduk's fatalistic expression exonerated him. He was waiting for the axe to fall, but he wouldn't move from her side. She wondered, suddenly, if that was what love was. She turned back to Mr. Calhoun and let the memory of the question do.

"Wonderful stuff, MEMS," Calhoun said. "Remember how they used it on

Kitmann's arm for feedback? They adapted that from pressure sensitive warning systems on propeller blades, VR models' body stockings, and other equipment. Any force that distorts the stored configuration beyond the specified range sets off an alarm."

Jacinta stared past Mr. Calhoun at the plume of *Ad Astra*. MEMS? She hadn't noticed them. But then, the first M stood for microscopic, didn't it? Not on the base. Too many cadets used it too casually. But the column. Places where climbers would put their feet, or hold on with their hands. Her glance at Sulbertson was accusatory. If those *had* been his initials on the plate at the tip, then he had to know about the warning system.

But accusations rolled off him. He simply shrugged once more and continued coiling up the rope. He knew, but hadn't warned her. Was that why he had agreed to accompany her? Just to see her expelled? But that made no sense. He had put himself at risk, as her accomplice. And if he had climbed the arc two years ago . . .

She addressed Mr. Calhoun. "You knew, but you didn't stop me."

"You looked to be doing all right," the superintendent allowed.

It was wrong to tempt the fates, but she had to ask. "Aren't I being expelled, sir?"

Calhoun's smile was fleeting. His glance flickered once over her shoulder to Sulbertson. "Should you be?"

"Stupid chances? Climbing at night?"

Calhoun didn't answer her directly. Instead, he checked the fastenings on her harness, the helmet straps, the night vision goggles. "Climbing gear," he said. "Two friends standing safety. What test is the rope?"

"Uh. Eighty-pound drop test. Climbing rope from the stores shed."

He nodded. "And how did you figure how much you'd need?"

"Basic trig, sir. Measured my shadow and the monument's shadow. Kitchen arithmetic."

"So, Ms. Rosario, we don't expel our cadets for taking risks. Taking risks will be part of your job description when you're done here. *Stupid* risks, that's another story. If you had gone up there alone . . . Or without adequate gear and preparation . . . Or even just out of a macho desire to show off . . . Well, Lonzo wouldn't have let you get that far; or Matusek and Izquierdo would have stepped in before you were ten feet up the shaft." Jacinta looked around for the two physical training instructors, but Calhoun said, "I dismissed them. Mr. Morrisey?"

Yungduk said, "Yes, sir?" in a small voice.

"You tried to talk Ms. Rosario out of this attempt."

He didn't bother asking how he knew. "Yes, sir."

"When she didn't take your advice, why didn't you call it quits and head back to the dorm?"

"Sir?" Yungduk frowned and his glance darted from one face to the other. It might have been the rose of dawn that made his face so ruddy. "Sir, I don't walk out on a friend."

"Even when she's doing something you think is stupid?"

"Sir. Especially then."

Calhoun grunted. "You'll make a hell of a first officer when Rosario here is captain."

"Sir. With all due respect, you have that backwards."

Calhoun's laugh was a rumbling bass. "God help me. You remind me of a polite version of Ned DuBois. Okay." He clapped his hands. "Mr. Sulbertson, clear the area. We don't want any early risers realizing what went down and getting dumb ideas. It's Monday morning, and cadets are especially stupid after a weekend. Ms. Rosario, stay with me for a moment."

Yungduk and Lonzo had already coiled the ropes. Now they took the helmet, goggles and harness from Jacinta and hurried off. Jacinta waited. The breeze freshened. Birds gave throat. In the distance, in the gap between Gagarin and Grissom Halls, an early morning jogger made a brief but earnest appearance. Calhoun coughed, folded his arms, and seemed to hunt for words. Finally— "What . . . did she look like?"

It wasn't a question Jacinta had been expecting. She studied his face. He was gazing off at the tip of the arc.

"Sir? She's the most beautiful woman I've ever seen. I don't mean fashion-beauty, but . . ."

"I understand." He drew a long breath. "If these bones of mine weren't so old . . ."

"You could use a cherry-picker, or a bo'sun chair." But he shook his head.

"That wouldn't be right."

"If you want," she offered with mischief in her voice, "I could run back up and doid a graphic for you."

The laugh was explosive. "You'd do it, too. Thank you, but . . . No, thanks." He tapped the noccs that dangled from his neck. "I saw you drop the camera disc on purpose, and I think you were right. A glimpse of Star of the Morning . . . That has to be earned." He clapped his hands together, rubbed them, turned suddenly gruff. "Well, morning sessions will be starting shortly, and you have to get ready. Bounce, Rosario! Oh, and I don't need to mention that this episode mustn't be discussed."

Jacinta shook her head and began to turn away, but Mr. Calhoun stopped her again.

"One last thing. If you ever do that calculation with the ratios of shadows and heights . . . ? Be careful. You might cast a longer shadow than you think."

On the jog back to her dorm, in a hasty shower and an even hastier breakfast, lost in the intricacies of Hohmann transfer orbits, she could not puzzle out what he meant.

21.

Common Cause

April was a month for new beginnings. Flowers broke above the earth. Birds returned from far-off climates. Fawns peeked hesitantly from the edge of the treeline. Old houses shut down; new ones opened. Possibilities emerged. And restless asteroids came 'round the sun.

Silverpond was bustling chaos. There were a thousand details involved in deeding it over to the new Conservancy Trust that the Van Huyten Trust and The People's Crusades had set up. Naturalists prowled the grounds, inventorying habitats and startling the fauna. Contractors prowled the house, planning renovations and startling the staff. Astronomers evaluated the rooftop observatory—though the stars, so far as Mariesa could tell, were not startled. The sale was not yet posted with the county clerk, but in some indefinable fashion the house was no longer entirely hers.

There were furnishings to dispose of. Silverpond had accumulated decor for a hundred years. Some of it would stay—drapes, carpets and the like—some of it would go. The ballroom portraits were destined for VHI headquarters, to join old Henryk at last in a sort of oil-on-canvas family reunion. Conrad's rare books would go to the university library at Rutgers. She would keep some things, give others to her cousins. But what was one to do with the hand-set bowling lane-cum-speakeasy that Gramper had, in a fit of Old Dutch romanticism, installed in the first sublevel back in the Twenties?

Roberta was coordinating the transfer for the Crusades. In her condition, the frequent commutes to Washington would be tiring. That gave her excuse enough to move into one of the long-disused spare bedrooms. On weekends, Phil joined her, and they and Mariesa often dined together. SkyWatch would obtain possession of the rooftop observatory under a sublease, so George Krishnarahman frequently stayed over, too, rather than fly back and forth to Phoenix. Since everyone frequently brought lawyers in tow, and the naturalists and the contractor and her people were often underfoot as well, Silverpond was more densely inhabited than at any time since Mariesa's distant childhood.

Mariesa, Roberta, and the contractor were discussing renovations over lunch on the veranda—and what would Mummy have thought of dining with the hired help?—when Armando bent over her shoulder to tell her that Charlie

Schwar was waiting for her in the library. She made her excuses to the others and hurried to meet him.

Schwar was a tall, square-faced man whose unruly mass of white hair gave him an old sheepdog look. A detective lieutenant on the Philadelphia police force for nineteen years before Chris had hired him to head up Cerberus Security, he had made a national reputation as a finder of missing persons. One year, he had located nearly three hundred runaway children on Market Street, largely through personal intuition. *They can change their location*, he once said of runaways, *but they can't change their habits.* Someone who *is* out of place *looks* out of place. Mariesa thought his skills largely wasted in administration, but that call was for Chris and Charlie to make between them. In any event, he had jumped at the task Mariesa had given him. The old war horse heareth the trumpet and paweth the ground and saith, Ha-ha!

Schwar was standing by one of the bookcases, reading the spines—a detective's curiosity, Mariesa supposed. When she entered, he turned and waited for her to be seated. He himself remained standing while he spoke, pacing sometimes back and forth and making odd motions with his hands that Mariesa eventually realized were those of a smoker who no longer smoked.

"What did you find for me?" she asked him.

"I had to bend a few rules here and there," Schwar cautioned her. "Nothing felonious, but there could be heavy fines if it came out."

Mariesa nodded. He was giving her the opportunity to avoid becoming an "accomplice after." "It's just for my personal knowledge," she said. "Nothing to be made public."

Schwar grunted and removed a flippad from his pocket, activating the screenlet with his ring stylus. "Okay, here's the skinny. Adam van Huyten worked for Ed Wilson on SpaceLab IV for a couple of months after his . . . After he left VHI. Helped out in blow-molding and, ummm, crystallography. Apparently, he's a fairly skilled mechanic." Surprise, that a rich man could do useful work. "Then he quit and lived the life of Riley. Officially."

"And unofficially?"

Schwar looked at her carefully. "This part is a judgement call. A hunch. Nineteen years on the street, sherlocking kids who are trying to get small, you learn when to play a hunch." He looked at his pad again and scrolled a page. "I was showing his face around and this one guy, a welder named Littlebear, goes how he never saw him before but he does looks a lot like a guy he worked with up on Goddard Free Port. Okay, so that rings a bell with an old fart like me excuse the language, and I ask him to describe the second dude. So, he does. Short hair. Different color eyes. A scar on the cheek. After a while, Littlebear talks himself out of it. Not the same guy at all. But my head, it's going ding-a-ling. You know what I mean?"

"Yes, I know what you mean. Who was the second man?"

"He calls himself David Desherite."

"Dezhuright?" Schwar spelled it for her and she laughed and pronounced it correctly. "That's French for 'disinherited.' I think your intuition is marvelous."

Schwar grunted. "So. Who was this 'Desherite' supposed to be?" He stressed the pronunciation and Mariesa wondered if he had taken her correction amiss. "I checked passenger manifests for SSTO lifts. He goes up; he comes down. Then he's on FreeFall resort. Wilson stuff. Just another otter; one of the guys."

"Why?" asked Mariesa.

Schwar looked up from his notepad. "Not ready for 'why,' yet. If I had to guess, I'd say he was getting his space legs, building some credibility, establishing a presence. And scouting out opportunities."

"Opportunities. For what?" Revenge, Roberta had told her at the funeral. From orbit? A sudden vision of a maniacal Adam hurling rocks down on VHI headquarters . . .

Schwar shrugged. He resumed scrolling. "I don't make him again until late last October, when he goes up to LEO—"

"LEO!"

"Yeah. Klon-Am country." That, in a knowing voice. "This time he's repping for some outfit calling itself Baleen—"

"Baleen?" Where had she heard that name before? Sometime recently, she was sure. Perhaps an investment in mariculture?

"Yeah," said Schwar. "Baleen. Supposedly he goes to LEO to check out the facilities, but bonebagging's not the most cost-effective way to do that, especially for a little start-up what isn't even on the web. So, I figure he goes to meet someone."

"Who?"

Schwar grinned and pulled an envelope from his jacket pocket. "I don't know where this came from," he said with a knowing smile, "but it's a list of everyone who was on Leo for at least part of the time Adam was there."

She read down the list. Faceless names, for the most part. She had met Shary once, but none of the other OMC people; and the Energia, Boeing, NASA, and other personnel were just names. Except one. Schwar smiled when she glanced up.

"Yes," he said. "Dr. Leland Hobart, from Argonaut Labs. One of the lab's biggest guns just happens to be on board LEO when his old boss shows up . . . My people asked around, and it seems this Hobart was a big fan of your nephew, from before. He went up, according to Deshpande, to work some sort of special project."

None of this was making sense. Was Hobart, too, conspiring with Klon-Am? But VHI companies, including Argonaut, rented volume on LEO. LEO Station might not be the only game in town, but there weren't all that many others. Perhaps Hobart did have an experiment aboard. Yet, what would that prove? Visiting his experiment could as easily have been an *excuse* for the trip as a *reason*. "What about Baleen? Did you check that out?"

Schwar gave her a teach-your-grandmother-to-suck-eggs look. "Not much," he said after another scroll. "My guess is, it's a virtual company. A small group of partners playing the key roles: planning, design, and the like, with everything else contracted out. I found a set of Baleen cargo manifests. Aerogel equipment lifted to Goddard Free Port just before Christmas, with some guy named Mercado hired to install it. I nosed around some with the OEM—acted like I was thinking of buying—and he told me two other sets of equipment had been built to the same specs, so I chased them down, too. One was gathering dust in a bonded warehouse in Leipzig. The manager there says it had a BOL to lift to LEO, but it kept getting postponed until just after Adam returned from LEO. Then it went up, with a Baleen guy name of Hawkins to babysit until the hand-off to LEO's staff."

"What are they making with the aerogel?" Mariesa wondered aloud. Whatever was going on, it didn't sound like mariculture.

"They've been lifting biocartridges to both the LEO and Goddard sites. BOLs read Kari Wincock, Pharmer. Probably another partner."

"I see. And the third set of equipment?"

Schwar shrugged. "Different customer. Cheetah Enterprises in . . ." A quick check of his scrolldex. ". . . in Kuala Lumpur. Just took delivery from the OEM. No connection to Baleen."

Mariesa sat silently trying to fit the unfittable together. Finally, she said, "And Jimmy Poole?"

Schwar shook his head. "No one gets a handle on the Wizard of Baud. Hardly ever leaves his house, and cybersleuthing *that* dude is out of the question. So what he's doing with Adam, I draw a blank."

Mariesa sighed. Discovering what Jimmy and Adam were up to together had been the whole point of going to Schwar. "I understand . . ." she started to say; but Schwar held up his hand.

"Not so fast. Front door's locked, there's always the back."

"What do you mean?"

"I sent a couple of my guys to stroke some of these Baleens."

"Not Adam!"

"No, not him. Not Poole, either. But the two riggers, Hawkins and Mercado, and the pharmer, Wincock. Now, before you ask; we really do know what we're doing at Cerberus; so, no, we didn't 'grill' them. We're talking about strangers-in-a-bar yacking over some beers. That kind of interrogation."

Mariesa nodded. "I see. What did you find out?"

"The usual. Nobody knows nothing." He laughed and Mariesa gave him a patient look. "Yeah. We laid some boon companions on them. Hawkins thinks he was talking to a 'sheila' from Brisbane who's gone 'otter space.' Just the sort he'd open up to; except he didn't. Wincock is a big, hairy guy, wears goofball, but he's sweet on unshaved chickens, so—"

Mariesa said, "I don't need to know this." Schwar gave her a silent look. Every professional liked inside neep and he'd been just starting to roll.

He closed his note pad. "All right. Bottom line is Kiersten—that's the sheila—thought Hawkins was surprised when she mentioned the other Baleen facility, the one that Mercado was running on Goddard. But as to what they're blowing aerogel for, and what's in those biocanisters, everyone imitated a giraffe."

Mariesa blinked. She couldn't not ask. "A giraffe?"

"No voicebox." Schwar chuckled. "Except, these guys, they didn't stick their necks out, either."

The humor was too much for the ex-detective. Mariesa waited for him to compose himself before she spoke. "Is that all?"

Schwar wiped an eye. "One last thread—and this one's the puzzler. I figure, if I can't get at Poole straight out, maybe I can learn something checking out his wife and his domestic staff. As far as the cook, the gardener, the babysitter, and the rest, nothing. But this Tanuja Pandya babe, that's different. She and Poole must be one fun couple, because she don't go out much, either. Writing a new book, they say. Then, last February, out of the blue, she flies off to Milwaukee."

Mariesa cocked an eyebrow. "Milwaukee?"

"Yeah. Hot tourist spot, right? Maybe she's hip for goofball music—wears lumberjack hats and checked flannel shirts; but I don't think so. Then again, five weeks ago, she jets off to Paris. I play a hunch and run down the passenger list. Sure enough there's a name from Milwaukee: Billie Whistle. So maybe she has a boy friend on the side . . . ?"

"No," said Mariesa. "Billie's a woman."

Schwar gave her a stole-my-thunder look. "You know this Whistle?" he said with accusation in his voice, as if she herself had now become a suspect in his investigation.

"Billie was a student at one of Belinda Karr's schools and a guest at Silverpond a few years ago. But how does she . . . ? Oh!"

Schwar poised his stylus over his notescreen. "Oh," he suggested.

"I just remembered. At Mother's funeral. Belinda mentioned that Billie was a partner in Baleen."

Schwar nodded and pursed his lips while he ran his ring down the slot in the pad. "It fits," he said. "How it fits, I don't know; but these factoids are coming together. Okay. I check out Whistle. We have the accident, the rehab, the grant from Opportunities Unlimited, the encephalo-training . . . ?" He glanced at her and she waved him on. "Okay. According to neighbors, this Whistle never left her apartment in three years until five weeks ago—then does she go to the corner grocery? No, she goes off to Paris with Pandya. Wait, it gets better. They're in Paris for a week and never charge a room or a meal?"

"Or they used assumed names."

Schwar smiled, as if she had passed a not-too-difficult test. "Right. It's awful hard to get into the EU with a phony name on your passport; but once you're there, you can call yourself Abraham-freaking-Lincoln if you have enough cash. So my guess is they went to Paris 'on the record,' then went somewhere else 'off the record.' They came back a week later, touched home bases; then vanished again. The keyword search engine comes back—no airplane tickets in either name. No bus or train tickets, either; and you gotta admit, their names aren't exactly Smith and Jones."

"Bottom line?"

"Bottom line is that Whistle is running an op for Poole and Pandya is their go-between. They go places where no one's supposed to know they went there. If we'd gotten that national ID card like they wanted back in the nineties 'for health care,' you wouldn't have people sneaking around like that. Whatever Adam and Baleen are up to, it involves Leo or the virtch; or both. Adam and Hobart on Leo; Poole and Whistle gaming the virtch. I nosed around but nothing's gone down big that I can find, either place. A few hobos rousted from classified deebies. A couple of attempted system break-ins, at NASA-Marshall and the Chicago Board of Trade. A rumor that someone tossed a bit-bomb at a hacker safe-house. Just the usual stuff. Nothing that ties to Baleen or this Whistle person."

Mariesa nodded slowly. "I see." It was less than she'd hoped for, but more than she'd expected. The tantalizing state of half-knowing. "You have a summary report for me?"

Schwar handed her a μCD. "Do you mind if I ask what this is all about?" He struck an assertive stance. He had rolled over some rocks for her and wanted to know why. Mariesa reminded herself that he was head of security for VHI and probably regarded Adam as a security risk. If the black sheep of the family was up to something, he wanted to know what it was, in case it was aimed at VHI. Mariesa sighed. She wanted to know, too.

"I was hoping you'd tell me." It might be that Baleen was nothing more than Adam making a new start and the secrecy, Schwar's suspicious notwithstanding, no more than protection for proprietary information. She turned the μCD Schwar had given her around and around as she thought. For the life of her, she couldn't see anything in Baleen's activities that made it an instrument of Adam's revenge on his father. One of its facilities was aboard LEO; but so were several of VHI's. For the first time, she wondered if the "revenge" Roberta had overheard had related to someone other than Chris and VHI. But, who? Klon-Am? Someone within Baleen? There was something about that second installation . . . If Hawkins really had been surprised, did that mean there was double dealing? Perhaps she should have Cheetah investigated, as well.

She would never be able to armchair this puzzle. She had no reason to suspect Adam of anything, either; only what Roberta had overheard. "Do you have any recommendations?"

"Yeah." Schwar tucked the note pad back in his jacket pocket. "When Adam lifted as David Desherite, he had to go through a Facemaker to get ID'd. How come it didn't kick his name out?"

Mariesa frowned. "Someone tampered with the master dataface . . . ?"

"Could be; and they tell me there aren't a lot of virtchuosos who could do that. But if I were you, I'd have someone talk to Ed Wilson."

The spinnaker ran up its halyards and, catching the warm Caribbean wind, blossomed like a great flower. The *Rita Marie* heeled over hard to port and Mariesa grabbed hold of the taffrail to keep her balance. Ed Wilson cranked the windlass two-handed. His man gave a half turn to the wheel and the ship eased off and settled into a steady, mile-eating flight down Tongue of the Ocean. The prow sliced cleanly through the waves, raising a fine mist; so that shortly Mariesa's blouse and shorts were damp with the spray, and her hair hopelessly ravelled by the wind.

Piet used to sail in an old ketch he had bought at salvage and refurbished with loving care. *Catch as Catch Can.* Mariesa sometimes wondered if his choice of vessel had been dictated by his choice of a name. He kept her at a marina in a shore town called Lovelady, named after an old Dutch sea captain and not, as the young Mariesa had romanced, after a beautiful woman. "Lovely Lady," she had called it until learning better. *Papa and I are going to see a lovely lady.* And who knew? Perhaps there had been one down there. Harriet had gone to sea only under duress—she hated the bobbing and the damp and the cold—but there had been one year when she had accompanied them several times running. Looking back, Mariesa thought she had been playing chaperone.

Piet would have made a fine playboy. He enjoyed sunshine and good drink and the company of pleasant tongues and bodies. He had backed several plays on and off-Broadway. His dinner guests dazzled and amazed. But most of all, he was a yachtsman. Sailing had been the only times that Mariesa could remember when her father had not been, so to speak, three sheets to the wind.

But Piet had never ventured too far to sea; nor too far from the bottle, and that was why, though Ed Wilson reminded her so of Piet in his enthusiasm for the water, she had always regarded him warily—neither ally nor enemy, but only a force to be reckoned with.

Rita Marie made the headland out of Kemps Bay and raised Big Wood Cay. Around her, ships danced on the waters—yawls out of Aruba; sloops come down from Grand Bahama; schooners, ketches, brigantines, a gaudy mix of sails ghosting silently with the steady breeze. Motor vessels threaded them retrograde with insolent ease and impertinent noise. Here and there, the behemoth yachts of the ostentatious rode on their sea anchors. A cruise ship, deck layered upon deck, steamed proudly north toward the Providence Channel.

The wind raised a light chop on the turquoise waters, tearing small drops from the crests and giving everything a salty, dank aroma of seaweed and water and fish. Wilson joined her at the rail, crossing the deck with the easy, rolling gait of a seaman, and handed her a hurricane glass containing one of his noxious, fruity drinks. It lacked only a paper umbrella. She had made the mistake one time of telling him she liked these concoctions, and politeness had metamorphosed somehow into obligation.

Forward, in the bow pulpit, Wayne Coper chatted amiably with Wilson's wife. Liliana was a small, dark woman half Wilson's years; but Ed was at an age when he needed to believe himself young. So was Wayne, who esteemed anything young and curved and feminine. A love of sun on Liliana's part and a minimum of clothing to block its warmth was simply a bonus. If Wilson harbored any reservations about the two huddled in the bow, he failed to show it. Yet, while he chatted with Mariesa, his own gaze seldom left his wife for long.

"You see there?" Wilson asked, pointing with his drink toward the line of Great Guana Cay a little way off toward the east. "See how the water changes color? There's fourteen hundred meters under our keel here in the Tongue. Over there, it's five meters—and it sounds just like that." A snap of his fingers, followed by a sip of fruited rum. "The sea," Wilson went on. "Just a lot of water with salt added, right? But it's as varied as the land to a practiced eye. It looks different. Smells different. It even tastes different." He turned to his coxswain. "Isn't that right, Master Sheffield?"

White teeth split the Islandman's broad face. "No bassa-bassa. Taste enough of it, fallin' overboard."

Wilson laughed and made a sign to the Bajan. "There are rivers in the ocean," he continued to Mariesa. "Even hills and valleys, if you know how to look. The water dips and rises as it rolls over seamounts and chasms—and the temperature changes with salinity and what have you, so it expands or contracts locally. A good seaman can study the waves and the spray and the fish running past and pretty much tell you—"

"How did you and Adam get on while he worked for you?"

Wilson paused at the sudden interruption and regarded her in silence for a long beat. He checked the sails, and the wake; checked his wife. He raised his glass to his lips and drank. "Yeah," he said, lowering the glass. "Yeah, we got on okay."

"Was it his idea or yours for him to adopt a *nom d'espace?*"

Wilson grunted. "You know about that? I thought he was on the outs with the rest of you."

"He and Chris fought."

"From what I heard, that's a considerable understatement." He stood away from the taffrail and wrapped an arm around a shroud for support. " 'Nom d'espace,' " he said. "I like that. It was his idea. My people helped him set it up."

"Why?"

"Why? So he could be a good little otter. What would it be like for him going around up there with a 'van Huyten' hanging off the south end of his name?"

"Just for incognito? Nothing more?"

Wilson looked at her. "Why should there be more?"

"Oh . . ." Mariesa waved an airy hand. A matter of no great importance, the fingers lied. "He's used it since."

Wilson tasted from his drink again; stared into the nearly empty bowl. "Maybe he liked being David more than he liked being Adam."

"Because David slew Goliath?"

Wilson chuckled. "2 Samuel," he said. "21:19."

Mariesa shook her head. "I don't understand."

"Sounding!" called the sailing master. "Fourteen-and-fifty!"

"Steady as she goes, Master," Wilson replied. He grinned with the unfeigned delight of a small boy. "I love this," he said. "I don't get down here enough. Today, fun in the sun. Next week, dickering with the Panch'en Lama over an orbital ram site. Shigatse is no picnic at any time of year and there are no flies on the Lama when it comes to the dime. Trouble is, you keep looking for the hand inside that makes him wiggle his arms. But the Roof of the World is such a grand place for a ram . . ." He took her glass. "Here, let me freshen that for you."

She followed him belowdecks into the master suite, where he went behind the bar and pulled out a clean glass. Mariesa sat on a padded bench against the cabin wall. "Just some white wine."

"Any particular vintage?"

"Industrial grade is fine."

He handed her a tall wine glass. "Why the interest in Adam?"

"He was with you for two years."

"Near enough."

"Why did he leave?"

Wilson pursed his lips and studied her narrowly. "I liked the guy," he said. "He had fire. Groundside, he was in the office weekends and into the evenings. He threw off ideas like a string of Chinese firecrackers. He wanted to *do* things, and—more important—he got others to want to do them, too. Most 'old money' just sits back and clips coupons, no offense. So if you're asking me, did I catch Adam diddling Wilson Enterprises and give him the boot, the answer is no. Your minor premise is wrong. I was sorry to see him go, but he had a deal that he wanted to shepherd and I had to respect that."

"I wasn't implying—"

"Of course not. But it seems to me you've never even questioned your major premise."

Mariesa stared out the porthole at the rolling waves. She did not understand Wilson's evident testiness. Unless . . . Could it be that a hard, practical man like Ed Wilson had fallen under Adam's magnetism? It seemed unlikely; yet, cynical old men had followed enthusiastic young ones before. Some of Alexander's generals had bounced him on their knees.

Wilson came up beside her. "He never spoke of his father," he said, "except with pity."

Mariesa's response was forestalled by her cell phone. "Excuse me," she said, and pressed the stud on her wrist strap. "Mariesa, here," she told the tracy. People called it that, she had heard, because the automatic link between 911 and the GPS meant that, in case of trouble, you could be "traced" by the nearest emergency response team. "Ed Wilson is with me." And that, in case the call was confidential. Wilson graciously crossed the cabin and perched on a stool by the bar, where he could pretend not to listen.

"Mariesa? Mariesa?" The voice was faint. "I can barely hear you. This is George."

George. It took her a moment to place him. The Arizona twang . . . "Oh, yes. George. Speak up. We have a bad channel."

"Can you come back?" the tinny voice asked her. "Right away?"

A request like that could never be good. George Krishnarahman hardly ever called her. Even appraising her rooftop observatory for the new educational center, he was sparing with his words. A host of scenarios chased through her mind. A fire. Robbery. Vandalism. Some problem with the courts or the tax authorities. Her fist tightened and she held the phone closer to her lips. "Has something happened at Silverpond?"

"I'm not at Silverpond. I'm in Washington. The commission wants to meet. Tomorrow. Can you be here?"

Now her fist was clenched so tightly the knuckles stood out white against her tan. "What is it, George?" Such precipitance did not sound like Solomon Dark.

"The sheep that was lost," Krishnarahman said, "is found again."

"The asteroid? 2004AS?"

"Yes."

"It *is* on a new orbit."

"Yes."

The ice had formed in her veins, but the words came out calm and reasonable. "Projection?"

"You had better come up right away."

Numb, she almost forgot to tell the phone to disconnect. George hadn't said a collision was forecast, but his evasion had confirmed the worst. When she looked up, Ed Wilson was biting his lip. He slid off the stool. "I'll tell the Master to turn us about."

"No," she said, laying a hand on his arm. "Drop me at Coakley Town and I'll hire a plane. I brought a change of clothing along for evening casual. That will suit me until I reach home. You can have my suitcases shipped back. Wayne will probably stay. This meeting doesn't concern him."

Wilson had taken a step toward the gangway, but paused. "I'd say it concerns all of us, wouldn't you? Whatever I can do . . . Just let me know."

This time she was not kept waiting. The White House guards had her badge ready and, after a pass through the μMRI scanner and a glance into the Face-maker to settle their nerves, she was escorted briskly through a series of sub-terranean tunnels and doors whose ups and downs and turns soon had her disoriented.

Solomon Dark was waiting in the meeting room, along with several mem-bers of the Extraordinary Commission and few others that Mariesa did not recognize. Dark stood at the far end of the room with his back to the doors and his hands clasped behind him, regarding the display on the broad pixwall: a lookdown view of the inner solar system on which small icons blinked along faint, pastel ellipses. He turned and saw Mariesa and nodded without speaking.

Unruffled. Mariesa took some vague comfort from that. Solomon Dark would show up for his own execution impeccably dressed and with shoes gleaming. She knew it was an affectation, that it was intended to have a calming effect; and it was spoiled only a little by the way the hands kept changing their grip on one another.

Mariesa found her name on a place card at the table. *M. van Huyten/VHI.* But that was wrong. She no longer held an official position at VHI. Her mem-bership on the Commission stemmed from her presidency of the Amateur Astronomical Association and its complimentary seat on SkyWatch. It wasn't like Solomon Dark to make an error of protocol. A portfolio lay open in front of her with a blank flatscreen and stylus. The covers were dark burgundy, padded, with metal caps on the corners. She closed it for a moment and saw embossed in gold on the front cover the letters NAPDC in a graceful script.

By ones and twos, others entered. Mariesa was waiting for Daryll Blessing, but George Krishnarahman appeared instead. "Daryll is ill," he whispered as he took a seat beside her. "He collapsed at his home last night."

Mariesa pursed her lips. "Will he be all right?" But George only shrugged.

"Why am I here?" she asked. "I am only an *ad hoc* member of the commis-sion . . ."

"Different commission."

Before she could ask the astronomer what he meant, the doors opened and admitted Phil Albright. Physically, he differed little from the last time Mariesa had seen him, two months ago; yet, his step was less steady and he leaned for support on the arms of Roberta Carson. It did not seem to Mariesa as if those arms were thick enough to support him, but they did.

Roberta walked with steel in her step, as if some of Phil's resiliant alloy had leached into her. Her face was flushed—perhaps at being in such an august setting—and a glow of contentment seemed to envelope her. Phil, once seated, helped her down. Roberta was on the opposite side of the table from Mariesa and three seats further toward the doors, but when Mariesa and she locked gazes for a moment, Roberta lifted her chin just a little and nodded.

Ed Bullock's entrance was the most unexpected of all, and from the look on his face, he was as puzzled as anyone else. At forty-two, his thin, delicate features had coarsened a little. He had lost the boyishness and the look of perpetual petulance and acquired in its place something of worry and maturity. His glance lingered briefly on Mariesa, and passed into a scowl when it reached Albright. But he unbuttoned his suit coat, tugged his vest, and took a chair near the foot of the table.

"I see we're all here," said Solomon Dark with a moment's consideration of his pocket watch. "So we may as well begin."

"All" included a few of the scientists from the commission; a Marine Corps general Mariesa recognized after a moment as the JCS chairman; the director of NASA; vice presidents from Boeing-MD, Lockheed-Martin, and Rockwell-Grumman; a short, gray-haired woman from the State Department; and the Director of FEMA. As the composition of the meeting sorted itself out in Mariesa's mind, she became steadily more afraid. She desperately wanted a drink to calm her nerves. A water glass sat before her place mat, but she feared to pick it up, lest she spill. She pressed her hands flat on the table until the knuckles stood out white.

"The President has asked me to brief you on the situation as we understand it. Some of you are already familiar with parts of it, but bear with us until we get everyone on the same page." Dark looked to Krishnarahman. "If you're ready . . . ?" At George's nod, he turned to a woman wearing a wireless skull-cap, who sat in one corner of the room surrounded by computer equipment. "Go ahead, Susan."

The woman did nothing that Mariesa could see, yet the lights dimmed and the pixwall reconfigured to a picture of the Earth floating in space, the famous "small blue planet" shot. The woman must be an encephalographic operator.

It was a dog and pony show. George covered the background on asteroid 2004AS and events of last December while the pixwall supported him with pixures, graphs, and brief film clips. It was old news; but Mariesa noted a few reminders and details on her pad. Others listened intently. Much of this they were hearing for the first time.

The Marine general interrupted. "Did you get any glimpse of the weapon inside the borehole?"

"It was an engine," said George, with a hint of disapproval. "Not a weapon."

The Marine snorted. "That's what weapons are, son. All depends on how you use 'em. Didn't see any evidence on your film clip, there"—he pointed to the wall, where a freeze frame showed a white-hot plume erupting from the west end of 2004AS—"that they checked whether the probe was manned or not before they vaporized it."

An uncomfortable moment of silence passed. Mariesa could see that some of the scientists itched to debate. It could have been an accident. A malfunction of a ten-thousand-year-old circuit. Yet what practical difference lay between accident, neglect, or design?

"We didn't get a look at the *engine*," Krishnarahman admitted. "But we did get an analysis of the gases—from a Chilean observatory that was watching the rendezvous through the Simon Bolivar Cooperative Orbital Array. The spectrum suggests the engine was burning iron."

"Iron!" That was Bullock.

George squinted to see who had spoken. "Yes. An oxy/iron propellant, at thirteen to one. I know it's a low specific impulse; but there's no shortage of fuel and no particular hurry." The scientists in the room chuckled, but Mariesa thought Bullock had been surprised less at using a low impulse fuel than at the idea of iron as a fuel at all. George began to say something about possible machinery to selectively ionize olivine and pyroxene to obtain both fuel and oxidizer, but Dark coughed peremptorily and the astronomer resumed the briefing.

George explained about the possible change of course and the long wait to reacquire the body, until earlier this month, when—

"How do you know it's the same asteroid?" asked the Lockheed VP. She brushed a lock of dark hair from her face. Her look was not quite defiance. It might have been the look of someone searching for a loophole. Everyone knew how many false alrms there had been over the decades. "It's just a dot of light, right?"

"It is very near the position we projected for 2004AS last December. Not quite," this with a scowl, "but very near. Either it's the same body or it's a terrible coincidence."

"Why 'terrible,' Doctor?" asked Phil Albright in a soft voice that demanded silence to be heard. He had steepled his fingers under his chin.

Krishnarahman hesitated and glanced at Dark, who gave him an under-the-table gesture that Mariesa interpreted as *Skip the rest of the briefing and cut to the chase*.

Krishnarahman took a deep breath. "Asteroid 2004AS will impact the Earth in six years. That is, unless no further course changes occur."

And that was why scientists could never quite mobilize the masses, Mariesa thought. They always qualified their statements. They could never let a ringing pronouncement stand without the brass clank of a "but" dragging behind it. Oddly, Mariesa felt no terror at the pronouncement so long dreaded, just a sort of numbness, as if everything were happening at a great distance. She held her hand level and saw not a tremble, so she reached for the water pitcher and poured herself a drink. When she set the pitcher down, she saw that Roberta had been watching her.

"Are you certain?" asked Bullock.

"Where will it hit?" asked JCS.

"How big is it?" asked Boeing.

"A water strike is most likely . . ." "Less damage . . ." "No, think of the tsunami and all that water vapor . . ." "Water vapor is the most efficient greenhouse gas . . ." "Yeah, but the dust plume would cut off sun . . ." "Another false alarm . . ." "What dust plume, if it hits the water . . . ?" Voice tumbled over voice, tripping, piling up into a heap until there were no words at all, only sound. A verbal tsunami created by the impact of the announcement. Through it all, only Mariesa and Roberta kept silent.

"People!" Solomon Dark raised his hands in an appeal for silence. "People! We have some material on likely scenarios that we want you to consider." When he had achieved a measure of attention, he gave the sign to continue with the briefing. When it was time for the last trump to blow, Mariesa supposed, there would be policy wonks to give briefings. They would prepare slides, perhaps design a logo. *The Last Days: America Prepares.* There would be speculations on the nature of the trumpet. (A cornet? A herald's horn?) On the tune to be played and the key it would play in. There would be profiles of Gabriel—background checks and likely scenarios.

And none of it would be of any use at all.

The American Planetary Defense Committee. That was the name Dark and Rutell had decided on, one of several regional and national groups being organized in the light of the new data. A committee to save the planet? The world was in deeper trouble than she had thought.

And yet, as the meeting wound on, she began to see Dark's wisdom. A great many ducks had to be put into rows in a very short time. Resources would have to be mobilized; efforts coordinated. More than one basket would be needed for their eggs.

Mariesa was present for VHI because—as she would have known had she ckecked her messages any time between Andros Island and Washington—Chris had designated her to act in this matter for VHI. *Only fitting,* she thought. *I've been rehearsing for it all my life.*

They spent the entire day in organizing and laying out a timeline. 17 October 2023. That was, as Lockheed so aptly phrased it, the "drop-dead date." Everything pegged off that. They nominalized major phases and subprojects, noted the interfaces, and set intermediate dates. They ended the day with three primary missions:

Land on and either destroy or divert the asteroid during the close approach of 2021.

Divert or destroy at long range from Earth orbit during the final approach of 2023.

Civil defense during, and rebuilding efforts after, Impact.

A host of other task lines tributaried off of those. Estimate likely site of the impact, should Prime 1 and Prime 2 fail. Determine probable consequences, short term and long term. Estimate resources needed for Prime 1 and plan the mission. Mariesa, would you champion that line? You'll work through UN Deep Space, of course. Prime 1 would be an international effort. Coordinate with the European, Russian, and other regional PDCs for planning staff.

Of course, she would. Could George rough out the orbits? If there were no launch window . . .

Ed Bullock and NASA would champion the orbital defense. Coordinate with Goddard, Tsiolkovky, and the other orbital stations. General, we need an assessment of weaponry, probable ranges, and effectivities. Bullock responded with a stunned look. He had still not taken it all in.

Lockheed and Boeing would champion the infrastructure support. There would be a lot of launches needed; hence, a lot of ships. Mariesa, would you assign liaisons from Pegasus and Aurora?

They had a working lunch; and later, a working dinner. Rutell joined them briefly at dinner, spoke cheerfully with Phil Albright, grazed on a veggie plate, shook hands and told them all how important their work was and that, for the time being, nothing must be said publicly. He would not meet Mariesa's eyes.

They had nearly completed the initial task of hammering out a policy and organization and would have continued pushing into the small hours, but Solomon Dark cautioned them against making policy recommendations when the brain was fogged. Washington's been there, done that, he told them, ending the session on a note of laughter. He really was a clever sort of man, Mariesa decided.

Rooms had been arranged at Blair House and other government buildings; even a change of clothing for those who, like Mariesa, had not thought to bring one.

That night, sleeping in a room that presidents and dignitaries had used, Mariesa dreamed of asteroids.

But it was not her usual nightmare. It was not the flame from the sky that turned the Earth to a wave of molten rock or flung her screaming into the air with scalding, hurricane winds; nor even the aftermath she sometimes saw: alone and cold and hungry in a world that had seen the sun for the last time.

This dream was different. Three astronauts bounded across the ragged surface of the asteroid. Young, grim, determined, they leapt like gazelles while above them the crescent Earth hovered in a black, airless sky. As her ghostly view tracked them across the scabrous landscape, she saw in the background, not one, but an entire fleet of vessels; and other astronauts busy at tasks she could not quite make out.

"It makes you proud, doesn't it?" Ned DuBois, improbably garbed in casual clothing, stood by her side also watching the three suited figures. "It's our one, best hope."

They were searching, those three. Searching for something important enough, something vital enough, to leave their other tasks undone. Just before Mariesa awoke, one of them stopped and turned to face Mariesa and said, quite distinctly in Roberta Carson's voice, "I found it."

The next morning, Mariesa and George Krishnarahman discussed their project over a breakfast served by pleasant, uniformed waiters.

"The rendezvous mission really is our one, best hope," Mariesa told him. He had chosen a fruit plate and yogurt. The fruit slices were arranged in a colorful and geometric pattern. Mariesa had ordered toast, lightly buttered, and a soft-boiled egg. The egg came in a china cup with the small end neatly snipped off. Strange, to think that some people considered such details important. But then, the cooks and waiters had not been in yesterday's meeting. "We really must get the resource and responsibility matrix completed today," she said. "It could take months just to organize the project and we don't have those months. What if, when we project lead times backward on the critical path, we find that we should have started six months ago?"

George smiled. "Project management is an area where I trust your judgement implicitly. Planning, marshalling resources, scheduling. You had plenty of experience along those lines running VHI." He paused with a slice of cantaloupe impaled on his fork and did not quite meet her eyes. "How did you sleep?" he asked casually, but with an undercurrent of concern.

Now that your nightmares have come true. The dependent clause lay unspoken.

And it was an odd thing, Mariesa suddenly realized, but she suddenly knew that her old *cauchemar* had been banished at last. She had awoken this day with an emotion other than the sheer terror with which she had grown so accustomed. And she knew what it was that the astronaut with Roberta's voice had found on that desolate, deadly rock.

She had found hope.

22.

Samson, in the Temple

Mariesa van Huyten was packing. Cartons were staged throughout Silverpond, strategically located to receive their wares. Workmen in dark green coveralls busied themselves with work orders and colored tags under the fierce supervision of Armando, Roy, and Ms. Whitmore. Walls bore a naked look; rims of faint discoloration marked the place where hangings and other ornamentation had for years blocked the light. Mariesa herself oversaw the packing in the library. An asteroid was coming to smite the Earth, and she was engaged with morocco and leather and bric-a-brac.

Yet, the world did not need her direct supervision, and this did. Others could calculate resources, estimate the number and power of lasers required, plot orbits for interceptions by nuclear-tipped missiles, develop simulations, analyze probable impact sites, lay out emergency evacuation plans. None of it required her direct input any more than, as chairman of VHI, she had been required to pour steel at Vulcan's mills. But, no one save she could decide which books to keep and which to give away.

I grew up here; and every day it grows more foreign.

"The horses have all been trailed, ma'am." Mariesa looked up from a first edition Dickens that Conrad had acquired. *It was the best of times; it was the worst of times . . .* LeRoy Thompson was the groundskeeper and groom. He dressed like a man outdoors—heavy jeans, checkered jacket, worn and scuffed boots. A kerchief circled his neck; a Stetson crowned his head. Roy had been at Silverpond since his teenage years; now he was a man with salt and pepper in his hair. "They're ready to go."

"Will you be riding with them to the new place?" She placed the Dickens carefully in the box that was to go to Rutgers.

"Got to see 'em properly stabled. And the new man, I'll have to train him."

"Leon is a perfectly competent horseman."

"Sure, but does he know that Daystar likes to bite people in the morning? Or that Gloriana throws out her chest when you tighten her cinch? Man, he'd be liable to slide down under her when she exhales. Can't do that to a bro'."

She laid a hand on his arm. "I wish you were coming with us, Roy," she said.

"Hunterdon County, man, that's too far off. And Clarissa, she wouldn't want to move so far from her folks. Besides, the new center here needs a manager; and who knows the place better'n me? I come with you, and I'll never be more than your stable boy."

She dropped the hand. "Roy!"

"Oh, you know what I mean, ma'am. This is an opportunity. I'll be ramrod, not segundo. Besides, Ms. Whitmore isn't going with you, either."

"No, but she was always closer to Mother than to me. She took Harriet's passing very hard. A clean break is best, I think. Perhaps she will finish that novel she's been writing."

Roy's teeth gleamed. "That'll be the day. She was writing that honker when I started here. Don't worry, ma'am. You and Armando'll break the new folks in."

"Yes, but . . ." Yes, but what? But it won't be the same? Why, it hadn't been the same for years. Sykes's retirement, Mother's stroke . . . And we mustn't forget Mrs. Pontavecchio or Laurence. Or Barry. People came and people went. It had not ever "been the same." And yet, each room she had walked through in the past few days whispered to her. Sometimes in Gramper's voice, sometimes in Harriet's. She heard Piet's intoxicated but well-meaning slur. And Mathilde's gentle tones. Once, a strange voice with a clipped, high-pitched accent that she took to be Conrad's, dimly remembered from her early childhood. Beneath them all, the chatter of several years' worth of Belinda's Kids.

"The best of luck to you, then." Impulsively, she hugged Roy, who stiffened for a moment before gingerly returning the gesture. He had strong arms. He had to, to handle the horses. Once those arms had lifted her, when miscarriage and hemorrhage had nearly killed her, and she had floated in them to the rooftop helipad.

She watched him go. Endings were also beginnings, and if there was an undertone of melancholy to the preparations, there was also a thrum of anticipation. A new setting, in the rolling hills by the Delaware, close by the maglev line that connected New York to the Allentown Ballistic Port so she could visit the city—or the entire world—whenever she wished; a jump pad so she could fly to Washington for PDC meetings.

"Ma'am?" It was one of the movers. He held a book to her. "This one isn't marked." There was a note of disapproval in his voice which she did not understand. She took the dusty volume and saw that it was Conrad's old Bible.

"Thank you. I'll take care of this."

"It must have fallen behind the other books on the shelf."

"Ah." That might explain the workman's tone. Perhaps he had been upset at the implied neglect. Or upset that she was a "religious nut" and possessed one at all. For some people, being offended was an avocation of sorts.

Opening the book's front cover she saw that Conrad had penned in the family's tree. Yes, she remembered Gramper showing her years ago. Black ink in a flowery script. Names that had long since passed from memory. Adelaide. Henry George. Anders. Roos. Christiana. Gramper had added others—in blue and in a hand less decorative. There she was, near the bottom of the page. A name and a birth year. Really, she ought to add Barry, if only for the record. It made no sense to pretend he had never been.

There was very little room at the bottom of the page. Fitting, because it would never be used. That line ended with her.

She shut the book with a clap and carried it to the packing box. It was an heirloom. It ought to stay in the family. Perhaps Chris ought to have it. It might be good to remind him that *his* line had not yet been irrevocably snipped short.

She paused before boxing it, recalling something Wilson had said last month. She paged through the volume, looking for the second book of Samuel, which earned her an odd glance from the workman who had brought it to her. The margins, she saw, had been heavily annotated in the same graceful black handwriting. Conrad had been something of a polymath, in perhaps the last generation in which the dedicated amateur could hope to make significant contributions to scholarship. He had written letters and published some few papers on diverse matters, including biblical issues. Strange that so unwordly a man had raised a son as pragmatic as Willem. Or perhaps not so strange at all.

She couldn't remember the chapter and verse Wilson had cited, only that it was twenty-something and it involved David and Goliath and it had some meaning regarding Adam. So she started reading at 20:1 until she found the verse in question. And then she saw that she had been half-right. It involved Goliath, but David was nowhere in sight.

> *Elhanan son of Jair of Bethlehem slew Goliath of Gath*
> *who had a spear with a shaft like a weaver's heddle-bar.*

Now, that was decidedly odd. *Two* men of Gath named Goliath? Both of them of giant stature, and both of them slain by Bethlehemites . . . Did the children of Gath run to such size then? The verse followed down to a footnote, handwritten in Conrad's elegant style.

> *King James translators inserted "the brother of" to make*
> *consistent with 1 Chronicles, 20:5 and David mythos. But*
> *Chronicles compiled much later. Original as here.*

Mariesa was not among those who expected literal exactitude in what was, after all, an anthology of writings by many individuals over many centuries living in as many political and social milieux; still, this was a striking bit of contradiction. *Samuel* and *Kings*, she read further, were Israelite, while *Chron-*

icles and *Ezra/Nehemiah* were Judahite. The two kingdoms had long been at odds, and Chronicles did not so much as mention the existence of a Kingdom of Israel. Mariesa smiled to herself when she read that. Even then, it seemed, there had been spin doctors.

So, this otherwise unknown Elhanan killed Goliath; and the David claque had later co-opted the story and inserted it into 1 Samuel 17, where it lay like an undigested lump, eclipsing not only poor Elhanan's fifteen minutes of fame, but contradicting the whole story in 1 Samuel 16.

She closed the book and frowned as she placed it in the box.

What *had* Wilson been trying to tell her? Damn everyone who spoke in riddles.

Mariesa tracked her nephew from Denver to Dillon to, finally, a turquoise tarn in the High Country, along a curving stretch of highway nestled under the peaks and overlooking a broad, bowl valley. The wind blew like a knife of ice, and flurries of dusty snow danced and twisted along the pass. The trees—twisted and cringing from the wind—stopped abrubtly just below the road. Above, nothing stood tall; though flowers blossomed defiance on the barren, rocky hillsides, and spots of bright violet and yellow relieved the dun sameness of rock and soil. Snow retreated with sullen reluctance into gullies and cracks and shadows to lurk awhile until its time came 'round again. In this country, it was never entirely summer.

It had been a long drive from Denver and she was now higher above that city than Denver was above sea level. The air here was thin, as well as cold; oxygen was an afterthought. The car passed through a gate reading KOBOLD MINES—RESPONSIBLE MINERAL EXTRACTION. A guard made a computer entry before waving her through. The driver, a Kobold employee, dropped her at the main administration building before fleeing to the interior and a thermos of coffee.

In Admin, they told her that the Baleen party had gone to the settling pond on the other side of the highway. Kobold provided an electric cart and an escort and took her through a tunnel under the road to the bowl valley.

The settling pond was easily an acre broad. It shimmered an unlikely, opaque turquoise and, despite the wind, did not have much of a chop. Around the edges, the fluid—it was not exactly right to call it "water"—became a sort of khaki before blending into dry, whitish flats. The air, too, was gritty with more than granular ice, and her escort handed her a facemask before they slid off the cart and joined the others.

Adam stepped forward to greet her and they shook hands briefly and formally. "David Desherite," he said with a significant glance at the others. In a lower voice, he added, "You didn't have to chase up here. You could have waited in Dillon."

Adam's smile was warm and his grip was firm, but Mariesa had always thought there was something just a little calculated about the warmth. Even as a boy, she remembered, he had seemed to be posing for someone's applause. Not that she objected in principle to well-mannered, polite young boys—Lord knew, there was a seller's market in that commodity!—but she had always suspected that under the soft-spoken exterior lay broken glass.

"I was curious to learn what you'd been up to. Kathryn said you were conducting a demonstration."

"Of our new filter, yes." Adam half-turned, then hesitated. "I figured that you knew when you called Kobold."

He meant about the Desherite persona, of course. Mariesa said nothing. There would be time to talk later. In the meantime, she would play along. "I've thought of investing," she said.

"Good. When the news gets out, we'll need capital for expansion." Adam introduced her to the others. A chemist and a district supervisor from Colorado DEP. A Bureau of Mines representative. The burly man in the heavy, checkered jacket was Baleen's pharmer, Karl Wincock. The fine-featured younger man who seemed to have Wincock's eye was a member of The Earthlings, an environmental group. The others were Kobold people.

They were clustered around a portable pump that had been set up on the edge of the settling pond. The intake hose lay deep under the blue-green surface. The discharge poured back into the pond. The discharge looked, Mariesa noted, markedly clearer.

The DEP chemist had a VCSEL laser array probing the effluent stream. The beam passed through the fluid stream and gave a breakdown to the processor in the receiver unit. The bounceback turbulence correction was the one used to stabilize ground-to-space power beams through the atmosphere. Police used a similar system, Mariesa remembered, to ticket polluting automobiles by spot-checking their exhaust plumes.

Adam took a glass out of a kit-bag and held it under the discharge for a moment. When he held it up to the light it appeared murky. "What do you think?" he asked the world in general. "Should I drink it?"

The DEP chemist, bent over her nanoprocessor, said, "I wouldn't."

Wincock shook his head and nudged the pump mechanic. "Take the flow rate down a notch or two. The stuff's going through too fast for my buggers to snack it all up."

"Mercury, trace amounts," the chemist announced. "Cadmium, 250 ppm. Molly-be-damned, nominal . . ."

Mariesa leaned close to Adam. "Molly be damned?"

"Molybdenum," he told her. "Don't worry. This filter wasn't designed for molly."

"The waste-water is mostly slurry and byproducts from the roaster," the Kobold man said on her other side. "Molly comes out of the ground as a sulfide. We roast it to get the oxide, then reduce the oxide with carbon. We sell the sulphur dioxide waste for air chip manufacture, and the rest is CO. Problem is, there's a lot of other crap in the ore; plus we got the coolants and all what-have-you."

"All what-have-you," Mariesa repeated, gazing across the green water. It was really quite lovely, if you didn't know what it was. Like a tropical lagoon, inexplicably misplaced to the alpine tundra. The Kobold man colored.

"That's a century's worth of accumulation. They been mining molly up here since who flung the chuck, and back then, they didn't have much in the way of remediation; nor thought too much about it. Way I look at it," and he crossed his arms, "we clean this up—show we can keep it clean—maybe we can up our permit on molly extraction. It's the only agent for steel alloy we don't gotta import."

The Earthling looked up. "More to it than the settling pond," he commented. "But each step's worth taking. Twenty years ago, Jim here and me, we'd be buttin' heads 'stead o' working this together. We'd both feel real good about ourselves afterward, but *nothing would get cleaned up*."

"Twenty years ago," Jim commented, "I'd be wiping Andy's butt for him, not buttin' his haid."

"Mercury, zero," the chemist announced. "Cadmium, zero. Tungsten, zero . . ."

The waste stream ran clear. "I still wouldn't drink it," Wincock said smugly. "Alkali metals . . . That's the next generation filter."

Mariesa and Adam met privately afterward in Kobold's conference room. It was not a very prepossessing room; about what you would expect at the tail end of nowhere. The paneling was peeling from the wall, and rock dust gathered in odd corners. Even the tabletop felt gritty. Jim, the plant manager, had a pot of coffee delivered to them, and it was the quality of coffee that the environs suggested. Harsh and metallic in flavor, with a bite that stayed long after. Mariesa did not take more than a swallow. She was not a coffee drinker, even of more user-friendly brews.

"How did you learn about Desherite and Baleen?" Adam asked.

Mariesa studied him quietly a moment before answering. Small talk aside, questions tended to tumble out in priority order; and Adam's question meant that the secrecy surrounding his identity weighed more than the exciting possibilities of the product itself. "Your filters were quite impressive," she said. "I may well invest. How many breeds does your pharmer grow?"

"We're up to seven. Karl's looking into customizing them to specific man-made compounds so the nellies can't fuss about them 'eating the whole world.' Aunt Mariesa, you didn't drive the whole way up here to witness a test you had no clue was happening."

"You're right, of course. I came to see you."

The chairs were short-backed plastic molds on pipe-thin legs. Not one, Mariesa thought, was plumb. Adam tilted back. "And . . . ?"

"And it was Charlie Schwar who made the connection, showing your pixure around."

Adam's lips pressed together. "You never let up, do you? So, Dad's been having me tailed."

Mariesa shook her head. "That was me. I haven't told Chris anything."

His eyes narrowed and he folded his hands under his lips, a gesture so like Chris's that Mariesa faltered for a moment. "Why?" he said.

" 'Desherite' was easy to figure out," she went on. " 'David' took a while longer. Ed Wilson gave me the clue."

"He was supposed to keep quiet." His fingertips, Mariesa noticed, had turned white.

"He did, after a fashion. He made a remark and I had to figure out what he meant by it. It seems King David never killed Goliath; it was some other warrior."

Adam's eyes glittered. The hands did not move. "And you took that to mean . . . what?"

"I took it to mean that 'David' did not do what popular legend credits him with." She waited for his reply and it did not come. Instead, his eyes bored into hers. They were hard eyes, carborundum; the tips of industrial drills. *Implacable*, she thought. Like a shelf of snow that had just broken loose. Finally, she spoke. "And Adam did not do what popular legend credits him with, either."

The hands parted, clapped, clapped again; and again and again, increasing the tempo into a fusillade. When he stopped, the silence unnerved her. "Are you telling me or asking me?"

"I think I've guessed right."

"It took you long enough."

"You never said anything."

"Should I have had to? I don't whine."

"I was out of the loop. Chris never released any details."

"The telephone is not a difficult instrument. A great many people have mastered the art."

Mariesa flushed and stood. "Do you so enjoy the role of wronged innocent?"

Adam hesitated, sighed, and waved her down. "I suppose I should be grateful that someone finally did ask. Not many have. It's just that I would rather have been asked sooner. Can you blame me?"

Of course she could. Being the wronged party did not relieve one of responsibilities. Mariesa resumed her seat. "I tried to get Chris to talk to you. So did Norbert."

"Reconciliation wasn't the issue. I didn't want Dad to *forgive* me. I wanted him to see that he was wrong."

"Do you hate him that much?"

Adam shook his head. "It's not hate. It's . . . whatever you get when you mix love with contempt."

"People have overheard you talking about revenge."

"He sees things in black and white, Dad does. It can force a man to see dichotomies when the reality is a continuum. It wasn't Dad who needed revenge. It was Bullock. And Dolores Pitchlynn."

"Dolores?" She had expected to hear Bullock's name before long; but that of a long-time president and confidant took her by surprise.

"She helped set me up. She wanted me out of her way." He shook his head. "Lord knows what coup she has in mind for Dad."

Mariesa saw the older woman in her mind's eye. Ambitious, determined; above all: patient. She had taken years squeezing João Pessoa and Daedalus Aerospace out of VHI. Would she engineer Chris's downfall, as Adam believed she had his, just for a chance at one or two years in the chairman's seat? Mariesa found that hard to accept.

"She always stood by me when I was chairman," Mariesa said.

"Did she?" Adam leaned forward in his seat, over the table that stood between them. "What was it that led to your own ouster?"

Mariesa felt the heat rise in her cheeks. "You know quite well. The president used my . . . my fears to put military weapons on Leo, which led to the *soyuski* raid, and . . ."

"And," said Adam smugly, "who was your staunchest supporter on *Steel Rain?* Who egged you on?"

"Dolores, yes, but . . ."

"But what? You think she didn't see your ouster as a possible outcome? Sure, maybe she didn't instigate the thing, and maybe she didn't plan on it turning out the way it did; but it was a win-win situation for her. One less van Huyten between her and the chair. After Dad brought me in, she never missed a chance to undermine my authority. I don't know if she approached Bullock or he approached her—I suspect it was her initiative—but—" His fist had risen, and his voice with it.

Adam's intensity was terrible to watch. It had begun to frighten her. She cut him off. "What do you plan to do about it?"

He unclenched his fist with palpable effort. "I've lived with this so long that it sometimes seems to have become my life." He turned the hand over, placed it flat on the table. "I'll bring them down, of course. Bullock and Pitchlynn, both."

"Living well," said Mariesa, "is the best revenge."

"A platitude? I thought about it. Build up Baleen, and maybe a handful of other enterprises, into a major economic force. I tried to let it go, but I couldn't."

"Why not?"

"Because it wasn't wealth they stole from me!" His fist on the table underlined each word. Then, more quietly, almost plaintively: "They stole my name, Aunt Mariesa. They stole my name. Who would ever trust me again?"

He drained his coffee, winced, and set the cup on the table with a sharp rap. "No, you've made up my mind for me. If you can noodle out who Desherite is, so can others. I've got to act now. Bullock has done something monumentally stupid. He can't keep it up forever. He's way out on a limb and the limb's bound to break."

"Then let it break. You'll have your revenge."

Adam shook his head. And his eyes gleamed unholy eager. "No," he said through an implacable smile. "I need to cut the limb off myself."

Afterward, Mariesa would sometimes blame herself for what happened. If she had not visited Adam and spooked him, he might not have sprung into action so quickly. But as she learned later, Bullock's house of cards was bound to collapse, whether Adam acted or no, and her nephew was no more to blame for that collapse than the surfer is to blame for the wave he rides.

Mariesa wondered if she herself should have done something beyond calling Chris and urging him once more to reconcile with his son. Perhaps it was only that the world was something greater than the sums of each individual's personal hurts and grievances, and now faced larger problems than who was right in a family quarrel, or who slicked who in a fraudulent stock transaction. In any event, she did not press the issue. Next to the impending impact crisis and the planning for FarTrip II, little else mattered to her. Yet, the larger tragedy, she thought later, might be not what happened to worlds, but what happened to the people who lived on them. And how from little things—the withholding a father's love—could grow strange and twisted results—and a likely boy could become an avenging angel. Even she herself did not recognize the first clattering stones for what they were.

KLON-AM STOCK PLUMMETS 37% ON NEWS OF FRAUDULENT LEASES

LONG-TIME PEGASUS CEO ANNOUNCES RETIREMENT

TURMOIL IN FEDERAL WEB AGENCY
TOP SLEUTH IMPLICATED IN LEO FRAUD; RESIGNS

Mariesa read the headlines with some uneasiness. OMC was in deep trouble and Klon-Am itself had taken a big hit. The Exchange had suspended trading in both the subsidiary and the parent. Yet OMC was supposed to coordinate the orbital laser defenses, just as VHI was coordinating FarTrip. She wanted to call Solomon, to find out if he had a contingency plan; but she suppressed the impulse for two reasons. In the first place, she was not the central player in Prime 2 and so she should not act like she was; and in the second place, that Solomon Dark had contingency plans was one of the few things on Earth that she was certain of.

Regarding Dolores's forced retirement, she felt a profound sorrow. A self-made woman who had clawed her way to the top in an era when genuine claws had been needed, Dolores had dreamed the same dreams and planned the same plans. She would build the ships, she had said at one of the Prometheus Project's early meetings. Correy would develop self-sustaining life support systems, and Chris would invent the new technologies, and Werewolf would build the power lasers, and Belinda would teach the kids, and Pegasus would build the ships, and the earth would be made safe.

It hadn't happened quite that way. Uncertainties regarding the U.S. government's attitude toward a private venture had caused Mariesa to move the ship-building responsibility to João Pessoa's Daedalus, in Brazil; and Dolores had never been happy with the second fiddle or the subcontracts that came her way. Perhaps that had been when the older woman began to part company and seek her own way.

They were gone now, so many of them. João and Belinda and Werewolf and others. And now Dolores, too. She had never been a *friend*. Her hard personality had precluded friendship. But she had been at least a comrade.

So, who was to blame? Bullock for stumbling into easy make-shifts? Adam for his vengeful triumphalism? Dolores for instigating the shell game? Chris for believing too easily when he should have doubted and remaining doubtful when he should have believed? Or even herself, for, in the end, doing nothing?

Ellis Harwood stood in Phil Albright's office and ran his finges through his thinning hair. Too thin, by far; just as the stomach muscles had loosened too much. Sometimes, when he remembered to think about it, he felt his age. "I think you're making the right decision about this asteroid business, Phil," he told the withered man behind the desk. And, Christ, it hurt him to see how the man was hurting. Phil was only five years his senior, and look how fast he had gone downhill. That wouldn't happen to Ellis Harwood. He'd kevork before he let his body degrade that far.

Phil Albright's lips twitched. "Thanks for telling me that, Ellis."

"The fact that the government wants it kept secret," Harwood said, "is reason enough to go public, but I've been giving it some thought and there's an aspect you may be overlooking"—he leaned closer—"and that's putting people to work."

Phil closed his eyes. "Unemployment's already pretty low. Unless you're talking about the defense effort sucking people out of civilian jobs."

"Absolutely." Phil's body might be failing him, but by God, the mind was still sharp! "There are going to be severe labor shortages, but the government is almost certain to throw on wage and price controls, because higher civilian wages will mean higher prices for consumer goods. We don't want the corporations picking our pockets."

Phil let out a long sigh, but made no response.

Did that signify a loss of patience? Harwood pressed on. "It's the Social Security angle. What were Blaise and his people worried about before this asteroid thing? The payroll tax might not cover the nut now that us Boomers are retiring, right? Well, what if we didn't retire? Don't you see? We fill in all those civilian jobs with our experience and wisdom, earning an income so we don't have to draw on the trust fund, plus we free up a lot of others to work on the asteroid defense."

Harwood looked for some sign he had interested Phil. Phil was usually ahead of the curve, but he couldn't think of everything and labor issues were Harwood's bailiwick. But Phil continued to sit placidly, eyes closed; just waiting for the pitch. Harwood took a deep breath and continued. "I don't know if the speech is already written up. Bertie—Roberta—was working on it last night. But I think when you tell America what's coming down their throats, you might also get in a word about the jobs that the defense effort would create and how we can all work together on this. Young and old. Common ground, isn't that what you always say, Phil? And this planet is the only good ground we've got.

"Phil . . . ?

"Phil!"

Harwood felt a sudden wave of sorrow and pity wash over him. "Oh, Jesus, Phil. Oh, Christ." He glanced once around the office: at the old, wooden desk, at the faded pictures tacked to the wall, at the jumble of postings and notes, and the poster that proclaimed THE CRUSADES TILT A LANCE FOR ALL THOSE IN NEED and it suddenly seemed empty, like an ancient temple fallen down. He brushed his cuff across his cheek; then strode to the office door and jerked it open. "Somebody," he hollered. "Go get Bertie and bring her here! Quick!"

E P I L O G U E : Cassandra, Weeping

Roberta Carson had always worn black. As far back as she could remember, the shades of night had been her color. Melancholic, neo-gothic, alcoholic . . . No other hue had been possible. Black shift, black spideweb stockings, black lipstick smeared so often around the long, hard neck of her secret bottle. And even later, when self-dramatization no longer appealed, because no one remained to hear the appeal, she had favored the color for its simplicity and its flexibility.

Now, of course, facing the doids, hands sweaty upon the lectern, heart banging in her chest, life stirring in her womb, the words stale and dull on her cheat sheet, she wore the color out of tradition. And respect.

The director held his right hand up, fingers splayed, and Roberta nodded. Her eyes danced down the speech typed in large easy-to-read letters. Phil's speech. *His* words, gone all misty on the page. She would have to put them in her mouth, taste him in their cadence—one last memory; one final resurrection.

Four minutes.

To the side, out of pickup range, Ellis Harwood stood, downcast, grave, worried, a sober black band around the arm of his tweed jacket, a duplicate of Phil's speech in his hand—in case Roberta could not finish. Eyes locked for a moment, and a single thought leapt between them. *Carry on.* Phil's voice. *Carry on the Crusade.* How could he be gone when . . .

Three minutes.

How could Phil be gone when she could still hear his voice, feel his caress, taste his love?

Isaac Kohl had told her one time, in one of his interminably lecturous modes, that time expanded toward infinity as you spiraled into a black hole. Here was experimental verification. While she spiraled in to the black discs of the digital cameras, these last few minutes consumed years of her life.

Two minutes.

She took a deep breath. Calm. Focus. Roberta was used to audiences smaller, more intimate, more personal. None this large or this remote. *Just pretend that the newsgroupies in the room are the only ones you're talking to.* The press conference would go out on broadcast, cable, web. Phil swung that much weight with those who made such decisions. One last favor called in from beyond the grave.

One minute.

That there had been no good-bye had hurt the worst. She ought to have

358

held his hand as he passed on, seen him off with loving words. Yet, he had slipped away with nothing more than Ellis Harwood's plaints in his ears. She knew Phil would have had it otherwise; but Phil had had no say in the matter. *You will know neither the day, nor the hour.* Roberta had given up on gods a long time ago; and yet that Book could still speak when you least expected it.

The director made a ball of his fist and brought it down like a hammer, his forefinger a spear aimed at Roberta's heart. Roberta looked straight into the pickups, waited a beat until the silence brought Ellis up from his own introspection.

Then she began to speak.

Good evening. And it is, in spite of everything, a good one.

(Oh, Phil, how could you have known when you wrote that?)

The words refused to stand firm. They dissolved and ran. Roberta clutched the papers. Ellis, alarmed, took a step forward from his post in the wings; but Roberta waved him back.

For those of you who expected to hear Phil Albright tonight, I have sad news. (These were her own words. They poured out of her.) *Earlier today, Phil Albright, my husband, the father of my child, died peacefully in his office. Some of you already know this. News travels at lightspeed through the fibrops and off the twenty-fours, and sometimes the truth travels with it. E-mail has been coming in faster than we can log it. For those of you who had hoped it was just another net-hoax . . .* (She paused and dropped her eyes, shook her head almost imperceptibly.)

Chris van Huyten, hunched over the papers and proposals and memos that had come to define his life, jerked his head up and stared at the pixwall, where the press conference was downloading. Had he heard right? Phil Albright dead? That was too bad. The man had done some good for this weary old planet. He was a man Chris could work with on the environment because, while they might disagree on means, they were both firmly fixed on the same ends. He wondered who would emerge in the power struggle that would inevitably follow. Someone doctrinaire, he supposed. Someone more interested in web-bytes than in accomplishing anything. He turned back to his work, picked up Khan's financials for the quarter. But after a moment, he dropped them back on the pile without having read them. Shortly, he rose and walked to the window, black with the outside night, nothing visible except his own reflection.

But there were things that Phil wanted to say, things that desperately needed saying, and the speaker's death should not stand in the way of his words. (Offstage, Ellis nodded gravely.) *So, for those of you who feel the grief of his passing and you others who feel a shameful elation, I ask you to set aside your own emotions and listen to what he wanted to say. It affects all of us.*

* * *

Mariesa, clad in T-shirt and jeans, had gone to the deck outside Ridgeview, where the night air off Musconetcong Mountain barely affected the dank, fleshy warmth of the summer fields. She wiped the perspiration from her brow with the back of her hand and listened for a moment to the whisper of the grasses in the dark breezes. A long, drawn-out sigh, like the passing of a soul. *Poor Roberta*, she thought. Poor Roberta. Perhaps she ought to offer Ridgeview as a retreat for the woman during the difficult time ahead—though the bustle of unpacking and organizing made it less than suitable for mourning. Through the tall French doors, Mariesa watched Armando direct the movers and their crates. What had impelled Roberta, in her grief, to stand before the cameras in her husband's place? An important announcement, Phil had hinted in his phone call two days ago. Two days ago, grave and cryptic; and now he was dead—grave and cryptic in another fashion. Phil might have lived another year, had he foregone the stress of running the Crusades. But he had chosen Achilles's path. She wondered whether Roberta harbored a secret resentment over that choice. And yet, an Albright that had quit to clutch a few final months would have been a stranger and would have deprived her just as surely of the man she loved.

An important announcement. Mariesa re-entered the house and, striding to the telenet screen, turned the volume up.

For more than twenty years, the Crusades have tilted the lance for those that luck or society have made victims. Sometimes, Phil clashed with the venal and the greedy and even with men of genuinely evil heart; but more often, as he learned, the enemy was shortsightedness, haste or foolishness, or ignorance. These can lead even the well-intentioned to do harm. He came to see, more and more, that all of us are victims.

Jimmy Poole lurked in the virtch, his senses encased and enhanced by helmet, goggs, and gloves, flitting like a spirit through the virtual press room. By juggling and blending the feeds, he could watch from a point in space just in front of the podium, where he had a very good view of Roberta Carson. *Tough breaks, Styxy*, he thought, *but that's what you get when you hook up with a geezer like Albright.* Widow's black, sooner or later, was pretty much a no-brainer.

He didn't buy the "We're all victims" crap—Jimmy Poole was no victim!—but Styx was dead nuts on about being shortsighted. Bullock building his house of cards, Adam shaking it down. Both of them feeding their appetites for greed or for revenge without thinking through the spin-offs. Jimmy, forewarned of Adam's plans, had dumped his Consortium holdings right off; and a good thing, too, since Klon-Am's stock had blackholed the very next day.

* * *

Now, it seems that we all might become victims in a more literal sense. Some of you have heard rumors on the net or elsewhere about an asteroid called 2004AS—

Blaise Rutell slammed his fist onto his desktop. "She's going to tell the whole friggin' world! Jesus, just like a woman . . . Why did Phil have to go and croak on us?"

Solomon Dark shuffled his papers and suppressed a smile. He was not a policy-maker, only an advisor; but he knew how to nudge policy-makers in the right direction, and presidents were not the only ones who sometimes called and asked for advice. Sometimes old friends did. "It's Phil's speech she's reading," he pointed out.

Yes, there have been asteroid alarms before. Premature announcements followed by retractions. But there is nothing premature about this. Astronomers have been following it since last December. (Roberta put down the cheat sheet, stared straight into the optic, oblivious now to the millions on the other end.) *This one's the Genuine Bean, folks. We've got six years. Six years, and then it hits the fan.*

Incredibly, Charlene relaxed and laughed. "Six years? She sure had me going there for a minute. How can they know what's going to happen six years from now when they can't say if it's even gonna rain next week?" Hobie looked at the stranger he had shared his life with. Didn't she have the slightest clue? Hobie was only a chemist, but he knew how orbital mechanics worked. "Thing is," he told his wife, "out in space, you always keep moving the same direction, 'cept when the sun or a planet yanks you by the scruff." Charlene's attention, momentarily captured, drifted back to the threedy set. Hobie raised his voice. For a moment there, they had almost communicated, and he tugged mightily on the thread of conversation. "So they just look ahead to see where that rock is going, and—"

"Bean," said Charlene. To Hobie's blank response, she coughed impatiently. "That white gal, she called it the Bean, not the Rock. The Rock's where that Calhoun went back in Ten."

Charlene was proof positive there was life elsewhere in the universe, Hobie reflected, 'cause she sure did live on another planet. Who the fuck *cared* what the name was? The Earth was going to get whacked upside the head, and she bitched about the label on the two-by-four. "They look ahead where the Bean is going," he insisted, granting her the right of nomenclature, "and where the Earth is going . . ." His two hands made ellipses in the air. ". . . and six years out . . ." He brought his fists together. "Bang." Charlene flinched, and maybe, from the brief look of fear in her eye, understood. "There's nothing else out there gonna change that Bean's course. Nothing at all—"

Hobie stiffened suddenly as lightning ran through him. *Unless . . .*

*   *   *

It's not a very big asteroid, as these things go; but something a little smaller once flattened an area of Siberia the size of New York City. So how much harm it does will depend on where it hits and what it's made of. One thing we know is, we can't just shrug our shoulders and hope it hits somewhere else. (Roberta studied her cheat sheet for a moment, granting a silence in which people listening could digest the news before she hit them between the eyes.) *We can't shrug our shoulders and hope, because whatever happens, this may only be the first.*

Billie Whistle sussed the deebies, flitting from node to node with the speed of thought, while on her pixwall the pale, dark-clad woman spoke her clarion call. An asteroid? Billie sat amidst her equipment pondering the image of a great rock hurtling toward them all like the ultimate drunk driver.

Deftly, she slipped through commercial security cordons, fingered the profiles on ISPs and BBSs. It wasn't a common name she sought. There couldn't be more than a few hundred people wearing it. She followed skeins to linking files and datafaces, and eliminated those whose parameters mismatched. Too old. Too young. Wrong hair or eye color. Occupations requiring a different life to win them. In the end, she had an edress.

Billie brushed at her cheek with her left arm and shivered momentarily at the weird, alien sensations that coursed through her from the MEMS neural feedback. Then she thought up an email blank and pondered the letters, one by one.

D-e-a-r—T-o-m . . .

The world's governments have been working quietly to organize a defense. Some good work has been done already. I was a—(I? Reading, she had forgotten who had written. She stopped, appalled at how suddenly memories could turn nasty and a mere pronoun slap you in the face.) *I mean, Phil was a member of the defense commission. Strategies were mapped out and coordinated with Mercosur, the European Union, the Russian Federation, and the Conference of Chinese States. But now* . . .

Ed Bullock knocked back his single-malt and stared at the pixwall with his mouth pressed into a thin line. "That little twit," he said. "And her do-gooder boyfriend . . . What does she think announcing Armageddon over the net will do to the market?"

The question was rhetorical. He did not expect Vanessa to answer. Policies and markets were not her arena. So when his wife spoke over the hiss of the fire and the chatter of the girl on the screen, he could not, for one weird instant, place the voice. "The work will continue, I trust. It would be a shame if the Earth were destroyed because 'a little penny-ante fraud' hobbled the defense efforts."

There was venom in her tones and, when he had turned to look at her, steel in her eyes. He stood and walked to the liquor cabinet, where he seized the whiskey decanter before J. G. could do more than take a single, scandalized step to intercept him. Bullock pulled the stopper and refilled his glass. "That will be all for the night, Glenn," he told the butler. "Mrs. Bullock and I can see to ourselves." Then, without waiting for the other man to leave, he put his back to the fire and poured the drink down his throat, warming himself inside and out. "Shary should have come straight to me," he complained, "the first time dell'Bosco ordered him to play games. There are times you ought to go out of channels, damn it. By the time I learned what was going on, we were in too deep."

"Poor dear." But there was no sympathy in her tones.

People, there's work to be done! Important work. World-saving work. You think you've seen us mount crusades? (Roberta leaned forward, gripping the sides of the lectern, as if restraining herself from a leap through the doids into everyone's office and living room.) *Friends, you ain't seen nothin' yet.*

Jacinta Rosario watched the webcast with the other cadets in the common room of Grissom dorm. "Aliens throwing rocks?" said Kenn Rowley. "That is so Out There."

Yungduk Morrisey, sitting beside Jacinta, reached over and squeezed her hand and Jacinta did not pull it away. "Remember what we overheard on The Man's plane?" he whispered. "They'll be sending ships—and we'll be on them."

A long and lonely journey, Jacinta thought, with the Earth a crescent dime among the stars. She imagined herself leaping gazelle-like across a barren rockscape far from all she knew.

Standing abruptly, she left the common room and the puzzled Yungduk, and strode to her own room, where she sat before her terminal. Before courage and newfound resolution left her, she called up a word processor and began to write.

Dear Mama . . .

But, after typing that single line, she sat paralyzed. Chit-chat out of the blue seemed disingenuous; but raking up old wounds and hurtling old challenges seemed equally foolish. Even if she finished the letter, there might never be a reply. And even if one did come, it might be nothing more than a continuation of the same argument, resumed as if it had never been interrupted.

Better that the long, loud silence continue.

And yet . . . And yet, with an asteroid on its way big enough to smash a city, old quarrels seemed somehow insignificant.

She began to write.

*   *   *

It's time to pull the sleeves up. Time to stand together. You and me and Great Aunt Mabel. There's work that needs doing and a lot of men and women willing to do it. Six years might seem like a long time, but it's just an eyeblink compared to how much we have to do. That asteroid that's going to hit us? It had to change course to come our way. Friends, someone is throwing rocks at us, and we don't know why. Until we do, we can't make them stop. And while we can't, we need to keep watch. And once we spot 'em, we need to swat them aside. And meanwhile—just in case—we need to get a few more of our eggs out of this handbasket of a planet.

Chris van Huyten pulled the drapes closed against the night sky and stared around his office as a man who has suddenly found himself inexplicably in a strange, new place. When he was very still, he could hear the distant rustle of other late-night employees.

Marianne was gone. On a vacation, she had said. To be alone. Restless, he left the office and sought the night air on the balcony outside. First Watchung Mountain was a dark looming presence. Fireflies danced across the lawn of the complex.

He looked over the railing at the edge of the balcony. The wind drifted off the face of the wooded hills, cooling the dank warmth of the night. It seemed to lift him up, as if he could fly, were he only to let himself go.

He stood that way for a long while, until, slowly, his muscles unclenched and he took an abrupt step backward. He looked up into the glittering, cloudless sky, pierced with gleaming fires. Is that what it took? The ultimate whap upside the head? A hell of a thing, just to get a stubborn father's attention.

He turned to the office and sat at his desk. He picked up a sheet of ordinary writing paper and uncapped his fountain pen.

Dear Adam . . . , he wrote.

He sat for a minute in silence, then crumpled the sheet into a ball and threw it to the waste can, where it hit the rim and bounced to the floor. Then he took up another sheet and wrote in flowing cursive.

Dear Son . . .

Maybe the hit won't be so bad. Maybe it'll splash down in mid-Pacific and drown a few islands and atolls. And maybe there won't be a next one.

But are you willing to bet your children's lives on that?

Because there will be a next one, and another after that. And maybe it'll be faster, or bigger, or come round the blind side with no warning. And our grandchildren will curse our name.

Or maybe they won't.

Maybe there won't be any grandchildren left.

*   *   *

José Eduardo Gonsalves y Mercado shook his head. He and Serafina locked glances over their two children, who sat between them on the sofa, not exactly grasping what the threedy was telling them. He saw fear in Serfina's eyes, and understanding, and—reluctantly—agreement. Though not a word was spoken, the issue had been debated, rebutted and decided. "They'll need ships," she told him. Flaco nodded, rose and crossed their small apartment to the wall phone. He picked up the receiver. "They'll need the men to build them."